Waking Isabella
...because beauty can't sleep

forever.

By

Melissa Muldoon

Matta Press · Austin

MelissaMuldoon.com

MelissaMuldoon.com

Cover Illustration, Cover Design,
Interior Design, Illustration,
Typography & Layout
by
Melissa Muldoon

MATTA

PRESS

Matta Press
2303 Ranch Road 620 S.
Suite 160 - 124
Austin, TX 78734

Cover Design by Melissa Muldoon
Interior Book Design by Melissa Muldoon

Manufactured in the United States of America

1st Edition
Muldoon, Melissa.
Waking Isabella

ISBN: 978-0-9976348-2-2

ISBN: 978-0-9976348-3-9 (E-Book)

Con Antico Ardore

Dedicated to those who appreciate
all kinds of beauty,
and those who seek
to uncover the beauty within.

To the Aretini and the city of Arezzo
that is rich in beauty and hidden treasures.

Art is the lie that makes us realize the truth.

– Pablo Picasso

It has been estimated that 100,000 works of art
lost during the war or taken by the Nazis
have not been returned to their rightful owners.

Isabella

Chapter 1

A Princess is Murdered

July 16, 1576

*W*hen Isabella woke that morning with intentions of washing her long dark hair, she hadn't imagined she would be dead before it was dry. Bending over the china basin as she poured lukewarm water over her head to remove the traces of lavender soap, her thoughts instead were of her lover.

Standing up, she tossed back her dripping mane, causing water to arc into the air and dribble over her forehead and down her back. She glanced at the mirror and lifted her chin. Tilting her head at a slight angle, she studied her nose and the curve of her long neck. Pleased with her appearance, and content she was aging well despite the fact she was approaching her thirty-fourth year, she pulled her night shift tighter to study the rest of her body.

The thin linen, now wet, clung to her, revealing the shape of a woman who had previously borne two children. She ran a hand down her side and over her hips, and a smile spread across her face as she thought about another who had recently traced his fingers over her bare midriff.

Picking up the letter Morgante the dwarf had left on the table by her bed, she read the first line. *"My dear lady, you are my most beautiful thought that will never be lost to me."*

Ah, il mio caro amore, Troilo, she thought wistfully. *Mi manchi tanto tanto. How I miss you.*

From the open window, she heard the rustling leaves of the oak trees that surrounded the villa set on the crest of the hill. Resting her hand on one of the wooden shutters, she could see the misty purple hues of the Tuscan valley floor that rolled all the way to the sea. This was her land.

She knew it well and had explored every valley and ridge on horseback.

Closing her eyes, she recalled a moment of pure joy, galloping across the plains, feeling the wind blowing across her cheeks and through her hair. When she had gazed over her shoulder, she had been delighted to see Troilo masterfully jumping over a downed tree, rapidly closing the distance between them. Calling out to him, she had said, *"Dai! Prendimi!* Catch me if you can, my dear sir!"

Although she had taken the lead, he was an adept horseman, her equal in the saddle—and in every other way. She knew when she had bounded away he would catch her easily. Or perhaps she wanted to be caught and had intentionally pulled back on her reins. Reaching the ridge, breathing hard, she waited for Troilo to come to a full stop beside her. Sidestepping his horse next to hers, he leaned over and kissed her fully on the mouth.

Isabella laughed with pleasure at the memory. Scanning his letter again, however, her joy quickly faded.

"Ho una paura terribile. I fear for you, my dearest lady. The tides are changing. There are vipers in your family, and they are preparing to strike."

"They are all a bunch of tiresome, miserly fools," she said, as if Troilo could hear her. "Power-hungry and conniving, the lot of them! When I return to Florence, I shall convince Francesco to hand over the money our father promised to me."

That is, if she could remove the new duke from the clutches of his Venetian whore. She shook her head in disgust and turned her attention back to Troilo's letter.

"Amore mio, the hour has become desperate, and it is time for you and the children to depart. You must leave everything immediately and come with me to Spain. There is no time to waste. Vi aspetto. I will be waiting for you at..."

Isabella stood motionless and in the silence she heard a floorboard groan ever so slightly. Her eyes traveled across the room and she knew full well someone was standing on the other side of the oak panel. Peering intently at the door, she watched as the handle turned slowly to the right, and then to the left, but the latch didn't budge. Earlier she had instructed

Morgante to lock the doors of her chamber when he left so no one could enter without her consent.

She paused, waiting to see what would happen next. But all was quiet on the other side. Only the ticking of the clock on the mantel punctuated the silence in her room. Standing in her thin linen slip, Isabella shuddered involuntarily from a chilly morning draft that blew in from the open window. As she waited, a tentacle of fear slithered up her spine, and she felt the first stab of panic.

As the moments passed and nothing happened, she cautiously sat down on her bed, trying to steady her racing heart. From the courtyard just outside, she could hear the groomsman's consoling words as he tried to calm the horses. His tone worked its magic on her as well and, regaining composure, she stood up to her full, regal height.

Pushing her damp hair off her face, she stared again into the mirror and reminded herself, "There is nothing to be afraid of. I am a Medici, am I not—the daughter of Cosimo and Eleonora? He would never dare harm me."

Seeking confirmation, Isabella glanced over at the portrait on the wall of herself and her beloved mamma. She cherished the picture and carried it with her wherever she traveled. Even though her mother had been dead many years, when Isabella looked at the picture, she still felt an unbroken connection. It gave her strength, reminding her of the beautiful and intelligent woman from whom she had descended. It seemed objects survived time more readily than people, and Isabella knew that as long as she had this painting, she too would live on through the ages.

In this moment of insecurity and panic, though, she needed her mother's courage more than ever. Fixing her gaze on her mother's alabaster face, she said, "I am your daughter, and you taught me well, mamma, and together we will see this through. I won't let them..." Isabella's words died on her lips at the sound of a fist pounding on her door.

"Isabella, let me in. We have something to discuss."

"Ah, so it *is* you, Paolo," she replied, trying to keep her tone cool. "I thought that might be you lurking outside in the hall. I was beginning to wonder when my husband might put in his appearance."

"Open the door, Isabella," he demanded. "I have received a message from Cafaggiolo and have news of your cousin Leonora."

"And what news might that be, that you must beat on my door like a barbarian?"

"There has been an accident," Paolo said flatly through the locked door. "*Leonora è morta*. Your cousin is dead."

Isabella inhaled sharply, and instantly her bravado drained away and was replaced by dread. She grabbed the china basin to steady herself as bile filled her stomach. When she caught sight of herself in the mirror, she shuddered at the reflection. She didn't recognize the woman at all. Her eyes were like dark saucers in an ashen gray mask, and it appeared a phantom was staring back at her.

When the hammering on the door began again, she instinctively clutched Troilo's message to her heart. She knew full well the argument that would ensue if Paolo discovered it in her possession. Moving across the room, she knelt before the wooden set of drawers. Lightly she touched the decorative panels and slid them in a well-memorized pattern. Soon a small drawer at the bottom sprang open. Gently she kissed the letter then tucked it inside for safe keeping.

At the sound of the bedroom door opening, she stood up and spun around. On the threshold of her bedroom stood her husband, his massive body filling the doorway. In his hand he held a key which he slowly wagged back and forth, mimicking the ticking of the clock that was once again audible. Seeing his wife's damp hair, and her not-so-modest wet slip, his beefy lips turned upward in a leer.

"I see you are as lovely as ever, despite your state of undress. Is all this primping for my benefit? *Vieni qui!* Come into my warm embrace and greet your devoted husband properly."

When Isabella raised her arms and crossed them protectively over her chest, Paolo laughed softly. Pleased he had caught her off guard, he took a step in her direction. To avoid his touch, Isabella moved around him, but despite his girth, he was too quick for her. He grabbed her by the hair and slammed her into the washstand, sending the pitcher crashing to the floor. Imprisoned in his rough embrace, she felt his moist fingers press into her bare arms and smelled the stench of his breath. Her stomach roiled again, and she felt like vomiting.

"*Lasciami! Non toccarmi!*" She twisted her shoulders and attempted to raise a knee to deal him a forceful blow. Before she could reach her target, he stopped her with a violent shake.

"Don't, my sweet," he warned in a menacing tone. "Come, now. It has been a fortnight since we last saw one another. Have you no kind words or kisses for me, or have you wasted them all on Troilo?"

Hearing Troilo's name, Isabella stopped struggling.

"*Ah, sì...* now I have your attention. *Non sono un'idiota.* I am not as foolish as you think. I am well aware how you have mocked me, cuckolding me for years—with my cousin, no less! Did you think me so blind that I didn't know you passed his spawn off as mine? The children we conceived ceased to thrive in your womb and were washed away by your blood. Yet, with him, you succeeded."

Dragging her roughly to the bed, he pushed her down and lowered himself on top of her. "Surely you can share your ripe fruit with me as well." Stroking her jaw, he continued, "You've both made me a laughing stock, you with your ludicrous affair and your dear *papà* stingily doling out little pieces of his fortune to me."

Wheezing heavily, he added, "For a change, it seems I have the upper hand—and believe me, now that Cosimo is dead, I plan on making you both pay."

When Isabella started to struggle again, he shook her roughly, making her head snap back. Raising a hand, he brushed back the wet hair that had fallen over her brow. "There, there, my love. If you fight me, it will only make things more difficult for you."

At his tone, Isabella narrowed her eyes and regarded him defiantly. "*Mi fai schifo.* You disgust me," she said. "You always were a narrow-minded man. Only one thing has ever consumed your thoughts. Taking your pleasure and hurting women—and money!"

A malicious grin spread across his flushed face, as if what she had just said greatly amused him. "Ah, you still haven't understood. You think I act alone?" he said. *"Per carità,* no, you stupid woman! Francesco sent me here today to deal with the Medici trash. My instructions are to put you in your place and make sure you are soundly punished."

At the mention of her brother's name, Isabella rolled her head to the side. Paolo raised his hand and turned her face back toward his, and with his tongue, he licked her neck. "Ah, you still taste sweet, my love."

His thick fingers pinched her jaw, and she squirmed beneath his massive weight. When he shifted slightly, she freed an arm and reached up and clawed his face with her sharp nails.

"Puttana! You miserable whore," Paolo cried out in pain as blood ran down his neck.

"M'lady, did you call me? Did you drop something? I thought I heard a disturbance, are you...?"

Craning his neck, Paolo chuckled when he saw Morgante standing in the doorway. Isabella screamed out to the dwarf for help, but Paolo covered her mouth, muffling her cries. Her faithful servant shuddered, unable to lift a finger to save her, paralyzed by his servitude to his more powerful master. He knew that if he attempted to help his mistress, he would be instantly killed.

"Vattene! Go. Get out of here," Paolo shouted. "You are not needed here, little man." Then, grabbing Isabella's arm and securing it firmly, he ripped away the linen shift from her body. Rolling back on top of her, he forced himself upon her. He rose up time and time again, hurting her brutally, enjoying her discomfort. Isabella thrashed from side to side, but with her arms pinned again, all she could manage was to bite him on his neck. Paolo retaliated by striking her with the back of his hand.

Whispering into her ear, Paolo cruelly tormented her. *"Non c'è nessuno qui a proteggerti.* There is no Troilo here to protect you, my sweet. Do you think he remained faithful to you—that he even cared? He was a paid lackey who took his orders from your brother. Come, come. Perhaps my cousin might have been infatuated by the luscious curves of your harlot's body, but your charms are nothing compared to the money offered by your kin. Coward that he is, Troilo has taken the purse and run to France to save his own hide."

Isabella gazed dully at the man she had been betrothed to at age eleven and whom she had married at sixteen. She saw him for what he was—a brutish man, a braggart, and a liar. All his life, it had been Paolo, the Orsini duke, who had danced to the tune of her father and brothers—always a pawn in the Medici game of power.

Now, as she scrutinized Paolo's red, angry face, she knew he was lying about Troilo—yet still, at the mention of his name, something inside her died. Disgusted by his brutality, still imprisoned by his weight on the bed, she spat at him. She observed with pleasure as he recoiled and wiped his cheek with the corner of one of her lace-edged pillows.

Paolo eyed her thoughtfully, seeing the fear that had previously clouded his wife's eyes replaced by haughty disdain. With a sneer, he reached for a cushion embroidered with the family logo and placed it over her nose and mouth. "You believe because you are a Medici your actions will be overlooked? Well, my dearest, nothing is forever. *You* brought this about, with your high and mighty ways."

As he applied firm pressure, in a cajoling tone he added, "Silly, foolish Isabella, to think she could play at a man's game and win."

Fighting for oxygen, instinctively Isabella thrashed and kicked her limbs but soon grew weak from the effort. When the pillow was finally lifted from her face, and she felt the weight of her husband's body leave her side, she felt tremendous relief. Thirstily she drank in great gulps of air, which caused her to cough violently. As coherent thought returned, Isabella tried to roll from the bed, but her body felt numb and lethargic as if a dray horse had trampled her.

She lay tiredly for a moment, thinking now that her humiliation and punishment had been carried out, Paolo would leave her. She waited for the door to slam, signaling his departure. But she was mistaken. He remained in the room, and she could hear him breathing heavily just a few steps away.

In a raspy voice, she whispered, "What else is there, Paolo? *Volevi la tua vendetta.* You wanted your revenge... now just go away."

Laughing softly, he said, "Oh, dearest Isabella, I'm just getting warmed up." With measured words, he said, "It is time for you to join Leonora."

At the mention of her beloved cousin's name, a tear slid down Isabella's cheek. She thought with despair of the preparations she would need to make for her funeral. But as the meaning of his words penetrated her pain, she slowly opened her heavy lids and blinked him into focus. Her sorrow quickly turned to horror as she watched him lift the portrait of her and her mother from the wall.

Brushing his hand over the surface of the canvas, he taunted her. "I fear after today... Well, you will no longer need this. *È un vero peccato. Sei così bella lo sai.* Such a pity. You are quite beautiful, you know. Too bad this must be destroyed as well."

Corralling her energy, Isabella pulled herself up and commanded, *"Non toccare!* Don't touch it. That is mine and mine alone! I'll have you..."

He cut her off with a mean laugh. "*What* exactly will you do to me, my pet? Isabella, don't you see? You have no control over me anymore. As for this," he said, looking at the painting, "I will return it to your brother as confirmation that our..." He smiled meanly at her again and continued, "Now that our little *chore* has been carried out. I'm sure he will view it as a trophy. It will be proof of his ultimate authority over you... if he doesn't destroy it first."

"Paolo, enough! I..."

"Shut up, Isabella, I've grown tired of you, and I really must hurry as I have other things to do this morning."

Peering up at the ceiling, he whistled loudly. From above, she heard shuffling footsteps. Following his gaze, Isabella saw a small hole had been drilled through the ceiling over her bed. It was barely noticeable, and now she watched with increasing panic as a thin rope was pushed through the opening. Her eyes widened further when she saw Paolo grab the cord and give it a sharp tug before fashioning it into a noose. It seemed her husband, a seasoned huntsman, had thought of everything. He had prepared quite a cruel trap to snare his prey.

She gasped at Paolo in disbelief, fully realizing for the first time he intended to kill her. *Could he really be so vicious?* In the next moment, he proved to be without morals or conscience as he slipped the rope over her head and tightened the knot.

Once again, Isabella fought back, but as she was helplessly hoisted upwards, the cord tightened, pressing into her slim neck cutting off her life's breath. As the pain increased, she was filled with unrelenting sadness. Her only crime had been that of being a woman and daring to live boldly, and for this she was being punished. By killing her, destroying her portrait, and telling lies about her, Isabella realized it was within their power to rewrite history.

To extinguish a life was to kill a small piece of beauty; no one person should have that power over another. Her life, perfect in its imperfection, had not been lived in vain. She had mattered and had loved deeply. No one could take that away from her.

Before she lost all consciousness, she felt her mother's presence and the light touch of her hand. "Isabella, dear child, remember, each life touches another, influencing and inspiring the other."

Drifting into the netherworld, Isabella closed her eyes to sleep forever, comforted by this final thought. As hard as they might try, they would never erase her completely. She wouldn't let them. A part of her would remain behind and, given time, someone would remember... and beauty would be awakened.

Chapter 2

Ghost Ships

April 2010

*T*he fog that shrouded the village of Half Moon Bay was just starting to lift and Nora, glancing up at the watery sky, was heartened when she saw a hint of silvery sun burning steadily through the California morning mist. It was still early, and she congratulated herself for having the stamina to get up at dawn to find a decent parking space just off the main square. The spring antique fair in Half Moon Bay, an eclectic seaside community just south of San Francisco, drew folks from all over the peninsula, searching for everything from artisan glass to handcrafted furniture.

Nora, always one with an eye for the unusual, loved antiquing. Usually, she liked to take her time, but today she was not here for pleasure. Nora was on a mission. She was scouting to find furniture to outfit the home in Palo Alto that she was preparing for resale. She wanted to give the house the appearance it had been lived in and well cared for by people who loved each other, even if in reality she and Richard had failed miserably at that.

As Nora approached Kelly Avenue, she could see the main drag leading to the beach had been blocked off. Normally, it was bustling with cars and pickup trucks. Today it was overrun with canvas tents filled with local crafts and vendors selling street food. Inhaling, Nora wrinkled her nose in distaste at the heavy, saturated smell of buttered popcorn and fried corn dogs. At nine in the morning, she wasn't ready for such greasy fare, so she stopped at a corner café and ordered a *macchiato* in a paper cup to go.

Despite being a double shot of espresso, to Nora it tasted weak and bitter, and after a few sips, she tossed it into the garbage. As the sun rose higher, the number of shoppers continued to increase, and determinedly she pushed on through the crowd. As she passed by the various vendors she admired the assortment of craft stalls filled with handmade felt jackets, stained glass ornaments, and wind chimes.

For the most part, she was good and walked on by the tables, refusing to be lured in by a whimsical purchase, but couldn't help but stop when confronted with a booth stocked with handmade clothes for toddlers and newborns. Gently she picked up a tiny smocked dress and fingered the fabric, admiring the whimsical pattern of red ladybugs. There was a time when she would have stockpiled such items, but now she just set down the delicate piece and turned and continued down the street.

Trying to stay focused on her objective, she turned off into a side street headed towards the used furniture section, but her steps faltered once again when she caught sight of a vendor selling artisan jewelry. Drawn nearer to the display of brightly colored gems, she picked up a pair of earrings set with a red stone and held it to her ear. Tilting her head from side to side, she admired the effect in the small mirror on the counter. She had an artistic and critical eye, and she, too, was a jewelry designer.

No, not really, she reminded herself. She was just a *wannabe* artist— jewelry design had been just a passing fad in college. In reality, she was an assistant researcher at Stanford. It sounded rather impressive, and what she told people when newly introduced, but if truth be told, she was nothing more than a glorified fact-checker.

There had been a time, though, back in college, when Nora had been quite taken with the idea of becoming a goldsmith. She had hoped her parents would be as thrilled as she when she gushed to them on the phone, telling them... How, had she phrased it? She had found her "true calling" and "authentic creative voice".

Instead of being pleased, they thought she was conjuring up some new-age drivel, chasing a pipe dream. "Be realistic, Nora," they had patiently responded. "You need to stay focused on your history degree, hone your research skills, and turn them into a well-paying job. You can't throw all that education away and start all over from scratch."

A bit reluctantly, Nora had seen their point and gone on to graduate school, thinking she'd be a teacher or perhaps find a job in an art museum. It seemed, however as in college, her passion and desire to create couldn't be dissuaded. During her first year, she took a documentary class and impressed her professor with her videography skills. She had always had an innate ability to perceive the feelings and energy of other people, making them come alive in her mind. Compounding this with her natural eye for staging and flair for drama, she created an impressive series of short films.

Aside from being considered the next up-and-coming documentary maker—rivaling Sofia Coppola—because of her knack for tracking down the most obscure bits of information, Nora also garnered a reputation as being an excellent researcher. It seemed her mind overflowed with obscure trivia, and once you got her started, she could talk for hours about sixteenth-century Italian Curule chairs, French commodes, and Delft ceramics. Without batting an eye, she could entertain you with facts about the symbolism in fifteenth-century paintings, which often escaped the modern viewer.

To some people, and most of her friends, such knowledge might be considered impressive cocktail party trivia—highly entertaining but hardly the kind of information that would land her a job in Silicon Valley. Still, her graduate advisor recognized her talents and told her there was nothing wrong with being a "keeper of the past". To further motivate her, he said he'd hire her after she finished her thesis.

Taking him at his word, she completed her doctorate degree and traveled to Italy to finalize research on the fashions and jewelry worn by women in Renaissance paintings. While she was there, she passed long hours in the Uffizi Gallery studying pictures and in the *Biblioteca Nazionale* taking notes. But her most memorable moments were spent in the studio of Signor Martelli, a Florentine jeweler. At the time, she thought it an inspired idea. What better way to understand the art of gold jewelry-making than to learn from an Italian craftsman who created faithful reproductions of the necklaces and earrings worn by the very women she was writing about?

Working with rare metals and semi-precious gems once again awakened her creative passions, and she seriously thought about ditching her graduate school work to remain in Florence and continue her apprenticeship. But, as in the past, it didn't sit well with her parents, and they had advised her to return to the States, reminding her she had a secure job waiting for her.

She replaced the earrings and thought, *Still, living in Florence would have been...*

"Hey, can I help you with anything?"

Glancing up, Nora saw a man with colorful designs inked on his arms was addressing her. "I've got a special price going on if you buy two or more."

Nora fingered a tag attached to a necklace and shook her head. The design wasn't all that original, and the craftsmanship was a bit sloppy. "I'm sorry, not today," she smiled wanly. "I'm just browsing." When she saw the man's face fall in disappointment, to be kind and not offend, as she turned to go, she added, "Nice tattoos."

She thought as she stepped back into the street, that if you looked hard enough, you could find beauty in the most unusual places. Turning around a little too quickly, she bumped into a woman pushing a stroller. When the child started to cry, she apologized profusely. Lately, it seemed she was asking forgiveness of everyone.

Suddenly the effects of having risen so early began to make themselves felt. Glancing at her watch, Nora saw it was barely ten o'clock, but already the pathways between booths were fully clogged with shoppers. Taking in the crowded scene, she felt claustrophobic, and a wave of exhaustion flooded over her. Despite her good intentions, bargain hunting now seemed too much of an ordeal. Needing a moment to regain her equilibrium, she clutched her purse tightly and shouldered her way through the throng, heading toward the beach.

Slipping out of her sandals, she walked for a distance, idly watching the waves roll in, mesmerized by the sound. As the outgoing tide swept debris out into the sea, she contemplated a bird balancing precariously on top of a buoy. Holding up her phone, Nora framed the shot and took a picture. She cropped and enhanced the image and, liking the effect, she debated whether to post it to Facebook.

Oh, what the hell, she thought. Although she was feeling quite the opposite, she typed the caption—*The gull sees farthest who flies highest*—and published it.

Listlessly she scrolled through her feed but didn't see anything of interest, just a bunch of pictures of cats and smiling babies and a couple of trite platitudes. She couldn't believe she was letting herself be dragged into social media again, trying to keep up appearances. "Oh, Nora! What is wrong with you?" she groaned. "You are pathetic."

Lately, she had been feeling melancholy and vulnerable, and it didn't seem like things were improving. Realizing that most of her life counseling was coming only from memes and the sage advice propagated by Facebook philosophers, she was seriously considering seeking professional help.

She was about to toss the phone into her purse when she heard a distinctive *ding* telling her she had just received a friend request. Tilting the screen against the glare of the sun, Nora saw the sender's name was Juliette Laurent.

Opening the message, Nora read, "*Ciao,* Nora! Hey, I just saw that post about the seagull. Seems like you are doing well out there in California. It's been a long time, let's connect. If your French is as terrible as I remember, we can always chat in Italian!"

Nora grimaced, realizing she should probably make her security controls tighter. Still, it pleased her that her picture of the seagull had flown across the ocean all the way to Vouvray, France, where Juliette lived. Once upon a time, they had been roommates in Florence and had shared a flat in *Le Cure,* the neighborhood to the north of town, near the soccer stadium.

She thought fondly of her friend. Juli had been the yin to her yang;

they complemented each other nicely. Her friend's blond hair and tall, lithe frame had been the perfect foil to Nora's long dark hair and petite figure, and while Nora had worked as a gold jeweler's apprentice, Juliette had interned with an Italian wine merchant.

Looking down at her phone, she wondered, *Was this some kind of cosmic sign?* Over the years, Nora had relegated Italy to the back of her mind. But lately, everywhere she turned it seemed she was struck by another reminder, like earlier this morning in the jeweler's booth and last week at the neighborhood wholesale warehouse.

She had stopped in for an oversized package of paper towels and a bottle of laundry detergent. Instead of running in and dashing out as she had intended, inundated by giant television monitors that continuously played splashy images of Tuscany, Nora had stood transfixed in the entrance. As she watched the video images of grape fields, hill towns, and quaint little churches play in a continuous loop, she was filled with deep regret and an aching longing. After a while, she forgot why she had even gone to the store in the first place.

Pushing her sunglasses on top of her head, Nora reread her friend's brief message and smiled. Just seeing Juliette's name reminded her of a time when she had used another language and had been unafraid to make a choice, travel the world, and take chances.

After she had returned home to California and had taken up with Richard, she had lost touch with her friend. Now it didn't seem possible seven years had passed since she had stood on the train platform in Santa Maria Novella waving goodbye to her old roommate. Where had the time gone, and what had happened to the young men they had dated? She imagined they were all married to lovely Italian women with two or three kids by now.

More than a little curious, Nora connected with Juliette and scrolled through her feed. She expected to see Juliette had returned to France, but to Nora's surprise, her friend's Facebook page was filled with pictures of Italy. "Well, now, let's just see what you have been doing on your vacation, Mademoiselle Laurent." Tilting the phone to see the screen better, she read out loud city names: "Florence, Montepulciano, Lucca, Arezzo."

Restlessly she shifted her feet, feeling the cold, loose sand between her toes, unable to shake the sudden powerful feeling of yearning—like unrequited love. Each Tuscan hill, rustic building, and smiling face seemed to Nora an open invitation to peer into the life of her friend. But instead of satisfying her cravings for Italy, they filled her with an edgy sensation, as if she were eavesdropping on a conversation she couldn't fully hear. It frustrated her.

Nora continued scanning but stopped when she came to a picture of her friend dressed in dirty jeans and a straw hat, standing in a vineyard between two men. She instinctively knew they were Italian by the effortless style they projected even dressed in t-shirts and jeans. One had long dark hair and was clean-shaven; the other had a hint of a beard and wavy hair.

Suddenly it dawned on Nora that these were no tourist pictures. Glancing at Juliette's profile description, she read, *"Works at Urlo alla Luna. In a relationship with Italy."*

Falling back into the sand, she realized Juliette wasn't vacationing in Italy. She lived there... She even worked at a winery there!

Holding the phone in front of her face, she studied the image again, noting that one of the men had his arm draped casually around Juliette. She had captioned the photo: *"Loving Arezzo... but I've got my hands full with these two!"* The post was followed by emojis of wine glasses and smiley faces, tagging it with two names: @MarcoOrlando and @GDonati.

She tasted envy on her tongue. It was like swallowing the last bitter dregs of coffee she had tossed away earlier. Out loud, she whispered, "That should be me."

Where had that thought come from? Discontent...regret? But this feeling wasn't just your average Facebook envy, where one coveted the images of someone else's picture-perfect life. No, this was different. Juliette's photos were conjuring up something she had long ago tamped down and denied. Restlessly, she wondered what her life might have been like if she had made different choices. What if she had stayed in Italy, and what if she hadn't moved back to San Francisco? What if she had never gotten married?

She paused a moment and let the last question linger in her head. If she hadn't married, what kind of person would she be now, and what would she be doing?

Nora thought back to the first time she had met Richard. She remembered their early days and the height of their happiness when they'd talked about traveling and seeing the world. In the end, their globe trotting plans never transpired. Instead, her husband had convinced her to embrace domestic life, buy a house, and start a vegetable garden.

Although she had wanted to take time off to go back to school to study design—or turn the hundreds of ideas and research notes she had written over the years into a book of her own, or make videos from ideas that filled her head—she had played it safe. Instead of realizing her personal dreams, she had stayed with her well-paying, if not mundane, research job to contribute her share to the mortgage.

Then there had been a whole host of problems. Years earlier she had suffered from a series of miscarriages in the early stages of pregnancy and was filled with an overwhelming sense of guilt, instinctively feeling his unexpressed blame. Rather than working through their differences and disappointments and growing stronger, their relationship took a downward turn. Nora drifted along, taking no action, letting herself be dragged into a lonely state of lethargy and depression.

She finally awoke one day, realizing she didn't like the person she had turned into. Knowing something had to change, daring to reinvest in herself, Nora had asked her husband for a break, telling him she needed some time on her own to sort things out. But, as the weeks slipped into months, during which Richard soothed his pride and flirted with a new love interest, their trial separation turned into something irreparable, and they agreed to end their marriage.

The decision had devastated her, but she had to let him go. If Nora was honest with herself, in the final analysis, she hadn't loved him enough to fight for him or their future together. She reminded herself he deserved someone who would.

Nora shaded her eyes and looked out at the ocean. It was then she saw it. Before her was her ghost ship—it was the life she had not chosen, sailing a parallel course to the one she was on now. Looking at it, she was filled with regret. She would never know about that other life filled with its complexities, joys, and sorrows.

Listening to the waves washing up onto the shore, she felt like the seagull balancing on the rocking buoy, trying desperately to hang on to something—but she wasn't even sure she knew what she was hanging onto. Was it a life alone, or did she want a partner? And children...? She shook her head and wondered if she could go through that all over again.

Gazing down at the photo open on the small screen of her phone, she thought morosely, *Do I even want to be here at all?*

Scrolling through Juliette's feed again, she felt another pang of longing. Italy. It was just one of the phantom ships she had not boarded. Perhaps if she had been bolder and booked passage on it, she would be a completely different, happier person.

She gazed at the horizon and watched as the mysterious shape of her hopes and regrets turned away, setting a course for a far-distant land, growing smaller and smaller until it vanished completely. Her vision clouded and she blinked back a tear of frustration. She stuffed her phone into her bag and rested her chin on her knees. All alone on the deserted beach, her choices continued to haunt her.

Chapter 3

Where Life is Beautiful

*T*hat evening, curled up on the couch sipping a glass of red wine, Nora turned the pages of an old photo album, of pictures she had taken in Italy. She and Julia had made many day trips from Florence, traipsing about the Tuscan countryside, and the images were stirring up fond memories. But there was one particular photo, taken in Arezzo, that captured *la gioia di vivere*—the carefree spirit—of their time together completely.

Where is it? she wondered as she turned to the last page. Then looking across the room at the hope chest her dad had built for her as a wedding present, she remembered she had tucked it inside one of the secret drawers where she kept all her special mementos.

Nora crossed the room and knelt before it and ran her hand over the lid, enjoying the silky smooth feel of the wood. Her father had started his woodworking hobby when she was just a little girl. From the beginning, into every piece of furniture he built, he had created a system of secret chambers. But, even as a child, she was never stumped for long and quickly solved his puzzles.

Raising the lid, and pulling open one of the little drawers, she found the picture she was searching for. Nora held the photo up to the light and gently caressed the image with her finger. Although the colors were fading to sepia, she remembered the moment vividly. Seeing the picture of Juliette, with a broad grin on her face, standing in the middle of the Piazza Grande in Arezzo holding a ridiculous lamp encrusted with seashells made her smile.

Out of all the things they had done together in Italy, one of their favorite adventures had been to hop the train out of Florence and head south for an afternoon of antiquing. The California market in Half Moon Bay didn't hold a candle to the treasures one could find in Arezzo. Amidst the jumble of rusty keys, cracked teapots, and old armoires, it was also intriguing to think you might find a valuable jewel or a forgotten letter tucked inside a secret drawer.

Setting the photo aside, Nora reached for her empty wine glass. "Looks like this *signorina* needs a refill," she said.

Settling back down on the couch, pushing the photo album aside, she turned on the TV. Halfheartedly, she traveled through the channels, but nothing held her interest for long. She continued zapping through infomercials, reruns of *Friends,* and CNN news highlights but stopped when she heard the hauntingly familiar theme song of a movie that had just started. Recognizing the soundtrack as that of the Italian film *Life Is Beautiful,* she thought, *I believe the universe is telling me again I could do with a little more beauty in my life.*

Pulling a pillow into her arms, she embraced it tightly and got ready for the romantic tragi-comedy starring Roberto Benigni that had been filmed in Arezzo. It was a story that started off lightly, causing her to laugh, but inevitably turned sad and made her cry.

As the opening credits rolled by and the initial scenes unfolded, Nora let the Italian words wash over her, relishing the familiar sounds. And true to form, just hearing the lyrical Italian accents made her incredibly happy, and ironically she felt her eyes grow misty. Absently, she brushed away an emotional tear feeling the tug of Italy once again, and then laughed in pleasure the next moment hearing the protagonist exclaim, *"Buongiorno, principessa!"* As a newcomer to town, luck was with him—even lovely young women were dropping out of the haylofts into his open arms!

Caught up in the rapid-fire dialogue, trying her best to keep up with what the actors were saying as they walked through the streets of Arezzo, she almost didn't hear the low hum of her cell phone set on vibrate. But when the buzzing started again, Nora was pulled away from the Piazza Grande and, back to the confines of her tiny apartment. She followed the sound to the kitchen and, moving her purse aside, she found her cell phone buried under a pile of junk mail, tucked inside a book.

Checking the display, she saw it was a friend from work, and instantly felt guilty. Earlier in the week, they had made plans to meet up for a drink, but now all she wanted was to watch her movie, return to Italy if only for a few hours, and have a therapeutic cry.

Quickly she invented an excuse and asked his forgiveness—again—promising she would make it up to him the following week. When the conversation concluded, in relief she placed her phone onto the kitchen counter next to her laptop. She was about to return to her movie but was distracted by the glossy cover of her book, where her phone had been hiding, featuring a Renaissance girl with an oval face and an aquiline nose. Nora patted the woman's cheek and, using her best Benigni impersonation said, *"Buongiorno, principessa!* It appears it is going to be just you and me tonight, lady."

Drawn to the image of the lovely Renaissance princess, Nora picked up the biography of Isabella de' Medici she was currently reading and lightly thumbed the pages. She enjoyed the swishing sound they made, almost as if Isabella was whispering a reply. She wasn't quite sure why she was so obsessed with the Medici princess, but lately, Nora was reading everything she could lay her hands on. Truth be told, she was feeling haunted by the woman.

It had all started a few months ago, when she had been fact-checking the number of villas and hunting lodges Cosimo de' Medici had built, that were peppered all around Tuscany. Following a series of links, Nora had eventually fallen into a site that featured the Medici sporting retreat located in the small town of Cerreto Guidi. She was about to click away but was caught by a startling passage that alluded to the murder of his daughter, Isabella, which had occurred in the villa. Nora's curiosity was further piqued when she discovered the brutal slaying had occurred at the hands of the woman's husband.

The story got even juicier when she learned the ghost of the Medici princess was supposedly trapped in the very spot where she had been hung. According to urban legend, Isabella still waited there for her lover,

Troilo to return. To make time pass and keep herself entertained, Isabella tended to pop up unexpectedly, scaring local tourists. At one point, sightings of the ethereal princess had been so dramatic and frequent, the townsfolk had dubbed her *La Dama Bianca*, the white lady.

Never one to let a good ghost story pass her by, Nora had continued reading and hours later, after sorting through numerous internet blogs, her interest still hadn't been satiated. But the legend of Isabella's phantom was just the lure to draw Nora in. She soon discovered that Isabella had been quite a diva and openly flaunted and broken the rules of Renaissance society.

Born in 1452 to Cosimo I, the Grand Duke of Tuscany, and Eleonora de' Toledo, she was the brightest of all her siblings. Lovely and liberated, Isabella stood toe to toe with her male counterparts, and she soon came to be known as the "Star of Florence". She had embraced life on her own terms, upsetting society's rules, and was a trend-setting feminist. For a fifteenth-century woman, when most wives were kept under lock and key, that was a dangerous thing indeed. And for Isabella, it did not play out well in the end.

Studying the photo on the book's jacket, Nora was once again struck by the princess's proud demeanor and the intelligence in her eyes. Caught by the fifteenth-century girl's penetrating stare, she couldn't look away. To Nora, it seemed Isabella was challenging her personally. Unnerved, she shifted the book slightly, and due to a trick of the light, it appeared Isabella had just winked at her.

Well, well, thought Nora, *what might you be suggesting? What could you possibly want from me?*

With her finger, she traced the curve of the young Medici woman's swan-like neck, adorned with a strand of iridescent pearls from which hung a heavy gold pendant set with a ruby, a symbol of her betrothal. Reaching for a pencil she had left on the counter, Nora picked up one of the envelopes from the pile of junk mail, turned it over, and copied the necklace with rapid, definitive strokes.

As she sketched, Nora replayed the details she knew about Isabella.

She realized the Renaissance princess would have known that marriage was rarely about romantic love and her role was to be a good and compliant wife. The "Star of Florence" would have clearly understood what her duty entailed, but still, it hadn't stopped her from stepping over the border of propriety and into the bed of her husband's cousin. She had been a strong-minded woman with self-serving notions.

The titillating details of Isabella's sexual escapades and the brutal way in which she had been killed had heightened local hysteria and given rise to her ghost story. Curiously, however, in more recent days, sightings of Isabella's phantom had diminished. Nora imagined the lady had grown weary of making public appearances. Or quite possibly the beautiful and well-educated princess, who delighted in making a scene, was just taking a break.

"This is only the intermission," Nora joked with her colleagues. "The third act is about to begin. She's probably waiting in the wings ready to make her grand re-entrance." Since Isabella was always the star of the show, Nora certainly wouldn't put it past her.

Studying the necklace she had just sketched, Nora thought, *Not bad*. To give the design more dimension, she emphasized it with a few more cross-hatchings, then tossed the envelope aside and reached for her wine glass. As she took a sip, Nora looked down at the envelope and saw the familiar university logo. Picking it up again, using her pencil as an opener, she drew out a flyer advertising next fall's Women's Week events. In bold letters, it read: *Bring to Life an Unsung Heroine!*

Nora's pulse quickened. The Medici princess was the epitome of the unsung heroine. Was this another sign? Was it a message from *La Dama Bianca*—her personal invitation to Nora to bring the princess' spirit back to life?

Laughing softly to herself, Nora thought, *I could tell Isabella's story. Well, why not?* She had the resources and the creative skills to make a video, but more importantly, she had already researched the material. Before she could talk herself out of the idea, Nora reached for her laptop and typed up an outline for a short documentary. She paused a moment and looked off into space. What would she call such a film? Nora pondered a moment, picked up her book, and studied the cover. Then, in a flash, it came to her, and she said softly, "I will call it *Waking Isabella: A Portrait of a Princess*. Yes, that's perfect!"

For two weeks straight, Nora worked on the proposal for her video. Once begun, she couldn't stop the flood of ideas. And after many late nights and getting up very early in the morning to complete the work, Nora was elated and gratified a month later to be awarded a grant to complete her documentary. The stipend was small, but it was enough to partially fund a trip to Italy where she planned to film.

Given the green light, Nora planned out her trip, but beyond buying her plane ticket and requesting a three-month sabbatical, her plans were still a little vague. She had a rough idea of how her summer would play out. She'd start in Rome and then make her way to Cerreto Guidi, where Isabella had been murdered. She absolutely had to see the place for herself and hoped, a bit unrealistically even, to meet Isabella's ghost.

Then Nora figured she'd move on to Florence where she would rent an apartment for the summer in the Oltrarno. There, in the shadow of the Pitti Palace, the Medici princess's home, Nora imagined herself splicing together video clips and adding voice-overs. In her mind's eye, she saw herself working during the mornings, taking long breaks to walk along the Ponte Vecchio in the afternoons, and lunching on tripe sandwiches bought from the *lampredotto* trucks parked near the Uffizi.

Right before departing, Nora contacted Juliette to let her know she was coming and suggested they meet up in Florence. Within a few hours, her friend sent back a message. "Listen, I know you are going to be busy with your film in Northern Tuscany and have your heart set on staying in Florence, but here's an idea—come spend the summer, instead, in Arezzo. I've moved out to the winery, and my apartment is available. You can finish your documentary in our corner of Tuscany—*dove la vita è bella*—where life is beautiful."

The offer was more than appealing, and Nora found it to be an invitation she couldn't refuse. Things were falling into place as if the

Medici princess herself were orchestrating the show, and at the end of May, Nora found herself sitting on the tarmac at San Francisco airport waiting for takeoff. From her window seat on a plane bound for Rome, she observed a flurry of airport workers loading bags and boxes onto the plane.

As Nora watched the luggage roll up the ramp to be stowed in the cargo hold, she congratulated herself. Although she planned to return to California in a few months, it felt like a step in the right direction. Just look how far she had already traveled, and she hadn't even left the gate in San Francisco. What else waited for her in Italy, she could only imagine.

Mentally reviewing the plans for her film and recalling what she knew about her capricious and elusive star, Nora thought a bit ironically, *Perhaps I will be the one to wake Isabella.*

Chapter 4

Incense and Regrets

October 2007 – Two and a Half Years Earlier

*L*uca sat rigidly on the pew in the dimly lit church and stared at his knuckles. He looked up briefly when the priest intoned an age-old prayer. Studying the old gentleman dressed in long flowing robes for a moment, he willed himself to listen. Then, giving up, he let out a long sigh then inhaled deeply, breathing in the scent of candle wax, incense, and old regrets.

"Signore onnipotente, Tu sei fonte di vita. Lord our God, you are the source of life. In Te, noi abbiamo la vita e prosperiamo. Amaci nella vita e nella morte, e per la Tua grazie, guidaci verso il Tuo regno, attraverso Tuo figlio Gesù Cristo. Nel nome del Padre, del figlio e dello Spirito Santo."

When the priest finished his holy appeal and made the sign of the cross, Luca mumbled out the age-old response, "Amen."

He, along with most of the town, had gathered in the church of San Donato to say goodbye to Carlotta, whom they had lost just the week before in a terrible accident. Some, like Luca, had known her very well, while others had known her only in passing. Arezzo was a small town, after all, and the folks who lived there were not impervious to her comings and goings. She was the kind of person who had lived her life in a big way and at some point or another, had made a lasting impression on almost every one of them. Her impact, whether good or bad, had depended on her mood on any particular day. And now, despite one's opinion of her, it was sobering to think that she was gone.

Those who knew her best had come to pay their respects to the dead woman. But, like him, Luca imagined each of the parishioners was also contemplating their own mortality and failings. So lost in thought, when the priest resumed the service, the words of solace cascaded over the grieving man in a senseless jumble of promises and prayers. Luca didn't even hear or turn around to look at the woman who hushed her child or see who the culprit was shuffling his feet and making the bench creak behind him.

Instead, he scrutinized the familiar stone arch at the front of the church depicting scenes from the life of San Donato. He stared at it curiously, admiring the elongated Gothic figures and quatrefoil arches, tracing the stonework with his eyes, wondering about the long-forgotten artist who had carved it.

Drowning in a sea of misgivings, he was barely aware when a parishioner got up and walked to the pulpit to read a passage from the *Bible*. Instead, his gaze drifted heavenward, and he focused his attention on the ceiling high above his head. Studying the angels and prophets in the quadrants, he realized they had always been there and would continue to be there long after he was gone. The thought gave him more comfort than the priest's or parishioner's words ever could. There was something timeless and reassuring knowing art endured while human lives were so fragile and frail.

Luca shifted his weight on the bench and remembered other moments when he'd sat here in this church, shoulder to shoulder with his grandmother Margherita. He had often accompanied her to mass each week to say a prayer to his grandfather and light a candle in his memory. Brushing back the hair from his forehead, his *nonna* Nita had told him he resembled Federico—the grandfather he had never known. "*Era un brav'uomo, tuo nonno.* He was a fine man," she said, "and you take after him in every way."

The young man had grown up listening to stories of his grandfather— an artist who had lived in Paris—whom his nonna Margherita met and fell in love with during the war—as well as memories of her father who had started the family's antique business back in the thirties. He smiled once again, remembering her feisty tenacity as well as her harrowing stories of the *partigiani*—the Italian rebels who had defied the Nazis on her very doorstep.

Aside from the weekly masses, there had been joyous moments in this church as well. In his younger days, he had been a talented horseman and participated in the city's famous jousting festival. For three years running, after each of the matches, here in this sanctified spot in front of a cheering crowd, he had held up the coveted prize—the Golden Lance, the symbol of triumph and victory.

Luca's thoughts continued to drift through the kaleidoscope of weddings, baptisms, and Christmas masses that had been held in this magnificent church, under its golden ceiling. He closed his eyes and steadied himself. Those had been happier times. Now it seemed he came here more often to mourn the loss of people he loved. First, his grandmother followed closely by the death of a beloved coach.

With deep regret, he remembered Antonio Giorgeschi, the man who had been the first to lift him up into a saddle and teach him to whisper to horses. And now, Luca sat on the same hard wooden pew, listening to the familiar words, going through the same exact motions mourning the loss of Carlotta.

The sound of the church door softly banging, announcing the arrival of a latecomer, finally interrupted Luca's reflections and caused him to look over his shoulder. When he did, he saw Egidio slipping into the chapel. When the elderly man's eyes met Luca's, he removed his hat and acknowledged Luca with a sympathetic smile. Egidio was a friend of his grandmother's, and despite his advanced age, he was dapperly dressed in crisp linen pants and coat. Around his neck was a blue and yellow tie fastened with a gold pin. Luca was pleased his old friend had made it back from Florence in time for the funeral. He was a part of the family, and his presence consoled him.

Before facing front again, Luca briefly scanned the crowd and saw his mother, father, and sister Serena seated just a short distance away. As his gaze traveled over the rest of the congregation, he paused when he saw Marco and Mariella, seated a few rows ahead of them. It had been a while since they last talked, and he noted that Marco's hair had grown a bit longer. It also seemed his old friend hadn't slept in days.

Once upon a time, they had shared great times together and, suddenly, memories of his youthful days came flooding back. With Carlotta as the ringleader, the three of them had conquered all. They'd galloped their horses through golden fields, swam in cool dark lakes in the ravines, and howled at the moon at midnight. Those had been such careless days, innocent and thrilling. Both of them had loved her well.

But that was then. Things had changed.

When Marco saw Luca glancing his way, he lifted his hand and raised his hand and waved slightly. Luca regarded him for a moment but didn't respond in kind. They had both lost Carlotta, but at the moment Luca had nothing to say to Marco. Even if he had the words, he didn't know where to pick up the pieces. He wasn't sure if they could ever go back to how things once were, or if he even wanted to.

Hearing the choir start to sing, Luca joined in halfheartedly, forcing himself to concentrate as the altar boys lit the candles, preparing for Holy Communion. When the congregation rose to its feet, he slowly stood, unaware or just not caring that another person was watching him from the shadows.

If he had turned around, Luca would have seen Carlotta's grandfather, Ruggero Falconi, leaning heavily on his cane at the back of the chapel. He would have also seen how the man narrowed his eyes in distaste as he looked at him. But, Luca didn't turn around, and he didn't see the old man take out his wallet, flip it open, and wistfully study the image of a lovely young girl.

Instead of joining in the refrain, sitting in isolation, the old man caressed the cheek of the woman with his finger and thought about his loss. But the photograph wasn't a recent color snapshot of his granddaughter; it was a faded black-and-white photo of the woman he had once loved. Studying her svelte figure standing next to a younger version of himself, he thought back to the moment when it had been taken.

What was the year? Ah, yes... It was May 10, 1940. Funny how he could recall the moment vividly, and yet he couldn't remember the current date. They had just returned from city hall where they had announced their wedding banns and Bernardo, her father, had taken the picture.

Ruggero continued to stare at the photo, and he shook his head in bitterness. Closing his eyes, he recalled past humiliations, fresh in his mind as if they had occurred yesterday. The future he had envisioned with the woman in the picture never transpired. He had lost her to another man, and the girl he had loved since childhood had slipped away.

He sucked in his breath when he felt a sharp pain as if his heart were trapped in a vise. He whispered, "*A cosa pensava? Avrei dovuto essere io!* Ridiculous that I should have been the one rejected. I am the one who had so much more to offer Margherita."

As people filed past him to the front of the church, Ruggero suddenly came back to the present. When he saw Luca returning to his seat, he inhaled sharply. For a moment he thought he'd seen a ghost. The face of the younger man reminded him of another. With shaking fingers, he replaced the photo into his wallet, letting dark memories and things he had never shared with anyone else slide away.

Once again, he clamped down the lid and locked them deep inside of him. It was so much easier to blame others than focus on his own past sins.

Whispering under his breath, he said, "Donati is the one to blame for Carlotta's death. *È lui il colpevole.*"

The organ swelled filling the church with solemn, melodic tones, indicating the service was over and soon the holy space was filled with the sound of people rising. Luca's melancholy thoughts were soon drowned out by the music and the murmur of sympathetic voices greeting one another. As the congregation filtered out of the church, Luca stood up too, adjusted his tie, and tugged down the sleeves of his jacket. He spoke with a few friends, biding his time until he could be alone with his melancholy thoughts again.

As the last few stragglers picked up their purses and coats and wandered out the door into the sunlight to resume their lives, he turned to his mother and hugged her slim shoulders. When Luca stepped back, she gave him a concerned frown, noticing the signs of a beard darkening his jaw.

"You are coming back to the house, *giusto? Ho preparato il pranzo.* Just something light to eat to keep up your strength."

"Certo, mamma," he agreed, although he hadn't had an appetite in days. Leaning in to kiss his sister, he murmured into her ear, "Take them home. I'll be there soon... I just need a moment."

Serena observed him sadly and said, "She worries, you know. Don't be too long."

Luca watched his family leave the church together and then turned back to the altar. Breathing in the sweet scent of lilies and the earthy smell of ferns, he studied the picture that had been set up on an easel next to the bank of flowers. It was a photo of Carlotta that Marco had taken several years before. She wore a long, white cotton dress and stood in a field of poppies, her face turned up to the sun, and her long, dark hair freely streamed over her shoulders.

In the empty, echoing space, he stared at the girl he had known all his life. She was wild and free, almost not of this earth. One would imagine by her radiant glow she had been a happy woman, but pictures could be deceiving.

Shaking his head, he wondered, *"Che cosa avrei potuto fare di diverso?* What could I have done differently to ease your pain?"

He had loved the girl, but had he loved the woman she'd become?

"Se solo..." But he never completed his thought. His concentration was broken by the sound of footsteps behind him and someone clearing their throat. Looking over his shoulder, he saw Marco and Mariella. The three of them stood in a small circle without saying anything, letting the ghost of Carlotta drift between them.

Finally, to break the awkward silence, Mariella reached up and kissed him on both cheeks. Marco followed her lead and, holding out his hand, he pulled his friend in close and gave him a quick hug.

Stepping back, they regarded each other tensely until Marco finally said, *"Mi dispiace. Senti* Luca, if you need anything, let me know. I just wanted to say..." He paused when he saw the despondency in Luca's eyes.

"Don't," Luca said. "*Lascia perdere*—let it go. I just can't..."

Marco waited to see if he would continue, but Luca said nothing more. Finally, he nodded, saying under his breath, "You have no idea how sorry I am."

Not expecting him to reply, Marco moved swiftly to the door. Mariella watched her brother retreat. Looking back at Luca, she shrugged apologetically and said, "He's taking her death hard. But, really, Luca, remember, if you need anything—anything at all—we are here. All you need to do is call. *Siamo qui. Chiamaci.*"

Luca only nodded and pivoted slowly around to face the altar again. Sadly, Mariella watched him then turned to follow her brother. Before she left the church, however, she paused in a small alcove to light a candle and pray for the dead. Striking a match and touching the flame to a wick, her eyes slid to the right as she watched Luca once again contemplating the picture of Carlotta.

Mariella had a compassionate heart but was also a woman of strong opinions, as well as a bit of a gossip. She had known Luca all her life and, from afar, had watched him turn from a reckless boy into a considerate man. Carlotta, on the other hand, had never changed. She had been a girl who started out wild and had never outgrown her careless nature.

Truth be told, Mariella's dislike for Carlotta took root when she had been only seven or eight. To this day, she could still hear the older girl teasing her about her weight, calling her *una grassa ciambella*—a fat doughnut. Aside from her personal feelings, Mariella had never been keen on the way Carlotta treated her brother, or, for that matter, Luca. Still, the woman's death was so terribly sad and tragic and swiftly, she touched her forehead and chest in a sign of the cross, asking the savior for forgiveness.

Tucked out of sight, glancing up at the patron Saint Donato, Mariella added on a special request to be forgiven for any unkind thoughts she might have had about the dead woman. She continued to pray, but hearing Luca start to speak, she glanced up in surprise, thinking he was addressing her. Looking over her shoulder, she saw instead he was still standing in front of Carlotta's photograph, talking to the dead woman.

Realizing his words were not intended for her ears, she tried not to listen. Still, being a curious person, couldn't tune out his words entirely and, through the quiet church, she heard him say, "I lost you a long time ago, Carlotta. A part of me will always love you. *Perdonami, amore mio.* Forgive me, my love."

Chapter 5

Backseat Driver

June 2010

*R*ome was as Nora remembered it—a bustling city alive with possibilities. Careening through the busy streets, she couldn't stop herself from taking terrible touristy pictures of ancient buildings and toppled pillars through the cab's dirty windows. She was excited to be back in Italy, listening once again to Italian spoken over the cab's radio, living the language and letting it swirl around her. She also thrilled to the sound of the street noises—the chorus of horns and wailing of police sirens—a symphony to her ears.

As her driver neared the historic city center, headed in the direction of the Campidoglio, they passed by the Theatre of Marcellus. Nora had noticed the ancient structure many times before but hadn't paid it much attention. To her, it had been just a part of Rome's picturesque stage setting of Doric columns and Corinthian arches. But, as the cab passed by, Nora sat up and took notice. She knew that constructed on top of the ruins was a Renaissance palace built by the Orsini family.

Paolo Orsini, who would one day marry Isabella de' Medici, could trace his lineage back to the eighth century. His family had been Roman bankers and could claim their fair share of popes, as well as sexual and political scandals. His grandmother, in fact, had been the illegitimate daughter of Pope Julius II. At the young age of nineteen, he was made Duke of Bracciano and given instructions to procreate and carry on the family line.

Nora rested her head on the back of the cab's vinyl seat, and an amused expression played over her face. In her punchy state of mind, she thought, *It is universally acknowledged that a single man invested with a dukedom must be in want of a wife.*

There had been a bevy of beauties for Paolo to choose from. But what made Isabella's candidacy stand out from all the rest wasn't the Florentine girl's sparkling wit and intellectual capabilities, nor was it that she played a fine tune on the lute. What had attracted the Orsini family to the eleven-year-old Medici princess was her excessively large silk purse, overflowing with gold florins.

The Orsini might have been an ancient Roman family, but by the end of the fifteenth century, their coffers were swiftly draining, and Paolo, in particular, was in desperate need of cash. A bit of a spendthrift, he liked the finer things in life; he enjoyed a robust wine, eating at an elegant table, and dressing in fancy brocades and lace.

But what he enjoyed most of all were the common prostitutes, like Camilla the Skinny, he purchased to warm his bed. They were as plentiful as the stallions that filled his stables, and if he were to beat one of his Roman courtesans or desire something a little more perverse, additional funds were required to pay the ghetto pimp. The answer to his financial problems presented itself in the form of Isabella's dowry.

From Cosimo de' Medici's standpoint, marrying his daughter to an Orsini would have been a feather in his cap. Nora could well imagine the Florentine leader chortling to his wife Eleonora about the political deal he had struck with the Roman Orsini.

"Just think, my love! Marrying Isabella to the Orsini duke will elevate our status in the eyes of our Sienese neighbors. Ha! We may be an upstart family descending from sheepherders, but now we are aligned with a family that can trace its roots back to Caesar!"

"Well, *tesoro mio*, you have been very clever indeed," replied Eleonora, tenderly massaging his shoulders. "I'd say it is quite the advantageous marriage. I do hope, however, our young daughter will be as fortunate as I. One must do one's duty to one's family and Florence, first and foremost... But my hope is that she too will find a pleasant man, with whom she may share a happy life."

With a wicked gleam, Cosimo turned her around and pulled the ties of her dressing gown so the flimsy robe fell open. Eyeing his wife lustfully, he drew her into his embrace. *"Davvero? Un uomo piacevole... A pleasant* man you say, *tesoro...?"*

Moving with her to the bed, he added, "Well, if that be the case... let me show you just how *pleasant* I can be."

Laughing together, they fell back onto the soft mattress. Seduced by his warm hands, she added with a coy smile, *"Oh, sì, signore.* Please show me! It is my duty after all. You know I'd do anything for the family—and for Florence!"

According to everyone involved, the marriage between Isabella and Paolo Orsini seemed a match made in heaven. For Cosimo, however, there was only one teeny-tiny problem—the Orsini duke's dark side.

This may have given him pause, and a reason to worry, but Cosimo was a clever man. To spare his precious daughter the insult of living with a misogynist and a womanizer, shortly after the marriage was consummated, he whisked Isabella back to Florence where he could protect her.

Nora, well versed in Renaissance history, knew full well it was highly unusual for a fifteenth-century bride to return home to her father and live independently of her husband. But for Isabella, Nora imagined, it must have been a dream come true. It was almost as if the marriage had never taken place. Free of her loutish husband, she lived a privileged life, enjoying unprecedented autonomy, of which she took full advantage.

As for Paolo, the arrangement may have insulted his honor, and it would have irked him that his father-in-law held the purse strings so tightly. But at the end of the day, Isabella remaining in Florence wasn't such a bad thing. With her living in the Pitti Palace next to the Arno, he had greater latitude to conduct his own dubious pursuits in his hometown of Rome near the Tiber. He had no real love for his Medici bride, but at least he had a wife who would bear him sons.

So absorbed by thoughts of Isabella's husband, when Nora's cab rounded the corner and jolted to a stop in front of her hotel just off of Piazza Navona, she blinked hard, half-expecting to see a Roman bordello and women like Camilla the Skinny and Pasqua the Garlic Eater waving to her from one of the windows. Instead, what she saw was a few stray tourists and a flock of pigeons strutting about.

Regaining her wits, Nora got out of the cab and concentrated on the mundane procedures of checking in. Greeting the porter at the desk, she signed the ledger, showed her passport, and transported her luggage from the lobby to the third floor in an ancient elevator the size of a linen closet.

In her room, before even turning on the lights or pulling back the drapes, she cranked on the air conditioning and connected to the hotel's WiFi. As she watched the life come back to her cell phone, the cool air revived her. It wasn't long before her device dinged, alerting her to a flurry of new messages.

Sorting them from least to most critical, she saw a couple from her mother and one from Richard. Wanting to get the worst over with first, she opened the message from her ex and learned they had a potential buyer for the house. He said he would keep her posted. He concluded his text by telling her where to go to get the best pizza in Rome.

"Unbelievable," Nora snorted. It was so like him. The man had never been to Italy, and *he* was telling *her* where to eat.

With a groan, she lay back on the bed.

Richard could be adamant and an authority on absolutely everything, from what brand of car to buy to the precise degree to set the thermostat. His intentions were good, but his suggestions often sounded like backhanded compliments. Even now she gritted her teeth, remembering some of his past comments.

"Sure, you look great in that outfit, only you can pull it off—but is that *really* what you are wearing tonight?" Or, her favorite one of all, "I don't know *where* you put it all—I wish I could eat *two* scoops of gelato every night like you and get away with it."

Turning over on her side, she curled into a ball, rested her head on her arm, and thought about their perfect beginning. It had been casual and light, and what attracted her at first had been his humor and charm. But perhaps she should have known better; early on there had been warning signs. They had only been dating a few weeks, and already Richard had planned out their entire future, locking her into a rigid ten-year family plan. He even went so far as to pick out the names for their children, and the ink had hardly been dry on their marriage certificate before he began preparing a nursery for those imagined kids.

Sadly, the room had remained empty for years, and after many doctor appointments and two miscarriages, they discovered they couldn't have a child. It wasn't that either one of them couldn't have a baby, just not together—something about their DNA wasn't compatible. The universe seemed to have played a cruel joke on them, letting them know practically from the outset that their union was unsuitable. It hurt her terribly, and she felt terribly guilty to realize she couldn't give Richard the child he wanted so desperately. As a result, fissures began to appear on the surface of their seemingly happy marriage.

Lying down on the bed in the darkened room, in her small hotel room in Rome, had been a big mistake. Not only was she starting to feel the onslaught of jet lag, but the thoughts of her ex-husband and all they had been through were severely dampening her mood. Rolling her head to look at the bedside clock, she saw it was still early. How easy it would be to slip into a comatose sleep to escape thoughts of past disappointments and pain.

Nora closed her eyes and started to drift off, but her lids fluttered open a few moments when she heard an internal voice whisper urgently, *"Svegliati! Non arrendersi mai!* Come on, Nora. Wake up! Never give up! What are you waiting for? It's time to check out this magnificent city."

She remained motionless on the bed, refocusing her priorities. Would Isabella have been reduced to such an apathetic puddle? *Come on. You are in Rome,* Nora told herself. *This is a moment not to be wasted.* Rallying all the energy she could muster as if commanded by the Medici princess herself, Nora stood up and picked up her purse, remembering at the last moment to grab her phone from the wall socket. Filled with a bit more energy, she felt her internal batteries, like those of her cell phone, were recharging.

Stepping onto the street, she pushed past the crowds in the Pantheon and the street vendors in Piazza Navona. As always, Italy's eclectic contrasts, combining the past and the present, appealed to her. One moment she walked past high-end boutiques featuring the futuristic fashions by Dolce and Gabbana, and the next she passed by a seventeenth-century Jesuit church. Rome never disappointed, and after only half an hour her photo library was filling with snapped images of archangels, cornices, and cobblestones. Following in the footsteps of Isabella, she relished her independence and even stopped to enjoy a *triple* scoop cone of gelato—*pistacchio* and *fragola!*

The next morning, Nora awoke feeling surprisingly refreshed and filled with anticipation to set off for Cerreto Guidi. Perhaps she was more awake due to the *passeggiata* she had taken the previous evening, feeling the vitality of Italy flowing around her, or maybe it had been the pep talk she had heard in her head and Isabella's admonishments telling her to get over herself and get on with things.

Whatever the case, a few hours later, opening the back door of her rented Fiat, she said with newfound determination, *"Sì, Isabella. Hai ragione.* You are right. It is time to move forward." Tossing her camera bags onto the floor, she added, "Okay, time for you to get in, too. Make yourself comfortable—we have a long drive ahead of us."

Sitting behind the wheel, contemplating the gridlock of cars and motorbikes clogging the streets, Nora panicked slightly and wondered if she was up to the task of navigating Roman traffic. But then she heard the voice of her backseat driver: "What are you waiting for? *Su. Avanti!* Stop wasting time. Let's go. *Andiamo!"*

Adjusting her rearview mirror, she could almost see the bossy princess seated behind her and agreed. Slowly, Nora released the clutch and, following the signs to the Autostrada, entered the expressway. Turning up the volume on the radio, she said to her unexpected passenger, *"Tranquilla. Posso farcela.* Relax, lady, I've got this!"

Halfway into her journey, Nora pulled over at an auto grill and refueled. At the well-appointed bar standing shoulder to shoulder with other highway travelers, she knocked back a shot of espresso, then stocked up on paper tubes filled with Baci candies. She relished the sounds of tiny clinking saucers and the taste of chocolate and hazelnut. Raising her small cup and saluting her reflection in the mirror over the bar, she said, "*Mi ricordo benissimo*. It's all coming back to me now."

By the time she arrived in Cerreto Guidi, the sun was hanging low in the early evening sky. The town had been named for the trees that once populated the area, the majority of which had long since been cut down. Anxious to get her first glimpse of the Medici hunting lodge before heading on to her lodgings located along the road that led to Vinci, the town where Leonardo had been born, Nora detoured through the center of town.

Before she knew it, however, after passing a couple of apartment buildings, one *trattoria* and a few sporting goods shops, she sailed right through the village and was headed back out into the country. Turning around in a farmer's dusty trailer track leading into a grape field, she realized Cerreto Guidi was even smaller than she had imagined. As she approached the town again at a much slower speed, gazing up, she could see the Medici hunting lodge, situated on top of a hill well above the cluster of newer buildings that had grown up around it.

Just one of many Cosimo de' Medici had built, the lodge had served as a place to avoid the heat of Florence while pursuing everyone's favorite pastime—that of cocking a gun and shooting a wild boar. It was Club Medici, Cosimo's pleasure palace—the original Club Med—and if a kiss was stolen, or more than a mare was mounted, no one was the wiser.

Rolling to a stop in front of the villa, Nora pulled up the parking brake and sat for a moment. She could hardly believe she was finally sitting in front of Isabella's home. "Well, my friend... we are finally here."

With her arms draped over the steering wheel, she admired the double staircase, paved in red brick that a horse could also climb. It was in this very spot that the Medici with their retinue of servants came in pursuit of forest prey. But on one particular summer morning, instead of venturing into the woods, a fairer species had been caught and killed inside the walls of the villa.

Getting out of the car, Nora said, "Are you ready for your close up, Miss de' Medici?"

She rested one hand on the top of the open door and listened. Illuminated by the setting sun, the façade of the house glowed with warm intensity. In the distance, she could hear the night birds calling and the whir of crickets. She took a deep breath, and her senses were awakened by a familiar Tuscan scent. It was the aroma of dirt, hay, and earthy mushrooms.

Nora was reminded of another moment in a similar hillside town when, years before, she and Juliette had been invited by friends from Florence to go truffle hunting. Although their yield had been meager and they went home covered in dirt, how they had shrieked as they slid down the slippery hills in the woods. Funny how a simple fragrance could awaken forgotten memories.

Taking in the surroundings, Nora imagined Isabella dressed in her riding gear, mounted on a magnificent stallion, surveying her land. Like Nora, had she too inhaled deeply, smelling the fresh loam and musty scent of oak leaves? Perhaps Isabella had made her way through the overgrown thicket, thinking about the next day's hunt—or maybe she had walked through the trees anticipating a clandestine meeting with her lover.

Studying the stark, uncompromising lines of the hunting lodge, now more than ever—due to the smells, the sounds, and the warmth of the sun—it felt as though she had tapped into Isabella's persona. Closing her eyes, she felt the full range of emotions that made Isabella such an intriguing woman.

At first, a wave of grief crashed over her, just as it had swept over Isabella when she learned her mother Eleonora had died of malaria after vacationing in the Maremma. All who traveled with her mamma that summer to the marshy seaside Medici resort had been stricken with the disease and had been taken too, including her beloved younger brother Giovanni. That had been a most heart-wrenching year.

But there had been other tragedies as well. Over the course of her very young life, Isabella had attended the funerals of three younger sisters, and those of her own unborn children. Nora could see the Medici princess's tears streaming down her cheeks after she lost another baby. Nora's eyes clouded over, too, and she wiped away a salty reminder of her own loss. Even years after the heartache of miscarriage, one never recovered from the death of a child.

Unlike Nora, the Star of Florence hadn't fallen into apathetic listlessness, too tired to move her life forward. Instead, feeling her calling, Isabella rose from tragedy to become the first lady of Florence. She hadn't shied away from her responsibilities or her potential but instead had ruled Florence with aplomb.

From the drawing rooms of the Medici palace, she had protected the arts and culture of the city through lively intellectual discussions and lavish theatrical performances. She had also laid the groundwork for the very first Italian dictionary and the *Academia Crusca* by hosting salons where the proper use of the language was debated.

Nora admired Isabella for her many positive qualities, but at the same time, she couldn't deny the thrill she had experienced reading Isabella's diary. In fact, Nora hadn't been able to put it down as it read very much like a contemporary torrid bodice-ripper. There was no doubt, in her mind, the Princess had been a lusty woman filled with romantic, if not erotic yearnings.

Opening her eyes suddenly, Nora was filled with a fierce sense of self-confidence, feeling Isabella's craving for power and control. She was Cosimo's daughter through and through. Like him, Isabella was a bit egotistical and didn't care a fig what others thought. She was known to flaunt her position, as well as her wealth, by driving through the streets of Florence in a horse-drawn conch shell.

It seemed to Nora the pursuit of power and self-gratification were the things that had motivated Isabella the most. They were the very reasons she rolled debauched and sometimes drunk out of bed late in the day, just in time to do it all over again. However, in the end, Isabella had greatly overplayed her hand and taken her extravagant lifestyle a step too far.

As long as Cosimo had been alive, Isabella and her partner in crime—

her cousin Leonora—were safe. When the old lion died, however, there was no one left to champion or protect them. After angering their male counterparts, namely her brothers Francesco and Pietro and her husband Paolo, she and Leonora were no longer seen as assets but instead as inconvenient and embarrassing financial burdens.

At that point, the Medici men, their egos significantly bruised and trampled upon, had plotted to rid themselves for good of their troublesome women. First, Leonora died mysteriously in the Medici villa in Cafaggiolo, and then Isabella at the hunting lodge in Cerreto Guidi. Both husbands claimed the deaths had been accidents, but no one really believed Leonora had tripped and tumbled down the stairs or that Isabella had fallen into her wash basin and cracked her skull early one morning while washing her hair.

As dusk descended and the last rays of sun faded into gray night, Nora slid back into the seat of her rental car and wondered, *What more will you reveal to me tomorrow, Isabella? Will I learn your secrets and what really happened that day? What would you tell me, if you could?*

Nora paused and listened, but all she heard in response was the wind rustling through the leaves of the trees. All else remained eerily quiet and wildly bleak.

Chapter 6

A Painting to Remember

*T*he following morning, Nora returned to the Medici villa ready to start filming. Driving from her lodgings, around every bend it seemed she saw the Medici princess's face. Mixed in with billboards advertising the local Co-op Supermarket, or *agriturisimi*, were signs displaying Isabella's likeness. There were those that invited motorists to visit the *Fattoria Isabella de' Medici* that produced wine and olive oil, and others that urged them to wash their clothes at the automated laundromat *"La Lavanderia di Isabella"*.

Since departing San Francisco, Nora had experienced the feeling that Isabella was traveling with her, and the sensation had only grown stronger during her trip up from Rome. Now, in this corner of Tuscany, confronted with visible evidence of the Star of Florence that popped up around every curve of the road, the feeling was positively uncanny.

As Nora hummed along to a song on the radio, seeing yet another posterized version of Isabella splashed on the side of the road, she thought of the many portraits of Isabella that had been painted over the years. Back in the Renaissance, there had been no cameras and no Facebook. Yet the human desire to communicate, brag, and share pictures of family and friends had been just as strong.

The Medici family, in particular, had loved to show off, and the court painter Bronzino was happy to oblige them. To create more flattering likenesses, with skill and imagination, he toned down their prominent noses and smoothed out their brows as competently as any modern Photoshop expert might do.

Evidence of the family's power and wealth was also proclaimed by portraits of Medici women draped in jewels and dressed in gold and silver gowns and cuddling their rosy-cheeked sons. Such images featuring the Medici male heirs shouted out to the world that Florence's first family was here to stay, presenting physical evidence of the fecundity of their wives, the potency of their men—that when combined helped to propagate and grow the family tree.

Over the past couple of months, Nora had poured over many art history books, studying pictures of Isabella at various ages, but there was one in particular that had especially intrigued her. It was a portrait done by the master painter Bronzino in which Isabella was seated next to her mother. The painting had caused quite a stir in its day. In and of itself, it was stunning, capturing the allure of the two Medici women exquisitely.

However, at the time the portrait had been an anomaly, as it was unheard of to show a mother with her daughter. After all, what kind of message would that send, and to what end would the painting serve? Females, at that time, were held with little regard, aside from their reproductive organs. By themselves, they were certainly not a symbol of intelligence and power.

But it had been a whim of Cosimo's to order a likeness of his wife and daughter together. He was, after all, the Grand Duke of Tuscany—ruler of the region and the one who made all the decisions—and there was no one who could stop him should he choose to be a nonconformist. And as a man who was head over heels in love with his wife, and who doted on his accomplished daughter, he saw no reason *not* to commission a portrait featuring the two most important females in his life.

Aside from being something of a peculiar commission, from the beginning, the painting, like the princess herself, had a capricious and complicated history. Shortly after Isabella's death, it went missing, then turned up years later in France, only to disappear again when the Nazis marched in and took over Paris. Much to the dismay of the Italian people, the details of how the painting had ended up in the Louvre were sketchy at best, and without a clear provenance, what exactly happened to the portrait had been lost in a dusty trail of misinformation.

This only heightened Nora's curiosity and hadn't dissuaded her in the slightest from developing a plotline of her own about what had happened to the errant painting. With a bit of deductive reasoning, she concluded that Francesco, Isabella's treacherous brother, had been the first to hide it. Perhaps he had intended to steal the painting as a means of exerting his power over his sister, but in the end, it only served as a guilty reminder of the unthinkable crime he had committed against her. Instead of flaunting it, unable to look upon her accusing face, he changed his mind and hid her away in the attic, out of sight and out of mind.

Wasting away in some forgotten corner of the Medici Palace, over time Isabella's painting was lost and forgotten. By luck, or rather misfortune, Nora mussed—depending on how you viewed it—a Medici descendant finally unearthed it. Needing some fast cash, he sold it to someone, who passed it along to someone else until it crossed the border into France and ended up in the Louvre.

But, after the war, once again the capricious portrait had taken flight and vanished from the French museum. At this point, although Nora had tried her best to put the pieces together, using her excellent research skills, she hadn't a clue as to where the canvas was now. Much like Isabella's ghost, the painting arbitrarily appeared and then disappeared, and for the moment like the whimsical princess, it too had gone underground again.

As she approached an intersection, hearing the grinding gears of a rusty old tractor, Nora slowed down and waited for the vehicle to turn the corner. Churning and chugging loudly, it moved out ahead and lumbered tipsily down the road.

Nora gritted her teeth and swore, *"Porca miseria!"*

Checking her watch, she saw she was already ten minutes late for her appointment at the villa. Getting stuck on the road going at a snail's pace behind this farmer was only going to make her later. Drumming her fingers on the steering wheel, she waited a second before attempting to pull out and pass by, but oncoming traffic caused her to retreat. Slipping back into position behind the tractor, she resigned herself to the delay.

As she crept anxiously along in the farmer's wake, longing to be free and unfettered, she wondered if Isabella had been as impatient as she, sitting for hours having her portrait painted, wishing she too could be doing other things.

When the tractor finally pulled over to let her pass, and Nora was once more sailing down the road, her imaginings took flight. She switched stations on the radio, and as she did, she tuned into the voices that emanated from a sixteenth-century artist's studio. As if she were standing in the room with the master painter and his will-o'-the-wisp subject Isabella, their very words echoed down through the ages and played out in her head.

"*Per carità!* Isabella, my dear girl, please sit still and stop fidgeting. I need just a few more minutes of your time, and then you are free to go." Bronzino looked down briefly at his palette, mixing a little more burnt umber into his pigment to deepen the color, than back at the girl and let out another exasperated sigh. "*Non ci posso credere.* You moved again!"

Walking quickly to the side of his subject, he readjusted her shoulders and tilted her head a little to the right so it was once again bathed in the warm summer sun that poured in from the window. "Hold your head just a little higher... Yes! Like that! There, that's much better. Stay put, and in just a quarter of an hour, we will be done for the day."

When he turned back to his canvas, Isabella rolled her eyes and stuck out her tongue. When the painter looked up again, she patted her hair, pursed her lips, and smiled sweetly at him. Used to her antics, Bronzino ignored her and gently stroked the canvas with his brush.

"Now try and stay put—*mi raccomando!*" the artist urged again as he continued to flush out the details. He hoped to finish the last little bit, taking advantage of her good humor, before she slipped out of his sight and his work would be suspended until the next day. After a moment, he raised his eyes and contemplated his subject again. "Isabella, lift your necklace just a little higher, so I can see it better."

Obediently, Isabella did as the painter requested and proudly touched the oversized, opulent pearl—the symbol of her betrothal—and repositioned herself on her cushion.

"Hold it between your fingers... Up just a touch more. *Sì. Perfetto!*"

Isabella sat a few moments longer, the model of grace and dignity, dressed in her heavy velvet gown, but when a shout from the garden below reached her ears, she squirmed and swiveled her head in the direction of the open window. Detecting the voice of Giovanni, her younger brother by two years, calling out to her to join them in a game of *Ring Alivio*, she gave the painter another pleading pout.

"Per piacere, Maestro, can we not be finished for this afternoon? I grow weary of the weight of this necklace and need a break. Surely you can't wish to torment me any longer when there is still much of the day to be enjoyed! Can you not hear my sisters and brothers have been released by their tutors from their studies? I promise I will not tell my father that we finished early..."

"What is this, my sweet?" asked a deep voice coming from the threshold of the studio. "Are you pestering our poor painter again? I don't know how he puts up with you."

A smile brightened the young girl's face. *"Papà!"* she cried. Isabella wanted to run to him, but seeing the painter's frown, she remained where she was.

Instead, from her perch, she peppered her father with questions. "When did you return? It seems like you have been away an age. How was Rome? Do tell me. What is the city like? Is it much different from Florence? Did you travel in a fine carriage... Did you..." Smiling prettily at him, she added, "Did you buy me a present?"

Holding up his hands, the Duke laughed. "Hold on, hold on. Only one question at a time."

Sauntering over to the artist's easel, from behind Bronzino's back, the duke studied the portrait. After a moment, he threw out his arms, signaling his approval. "Well done, Bronzino! You have captured my daughter well. She is a lovely girl, becoming a handsome young woman, but I can see the sparkle of a child's wit lighting her intelligent eyes."

Glancing from the canvas to his little girl seated a few steps away, he noted the way she tapped her foot and her body quivered with the desire to be free. He chuckled again at her impatience.

"Well, Agostino? Is it time to untether this lovely dove?"

The artist, seeing he wasn't going to get any more work done on his portrait, bowed his head acquiescing to the Grand Duke. "As you wish, My Lord." He looked at Isabella and when she gave him a gleeful look, he rolled his eyes heavenward. Setting down his brush he admonished, *"Vi prego, cara Isabella.* Return here tomorrow at the same hour. I beg you not to forget."

"See, Isabella?" said the Grand Duke. "Maestro Bronzino isn't as cruel and demanding as you may think. He is quite a reasonable man and an excellent painter. Now, come, give your father the hug he has longed for."

Delighted to be free, Isabella lost no time slipping off her velvet chair eager to run into his open arms. Then, standing back, she did a little pirouette. *"Papà,* what do you think of my gown?"

"Very pretty, indeed," said the Duke. "It is a dress fit for a princess."

"Now that you are home, I can't wait for you to hear the new song I have composed. I worked on it the entire week. I have so many things to tell you. Just the other day, I was speaking in French with my tutor, and he tells me I'm almost better than he. I'm also reading a new book of Latin poems, given to me by Signor..."

"Aspetta! Piano per favore! Slow down, Isabella. All in good time, my darling girl. There will be plenty of days ahead for you to share with me all your accomplishments. We will begin this evening, and you may play a fine tune on your lute to entertain us all. How good it is to see you again—I've missed you very much."

Reaching out, he caressed her cheek and then, seeing the gold pendant hanging from her neck, he lifted it up and regarded it thoughtfully.

"You, my pet, are as rare as this pearl." He frowned slightly as he fingered the lovely medallion.

"What's wrong, *papà*? Do you not like my betrothal gift? Does it displease you?"

Seeing her agitation, he fixed an easy smile on his face. To ease her concerns, he then adeptly replied, "On the contrary. I think the necklace the Duke of Bracciano sent you is magnificent. Just imagine," he said, "soon, like your mother, you too will be a duchess."

Turning to Bronzino, he reminded the artist, "Make sure you highlight this necklace particularly well in my daughter's portrait. We want to show the Orsini the Medici are flattered and honored by their generous offering."

Giddy at the thought of marriage, Isabella's rosy lips turned upward. *"Oh, sì papà.* It is a beautiful necklace, and to be a bride of such an important man will be a privilege. When will I meet my betrothed? Will he be handsome, and shall I sing and share with him the things I have read? I can only imagine how wonderful life will be to have a husband as kind and loving as you. Just the other day, Morgante and I reenacted the wedding ceremony—Giovanni, of course, stood in as my bridegroom."

At first, the Duke didn't respond. The spark of joy that had illuminated his eyes dimmed just a touch. But seeing his daughter's hopeful expression, he quickly recovered and replied, "All in good time, my sweet. I'm not quite willing to part with you yet. Good heavens, will I ever be?"

Cosimo kissed his daughter on the forehead and continued, "Isabella, know this. You will never want for anything. I will always be here to protect you. You are simply too precious and too intelligent to be kept under lock and key, and no one will ever..."

When a dark-haired woman in a golden gown stepped lightly over the threshold, all eyes turned in her direction. The painter Bronzino bowed his head courteously, and Cosimo exclaimed, "Ah, Eleonora, sweet wife! I was just coming to your chambers."

Surprised to see him there, Eleonora exclaimed, "Cosimo, *amore mio.* You have returned! The children and I have been counting the hours until we would see you again."

"As have I," he said. Crossing the room in just a few strides, Cosimo reached his wife's side and bent her back, giving her a kiss that made even the painter blush. Isabella only giggled and thought about the day her husband would kiss her the way her father kissed her mother.

"My trip home was delayed a day or two in Arezzo," he said. "I was inspecting the command post and the wall I am building there to secure the town." To Isabella, he said, "One day I will take you there, my pet. The fortress is progressing well and nearly finished."

"*Oh, papà!* I'd like that. Tell me, what does it look like?"

"Maestro Sangallo has created a massive structure with five impressive bastions. It is shaped like a star, and it is a formidable thing to see sitting on top of the town's highest hill. From that vantage point, we have a clear view of the entire valley below."

Reaching his hand out for Isabella's, he twirled her around in a circle. "You know, Arezzo is quite a charming town. Oh, nothing like Florence at all," he hastened to clarify. "Still, the Aretini are quite a diverting people. They entertained me with song and good food. But the most fantastic thing of all was the knights' tournament. Jousters from the four gates of the city compete against one another by charging their horse at a target with their lances. *È uno spettacolo fantastico!* You would find the competition very invigorating—and thrilling."

Letting Isabella spin off in a series of pirouettes, Cosimo watched for a moment, chuckling. "The joust certainly put me in a good mood and made me feel like a much younger man. I was almost tempted to try my hand at the sport."

Eleonora stepped over to his side, tucked her arm in his, and said, "Ah, I believe the merrymaking in Arezzo has helped ease your burdens, as well as kept you amused. You know the hours pass by so tediously when you are gone—I get so lonely."

Flirtatiously, she added, "But I've kept myself busy and occupied since you've been away. I've indulged in a few amusing diversions myself."

He scrutinized her, and she added in mock offense, "Oh, sir! Don't worry. I've managed to keep myself out of trouble. Be assured the Medici fortunes are still intact. I haven't gambled *all* our money away."

With a wave of her hand, she gestured to a canvas at the back of the room. "On the contrary, I've been kept quite captive by our handsome painter here. Signor Bronzino has just finished the portrait of our beloved little Giovanni and me."

Sashaying her skirts, she moved briskly to the far wall, calling over her shoulder for her husband to join her. "Come, my love. See what you think."

Cosimo followed her and watched as she removed a cloth covering a large canvas. He was silent a moment, and everyone held their breath. Then, calling over his shoulder, he bellowed out, "Bronzino, you've delighted me once again! Your work is simply astounding. *Bravo! Complimenti*. Well done."

Holding his hands up as if framing his wife's face with his fingers, Cosimo added, "And you, my dear, are a vision. I am a most fortunate husband. You do have many, many charms."

The Duchess gave him a coy smirk to which he responded with a sly smile. Then he said, "To keep you out of trouble *and* away from the gambling table, I think another painting is in order. Would you do me the honor of sitting for another?"

"As you wish, my dear sir," replied Eleonora. "And which of our boys should we include? Francesco, perhaps? After all, he will be the next Grand Duke."

"No, no, my love. I have something else in mind. Nothing would make me happier than having a painting of you with Isabella seated by your side."

"*Che meraviglia!*" exclaimed Eleonora. "A painting of your wife and daughter. Francesco will be so disappointed." Addressing the painter, she asked, "*Signor Bronzino, Maestro!* Isn't this a most unusual request? A portrait featuring a mother and her daughter is rather unheard of, is it not?"

On the opposite side of the room, Isabella, who had resumed dancing with an imaginary partner, ceased her twirling to listen to her parents' exchange. Secretly, she was quite pleased by the idea of sitting with her mother for a portrait and more than a little happy to be usurping her brother's position.

Cosimo exclaimed, "What care I care if it isn't the fashion? I make the rules, do I not? Nothing would make this old Duke happier."

Challenging the Medici court painter, he said, "What do you say, Bronzino? Do you think you can do justice to these two lovely women seated together, capturing their rare spirits as well as their inner beauty? Not an easy task, I fear."

Bronzino smiled in pleasure. "My dear Duke, I have painted many pictures of Isabella, as well as those of your wife with your sons, but it would be my extreme pleasure to paint the two of them side by side. It will set this city on its ear! They will talk of nothing else for years to come. Believe me, it will be a painting to remember."

Chapter 7

Prelude to a Storm

Approaching the villa in Cerreto Guidi, Bronzino's words faded back into time, but thoughts of Isabella's painting remained in the forefront of Nora's mind. Glancing at the dashboard clock in her rented car, she saw it was nearly twelve o' clock—the height of a scorching Tuscan day. She parked her car in the shade, then climbed the stairs to the expansive courtyard. As she did, she could feel the oppressive heat emanating from the stones of the terrace. The courtyard appeared deserted except for two teenagers engrossed in their cell phones sitting in the shade of the portico of the church next to the main house.

When she entered the main hall, Nora was immediately greeted politely by a lone caretaker. She introduced herself as Leonora Havilland, the American who was making a documentary about Isabella de' Medici. Reaching into her bag, she pulled out her permission slips and said, "I called the department of communications of Florentine museums a month ago to get permission to film."

Nora waited for the guard to shuffle through the documents, recalling the hoops she had to jump through to obtain the necessary approval. She had been passed around from one Italian museum project coordinator to another until finally, with great perseverance, she talked with the right person with authority to grant unlimited access to the property to make her film.

Seeing the man frown slightly, as he studied the papers in English, she said, "*Spero che abbiano detto che stavo per arrivare oggi.*"

Hearing her speak Italian, the guard looked up at her in relief and smiled. Handing back the papers, the stocky man said, "*Bene parla Italiano!* You speak Italian! That's a relief! *Si, Signora.* I got the message and have been expecting you."

"*Meno male!* I was starting to think there might be a problem..."

"Oh, no! On the contrary, from what I understand, the administrators in Florence are quite pleased with the idea and premise of your documentary. Personally, I think Isabella would be delighted as well. As for me, I am ready to assist you. Just let me know if you have any questions or need anything. I will do my best to help make your stay here in Cerreto Guidi as pleasant as possible."

Holding out his hand, he introduced himself. "*Sono Giuseppe. Giuseppe Gargiulo.* I'm the curator of the hunting museum. Here you'll find a collection of weaponry, dating back to the Middle Ages."

"*Bene, grazie, Signor* Gargiulo. Can I leave my camera bag with you here at the desk? Before I get started, I want to look around and familiarize myself with the layout of the villa. I have some specific ideas where I want to film, and I want to check out the lighting before I set up my equipment."

"*Certo! Faccia come se fosse casa sua.* Make yourself at home," he said, handing her an official museum badge to wear around her neck.

Already feeling the magical draw of the place, Nora set down her heavy bag and strolled into the first room. Moving in a circular pattern through the chambers on the main level, she paused now and then to focus her attention on a piece of antique furniture or admire the glass cases positioned in the middle of the room and against the wall, filled with old guns, hunting daggers, and swords. By the excessive number of paintings that hung on the wall of horses and hounds, she saw where the real passions of the Medici lay.

When she arrived back in the main hallway, she was pleased to be greeted by two enormous portraits of Isabella's parents, Eleonora and her husband, Cosimo. Next to them were depictions of their eleven children they had produced in the course of twenty-three years. Lost in thought, Nora contemplated the paintings and didn't hear the museum curator approach until he was standing just a few steps away. Following her gaze, Giuseppe thoughtfully regarded the members of the Medici family too.

After a moment, he said, *"Sono stupendi, no?"* Seeing her nod, he pointed to a painting of Isabella, dressed in an elaborate gown with frills and lace that hung a short distance away. *"Guardi quello.* Take a closer view at that one. We recently made quite a remarkable discovery."

"What did you find?" she asked, leaning in to examine the classically elegant features of the young princess who couldn't have been more than fifteen or sixteen.

"The curators saw a ghosting of another image beneath the surface. A bit of *pentimento*... Some of the underpainting was beginning to show through. It was the clue that tipped them off that something lay beneath the surface of the top layer of paint."

Nora repeated the word, savoring the sound—in Italian *pentimento* meant to repent. She thought it was a perfect way to describe an artist's choice to change his mind and paint over his original design.

Giuseppe continued, "After examining the canvas, they got suspicious, so they ordered a thorough cleaning and discovered someone had painted over the original version of Isabella. In fact, they went so far as to change her features, completely adding a new visage on top of the original one. It seems the color of the background was also changed."

Looking at the painting with new eyes, Nora said, "They restored Isabella beautifully. I'm sure she didn't appreciate being covered up all those years."

"I'm sure she didn't," agreed Giuseppe. Glancing at Nora, he added, "The restorers did the work here, in one of the back rooms, and I was invited to watch as they carefully washed away the top coat to reveal the princess's face."

"It must have been like finding buried treasure—a gift that time restored."

He smiled at her analogy. Then shrugging his shoulders, he added, *"Non riesco a capire!* For the life of me, I will never understand why people do such things. How can such amateurs have the nerve to tamper with a masterpiece?"

"It is a real shame, isn't it? Most likely the painting was altered to suit modern tastes. They often did that around the turn of the century. Isabella had a lovely face, but her features were typical of the Medici, strong and bold. The Victorians, on the other hand, fancied a frillier style—cupids, clouds, and bows—like Fragonard's sweet, dainty ladies. If this portrait of Isabella was painted over, it was probably done to sell the painting to fit the color scheme and décor of someone's parlor."

"*Ovviamente,*" he said in a joking manner. "Paintings must match the drapes after all." Reaching behind the desk, he retrieved her camera bag and said, "If you are here to make a documentary about Isabella, then you probably already know the princess well."

Amusement lit her eyes, and she said, "Yes, it seems so. Lately, Isabella has been my constant companion, and each day I learn a little more about her as if she were whispering things into my ear. I've done extensive research, and have become quite an authority on the lady. *Chissà?* Who knows, perhaps we were friends in a previous life."

With a small shrug, she added, "Anyway, that's why I'm making this film. I see the many sides of Isabella and want to introduce the woman I've gotten acquainted with to others, so they can appreciate her as I do."

Giuseppe seemed pleased by her response, happy to finally have a captive visitor, even if it was only an audience of one. Cerreto Guidi was not by any definition of the term your typical tourist trap. Because the hunting museum was in the middle of a remote area of Tuscany, not serviced by trains or even with much frequency a local bus, he rarely had to deal with large crowds like in Florence. Certainly, people dribbled in to see the weapons on display, and then there were the thrill-seekers wanting to get a peek at Isabella's phantom. Aside from the ghost story, that to this day continued to be perpetuated, few people actually knew much about the woman or her accomplishments.

"*Viene qua.* This way to the *Camera del cappio,* the room of strangulation. *Lei è pronta?* Are you ready? There are more paintings of *la mia Isabella* in her bedroom."

Sweeping out his arm, he indicated the corridor to his left. Interested to actually step foot into the Princess' chambers, the place where she was murdered, Nora followed him to a small antechamber located in the other wing of the house.

As they entered the room filled with more dark paintings, the guard slowed his steps and stopped. "That is Paolo Orsini, Isabella's husband, the Duke of Bracciano."

Nora studied the face of Isabella's husband. She could see the artist had not been kind, and there had been no touch-ups by a more modern brush to enhance the Duke's appearance. He appeared to be a proud, if not a pudgy, little man. His expression was pinched and world-weary, an effect created by a pair of bloated eyelids and a mustache that hid his upper lip. Even with Nora's vivid imagination, it was hard to see Paolo turning the head of any young woman, let alone frolicking in bed and steaming up the sheets with a prostitute.

"*Siamo fortunati,*" said Giuseppe. "We are lucky to have many of these paintings. The only reason they are here is that they were hidden from the Nazis during the German occupation. To keep them safe, they were concealed in a farmer's cantina near Vinci."

Nora regarded the portrait with greater interest. She had seen a movie once, about the Italian partisans who had hidden precious paintings and priceless artifacts during the time of the German occupation. But it seemed real life was more fascinating than fiction.

To stave off the sweat that trickled down her neck, Nora reached into her bag, drew out a paper fan, and vigorously waved it in front of her. She noticed Giuseppe, dressed in long pants and a button-down shirt, unlike her, seemed cool as a cucumber. In fact, even in the height of summer heat, he had a scarf wrapped around his neck to avoid a draft of air.

Directing her thoughts back to the portrait, Nora said, "Perhaps this painting of Paolo should have been stolen by Hitler." Hastily, she clarified, "I'm sorry, of course it should have been protected. It just seems to me, from what I've learned about Isabella's husband after reading the testimonies of a few Roman courtesans, he was quite a wicked man, a monster himself."

"*Sì*, I couldn't agree with you more—*povera Isabella*—married to such a man."

Turning to face her, Giuseppe added, "When Hitler arrived with his troops, he sent out teams of soldiers led by German art experts and ordered them to collect as many paintings and sculptures as possible to ship it all back to Berlin."

"The German dictator was truly obsessed. He intended to create the world's largest art museum, keeping all the great art for himself."

"*Il bastardo* had the nerve to outright steal masterpieces from churches and museums—even people's private homes. Once it started happening, members of the resistance began hiding some of the more important pieces before they could get their hands on them."

Nora frowned as she thought about it, imagining the heartbreak she would have felt if someone had pounded upon her door in the middle of the night, demanding to be let in. How horrible to watch as soldiers stormed in, turning over furniture, upending drawers, looking for things to confiscate—silver, musical instruments, paintings, and more. Then, to stand utterly helpless and watch as, one by one, treasured possessions were thrust into the back of a waiting truck to be driven off to Berlin and never to be seen again.

Watching her eyes cloud over in sympathy, Giuseppe continued, "It was a very dark, dangerous time, *signora*. Nothing and no one was safe. Battles were taking place on Italy's frontier, but there was also fighting right here in Tuscany. After Mussolini fell from power, many people were thrilled at first, but when he was reinstated by Hitler, well... The *partigiani* reacted violently and started taking things into their own hands."

"That was the start of the *guerra civile*," Nora said. "The war between the fascists and everyone else who wanted to free Italy of foreign powers and dictators."

"*Sì, esatto.*" Taking a few steps closer to the door of Isabella's bedroom, Giuseppe said, "They didn't want to wait around for the allies to arrive, so they waged their own war on the Nazis. Many people were involved in the underground movement from farmers, factory workers to parish priests—even the Principessa di Piemonte, the last Italian royalty, and her ladies in waiting took part in the partisan movement."

"Marie Josè—the last Queen of Italy—was a part of the resistance?"

Giuseppe nodded. "She sympathized with the partisans, yes. She even smuggled weapons, money, and food to them."

Impressed, Nora couldn't help but think Isabella, the Medici Princess, would have done the same.

"They were all very brave—but such risks they took. The rebels made small ambushes and disrupted their military operations, but every time they did the Germans retaliated viciously. If the resisters were caught, they were beaten, shot, or deported to German camps in the north. They even went as far as to massacre entire villages. Even kids."

"I had no idea about the slaughtering of so many people in this area." The thought of killing an innocent child sobered Nora.

"*Oh, si, signora.* As I said, no one was safe. But that didn't stop the resistance forces. To avoid being caught, they went into hiding and escaped into the hills. In the towns, people began meeting secretly, hiding their communications in books or the soles of their shoes. They had to be careful, though. There were informants everywhere. If suspected of even the simplest act of kindness, like offering bread to the British prisoners, a spy who worked for Mussolini's government would expose you."

Giuseppe fell silent for a moment, then gesturing to a portrait outside Isabella's door, he added, "Even the act of hiding a painting was a sign of defiance and might put you at the wrong end of a German Tommy gun."

Nora tried to imagine the peaceful hills of Tuscany that Isabella had once galloped her horse through being overrun with Nazi tanks and fascist spies. She shuddered ever so slightly, hearing the cries of women and children being tortured and shot.

"It seems insane," said Nora. To herself, she thought, *So much hatred and greed—so many lives destroyed... So much art lost too. And for what? The tyranny of a bigoted and egotistical man?*

Nora replaced the fan in her purse and adjusted the camera bag that had slipped down her shoulder. Looking over at Giuseppe, she said, "I've been wondering about something lately."

"*Mi dica, signora.*"

"Perhaps you can help shed some light on a question I have about a particular painting of Isabella and..."

Without her saying a word more, Giuseppe nodded his head in understanding. "Ah, I believe you refer to the painting of Isabella and her mother, Eleonora—the missing masterpiece."

"Yes, actually," replied Nora. "The portrait painted by Bronzino."

"*Ma dai! È un ritratto fantastico.* Of course, I know the one," the guard said quickly.

"It used to hang in the Louvre and..."

"The Italians were not happy at all about *that*!" responded Giuseppe passionately. "*Non era giusto!* That picture, just like the *Mona Lisa* by Leonardo, belongs to the Italian people and should have been returned to the Uffizi in Florence a long time ago."

"Do you know anything more about it? I am trying to find out what happened to it during the war and why it is still missing."

Giuseppe only shook his head. "When the Nazis took over Paris, there was great confusion. Most likely it was destroyed. "

"Or maybe," Nora said hopefully, "it is hidden away somewhere in someone's attic, ready to make a dramatic re-appearance."

"*Magari, signora!* Let us hope so." Opening the door to Isabella's bedroom, Giuseppe added, "Are you ready? *Entri pure!*"

Nora paused for a moment before crossing the threshold, preparing herself mentally for the emotions she might feel. When she walked into the room, however, she was surprised by how ordinary it seemed. She glanced about at the floral wallpaper and coffered wooden ceiling decorated with delicate hand-painted blooms. There were several cabinets and a few chairs, and on the large dresser rested a silver brush and a comb. As her eyes drifted about the room, they came to rest on the canopied bed draped in red silk. It seemed peaceful and serene, the boudoir of any noble lady.

When the guard's cell phone rang, he said, "*Scusi, signora.* If you need me, I'll be just down the hall." He laughed good-naturedly. "If Isabella decides to put in an appearance, you know where to find me."

As he turned away, she heard him say into his phone, *"Dimmi... Ah! Jacopo, sei proprio tu... Senti..."*

Alone in the room, Nora pulled out a tripod and a few lenses and set up her video equipment. Paging through her script and rehearsing her opening dialogue, she suddenly had a feeling as if she were being spied on from above. A sudden coldness swept through her body, and an odd sense of foreboding came over her. Looking up, she saw for the first time the hole in the ceiling from which Paolo had drawn the cord to hang Isabella.

Nora's heart skipped a beat, and for a split second she felt the pressure of a noose at the base of her collar. Placing a hand to her neck, she gently caressed it as she tried to shake off the sudden oppressive feeling of dread. What exactly had happened inside this room? Feeling a curious energy swirling through the air, she closed her eyes and listened. It seemed the words came in waves from the past, and she could hear the heated exchange between a husband and wife in an overture to murder.

"Isabella, let me in. We have something to discuss."

"Ah, so it *is* you, Paolo. I was wondering when you would arrive."

"Let me in, Isabella! I have news of your cousin Leonora. There has been an accident. She is dead."

Nora slowly opened her eyes. Had she just conjured up the final act of Isabella's play? Previously, the things she had read about the Medici Princess and her murder had been dusty facts—mere words on yellowed pages. Now, however, they seemed shockingly real. Tapping into Isabella's psyche once again, Nora began filming her documentary.

At the end of the afternoon, she returned to the bedroom to gather the gear she had left there. She took a few moments to fast-forward through a few of the clips and was pleased with what she had captured so far. Nora planned on coming back to get more footage, but she had enough to get started. In Arezzo, she would begin the editing process, applying the music, graphics, and finishing touches. Nora made a mental note to let Giuseppe know the dates she would return.

As she packed away her camera, she thought a bit ruefully, *While it had been a productive day, it had also been relatively uneventful.* In the villa, Nora had felt Isabella's presence around her, but she hadn't actually seen a vision of the white lady.

Even though she had peeked into closets and probed into dark corners, she hadn't encountered any apparitions, not even the tiniest wisp of one. Of course, the urban legend of Isabella's phantom was just a silly invention, fabricated to sell a few tabloids. Still, she couldn't help but feel a tiny bit disappointed.

Standing in the middle of the room, Nora called out, "Really, Isabella? This is how you treat your guests? I've come all the way from California. The least you could have done was introduce yourself in person."

Nora bent over to pick up her bulky equipment and, as she did, a gush of wind swept through the house, causing the door to bang shut. Startled, she dropped her tripod, and it clattered to the floor. Hearing the noise, Giuseppe opened the door and asked a bit worriedly, *"Tutto bene?"*

Placing a hand over her racing heart, Nora laughed in spite of herself. *"Sì, Giuseppe. Tutto a posto.* Everything is okay, I just had quite a start."

Glancing around, she commented, "Still, it would have been fun to see *La Dama Bianca.*"

The guard grinned. "You aren't the only one. Everyone wants to see Isabella. She is a mysterious lady, but only comes out to play now and again."

He had barely finished his words before another gust of wind blew in through the window, causing the drapes on the bed's canopy to flutter. Stepping over to the window to close and latch the shutters, he paused for a moment to admire the view. Nora looked over too and saw the darkening clouds that cast a shadow over the valley below.

"Up on this hill, we often get strong breezes." Turning back to Nora, he added, "Can you feel it? There is going to be a change in the weather. Tonight there will be rain. Here in Tuscany, the cloudbursts can be quite fierce. I hope you aren't afraid of a little lightning and thunder."

"Well... I was prepared to meet a ghost today," Nora said, "so I don't think a little rain shower will scare me."

As if to test her, an even more powerful surge of air whistled into Isabella's chamber, blowing back the heavy wooden shutter, slamming it loudly against the wall.

Hastening to secure it, Giuseppe said, *"Signora,* get ready. This is just the prelude to a storm."

Chapter 8

La Dama Bianca

*A*s the wind picked up and the storm clouds accumulated, moving ever closer toward Ceretto Guidi, Nora returned to her lodgings a couple of miles out of town. After consuming a hearty plate of Tuscan *tagliatelle* smothered in rich boar sauce, followed by a *torta* made from lemons grown in the garden of the restaurant, she fell into bed feeling incredibly full. But she reminded herself she was in Italy after all, where all the walking she did would counteract the effects of pasta and gelato. If not, there was certainly no God at all.

Turning out the light in her quaintly decorated room, she settled into the narrow bed trying to make herself comfortable. From outside her window, she could hear the leaves rustling in the trees. She was exhausted, but still, she couldn't sleep.

In the darkness, Nora became aware of the irritating whine of a mosquito dive-bombing her ear and wildly waved her arms in the air. The room was silent for a moment, and she congratulated herself for fending off her would-be assailant, but then the pesky buzzing started again. She groaned and pulled the covers over her head. However, after a few moments, she grew hot and, feeling suffocated, she flung them off again and rolled onto her side.

Eyeing the clock, she realized it was still early—only ten o'clock. To pass the time, she counted the chimes of the church bells, marking the quarter hours. As she did, her thoughts drifted back to the Medici villa. It had been a particularly enlightening afternoon, and she had enjoyed her conversation with Giuseppe, the museum guard. It had also been a little chilling to see the portrait of Paolo, the man who had murdered his wife in cold blood.

Nora wondered what it would have been like to be married to such a man. After seeing the face of the Duke of Orsini, and from what she had read about him, Nora knew he certainly had not been Isabella's idea of the perfect cavalier, or a match for her intellect and wit. His cousin, Troilo, on the other hand—now, he had cut quite a fine figure. Handsome, cultured, and educated, as well as a bit of a charmer, he was a much more suitable match for the Medici princess.

In fact, it seemed Troilo had stepped right out of one of Isabella's romantic girlhood fantasies—she couldn't have cast a more appealing and sympathetic hero. Out of her dreams and into her arms, Paolo's cousin had made himself quite comfortable, and together they had found great happiness.

It was funny, Nora thought, *it had been Paolo's idea in the first place to introduce the two. What had the man been thinking?* she wondered. But Paolo, because of his frequent absences remaining in Rome while Isabella lived with her father, feared his wife would take a lover. Not wanting to become a cuckolded husband or the object of hilarity among his friends, had sent his trusted cousin Troilo to the Medici court to keep a watchful eye on his wife. Paolo told his kin to befriend Isabella and gain her confidence. He intimated that Troilo might flirt with her, even flatter her with poetic words, but other than that, his wife was strictly off-limits: *intoccabile*—untouchable.

Apparently, the Duke of Bracciano had been a dolt, and the joke had undoubtedly been upon him, for as soon as Isabella and Troilo laid eyes upon one another, a spark ignited, and the chemistry between them exploded. Very quickly the two were engaged in much more than ballroom dancing and playful innuendos.

Letting her imagination take over, Nora could see Isabella's delighted expression as the Medici Princess admired for the first time the way Troilo's jacket fit across his broad shoulders. Closing her eyes, she could practically hear the teasing words Isabella had whispered into the handsome man's ear, just hours after their introduction.

"Why, dear sir, you do seem to be in excellent form and capable of defending a lady's honor. I believe I am quite taken with your sword. It seems a mighty weapon."

"*Ah, sì,* kind lady," replied Troilo, warmly rising to the occasion. "With it, I am quite agile and could slay the mightiest of foes, to lay at your feet."

"Is that so? Perhaps you might teach me the fine art of how to handle such a fierce and mighty sword."

"*Certo,* m'lady. I would be more than happy to instruct you in the art of dueling, should you so desire. This sword of mine is ready to be put to good use. A skilled warrior must accept any challenge, ready to stand up and defend his lady, willing to satisfy her every need."

Isabella blushed beautifully and arched a well-defined brow. "Well, signore, I for one am ready for my first lesson."

Before the musicians could sound the next dulcet chord on their lutes, Isabella and Troilo had slipped out the door and up the stairs. Behind closed doors, away from prying eyes, they tumbled into bed, entwined in silky sheets. There they remained entangled for more than ten years. Where she had failed at conceiving a child with her husband, she succeeded in the arms of her lover—producing two healthy children.

They tried their best to keep their affair under wraps, and if anyone could have put a stop to their meetings, it would have been Cosimo. Instead, he turned a blind eye, allowing his daughter to find pleasure where she could, knowing full well she wouldn't find it with her husband.

The stolen moments Isabella spent in the arms of her lover were treasured, and when they were separated, they exchanged long passionate letters. Her unique gift for verse flowed from her pen in honeyed words: "*I am your slave and eternally intoxicated by he who has deigned his kindness to offer me his love.*"

Often their love notes contained code words that only they recognized, disguising private jokes that poked fun at Paolo. But, although Isabella was prolific with her words of affection, she never dared to address Troilo directly using his given name, nor did she sign her letters with hers. For if her impassioned declarations fell into the wrong hands, the consequences would be dire.

She also never risked writing the letters herself, as her distinctive sloping handwriting might easily give her away. Instead, to maintain anonymity, she dictated her words to her faithful servant Morgante. He was an intelligent little fellow, educated and wise, who was well loved by the Medici family. Not merely Isabella's special companion, he also entertained them all at court with his witty banter and sly parodies. At times he even accompanied the Grand Duke himself on diplomatic missions. Because he was such an essential part of Medici life, he was granted the privilege of marrying and was also given a small parcel of land.

Nora rolled onto her back, remembering a particularly juicy passage from one of Isabella's love notes.

"Dear sir, your letter gave me such great contentment. It gave me the presence of him who is desired by me more than life itself. Every hour seems like a thousand. If it were not for the high hopes of seeing you again, I would be finished at this time. Do tell me that your return will be the quickest possible, so dear is it to my life."

Staring absently into space, Nora spoke Isabella's words out loud: "Him who is more desired than life itself. I am your slave. I am eternally intoxicated by he who has *deigned* his kindness to offer me his love."

How could anyone write those words? Granted, it was the sixteenth-century, and people tended to be a bit more effusively demonstrative— yet still, the heart-wrenching emotions were there, real and true. It was clear the Medici princess had been a woman deeply in love, and over the years her affections had only grown stronger.

Nora couldn't help but feel a bit envious of Isabella. How had a Renaissance woman found such a romantic love and she, a forward thinking, liberated woman, had failed so miserably at it? She studied the ceiling. Had Richard ever sent her such messages? She thought back to the early days of their courtship. They'd never really spent any time apart, so the only things he'd ever penned to her were short, itemized grocery lists. Digital texts that reminded her to pick up deodorant and dandruff shampoo hardly compared to the kind of love notes that had made Isabella swoon.

She plumped up the pillow under her head and wondered, *Does a love like Isabella's and Troilo's really exist?*

But that was the fantasy, wasn't it? Even today, in this modern age, women dreamed of finding a wildly handsome man that would intellectually challenge and complete them, not to mention fulfill them in bed. Dispiritedly, she thought, *What a bunch of Hollywood drivel.*

Yet, she reminded herself, a life lived entirely on her own could be lonely. If she were honest with herself, she too wanted that dream. She wanted to feel a deep aching love like Isabella's—but she also wanted mutual respect, independence, and freedom. She reasoned that if a complicated woman like Isabella de' Medici had found love and an intellectual equal—perhaps there still might be hope for her as well.

Distracted by the fluttering of the curtains, Nora felt the caress of a gush of warm air blown in through the open window. It seemed the museum guard had been right about the thunderstorm. She sat up and looked out the window and listened to the branches in the garden below thrashing restlessly in the uneven evening breeze. From the far edge of the valley, she heard an ominous rumble roll across the fields. It wasn't long after that a sweet, pungent scent filled the air, and she heard the sounds of water splattering on the ground.

As the rhythm of the rain steadily increased, she fell tiredly back onto the bed. To shield her eyes from the flashes of lightning stabbing the night sky, she pulled the cushion over her head again and relaxed into the soft mattress. Tucked inside a safe cocoon, she was vaguely aware of the storm's commotion, but it wasn't until she heard the woman speak that she groggily opened her eyes.

"*Svegliati!* Wake up, Nora. I have something important to tell you."

Coming slowly to her senses, Nora sleepily replied, "Something important? I don't understand." Running a hand over her face, she opened her eyes and blinked in surprise. Standing in front of her was a woman in white, and she was no longer in bed. How she had come to be there speaking to a woman who was soaking wet, dressed in a flowing white gown, she hadn't a clue.

A bit groggily she asked, "Am I dreaming?"

Ignoring her question, the woman replied, "We must be quick. There is no time to waste. He will be here soon."

What was she talking about? Nora wondered. *Who will be here soon?*

Nora assessed the woman, observing how raindrops—or were they tears—dribbled down her cheeks. And, when the vision impatiently tossed her dripping mane over her shoulder, in fascination, Nora watched as the beads of water arched high into the air and remained suspended as if by magic. To Nora, they seemed like precious gems, that glistened and sparkled in the dim light.

"Nora!" the woman admonished, taking a step closer and gently shaking her shoulder. "*Sbrigati!* There is no time to waste."

Refocusing her attention, Nora attempted to listen, as in hushed tones the vision continued, "You can trust no one, *mia cara!* Do you hear me? They want revenge. There is no time... Hurry... Francesco..."

As the misty vision continued mouthing words, Nora strained her ears, but she couldn't understand completely the cryptic message the woman seemed so intent on delivering. Instead of becoming clearer, the woman's strange message grew more convoluted and confusing. It seemed to Nora she was listening to a weak and crackling radio transmission and the words were coming from a place far far away.

"*Aiutami, Nora!* Help me. Paolo has come... Leonora dead... Hide letter..."

"Letter? *What* letter? I don't understand you."

The filmy vision only smiled obliquely and withdrew a piece of parchment paper from behind her back. Rapidly she scanned the contents, before kissing it, then extended it to Nora, as if she wanted her to read it too. But, just as Nora was about to take the note from her outstretched hand, the woman drew back and turned instead to a wooden chest by the side of the bed. In a graceful motion, she knelt before it and slid her hand along the back until a secret compartment sprung open.

With the hiding place fully revealed she peered over her shoulder to make sure Nora was watching her, then slipped the letter inside. In a satisfied tone, she said, "There. That is done. The letter is safe."

Cryptically, she added, "Now, all my secrets are hidden, and only those who really know where to look will ever find them again."

In slow motion, the woman spun around in a circle and Nora moved in her orbit. They continued their slow spinning dance, but when the woman looked over her shoulder, she came to a sudden stop. Pointing to the far wall, the vision cried out, "The painting is gone!"

Nora swiveled around but saw nothing in the darkness. From behind, the woman crept up to her and wrapped her arms around Nora and embraced her tightly. In the dark room, she could feel the woman's cold, trembling body and the misery that flooded her mind. Softly, the lady in white moaned in her ear, "Do something, Nora. Help me. He has taken it!"

Hearing a low rumble, the woman moved swiftly to the door and rested her ear against it. When she turned, Nora could see her eyes were now wide with fright.

"He is coming. Hurry! We must hide."

A flash of light blinded Nora.

"Find the painting, Nora. Don't let them destroy it. Don't let them win. Let them know..."

When a thunderous pounding on the door began, both women swung around. As another blaze of white-hot light illuminated the room, Nora fell dizzily to the ground. She tried to take a gulp of air but was suffocating under the weight of something covering her face. With all her might, she pushed back at her aggressor.

Now fully awake, she looked down at the floor and saw her pillow lying next to the bed. Her assailant had been a sack full of feathers. Sighing in relief, she flopped back on the bed and thought, *It was just a dream.*

Nora lay for a moment watching the shadows dance on the ceiling and listened to the steady beat of rain. Gradually, the sound calmed her jangled nerves. In the distance, she heard the soft purring of thunder. The storm had passed and was moving farther down the valley. Once again, the tolling of the church bells chiming out the hour in the moist night was discernible.

Getting out of bed, Nora padded over to the window and pushed the shutters aside. She glanced up and saw a sliver of moonlight peeking through the night clouds. As they shifted, a beam of light cascaded down from the sky and illuminated the Medici villa perched on top of the hill high above her.

As the last remnants of her unsettling dream faded away, Nora thought about the tragic fate that had befallen the Medici princess and the mystery of her missing portrait. Today she had undoubtedly stirred up the past, and now it seemed she was hearing the echoes from a nebulous realm.

"Pull yourself together, Nora," she admonished herself.

Still, she couldn't help but think Isabella was reaching out to her, urging her to... To do what exactly? Find her painting? She hadn't a clue where to begin.

Standing in the open window, Nora was enveloped by a current of humid night air, which carried with it the perfume of wet oak leaves. Regardless of time and place, Isabella's life was touching her own. She had been moved by Isabella's story back in California, and now, here in Italy, the filament that held them together was growing stronger.

Perhaps they were destined to help one another.

Looking back up at the villa again, Nora watched the flickering shadows play over the hill. As she did, it seemed a dark stallion stepped out of a small copse of trees into the pale moonlight. Seated proudly in the saddle was a woman in filmy white.

"*Caspita!*" Nora softly exclaimed. She leaned over the edge for a better view, but the moody clouds shifted again, casting the villa into total darkness. What was surreal blended into the sublime.

Chapter 9

The Rules of the Game

*W*hat had seemed so real last evening, in the light of day melted away like the nocturnal rainstorm. Now, seated on the terrace of the bed and breakfast, with her suitcases and camera equipment piled in the lobby, Nora looked out over the emerald-green valley and the misty blue sky, heavy with humidity, and shook her head at the silly idea she had actually encountered the *Dama Bianca*.

Taking a deep breath, she noticed the air smelled sweet, like wet grass and lavender, and the stone terrace glistened with moisture from the rain. In the distance, she could hear the whine of the cicadas. There was a cool breeze now, but she could feel the temperature rising. It was just a matter of time before it turned into another hot, muggy Tuscan day.

Nora peeled off her light cotton sweater, stuffed it back into her bag, and smoothed a hand over her hair. Despite the efforts she had taken to dry and force it into submission, she could already feel it curling. It had a mind of its own and was a more effective gauge of the weather than any barometer ever could be. She pushed it back from her face and secured it using her sunglasses as a headband, realizing sometimes you just had to give in and go with the flow.

She picked up her espresso cup to finish it off, but hearing her phone chime, she pulled it out of her purse and saw a text message from Richard. Nora winced slightly as she opened up the text, preparing herself for the worst. Surprisingly, however, he had sent her an upbeat note, letting her know the sale of the house had gone through. On top of that, his sentiments were warm and encouraging.

"So, I guess this is it, Nora. We had a good run for a while there, and now it is time for both of us to move on. I hope you find what you are searching for in Italy. Good luck with the film."

Gazing out over the landscape, Nora thought about their story. It seemed this was indeed the last line of their final chapter. When she heard her phone ding again, she looked down and saw yet another message from her ex-husband: "I'll send the accounting work later. My pleasure. I know math was never your strength."

What a guy, she thought. That was so typical Richard—of course, he couldn't just leave well enough alone.

Nora set the phone down and dug out the car keys from her purse and tossed them between her hands a couple of times, trying to analyze her feelings. She also wasn't sorry for the years they had spent together. Richard would always be a part of her journey. *I feel optimistically sad*, she finally decided. It was a strange cocktail of emotions, a bit of melancholy mingled with relief, as well as a bit of anticipation.

Raising a key to her forehead in a salute to her ex, she thought, *Well, if our final goodbye had to be done somewhere, what better place than standing on this terrace in Tuscany?*

Picking up her phone again, she scrolled through the rest of her messages. She deleted a few, but when she came to one from her mother, she paused. She hadn't sent her parents a text after she had landed—for that, she felt incredibly guilty. Hastily, she tapped out a reply, and just as she pushed the send button, her phone rang.

Looking at the small screen, she was pleased to see the caller was Juliette. "*Ciao, bella. Come stai?* How are things in Arezzo? I was just about to call you. Can you believe I'm back in Italy again?"

"*Era ora!* About time, I'd say. I can't wait to see you," gushed to Juliette. "When do you plan on arriving here?"

"I'm just getting ready to leave. I was thinking about stopping in Florence for lunch to take a walk and visit our old stomping grounds. If I don't get stuck in rush-hour traffic, I should be in Arezzo around six."

Running a hand through her hair, she told Juliette about the long flight from California, how she had passed her time in Rome, and her recent message from Richard.

"And the villa?" Juliette asked. "How did the filming go?"

"The hunting lodge was incredible, and the museum guard is a great guy. He gave me a lot of background information, and the filming went very well."

"So, did you meet the ghost herself, Ms. Isabella—*La Dama Bianca?*"

"Only in my dreams," Nora retorted. "It was quite a sensation to find myself standing in the very room where the Medici princess was murdered. It gave me a chill as if I could almost hear her speaking to me."

"You always did have a vivid imagination. I've never been up to Cerreto Guidi," said Juliette.

"I'll be going back to finish up some more filming. If you have time, come with me. In just a few weeks, the town will throw a party to honor Isabella. It's a festival with food, as well as a historical reenactment."

Although it was ordinarily a sleepy little place, Nora had learned from Giuseppe that each year the city selected a young woman to dress up like Isabella. On the back of a horse, she paraded through the streets, presiding over a festival created to honor the Medici princess's memory. There were music and dancing in the streets, as well as theatrical performances, reenacting the story of Isabella's death.

"Isabella's celebration sounds like the spectacle going on here. Once again they are pulling out the medieval costumes in Arezzo," said Juliette. "Things are well underway for the *Giostra del Saracino*. Tonight you will see the city streets decked out with all the neighborhood banners. The flag throwers and musicians are practicing in Piazza Grande too, later this evening. If you get here early enough, we can have a drink and watch the jousters practice their trial runs across the piazza."

"I can't believe I'll be in town for the June joust. I couldn't have timed my arrival any better," said Nora.

"Ehi, do you remember that time we met those two jousters in that bar?" asked Juliette.

Nora did, and she smiled at the memory.

The two girls had once spent a magical weekend in Arezzo, antiquing and attending the town's festival—*la Giostra*. It had been like falling back in time, and Nora had been completely entranced to learn that twice a year, in June and September, the town came alive with old-fashioned glamor and regalia that harkened back to the Middle Ages.

They had come to shop but had been quickly distracted by the colorful banners decorating the main square celebrating the neighborhoods that competed in the tournament. It had been quite a romantic scene, especially for two young women seeking a little adventure, and perhaps score a date with a handsome jouster.

She and Juliette had been particularly smitten by two young riders they had spied leaving the Piazza Grande after one of the preliminary practices. Following the men to a nearby bar, they broke the ice by asking them to explain the rules of the game. Flattered and enjoying the attention of two attractive foreign girls, the jousters, dressed in embroidered doublets and colorful leggings, were more than happy to oblige.

"The way the joust is organized is pretty straightforward," the dark-haired man had explained. "The town is divided into four districts representing the city's ancient noble families. We compete against one another on horseback with lances in an ancient game of skill and endurance."

He pointed to his blue and yellow costume and said, "I'm from Porta Santo Spirito, and my friend over there at the bar wearing green and white is from Porta S'Andrea. My name is Saverio, by the way, and that's Dario. Our teams are named for the medieval gates located at each corner of the city, and we all have distinctive colors."

"Seems a convenient way to keep all the fans and horsemen sorted out, and know who is friend or foe," teased Nora. "How many players are there?"

Juliette chimed in, "You know, strictly for research purposes. We might have to interview a few other jousters to make sure you are giving us the right information."

Saverio threw up his hands in mock offense. "What? Don't you trust a man sworn to protect the city from intruders to tell you the truth? *Fidati di me! Dai!*"

Juliette tilted her head playfully and said, "Well, it does appear you have quite an impressive lance—and you seem quite capable of using it."

He laughed at her quip and said, "Handling a lance takes quite a lot of practice. Only the most skilled riders make the cut."

"For the record, how many of you jousters are there?" asked Juliette.

"There are two jousters from each neighborhood—so that makes eight of us all together. During the actual match, we each take turns running up the *lizza*—the race track."

"It must be quite an honor to wear those beautiful costumes," added Nora, slightly in awe she was actually talking to one of the town's talented horsemen.

"It is," the man said as he stretched out a booted limb to reveal a well-toned muscular thigh encased in colorful leggings. "It's kind of hard to miss us riding down the street on horseback dressed like this—we tend to stop traffic. Still, while we might be the ones in the spotlight, there are many dedicated people involved in Arezzo's joust."

"Like who?" asked Nora.

"Let's see... For starters, the mayor of Arezzo presides over everything. Then there is the Master of Ceremonies—*il Maestro del Campo*—and all the team directors and coaches. But none of this would be possible without the support of all the people in our neighborhoods who work all year long, helping out."

Looking up, Nora saw Dario had joined them. In his hands, he carried two beer mugs and was giving his friend a questioning look.

"Seems we have acquired a few new joust enthusiasts," said Saverio.

"*Ah, sì?*" said Dario. Setting the beer mugs down, he turned a chair backward and straddled it. Looking at Nora, he said, "This guy is from Porta Santo Spirito, and is new to the game. Donati, one of their best jousters, just left to attend university in Rome."

Toasting Saverio with his glass, he joked, "*Hai una bella patata bollente da gestire, questo è certo!*"

"A boiling potato to take care of?" asked Nora curiously.

Dario laughed. "*Sì!* It just means he's got some big shoes to fill."

Glancing back at Saverio, he exclaimed, *"Che eredità impegnativa!* Gianluca is a tough act to follow—he was one of the best.'"

Raising his glass, he said, *"Comunque* as for me, I've been at this for a couple of years. It runs in our family. My great-grandfather helped revive the tradition back in the thirties."

Taking a sip of his beer, he asked, *"Che cos'altro volete sapere?* So, what else do you want to know?"

"If it was brought back during the thirties, when did it originally get started?"

"Our city's tournament goes way back, and I mean way, way back in time," said Dario. "It originated during the time of the Crusades. Seems it was a necessary means of defense to protect the city from the raids of the Saracens—the Muslims. It's kind of hard to believe they made it all the way here to Arezzo, right? At first, it was born as a military training exercise to keep the knights in shining armor fit and ready. Over time, though, it turned into this festival—a means of showing off for visiting dignitaries, like our Florentine neighbors. Probably even the Duke of Tuscany, Cosimo de' Medici himself."

"How does the joust work exactly? Are you guys just crazily going at it in the piazza, charging at one another with those wicked-looking lances?"

"Not exactly," Saverio said in amusement. "The object of the game is to strike a scorecard held by the *buratto.* He's the wooden dummy set up at the end of the racetrack who represents the King of India. We try to hit it squarely in the middle with our lances. But it isn't an easy thing to hold a spear longer than the height of a man—and almost as heavy—while charging up the hill on the back of a horse trying to hit a target the size of a coin."

"It's made even more difficult," continued Dario, "by the fact that the swiveling Saracen dummy holds a cat-o'-nine tails that whips a rider if he is too slow. Believe me—it doesn't feel all that great. The other day out at our practice field, I got hit with it."

Slapping his friend on the back, making him wince from his recent injury, Saverio said, "And he calls me *il principiante*—the novice."

"Yes, well, that's what makes the joust so interesting. Despite how experienced you are, it is almost impossible to foresee what the result of the joust will be—it all depends on the ability and the good luck of the eight jousters. There are penalties, of course. For instance, if you drop your lance, or if you ride accidentally off the jousting track."

"But," added Saverio, "you can also double your points if you break your lance by violently hitting the Saracen."

"And for the winning team...?" asked Juliette. "There must be some kind of prize."

"*Certo. La lancia d'oro*—the Golden Lance."

"Sounds like something I'd like to see," said Juliette. When Nora kicked her under the table, she smothered a laugh. Recovering quickly, she asked, "When it is all over, what do you do then?"

"The winners celebrate, the losers cry into their beer vowing to win the next match, and the tourists finally leave town and Arezzo returns to normal," he said. "Dario and me, and, well, all the other jousters go back to our normal jobs."

"But the practicing never ends," the other man said. "I practically live out at the stables. From October until March I'm in the saddle about three times a week, and from March, until September I ride every day, except, of course, for Sundays."

"But for me, it's a pleasure," said Saverio. "There is nothing better than training with the horses at dawn when the dew is thick on the grass and the morning fog is still hanging over the field. Or sometimes in the evening, when no one else is around, a calm descends over the pasture— that is, until you let the horse fly and you are the only one in control of your destiny competing with no one but yourself."

"*Vedete?*" he continued. "You have to have a lot of dedication and a certain passion for carrying on this tradition." Flashing them a brilliant smile, he offered, "*Sentite, offro io.* Can I buy you girls a drink?"

It was at that precise moment Nora had developed an intense crush on the handsome jouster from Porta Santo Spirito, whose team wore blue and yellow. She hadn't exactly fallen in love with the young man himself, but rather the ideals he represented and the very town itself.

It had thrilled her to know there existed a place where time stood still, where people embraced this ancient tradition. How appropriate the team she had decided to root for had the slogan *"con antico ardore"*—with ancient ardor—because something deep inside of her, too, responded to the sound of the drums, the pageantry and the devotion expressed by these talented cavaliers.

Nora came back to the present reluctantly. Once again, Italy was stirring her senses. Just as the tastes, sights, and smells had spoken to her ever since her arrival, now thinking about Arezzo and its joust was bringing back old yearnings, awakening the ancient ardor inside her heart.

Speaking again to Juliette on the phone, Nora admitted, "I'm looking forward to returning to Arezzo. It's been too long. I definitely feel the town calling me home."

"And just think of all the new double entendres we can come up with about men and their lances," Juliette said.

"Don't get me started," Nora warned. Glancing at her watch, she said, "Listen, we can catch up some more tonight. Isabella and I can't wait to move into your place. We can squeeze her in, can't we?"

"The more the merrier. Bring that old Tuscan ghost along with you. Let *La Dama Bianca* know she is invited to join us in Arezzo, too!"

Chapter 10

Buongiorno Principessa!

*W*hen Nora arrived in Arezzo later that afternoon, true to Juliette's word, the city was more lively than usual decked out in a sea of blue, yellow, green, and red banners. Walking up the main street to the Piazza Grande, she sidestepped a man wearing a Rolling Stones t-shirt leading a horse, and almost collided with a woman dressed in a long blue medieval gown who carried a Gucci purse. It seemed a quirky mixing of the past with the present. But, unlike a fabricated Disneyland setting, what was transpiring here in Arezzo, in this medieval town, was authentic and real, based on hundreds of years of traditions.

Entering the main piazza in the middle of town, Nora saw delivery vans and men in orange work pants had overtaken the large open space. The place was alive with activity, and each individual appeared to be focused on his particular task. Along the perimeter, metal scaffolding was in various stages of construction, and she could hear the ringing of hammers and the clatter of metal girders. When finished, the stands would accommodate the thousands of people who came from all over Italy to watch the event.

In the center of it all, spanning the gently sloping Piazza Grande was the horse track, constructed of packed sand and dirt that had been brought in by the truckload. Workers had covered up the ancient cobblestones so that the piazza was at least a foot higher, creating an impressively broad and stable path. Now the horses and their riders could gain the traction they needed to race across it at lightning speeds.

Nora glanced around, getting her bearings, and then climbed the metal stairs of one of the bleachers to get a better view. As she settled herself on the bench, she slipped on her sunglasses and watched as a horseman took his practice runs up the track. She couldn't help but feel a thrill as the rider skimmed up the steep slope of the piazza, repeatedly charging at the Saracen dummy. It was a preliminary exhibition, and the rider didn't carry an actual lance. Instead, his hand was held at the ready, and she could see he eyed his mark with unrelenting precision, preparing himself mentally to pierce the center of the target with the lance he would hold the following day.

When the jouster reached the top of the piazza, close to the Vasari Loggia, she observed how he skillfully reined in his horse. It was a mesmerizing sight, and she found she couldn't look away. It appeared she wasn't the only one, as a small crowd had settled near her. Around the piazza's perimeter, she also saw a group of townspeople as well as tourists taking pictures and cheering the man's performance.

Just as the crenelated buildings that circled the piazza began to cast long shadows, Nora realized, with a start, she should be keeping an eye out for Juliette. Looking back at the loggia where they had planned to meet, then back at her watch, she knew she was now running late. She estimated it would take another ten minutes to elbow her way through the crowd on the main street—*via del Corso*. To save time, she decided to take a shortcut across the back of the piazza.

Without giving it further thought, she ducked under the railing of the makeshift stand and jumped down. But instead of landing squarely on her feet, she skidded out of control on the slippery pavement, made more treacherous by the loose layer of sand. *This is not going to end well,* she thought as she headed downwards.

In the next instant, much to her surprise, she was caught from behind and heard the familiar words, *"Buongiorno, principessa!"*

Despite the awkwardness of the situation, she laughed, recognizing the line from her favorite movie. The man lifted her up, holding her hand as she regained her balance and footing.

"*Tutto bene,* are you okay?" he asked.

Swiveling around to face the person who had caught her, the words Nora was about to speak never made it past her lips. She hadn't anticipated the man to be quite so attractive, and she couldn't deny the spark of immediate attraction she felt. He was tall and physically fit, with a jawline that made her think of a Roman centurion. By the grin on his face, Nora could tell he was amused by her wide-eyed, embarrassed expression.

Not one to be so easily tongue-tied, she quickly found her voice and her wits. In an attempt to hide her confusion, and the fact that she was staring, Nora said a little too brightly, "*Sì, grazie signore.* Thanks, I'm fine, just feeling a little stupid, that's all."

She reached for her purse, which had dropped to the ground. Brushing the sand off it, she said, "You sure know how to flatter a girl. That's a great pickup line. *Complimenti!* You just made my day—even if you stole Benigni's line!"

The man laughed. "So, you are familiar with the movie?"

"Of course!" she exclaimed. "I've seen it many times. Roberto is a hard act to follow, but you delivered the line beautifully."

Looking him up and down, she saw he was dressed in jeans and a polo shirt with the team's neighborhood emblem. Around his neck was a loosely tied blue and yellow scarf. "I see you are from the Santo Spirito *contrada*," she said. "Are you a trainer or a coach?"

"Ex jouster. Avid Giostra del Saracino enthusiast," he said. "I'm part of the staff now and help with the horses. I'm the one who leads the riders down the track to the start line."

He pointed to the far end of the track. "See down there, at the bottom of the piazza near the fountain? That's the starting point, and I help from the ground—controlling the fans who go a little crazy, as well as with horses who get frightened by the noise."

"So, you can touch the horse..."

"Yes, but never the lance," he said quickly. "That's strictly prohibited. I'm there at ground zero, so to speak... it's my job to watch the *maestro di campo*, and, when he lowers his scepter, I signal the rider he is good to go."

To block the late afternoon sun, he shaded his eyes with a hand and asked, "Are you partial to any particular team?"

"If I wasn't before, I certainly will be rooting for the *Blu* and *Giallo* team now. The knights in Santo Spirito are proving to be quite chivalrous," she teased. "Besides, I like your team's colors the best, but..."

Nora stopped mid-sentence as she got the odd feeling that she had met him before. His hair was short, and he was clean-shaven, but there was something about the expression on his face, the shape of his nose and the line of his jaw. "Wait a minute. I think I might know you..."

The man appeared doubtful. "I don't think we've met before. You speak Italian very well, but I can tell you are a foreigner. Are you French, or perhaps English?"

She was about to respond when her cell phone rang. *"Scusami, solo un attimo,"* she said as she took the call. *"Ciao, bella.* Yes, I'm here. Sorry, I know I'm late. The jousters distracted me..." She looked up and caught the man's eye and blushed again in embarrassment.

Then, into the phone, she hastened to respond, "Yes, of course. I'll wait for you here. I'm in the *piazza,* close to the *buratto* target." She listened for a moment and then said, "Okay, see you soon."

Clicking off her phone, she regarded the man again. Then a slow smile spread across her face. *"Now* I remember where I've seen you before."

He raised an eyebrow and gave her a puzzled look.

"If I'm not mistaken, I believe we have a mutual friend. Do you know Juliette Laurent?"

The man tilted his head in surprise. "Sure, I know Juli."

"Tutto chiaro. That explains it. I've seen pictures of you on her Facebook page."

"Facebook. *Ho capito.* Got it."

"Juli and I met in Florence years ago. We were roommates."

"Aspetta! Sei la sua amica che fa il documentario. You must be the friend who is staying in her apartment, *giusto*? You're the one working on a documentary?"

"Yes, that's me. I'm Nora, by the way. Well, Leonora actually. Leonora Havilland—but I go by Nora for the most part."

"Leonora. That's a beautiful name." Shaking her hand, he said, *"Che piacere, sono Gianluca.* Gianluca Donati, but Luca to my friends."

Gesturing back across the piazza, he said, "As I said, once upon a time I used to compete in this competition. That was a while ago—but once a jouster, always a jouster. I can't stay away from the horses and this festival..."

"It's really something," Nora agreed. "I may be a foreigner, but there is something so special about this whole event... I can see why the people of this town take it so seriously. It is something to be proud of."

Glancing down at his dirty jeans and leather riding boots, he said, "*Ti giuro.* I swear. Most days you will see me in a suit and tie. I own an antique shop here in town."

"A jouster *and* an antiquarian? What an unusual combination. Only in Italy, that's for sure. So, where is your shop?"

"It is The Shop around the Corner."

"Which corner?"

"No," he corrected her, "our store is known as The Shop around the Corner. It is in via Bicchieraia. When you go out of the Piazza, you go up the street a bit and then turn left."

"Ah, I see, *il negozio dietro l'angolo*. I get it now. That's clever and easy to remember. I love antiques, by the way. Juli and I used to come to Arezzo to wander through your antique market here in the Piazza Grande. That is how I first found out about this gem of a town. I fell in love here..." She quickly added, "Well, with the city, I mean."

"There is much to like about Arezzo. I grew up here." Smiling, he said, "I may be a bit biased, but I am quite partial to the place. My father took over the business from his grandfather. Now I'm in charge of running the show. It seems we Donati have a thing for the past."

"Nothing wrong with that—history is my thing too. I've just come from Cerreto Guidi where I started filming..." She stopped mid-sentence and let out a little scream when she saw Juliette running across the piazza in her direction. "Juli!"

"Nora, it is so wonderful to see you. I can't believe you are finally here. Welcome back."

Wrapping her friend in a warm embrace, Nora said, "*Oh mio Dio,*

Juli! It's been too long."

Juliette looked back at the man behind her and grabbed his arm, pulling him forward. "Marco, I want you to meet my friend."

Nora instantly recognized him as the other man from Juliette's Facebook page. Stepping over, Marco kissed Nora first on one cheek then the other. *"Benvenuta ad Arezzo.* In a short time, I've heard so much about you—seems like we are already friends."

Nora narrowed her eyes at Juliette. "Well, I hope she hasn't told you *everything...*"

Juliette smothered a laugh. "Oh, just the good stuff. We will let him find out all the rest gradually. This is Marco Orlando, and, well, technically he is my boss. We work together at his winery, Urlo alla Luna. It's just a short distance outside the city." Gesturing vaguely in the direction of the *Duomo* at the top of the Arezzo, she said, "It's up in the hills over there in that general direction."

"Il capo? Dai!" Marco said. "Juli, who is the real boss of the winery these days?"

"Oui, d'accord, je l'avoue," Juliette said. "Okay, I admit it. I can be a little bit of a control freak. Out at the winery, I'm the *Capo.* But let's face it, *amore,* someone around here has to be the adult." She swatted him on the cheek and then kissed him.

Well, this was an interesting development, Nora thought. It was apparent that Juliette and Marco were much more than boss and employee. Her friend hadn't told her this during their recent flurry of messaging and emails. Now she understood the reason her friend's apartment was free for her to use this summer.

Looking over at Luca standing next to Nora, Juliette said delightedly, *"Ah sei tu!* It's been a couple of weeks since we saw you last. How are you doing?" Stepping over, she embraced him. "We thought we would find you hanging around the *piazza* helping with the horses."

Her eyes moved from Luca back to Nora, and observed with a pleased smile, "So you two have already met. *Bene,* that's great."

To Nora, she explained, "Gianluca is a friend of ours. He and Marco go way back—they grew up together. Once upon a time, they both were jousters, and competed against one another."

"*Giusto?*" Juliette said to Luca as she gave the ends of his scarf a gentle tug. "Nice touch, by the way. I like your colors. I see you are ready for the *giostra.*"

Giving her a knowing look, she added slyly, "Nora, we will have to pick up a blue and yellow scarf for you, too. I seem to recall you have a partiality for the team *and* in particular their jousters. Plus my apartment is down in the Santo Spirito neighborhood, so officially, you are a fan of Luca's team."

Marco scoffed. "Juli, really, you are starting to offend me. What about my team, Porta Crucifera?"

"Better to wear the colors of champions," Luca interjected with a mocking grin.

Skeptically, Marco scrutinized his friend. "Really now! Since when? It seems Porta Crucifera had a pretty good run last year. *Fammi pensare—* let me think... Didn't *we* win both the tournaments last year? Oh, that's right, we did! Your *contrada* came in second both times, as I recall."

Listening to their exchange, Nora could tell the two men took immense pride in their teams and were also highly competitive. Realizing she was probably throwing oil onto the fire, she innocently inquired of the two men, "*Allora, ragazzi*—who is predicted to win the joust this weekend?"

In unison, they each said the name of their team.

"*Vabbè, comunque è stato solo un colpo di fortuna che abbiate vinto.* It was just a fluke you guys won last time," said Luca. "Do you think you really have what it takes to win again?"

"*Cazzo, dici un sacco di cavolate.* You are so full of it sometimes," Marco retorted.

Listening to their colorful insults, which continued to escalate, becoming increasingly more profane, Nora stood back and threw up her hands. Juliette, apparently used to such heated exchanges, just laughed and said, "Oh, come on, guys. Easy now, play nice."

Putting his arm around her shoulders, Marco said, "*Senti,* Juli, you know we are just having a little fun." Glancing at his friend, he said, "Right, Luca?"

Luca gestured dismissively. "*Certo.* Friends. Of course."

Nora looked from one man to the other. She could see why Juliette had made a comment on her Facebook page that she had her hands full with these two. She sensed an apparent camaraderie, and it was evident they had been friends for a long time, but like competitive siblings, they quickly got under one another's skin.

Tugging on her arm, Juliette pulled Nora aside and handed her the keys to her apartment. As she explained a few quirks about how the locks on her apartment worked, Nora studied the two men standing a few steps away. Left alone, without the women to interact with, a subtle change had come over them. Their good humor had ratcheted down a few degrees, and the demeanors had turned a little cool. Nora couldn't hear what they were saying, but it seemed—well, what did they seem? What it was she wasn't quite sure, she just sensed something was a little off between the two.

Nora's thoughts were interrupted when she heard Juliette mention something about the celebratory neighborhood dinner—*la cena propiziatoria*—held in each neighborhood quarter the night before the big jousting tournament. "We can meet up tomorrow night and..."

Looking over at Marco, she cried out, "*Merde!* I just realized something. We have a big group of tourists coming to the winery tomorrow tonight. We won't be in town for the big party."

"That's right, *Capo*. That was *your* idea. Remember?" retorted Marco.

Juliette ignored him and continued, "You remember the good luck dinner we went to once?"

"Of course," Nora said, vividly recalling the event to celebrate the jousters and the fans of each neighborhood team. She also remembered fondly the long tables set up in the parks all over town, and all the great food and wine, as well as the dancing in the streets.

"Luca," Juliette asked, "isn't Claudio the deejay again tomorrow in

Santo Spirito?"

When he nodded, she said, "I love that guy—he always plays great music." With a forlorn look, she said, "Nora, I feel bad leaving you alone just after you've arrived. But you should still go. Listen, here's what I'll do. Tomorrow morning, I'll get you a ticket, and after the event at the winery, I could try..."

"I'm going," interrupted Luca. "Leonora, why don't you come along with me? You are a Santo Spirito fan now, after all."

Nora looked at him in surprise.

"I'd love the company," he continued. "I'd be more than happy to show you around and introduce you to some of our mutual friends."

The invitation sounded very tempting, and Nora glanced back at Juliette and gave her a questioning look. Interrupting the silent message telegraphed between the two friends, Luca said with a smile, "I'm no substitute for Juliette, but I promise you will have a good time. What do you say, *principessa*?"

Nora smiled at the reference to the line he had used before. "Well, sure, why not? That is, if you really don't mind me tagging along?"

"*Figurati*. Women dropping out of the sky into my arms doesn't happen every day. I think it is an excellent sign for Santo Spirito. You will be a good luck charm for the team."

"When you put it like that, how can I resist?" Nora said with a laugh.

"We can meet at the park tomorrow at the antique fair. It's tomorrow."

"I thought it was held the first weekend of every month?"

"*Sei molto fortunata*. They moved it back three weeks just to accommodate your schedule," he said.

"Really? To think Arezzo would do that just for me..." she teased.

He smiled at her. "Well, actually the fair is usually the first weekend, but there was a special event in the *piazza* earlier this month, and Bucciarelli the *assessore del comune* decided to change the date. Come by the Donati booth, say around seven, and we can walk back to the neighborhood together."

"It seems luck really is with me—jousting and antiquing on the same day. I couldn't ask for more. *Non vedo l'ora*—I can't wait," said Nora.

Across the square, a man shouted out to Luca. Glancing behind him, he waved. "*Arrivo*, I'll be right there, Nico."

Apologetically, he said to the group, "Sorry, the team is just about done. *Me ne vado.* I've gotta go and help pack things up." Placing a hand on Marco's shoulder, he added, "*Sei pronto?* Ready to lose tomorrow?"

Not missing a beat, Marco quickly responded, "*Vedremo.* We'll see about that. I think you guys are about to be whipped again. You never could hang on to anything important."

Holding Marco's gaze, Luca said, *"Sei un bastardo."*

Marco narrowed his eyes and said, "Son of a bitch, Luca. Give it up—it was just a joke, just let it go."

Juliette grabbed Marco's arm impatiently. "Guys, come on, enough already. Let's not start that up again."

Slowly they turned their heads in Juliette's direction, refocusing their attention on her. "Go on, gentlemen. Shake hands. May the best team win and all," she said.

Seeing her exasperation, they relaxed, and Marco extended his hand. "*Auguri*, see you day after tomorrow at the joust."

Luca in turn shook Marco's hand. "*Anche a te*—you too. See you in the Piazza." Still regarding him intently, he said, "*Sei proprio uno stronzo lo sai.* You are a real ass sometimes."

Marco unflinchingly agreed: "*Lo so.* I know." Then he added, "But I'm trying to change. So we are good then?"

Luca studied him for a moment. "Yeah, we are good."

Turning, Luca strode across the piazza to the far end, where the others were collecting the horses and gear. Nora listened in amusement to Marco and Juliette as they bickered about where they should eat. After a moment, however, she looked back over her shoulder and thoughtfully regarded the man she had just met.

In the distance, amongst the others, she could see Luca holding the reins of a horse, brushing its flank. *Interesting,* Nora thought. She couldn't quite put her finger on it, and she had only just arrived, but once again her intuition was telling her there was something more going on between the two men than just friendly neighborhood feuding.

Chapter 11

Sinners and Saints

*T*he next morning, seated in a little outdoor café near Juliette's apartment, Nora took a bite of her chocolate-infused brioche, and her lips turned upward in sticky pleasure. "Italian sweets are the best. Oh, how I have missed them." Glancing inside the bar at the *barista*, clinking cups behind the counter, she continued, "I mean, just look at that case filled with beautiful pastries, and did you *see* the design the guy made in my *cappuccino*? The man is an artist. It is almost a shame to drink. It's true. If you slow down long enough, you will discover—*l'arte è ovvunque*—art is all around us, even in the smallest of things. You just have to take time to see and appreciate them."

"It's a little too early to be philosophizing," Juliette said, smothering a yawn. Taking a long sip of her coffee, she looked over the brim and said, "*Je suis très contente que...*"

"Listen, Juli, pick either English or Italian—my French is rather limited, as you may remember."

"I remember," Juliette said with an exaggerated groan. "Your French never was as good as your Italian—still I kind of missed your terrible accent."

"Ehi!" Nora said and nudged her arm, causing the coffee in her friend's cup to slosh over the brim. Juliette sighed in mock exasperation and pulled out a napkin to wipe up the mess. "You always were a little too sensitive. But, for the record, I just wanted to say I'm glad you decided to come to Arezzo this summer. I'd almost forgotten how much fun we had together. And, by the way, I think this film of yours—*Waking Isabella*—is going to turn out just great. It's just what you needed to take your mind off..."

Catching her eye, Juliette said carefully, "I know a lot of stuff has happened to the both of us during the past couple of years, and it's been a while, but I can sense a new... *Merde!* I don't know how to put it into Italian or English. Let's just say I can sense a new kind of positive energy. After telling me about Richard and the baby... Well, I can tell already you are in a much better place now."

Reaching for a packet of sugar, she tore it open and poured a small amount into her drink. As she stirred her coffee with a little spoon, she said, "If you ask me, instead of you bringing Isabella to life, I think it is the other way around. I think it is Isabella who has brought *you* back to the land of the living."

Giving her friend a quick hug, Nora said, "Thanks, Juli. It's starting to feel like that." Taking a sip of espresso, she added, "I've missed you, and I've missed our long talks. How did we ever lose touch?"

"Life, I guess," said Juliette, dumping the rest of the sugar packet into her coffee. "What time did we send Marco back to the winery?"

"It was long after dinner. I couldn't tell if he was pleased to be free of us and our reminiscing or if he was truly reluctant to go," said Nora.

"Knowing Marco, probably a little bit of both. I can see he likes you."

Placing her elbows on the table, Nora leaned in and said, "You were holding out on me. Why didn't you tell me you were involved with Marco? He's a great guy. I'm half in love with him already."

Imitating her friend, Juliette leaned in too, and said, "I know. I was waiting until you got here because I was a little embarrassed. So typical, isn't it? It's what everyone tells you not to do—don't go falling for your boss, especially an Italian one. *Mais c'est la vie?*"

"But you never were one to follow conventions," said Nora. "I remember back in Florence, you always knew what you wanted and went after it. You wanted to manage a winery. Now, look. You're doing it."

"*Oui,* I came for the winery but then got blind sided by this Italian man," said Juliette. "*Oh, mon Dieu. Qui aurait pensé?* Because I'm French and a bossy business manager and he is Italian and easygoing and creative, you would think we'd be like oil and water, but you know what? When he isn't off daydreaming up some new idea, I'm teaching him some of my marketing tricks that are helping to grow our business. "

Juliette took another sip of her coffee. "He's very kind and funny, you know? He has this way of making me laugh even when he gets under my skin. It's always a surprise with him."

"When you find someone like Marco who makes you smile and builds you up, you've got to hang on to them. Believe me, those kinds of men are a rare commodity."

"There are times, however, when I would like to strangle him... Just the other day, Marco..."

"Did I hear my name?"

"Marco! *Tesoro*. Look, Nora—it's the devil himself!"

"*Ciao amore!*" he said, leaning down to kiss her on the lips. "I knew I'd find you here. I missed you last night."

Smiling at Nora, he said, "I'll let you borrow her now and then, but it's lonely out there on the hill all by myself."

Juliette laughed. "You are a big boy now—you can manage without me for one night. Besides, Nora and I spent most of the night catching up. We had a lot of ground to cover since we last saw one another. What are you doing here anyway? I didn't think I'd see you until later this afternoon."

"I had a couple of errands to run in town, and then I heard the sound of your voices as I was walking up from the parking lot. If you are done, why don't we take a walk around and show Nora a few of the sights. I'd like to get to know your friend better. Last night at dinner, I could barely get in a word edgewise."

"Yeah, sorry about that," said Nora. "I didn't mean to monopolize Juliette. I'd love to see what's new and visit some of my favorite spots."

"Alright," said Juliette, standing up and brushing the crumbs from her hands. "Let's climb up to the Prato near San Donato—the cathedral. The antique fair is under way by now. After that, the return trip back to my apartment will be a lot easier."

Linking her arm in his, she added, "Marco loves to play tour guide. He knows lots of fascinating things about this town."

"Where should I begin?" Marco mussed.

"Start with San Donato," suggested Nora. "Tell me about him. I gather he is Arezzo's patron saint."

"That's right. The cathedral is named after Donato, and part of him resides in a casket inside the altar."

"I remember going into the church after the last joust we attended..." Nora said, looking over at Juliette for confirmation. "That's the one, right?"

"Yes," Juliette replied. "After the competition ends..."

"And my team wins, of course," said Marco with a grin.

"*Certo, amore mio*!" said Juliette. "After Porta Crucifera wins, everyone in Marco's neighborhood crowds into the church to celebrate. People stand on the pews, waving banners and singing. Then the jousters arrive—even their horses are allowed to enter the church."

"The horses go inside? I don't remember that."

"Naturally, they are champions, too! It is there in the cathedral the jousters are presented with the golden lance."

"You probably don't remember seeing the horses, Nora, because you had eyes only for the cute jouster."

"And, as I recall, Juli, I believe you stayed up all night celebrating with..."

Juliette put her hand on Nora's arm, stopping her, and said, "Um, hold on right there. We don't need to go into *all* the details." Smiling innocently at Marco, she continued, "*Amore*, weren't you telling Nora something about Saint Donato?"

"Sounds like Nora and I need to have a talk about your past, Mademoiselle Laurent—but we'll save that conversation for another day," said Marco.

"Oh, I bet when you were in college, Marco, you weren't always so saintly. If we checked into your dark closet, we might find a few skeletons," Juliette joked.

Marco gave her an oblique look but didn't say anything. He looked instead at Nora, and said, "So, you wanted to know about San Donato?"

When she nodded her head, they walked through the heart of

town, climbing the slope to the upper part of the city, and he smoothly launched into a colorful story about a priest who had performed the "miracle of the crystal goblet".

"A magic goblet, imagine that," Nora said.

Smiling Marco, continued, "They say that San Donato, a priest from the first century, picked up a broken goblet that had a large hole in the bottom. But, still, when he poured wine into the glass chalice, amazingly it remained contained inside, and not a drop was wasted. In awe, the pagans in the church fell down on their knees and prayed. Having seen the light at that moment, they promptly converted to Christianity."

Looking at Juliette, he joked, "Pretty neat party trick, don't you think, to mend a broken glass? We could benefit from a few acts of God like that out at the winery. It sure would cut down on costs for our stemware."

Nora laughed at his joke, but Juliette only rolled her eyes, apparently having heard that line a couple of times before.

"So, what happened next—to Donato, I mean?" asked Nora, her interest clearly piqued.

Delighted to have entertained her, and by her question, Marco continued. "Well, as you can well imagine, a miracle-performing priest tended to make the regional Roman prefects a little uncomfortable. It didn't bode well for them or their provincial government if a Christian like Donato was allowed to stir up the peasants, converting them quickly to a religion the Romans condemned. So, rather than let Donato hang around to dazzle, distract, or save any more souls, they arrested him."

"And..." prompted Nora.

"Cutting to the end, so to speak, shortly after that they chopped off his head... According to a popular legend, Donato's head bounced a few times before rolling down the hill in the direction of the Piazza Grande and *la Pieve*—the church of the people."

"No, you can't be serious," Nora groaned.

"Oh, but I am. Do you want to hear what happened next?"

"I'm almost afraid to," said Nora.

"It isn't that bad. Quite the opposite—the people of Arezzo scooped up the head of Donato, for safekeeping."

"And where is this relic now?" asked Nora.

"Would you like to see it?" Marco said, pointing to the church of *la Pieve* they were just passing by. "It's kept in there."

Nora glanced over at the church's facade, built with three loggias, with a series of columns that increased with each elevation. She realized this was the church that faced onto the main street, whose characteristic rounded apse could be seen from the main piazza, giving the square its distinctive appearance.

"You can go inside and see San Donato's head," said Juliette. "Well, not his actual head—it is kept inside a silver bust that resembles him. But, if you *really* want to meet a real saint, up close and in person, from the tip of her nose to the bottom of her toes, I'll take you to Cortona to see Santa Margherita. Her mummy is preserved in a glass case in a church dedicated to her."

"Really, she is actually displayed right there in the church for all to pay their respect?"

"*Sì!* Like sleeping beauty, Margherita lies peacefully on a satin bed, her head on a velvet cushion, laid out for all the parishioners to see."

Shaking her head Nora said, "These are the things that I find so intriguing about Italy, the devotion to saints and their body parts. In America," she continued, "we just don't have that kind of sacred devotion, it just isn't a part of our religious culture."

When they reached the Prato at the top of the hill, where the antique fair was indeed in full swing, they strolled on past the crowds and into the cathedral next door where they walked around and admired the magnificently carved altar depicting scenes of Donato's life.

The images made a lot more sense to Nora, now that she had a better appreciation of the miracles Donato had performed in this very spot. She admired his courage. And even if it had ended badly for him, his legacy still lived on in two churches in Arezzo—his body in one, his head in another, and his heart continued to beat for the city.

Continuing their pilgrimage, they left the large airy church and walked on to the smaller neighborhood church of San Domenico, just a few steps away, where Nora remembered they'd find the famous cross painted by Cimabue—the artist who had inspired Michelangelo and Caravaggio.

When they entered the more humbly decorated church, compared to the one they had just been in, Nora walked the length of the nave and quietly stood in front of the crucifix. She never got tired of looking at this lovely piece that depicted the gently curving figure of the flanked by the portraits of Mary and St. John.

Pointing reverently to it, she said, "Look. You can see traces of the old Byzantine style in Cimabue's work in the gold leaf that he used in the background. But this piece is actually innovative."

"What do you mean?" asked Marco.

"You can also see he was beginning to experiment with new ideas. There is a new sense of realism—see the Madonna's sorrowful eyes? You can almost feel her pain. This isn't a triumphant Christ rising up, but a man who has suffered greatly, and we too suffer and empathize with him. The artist has managed to turn the moment of death and sadness into something beautiful and moving."

Inhaling deeply, taking in the scent of incense and dust, Nora continued, "I've never been all that religious, or read the *Bible* much, but standing here gazing up at this cross makes me want to believe in something bigger than myself. In this sacred spot, I'm ready to embrace the power of the saints."

"There is definitely something in the air here," agreed Juliette, walking to the far wall where she inserted a coin into a box to activate a spotlight that illuminated the cross.

Studying Cimabue's work, which now seemed to glow, Marco said in hushed tones, "We are lucky to have this crucifix. It is very similar to the one he painted a few years later, which hangs in Santa Croce church in Florence—it was practically destroyed in the flood."

Sitting down on a wooden bench and draping his hands over the back of the pew in front of him, he went on. "But, this cross, too, was once put in harm's way and almost stolen from the town. In fact, we have Luca's great-grandfather, Bernardo Lancini, and his grandfather Federico Donato to thank for saving it. During the war, with the help of the partisans and the parish priest, they kept it out of the hands of the Nazis, hiding it in an underground railway spur to the north of town. The Lancini's also helped save the Piero della Francesca frescos in the church in the middle of town."

"Just yesterday I was talking to someone about this very thing," said Nora. Looking over at Juliette, she reminded her, "You know, the curator of the Medici museum in Cerreto Guidi. He was telling me about the rebel bands who saved the Medici portraits in the villa there."

Turning back to face Marco, she asked, "It is rather fascinating to meet people who were so directly involved in the resistance movement. Were your family *partigiani*, too?"

"*Sì*," he said, "There was an underground network that thrived here in Arezzo. In fact, my great-aunt on my mother's side—Maria Rosa—she used to deliver pamphlets and bread in the false bottom of her bicycle basket to those hidden in the hills. The partisans relied on village women, even children, to shuttle notes from camp to camp. But eventually she was apprehended."

"What happened to her?"

"They held her at Villa Godiola at first and then she just disappeared. After that, the family never heard from her again."

"Villa Godiola—was that a German headquarters?"

"It was just one of the many villas around here that the Nazis used."

Juliette glanced up from a hymnal she had been paging through. "In France, it was awful, too. Just like the partisans in Italy, the French did their best to protect national treasures. Because of them, the *Mona Lisa* was kept out of the Führer's hands. She was moved five or six times to various secret locations to keep her safe."

"I've never understood why Hitler was so obsessed with paintings and art," said Marco.

"Believe it or not," said Nora, "he wanted to be an artist himself."

When she saw Marco's incredulous face, she explained, "It's true. The man who became the dictator of Germany originally had artistic intentions and wanted to attend Vienna's Academy of Fine Arts."

"Why didn't he?"

"He failed the entrance exam because they believed his work lacked creativity and style," said Nora. "The admitting committee dismissed his watercolors of flowers and country cottages in favor of bolder modern expressionist art."

"I wonder whatever happened to the instructors who rejected him? I'm sure it didn't end well for them."

"It didn't. Hitler was so infuriated that the Academy preferred paintings with 'no subject matter' over his—eventually, he took his revenge and began to wage war on modern artists. He called them degenerates, and loathed their 'deviant' style of art."

"Deviant art? I'm not sure I follow... It sounds kind of gruesome. I don't think I've ever come across or seen..."

"Have you ever seen a painting by Matisse or Vincent van Gogh?"

"*That's* deviant art? Surely, now you are the one who is joking."

"Not at all," said Nora. "What we take for granted and sell all over the place today—on coffee mugs, posters, and calendars—Hitler considered the downfall of modern civilization, something to fear, deny, and destroy."

Gazing back at the cross, Nora said, "But what really drove the fascist regime crazy were the men behind the pictures. They saw them as a dangerous breed who challenged the status quo and invited the viewer to think for himself. Just like San Donato..."

"Because, you know," interjected Juliette, walking to the far wall to study a portion of a faded fresco on the wall of the church, "art, freedom, and creativity will change society faster than politics."

"Exactly," said Nora, standing up to join her. "But here's the irony. As much as Hitler wanted to amass the biggest collection of art for himself, he destroyed almost as much. He was intent on purifying the German culture, hence all the book burnings, but he also raged a war on modern artists, destroying and desecrating so many paintings. Eventually, artists went underground and painted in secret, afraid to express themselves freely."

"*Oui.* That is exactly what happened in Paris," Juliette agreed. "The Nazis kept a close watch on the areas where the artist communes existed, carrying out raids and harassing artists like Picasso, Dalì, and Miro. They were like bloodhounds following a scent, trying to keep a lid on their modern ideas and squashing free thought and creativity."

"Can you imagine if Hitler had achieved his goal?" asked Marco. "What if he had managed to wipe out freedom of expression completely?"

"A world without Picasso," murmured Nora. "What a loss that would be. Certainly not a world I want to live in."

A loud click echoed through the church when the timed light that had been focused on the cross blinked off. Marco indicated the direction of the exit, and the two girls followed his lead. Stepping into the sunny piazza, Marco looked at his watch and said, "Who's hungry? I know a little place near..."

Before he could continue, Juliette, pointing excitedly to a street vendor selling banners and souvenirs for the next day's joust, cried out, "*Guarda*! Check out those scarves, Nora. See, I told you they would be easy to find! Let's get you a blue and yellow one right now—my treat."

Marco rolled his eyes in mock disdain. "Are you sure you don't want to wear my team's colors, Nora? Green and red..."

"Oh, pipe down, Marco," said Juliette. "Don't worry, tomorrow I'll wear your colors. In fact, give me some money, and I'll pick myself up a green and red scarf, too."

"Amore, you *do* love me." Smiling, he kissed Juliette.

"*Mais bien sûr, je t'aime aussi mon amour,*" Juliette replied sweetly. She graced him with a charming smile before turning back to examine the array of colorful scarves.

Marco glanced sideways at Nora and confessed, "I just love it when she speaks to me in French." Smiling, he added, "Go ahead, then, and wear the colors of Santo Spirito. I know it will make Luca happy the next time you see him. We may come from different parts of town and root for different teams, but despite that, for the most part, we've been best friends since we were kids. I remember this one time—we must have been about fourteen—we decided to liberate some horses from the Porta del Foro stables and..."

"And by 'liberate' you mean 'steal'?" Juliette said, holding up a scarf. "What do you think, Nora? Do you like this one or... or this one here? Which is better?"

Throwing out his arms in mock defense, Marco said, "Okay, for the record, let's just say we 'borrowed' them for the afternoon."

Considering the selections, Nora pointed at the scarf Juliette held in her left hand. "I like that one."

"Marco, get your wallet out," her friend called over her shoulder. "I need another *euro*."

"Come on, you two. I'm telling a story here. Where was I?"

"Something about stealing horses, I believe," Nora reminded him.

"Right," he said. "Anyway, Luca and I were always competitive and up to no good. We weren't always the saints we are today. But come to think of it, it was all Carlotta's idea. She was the one who decided to prank the stablemen at the *scuderia* that day and take their horses on a joy ride. So we..."

"Carlotta? Who was Carlotta?" Nora interrupted.

"She was a friend of ours," Marco said, a little too casually. "When we were kids, we were all pretty tight. It was always me, Luca, and Carlotta. She rode horses, too. We were all pretty crazy back then..." He shook his head at the memory, then added, "But, it always seemed Carlotta was the one devising the schemes that got us all into trouble."

"She sounds like a handful."

"Carlotta could be very persuasive," Marco agreed.

"Women like *that* are dangerous."

Marco was quiet a moment, lost in a memory. "She was beautiful and bold. Stubborn as the day is long. Sometimes I used to think the devil possessed her."

"I look forward to meeting her," said Nora. "Does she still live here?"

Her question hung in the air for a moment, then he replied flatly, "Carlotta died a few years ago."

Nora's eyes grew big, and she put a hand on his shoulder. "I'm so sorry. It's hard to lose someone so young—especially a close childhood friend. What happened?"

Nora waited and, after a moment when he finally responded, it seemed he chose his words carefully. "Carlotta was a rare kind of person, the kind you really had to know to appreciate. I wish..."

"*Ehi, Marco! Senti amore*—don't put your wallet away," Juliette called out. "I'm not done here."

With a tilt of his head in Juliette's direction, he said, "I guess the boss needs me."

Quickly he stepped to Juliette's side, put his hand on her back, and said, "*Dimmi tesoro*. How much money do you need?"

Nora watched as Marco's mood lightened instantly as he animatedly chatted with the vendor behind the booth. As he handed the man change, Juliette approached her and draped the newly acquired blue-and-yellow scarf around Nora's shoulders. Tying it in a loose knot, she adjusted the folds, then stepped back and said, "There, that looks perfect on you."

As she fingered the soft material, Nora's thoughts remained focused on a woman named Carlotta. Just saying her name seemed to stir up mixed memories for Marco. She had picked up on a curious vibe, as she had the other day after first seeing Marco and Luca together.

She couldn't quite explain it, but Nora had a premonition that this childhood friend was the cause of the subtle tension between the two men. Had Carlotta taken only horses—or had she in fact stolen one of their hearts?

As the threesome walked back toward the Piazza Grande, Nora wondered if Carlotta had been a sinner or a saint. Or, like Isabella, had she been a little bit of both?

Chapter 12

Family Business

*A*n hour or so before sunset, Nora climbed back to the top of the hill to the park next to the cathedral to meet Luca at his booth at the antique fair. In support of Porta Santo Spirito's team, she had changed into a blue t-shirt, and around her neck was the scarf Juliette purchased for her earlier. If she was to attend the *Propiziatoria del Saracino*—with one of its ex-jousters—she figured she needed to dress appropriately.

As Nora approached the *belvedere* at the top of Arezzo's hill, colorful balloons and a large crowd greeted her. She stood for a moment surveying the picturesque scene, observing with pleasure the multitude of booths and tables set up under the canopy of trees. Taking her time, Nora began weaving her way through tables filled with silver, embroidered linens, and old phones. At first, she resisted temptation, but after ten minutes, drawn in by the warm patina of a pair of brass wall hooks, her willpower gave way. Inquiring about the price, at ten euro each, she decided they were a steal, and she reasoned they were small enough to pack.

Clutching a plastic bag with her purchase, she walked determinedly on in search of Luca, but stopped again a few yards away, distracted by a booth filled with luminous chandeliers. Dazzled by the shimmering crystal teardrops, she didn't hear her name being called. It wasn't until the man selling the lamps touched her lightly on the arm that she turned around and saw Luca standing a short distance away.

"Leonora, it's hard to get your attention," he called out. "It seems you are quite enthralled with our antique fair." Seeing the colors she wore, he praised, *"Complimenti*! I see you are getting into the spirit of things."

"Sorry, I didn't recognize my name—I'm used to everyone calling me Nora." Toying with the scarf, she said, "Do you like it? Juliette bought it for me earlier today."

"I think it suits you perfectly," he said. "It was the missing touch you needed. Now you look like a real Aretina." Eyeing her bag, he added, "I see you've acquired a few other things, too."

"Oh, I've been tempted by a lot of things here in the market." Opening the plastic sack, she showed him the brass pieces she had just purchased. "But at least *these* will fit in my luggage."

"Come, let me show you what we are selling today," said Luca.

Nora followed him into the Donati booth, located just a short distance away, that was filled with furniture and old mirrors. Running her hand over a table, she said, "This piece is gorgeous—the woodworking and craftsmanship are exquisite."

Glancing up, she saw a Renaissance *cassapanca*—something Isabella might have used as a hope chest. "And this!" Skirting around a pair of chairs, she bent down to examine it more closely. "My dad is a woodworker, and he would absolutely love this piece."

"Really?" said Luca. "My grandfather was too. He used to make these chests with hidden compartments. They were quite ingenious, really."

"That's funny, so did my dad!" Turning her head to the right, she exclaimed again, "And look at that little table, I would just die to have that as well. Too bad I can't fold that up and carry it onto the plane. Do you ship to the...?"

She was interrupted by the yapping of a little dog. Standing up, she saw an older couple come into the booth. Nora watched as the woman handed a leash attached to a dancing white terrier to her companion. "Here, Edi, take Rocco for a minute." Walking up to Luca, she gave him an affectionate hug. *"Ciao, amore,* how are you?" The woman looked over at Nora who had turned back to admire the table and said, *"Buona sera, Signora.* Isn't that a lovely piece?"

When Nora nodded, the woman said to Luca, *"Scusami,* I didn't mean to intrude, we just wanted to stop by and see you before we leave tomorrow."

"Figurati, mamma." Addressing Nora, he said, "I'd like you to meet my parents, Edoardo and Elena." Then, to his mother, he said, "Leonora

has just arrived from California and will be living in Juliette's apartment for the summer. She's the one working on the documentary. Marco and Juliette are occupied with their guests out at the winery, so she's coming with me to the dinner in the Santo Spirito neighborhood tonight."

Elena eyed Nora with increased interest. *"Ah, sì?* We saw them setting up the tables down in the street earlier today." Noticing Nora's scarf, Elena inquired, "I see you are supporting the *gialloblù* team—or has Gianluca coerced you into wearing our colors?"

"Not at all," Nora said. "I've been a fan for some time now." Glancing at Luca, she added, "I find the cavaliers of Santo Spirito especially obliging."

Luca smiled at their private joke, then said to his father, "We've had a pretty good day. I sold a table and a sideboard. That put us over the top for the month. They are coming by tomorrow to pick them up."

Edoardo seemed immensely pleased by this. *"Bene!"* He turned to Nora and, with a broad sweep of his arm, taking in the commotion around them, he asked, *"Che ne pensi?* Are you enjoying the fair?"

"There is nothing like it," exclaimed Nora. "I was just admiring several items for sale in your booth—the chest over there, and this lovely table. You just can't find such treasures like this back in the States."

"Keep in mind, this is just a sampling of all that we offer. You must visit our store in via Bicchieraia."

"Has it always been in your family?"

"For years! My grandfather Bernardo—Luca's *bisnonno*—started the business back in the early thirties. He, along with my mother Margherita, ran the place. He had impeccable taste, and she—well, she was a force to be reckoned with! She had a remarkable sense for business and talent with numbers. After the war, she rebuilt and kept things running smoothly, and eventually I took things over from her."

Glancing at his son, he added, "Now it is Gianluca's turn to pick up the reins."

"Your business really is a family affair—I love that about Italy, how things are passed down from generation to generation."

"Gianluca's doing a fine job. In the past few years, he's made lots of innovations. I think that he gets his head for business from his grandmother. Like my father and grandfather, he too has a talent for finding hidden gems—like some of the things you've just been admiring."

"I look forward to stopping by your shop in town and seeing where it all got started."

Taking in the well-appointed booth Luca had organized for the antique fair, she imagined the Donati shop would be even more delightful—a place to lose oneself for an hour—filled with cut glassware, brass candlesticks, and mahogany tables. There would be stunning paintings from the fifteenth century hanging on the walls, and sprinkled around the room would be a vast assortment of pedestals displaying marble busts of Roman emperors.

In her mind's eye, she could also see the original Donati family members—Margherita with a pencil behind her ear, tabulating the day's earnings, and her father Bernardo, who chatted with clients in the middle of the shop, extolling the virtues of a porcelain vase.

When the little dog whined at the sight of a poodle passing by, Nora looked over at Elena. She watched in amusement as Luca's mother took the leash from her husband and gave it a slight tug. "Zitto! Rocco. Have you no manners?" Addressing her husband, she said, "Edi, I think it's time to go. Rocco needs his dinner." Placing a hand on Nora's arm, she said, "It has been nice chatting with you, Leonora."

"Likewise. Perhaps we will meet again soon. Will you be attending the joust tomorrow night?"

"Not this time. We are leaving early tomorrow for London." Nodding toward her son, she said, "Gianluca has probably told you this, but he was a jouster for several years—and I miss watching him ride in the piazza on that famous horse of his, Bright Dawn."

"That horse was a magnificent animal," agreed Edoardo. Putting his hand on his son's shoulder, he added, "Did you know teamed with that horse Gianluca won six jousts in a row? Those were exciting days for the family."

Luca shrugged nonchalantly. Nora could tell he was embarrassed by his parents' praise; still, it was a remarkable accomplishment—something worthy only of a highly trained and skilled athlete, and she could tell deep down inside he also was quite proud.

"Anyway," said Elena, "we are off early in the morning to visit Serena, Luca's sister, and…"

"And after England," interrupted Edoardo, "I'm taking Elena to Venice for a romantic holiday."

Elena looked at her husband and shook her head in amusement. Leaning in, she said in a stage whisper to Nora, "He'll be asleep by nine every night, I guarantee. I plan to go out and dance in Piazza San Marco—maybe even take a gondola ride…"

Edoardo chuckled. "You, *tesoro*, have no sense of direction. If you go out on your own, you will just end up in the canal, and I'll have to be the one to fish you out."

Nora smiled at their teasing remarks. "Perhaps I will see you when you return. I'm staying in Italy until mid-September."

"*Bene!*" said Elena. "Excellent! You will still be here for the joust at the end of the summer—we will be here too, and we can all go together."

Looking over at Luca, she said, "When we get back from London, bring Nora to the house. You remind me when I return, *va bene?* We will have a nice dinner together when we get back."

Luca held up his hands. "*Sì, mamma,* whatever you like."

As the couple turned to go, Nora called after them, "*Buon viaggio!*" Glancing back, seeing Luca's amused expression, she asked, "What's so funny?"

"You've only been here a short while and have already been invited to two dinners—and both times you obtained these invites in less than ten minutes."

Nora laughed. "Just for the record, I don't accept dates from just anyone. Your parents seem delightful and I'd like to get to know them better—plus, I love Italian hospitality and an authentic homemade meal. You are crazy if you think I'd pass that up!"

As she spoke, out of the corner of her eye Nora watched a young man enter the booth and start placing items into a box. Without saying a word, he closed the lid and walked briskly to a van parked a short distance away. Tilting her head at the man, she gave Luca a questioning look.

Following her gaze, he said, "Oh, don't worry. That's Franco—he works for us. The market will be closing soon, and I called him a short while ago to help take down the booth and start packing up our merchandise to take back to the store."

Checking his watch, Luca said to Nora, "It's still a little early. The dinner gets started around seven. Would you like to get a drink first?"

"I'd love one."

When Franco returned to load up more things, Luca called out, "Giovanni will be here in a minute. Do you need any more help?"

Franco waved a hand. *"Tranquillo, capo!* We've got everything covered. See you later tonight."

Nodding toward the cathedral, they walked side by side in the direction of the church of San Donato. Descending the stairs to the street, a passerby called out a friendly greeting. In return, Luca waved his hand. As they approached the church built of sandstone and columns removed from an ancient Roman temple, Nora looked up. She admired the roof line of the church and the bell tower—the distinctive red-roofed pinnacle that rose up majestically as if to touch the heavens above.

Glancing over at Luca, she said, "I was inside the cathedral earlier. Marco and Juli gave me a tour."

"At this time tomorrow, after the joust, it will be full of the fans of Santo Spirito! All you will see will be blue and yellow flags."

"Funny," Nora said. "That's the same thing Marco said, but he implied I'd be seeing a sea of red and green celebrating his team's victory."

Luca didn't verbally respond, just shrugged his shoulders, as if he didn't believe it for a moment. Indicating a table set out in the street in front of a nearby café, he gestured for her to take a seat. Nora smiled again at their unashamed rivalry, as she sat down on a chair whose legs had been altered, the front shorter than the back, to accommodate the steep incline of the hill. Still, both the chair and the table wobbled just a bit.

Joking with the waiter, who also seemed to be a close friend, Luca placed an order for two spritzes. When their drinks arrived, the two men talked for a moment about the upcoming joust. As they did, Nora held up her glass, admiring the deep amber color of her apéritif. Taking a sip, and then another, she enjoyed the warm sensation that spread through her body as the *Aperol* liquor began to take effect.

When his friend returned inside the bar, Luca sat back in his chair, picked up his own drink, and they clinked their glasses together in a toast. "Seems like you know everyone here. You are quite the 'Big Man on Campus.'"

He appeared puzzled by the American idiom. Nora mused, "How can I explain this expression? You seem to be very popular—a man about town—well known and respected."

"*Ah, sì,*" he said. "Sure, I know everyone here. I told you yesterday... I've lived here all my life."

"It seems an important part of Italian identity to be so loyal to the place where you were born."

He gave her a scrutinizing look. "Now, don't go stereotyping me. I've traveled all over Europe and studied in Rome, but I'm always happy to come home." Gesturing around, he continued, "Can you blame me for having a soft spot for this place?"

"On the contrary," Nora replied, "I envy the pride you have for your town." Considering the golden stone building on the opposite side of the street he pointed to, that matched the color of her drink and was almost as intoxicating, Nora added, "To me, it makes perfect sense. I love all the medieval and Renaissance buildings—I wish *I* could call it my home."

With a smile, she added, "It is certainly a place worth defending."

"Arezzo has always done its best to protect itself. We built a wall around the town..."

"And trained jousters to defend it against its foes and the infidels."

Luca smiled. "Well, the Aretini have always put up a good fight. Unfortunately, we didn't have the numbers to keep the Florentine troops out of our fair city, and ultimately, Cosimo's army overran us.

Gesturing with his straw, he added, "He built a fortress at the top of the hill over there. At first, we didn't take too kindly to Medici. It took a while, but we all learned to get along—eventually."

"So, nowadays, instead of fighting the Medici or the Saracen, you are reduced to showing off your bravery racing horses up a track and piercing a wooden dummy," Nora said innocently.

"That," he retorted, "or gallantly rescuing women who clumsily slip off spectator stands."

"*Touché,*" said Nora with a small laugh. "Don't get me wrong, I think the joust is wonderful, and I am impressed by your accomplishments, really—and I can tell your parents are proud of you also. So, do you all live together?"

"Now, that's one Italian stereotype I'm happy to say I have broken. I haven't lived with my mom and dad for years. My parents still keep the family apartments where I grew up, and my *nonna* lived on the top floor where they could keep an eye on her." He paused, reconsidering. "But come to think of it—really, it was the other way around. I believe it was actually *nonna* who was taking care of all of us."

Luca swirled the ice around in his glass and smiled at the memory of his grandmother. "Her name was Margherita, but everyone called her Nita." Taking a drink, he added, "She would have liked you too. She always wanted to visit California—go to San Francisco, especially Los Angeles. If you ask me, I think she wanted to go to Hollywood and meet Cary Grant."

"Who wouldn't?" Nora replied. "Did she ever go?"

"No, unfortunately, she never did. But she read a lot of stories and watched many American films. Even though *she* never got the chance, she was always encouraging Serena and me to go."

When the waiter placed a small bowl of chips on the table, Luca glanced up. He thanked the man and then said, "In answer to your question, I live in the apartment over the antique shop. Back in the nineties, my dad converted the workrooms on the second floor into apartments. We used to rent it out to people on holidays, but I moved back there about two years ago. It was just after..."

He hesitated a beat and Nora waited for him to continue. When he said nothing, she encouraged, "Yes, just after..."

"Just after I took over the business," he said, finishing his thought quickly. My dad still likes to stay involved, of course, and I try to keep him in the loop. Still, I try not to trouble him with things too much."

"Things not going well?"

"Sales have been a little slow..."

"Slow? From what I could tell, you have some remarkable pieces. You have a good eye. Didn't you say earlier you sold a piece that brought in a pretty good price?"

"The antique fair draws a large crowd. We always do well selling to tourists as well as more prestigious collectors, looking for a rare and well-crafted piece. And during the week we make a good profit on smaller items, like lamps and smaller decorative pieces, but recently I've noticed a downward trend. With more Italian women working and changing tastes, no one wants to dust or polish antiques anymore. Plus, people are more minimalist now: a simple table, clean lines, and a single vase, that's how people decorate."

"I see your point."

"And a few weeks ago," he added, "we had a break-in. I got to work one morning to find the front window shattered and a couple of pieces stolen from the display. Of course, when my father found out, it upset him greatly."

"A break-in? Really?"

"Fortunately, the intruders didn't get away with much, and there wasn't that much damage, aside from replacing the window. But the real headache was filling out all the paperwork and talking with the police."

Seeing her growing concern, Luca quickly added, *"Non importa.* It was an isolated event. Arezzo is really a safe place. Owning a shop like ours, it comes with the territory. After the incident, I realized I needed to upgrade our security. So, in the end, some good came out of it."

"I can tell you love what you do," said Nora. "The family business is in good hands."

Leaning in, Luca said, "I studied business and marketing development in Rome, but what I really enjoy is scouting the area and finding unusual things in out-of-the-way places. In fact, I've just acquired a new lot of..."

When a shadow fell over the table, he came to a stop. In unison, they looked up to see a dark figure standing a few steps away, silhouetted by the setting sun. By the way he bent over his cane, breathing heavily, it seemed the man was tired from walking up the steep hill.

Taking a step closer, Nora could better see his weathered face and noticed that on his lapel he wore a pin with the colors red and yellow from another *contrada*. She looked back at Luca curiously, waiting for a cue. But, instead of greeting the man pleasantly, as she had seen him do earlier with others, he only toyed with his drink, and he impassively regarded the older man. To her, it seemed he was steeling himself for what the man would do or say next.

After a moment, when the silence became too awkward, he finally made introductions. "*Scusami,* Leonora, this is Ruggero Falconi."

Politely, Nora reached out to shake the old man's. He accepted the gesture but continued to stare at Luca. As he withdrew his hand, he said, "Signora, you should pick your friends wisely. You wouldn't want to get mixed up with bad company. One never knows these days who they can trust."

Confused by the man's comment, Nora caught Luca's eye, silently asking for an explanation. Showing no emotion, he shook his head slightly and murmured in English, "He's a little old and a bit touched and takes the neighborhood rivalries very seriously. Just ignore him."

Glancing back at the man's lapel pin, Nora suddenly realized, because of the opposing team colors he wore, perhaps he was joking. Confirming her suspicions, Luca said, "Leonora, as you can see by the yellow and crimson colors Signor Falconi wears, he is from Porta del Foro."

Nora acknowledged the man politely. "*Signore,* will you be at the joust tomorrow? I am new to town and am looking forward to..."

"Of course, *Signora,*" he said in a gruff voice. "Haven't missed a tournament in twenty years."

Turning his attention back to Luca, he regarded him silently again. But, instead of speaking of the next days' joust, as Nora expected him to do, he abruptly changed topics. "Tell me, *figlio mio*. How's business these days?"

Luca studied him intently. "You of all people should know the answer to that. I was just telling Leonora about the break-in we had last week..."

"Yes, I heard about it. Nasty business that," he said. "You know, Luca, you should take better care of your things—when you are careless they just seem to slip through your fingers."

How odd, Nora thought. The comment sounded vaguely familiar. Hadn't Marco intimated to Luca practically the same thing?

"Don't worry," Luca said evenly. "We cleaned up the mess, filed the insurance reports—the shop is running better than ever..."

"That blasted shop! Always focused on business. If only you had cared as much about Carlotta..."

Nora, who had been nervously playing with her napkin, listening to their strange conversation, glanced up quickly. Carlotta? She waited for Luca to respond, but instead of answering he shook his head tiredly at the old man's words.

After a moment, Signor Falconi, growing tired of the oblique game they were playing, stamped his cane on the ground and let out a frustrated sigh. Stiffly, he took a step back, and without another word continued climbing the hill, stopping every so often to catch his breath. As she watched him go, Nora wondered where he might be going—perhaps to evening mass in San Donato?

Pushing her empty glass away, she regarded Luca thoughtfully. Finally, she asked, "What was all that about? Who is Carlotta? Marco mentioned her this morning too. He told me she was a friend of yours?"

Luca looked at her for a long moment before responding. "That's right. We were friends with her."

"What is the connection with Signor...?"

"Carlotta was the old man's granddaughter."

Knocking back the last of his drink, without looking at her directly, he added, "Carlotta was also my wife."

Chapter 13

Legends

*W*ithout further comment, dismissing the entire strange incident entirely, Luca raised his hand and motioned to the waiter to bring the *conto*. Glancing at Nora, he said, "Come on, it's time to go. Let's get out of here. There will be more going on in the Porta Santa Spirito neighborhood by now and Claudio will be starting the music soon."

Flipping open his wallet, he paid the bill, despite Nora's protests. "My treat, I've got this. Next time, *tocca a te*. It will be on you. Are you hungry? They will already have the fires heated up for grilling the *bistecca*."

"Of course," she said pleasantly, following his lead, pretending she hadn't witnessed the encounter with Signor Falconi only moments before. Instead, she focused her attention on the celebratory dinner they were headed to in the piazza in Luca's neighborhood.

"I've worked up my appetite climbing up and down Arezzo's hill today."

Despite what she said, what was actually eating her was her curiosity about the woman named Carlotta, who had turned out to not be just a childhood friend, but also Luca's wife. That was quite a dramatic bombshell. Marco hadn't told her *that* this morning.

Unable to curtain her questions any longer, she casually asked, "So, Carlotta was your wife... and you were all friends? Marco started to tell me about her this morning. I'm so sorry for your loss. How long were you two...?"

Luca turned slowly toward her, and the expression on his face stopped her in her tracks. "*Lascia stare*, let it be. Look. It's all in the past. That's all you really need to know."

Nora closed her mouth and felt the heat rising on her cheeks. She sensed the tension vibrating within him. It was apparent Signor Falconi had triggered something unpleasant, and her innocent question had only aggravated him more.

"I'm sorry... I didn't mean..." she stuttered like an idiot.

Luca didn't say anything more. He only nodded, acknowledging then quickly dismissing her words of apology. Then, with a small gesture, he indicated the street and suggested they continue their descent down the hill.

Nora marveled at his mood change. To be fair, just as with Marco earlier that morning, it wasn't her place to go probing into their private lives. By their reactions, it was obvious the two men were still troubled by the death of a girl they had known well in their youth. And in Luca's case—the woman he had married.

Knowing she had blundered, to return to an even keel Nora cast about for a safer topic. Remembering their earlier conversation, before they had been interrupted, she asked, "Tell me more about the antique shipment you are expecting."

"I've been talking too much. I should be asking you about your work," he said."

She smiled at his evasive technique to put her on the spot.

"Well... as Juliette has probably told you already, I'm working on a short film about Isabella de' Medici. She was the daughter of Cosimo, you know the duke who built the fortress on top of Arezzo's hill you were talking about earlier. Have you heard about her?"

"Just a little. Mostly, I've heard the stories about Isabella's ghost. Everyone around here knows the urban legend."

"The lady has developed quite a reputation," agreed Nora. "Apparently, she shows up from time to time when least expected."

"From what I gather, though, it happens mostly to people who have had too much to drink."

"That's right, they call her *La Dama Bianca*," Nora said. "I was kind of hoping to meet her the other day."

When he gave her a questioning look, she added, with a small laugh, "Oh, not that I was drunk or anything. This was strictly a professional encounter I was hoping to have with her. After I arrived in Rome, before coming here, I went directly to Cerreto Guidi to start filming."

"So, Isabella didn't show up for her interview?" Luca said.

Seeing the spark of amusement return to his eye, Nora added, "I didn't encounter her in the villa and was a bit disappointed. But, later, I had the strangest dream."

She looked at him and shrugged. "Chalk it up to jet lag or the dinner I had in Vinci. Have you ever been there? I'm hoping to return with Juliette in a few weeks."

"As a matter of fact, the shipment of antiques I was starting to tell you about comes from a fifteenth-century home near there. The house and land are up for sale. There was an auction and I bought up some really nice pieces as well as a few paintings. I also picked up some sight-unseen lots, which potentially could be quite lucrative."

"Sounds promising," Nora said as she walked beside him.

"I'm taking a bit of a gamble, but I think it will prove interesting in the end."

"Do you know anything more about Isabella? I mean, besides the ghost stories? They just don't do her justice. She was a woman ahead of her time."

"Not much. Only what I learned from Carlotta. She was fascinated by Isabella's ghost, and when she was a kid she was always inventing horror stories..."

Nora waited for him to elaborate, but once again he fell into silence. As they passed by the church of San Francesco, she remembered Marco telling her about the frescos Luca's bisnonno Bernardo had rescued. Seeing it as a means of animating their conversation again, she quickly said, "Marco told me some things about your grandfather. How, during the war, he had a hand in protecting the paintings inside that church."

Eyeing the façade of the building, Luca said, "During the German occupation, the soldiers used it as a barracks. They were very disrespectful and destroyed much of the interior. But Bernardo—my great grandfather—took protective measures. Together with my grandfather

Federico, they secured the frescos painted by Piero della Francesca with sandbags to keep them from falling off the wall during the bombing raids. They managed to hide many other important paintings and pieces of art from the Nazis as well."

"Marco mentioned that too. I think it's awe-inspiring your family had a hand in that," said Nora.

"They were quite extraordinary, legends in their own time," said Luca with certain pride.

As they passed by an *osteria*, momentarily distracted by the pungent perfume of freshly cut pecorino cheese and the tangy scent of boar sausage, Nora's steps faltered. When she turned her attention back to Luca, she saw his teasing look had returned.

"*Beccata!*" he said. "Caught you. Don't worry. There will be lots to eat in just a bit."

"If the dinner is anything like the last time I was here, I'm going to have to climb this hill a couple more times tomorrow to work it all off."

He glanced sideways at her appreciatively and commented, "I don't think you have anything to worry about."

"Well, thanks," said Nora, feeling flattered.

"Besides, tonight we are celebrating. *Lasci andare un po'.* It's time to let go and celebrate with the neighborhood fans of Santo Spirito."

"I couldn't agree with you more. It's been too long since I was so carefree."

Italy will be good for you then," he said. "Everyone needs a chance to start over. Juliette told me a little bit about your past."

Nora was quiet a moment. Now it was her turn to become reticent. Like him, she realized, she didn't want to ruin the night by sharing all the intimate details of her life up to that point. Finally, she just said, "Let's just say I'm right where I need to be. It's taken me far too long to return."

"I guess we have the Medici Princess to thank for your return," said Luca with a grin.

"As funny as that sounds, it's actually true. I'm happy to repay her by telling her story, making my documentary. Wouldn't it be something too if I could find out something more about her missing painting."

"You mean the missing Bronzino?" asked Luca.

"You know the painting?"

"Of course. It is a very famous one."

"It disappeared from the Louvre during the war. Maybe the French partisans hid it somewhere in Paris and it's still there in some forgotten attic."

"Perhaps," he said a bit evasively. Something in his tone made Nora look over at him curiously. "I'd love to hear more about the work your grandparents did," she added. "It would make a wonderful foundation for my next documentary."

"Sure," said Luca. "I've got many stories. I grew up hearing them from my grandmother Margherita. She used to tell me how important it was to keep their memories alive and continue passing down their stories. I think she'd like the idea of you recording them for future generations."

"Were they always from Arezzo?"

"My grandmother was, but Federico, her husband, was from Lazio. He was an artist who studied at the Accademia in Rome, but in his youth—sometime in the mid-to-late thirties—he moved to Paris, and it was there he experimented with modern painting styles—Expressionism, Fauvism..."

"Really?" said Nora. "He lived in Paris—what part of town?"

"In the poorer part, where most of the painters and poets lived. He was just one of many starving artists. According to *nonna*, he had a place in La Ruche."

"I've been to Paris once—I spent winter break there with Juliette's family when we were roommates. It's a beautiful city, and she and I wandered around and even visited that neighborhood as well as the Montparnasse. Did you know it's still an artist's colony? These days, it is considered rather high end, but back then it was a bit of a dump."

"Rent was cheap, it didn't have heat..."

"*And* was probably infested with rats and fleas," said Nora.

"Yes, but it was the only thing he could afford," said Luca. "He didn't have a lot of money. Like all the other struggling artists he sold his work for hardly anything—perhaps a few francs—just enough to keep a leaky roof over his head and buy some bread."

"I'm sure for him it was worth the trade-off," said Nora. "Where else but in Paris could you rub shoulders with or hope to catch a glimpse of fascinating intellectuals like Picasso, simply by having a glass of wine in little cafes like Le Dôme and La Ronde?"

"*Sì.* My grandmother said they were great friends."

Nora stopped in her tracks. "Your grandfather *knew* Picasso and was friends with him?"

Luca turned around, and seeing the dumbfounded expression on her face, he laughed. "That's right."

As a drumbeat struck up in the distance, Luca paused to listen. "Hear that? The *sbandieratori*—the flag throwers will be passing by here shortly. If we hurry, we can see them practicing."

Picking up her pace, Nora said, "You know, I would give anything to go back in time to one of those bars and meet the people in them. Imagine having a conversation with Picasso or Man Ray, Dalì, even Severini."

"Margherita told me once, that when Federico couldn't pay his bills, he left one of his drawings on the table as collateral. I guess it was a common practice—lots of artists did that."

"Can you imagine walking into one of those places and seeing the work of the work of Georges Braque, Raoul Dufy, and Jaun Gris all together hanging on the wall of a bar?"

"It would make any curator drool with envy—including me."

At the bottom of the hill, at the corner of Via Roma where the pedestrian part of the city ended, and traffic began, they stopped at the traffic light. On the opposite side of the street, blue and yellow banners fluttered from the buildings and Nora could see they were about to enter the Santo Spirito quarter. In the distance, she could hear music and the drumbeats of the roving musicians growing louder. In response, her own heart began to hammer in time to the thundering roar, filling her with an inexplicable sensation of anticipation.

Waiting to cross the street, impatient see them, Nora glanced up at

Luca and asked, "When did you grandfather return to Italy from France?"

"A year after the Germans took over Paris. About that time things got pretty dangerous for the *avant garde* artists who lived there."

So absorbed by his story and the drumbeats that called out to her, when the light turned green, Nora stepped absently off the curb into the path of an errant Vespa rider. Gunning his engine, he zoomed toward her, but before they collided, Luca reached out an arm and hauled her back, hugging her tightly to his side. To the man on the motorbike, he angrily yelled, *"Stronzo! Fai attenzione!"*

Looking back at her, he asked, *"Tutto bene?* Are you okay?"

Nora's heart, hammering in her chest, quickly replied, "Yes, of course. Sorry, I should have been watching where I was going."

For the second time in two days, she felt like an idiot and could only imagine the impression she was making on the man. First, she had fallen out of the stands in the piazza, and now she had nearly gotten herself run down in the street.

Recovering her wits, Nora said, "I was testing your reflexes. You just passed—again."

She looked up at him and met his eyes, and once again her heart began to pound. Lost in his gaze, she forgot what they had been talking about. As the crowd ebbed and flowed around them, they were oblivious to their surroundings.

Then looking over at the light, before it could change again, Luca took her elbow and guided her across the street.

"You were saying..." Nora said, slowly recovering her senses.

"Ah..." it seemed to her Luca, was also having difficulty picking up the strand of their previous conversation. "Where was I...?"

"I believe... ah... you were telling me about why your grandfather left Paris," she said distractedly.

"Right," he said. "Well... um let's see... Federico left Paris in '41 and arrived here in Arezzo later that summer. Lucky for me, too. Shortly after he got here, he met my grandmother. They fell in love and married, and nine months after that, my dad, Edoardo was born."

"They didn't lose any time," Nora teased regaining her sense of humor. "But why did Federico stop off here in Arezzo? Don't get me wrong. I love it here. It's just, well… It isn't exactly Paris or Florence. Why didn't he go back to Rome to his family?"

"Federico was on a special mission. He was entrusted with the task of smuggling three masterpieces out of Paris."

"Are you kidding me?" Nora exclaimed. He was a smuggler—an art thief—*and* knew Picasso?"

"According to my grandmother, he slipped them through border control right under the noses of the Gestapo."

"And how did he manage that?"

"By hiding them between two mattresses in a Red Cross lorry."

"Very ingenious but very dangerous," said Nora. As she continued to listen, the scene materialized in her mind.

In the dead of night, she clearly saw a van sat idling in front of a closed toll gate as German border patrol soldiers interrogated the artist. Tapping his hands on the steering wheel, waiting for the guards to check his documents, Luca's grandfather must have been as stern and impassive as Luca had been just a few moments before during his run-in with Signor Falconi. Despite his calm exterior, however, Federico's pulse must have quickened when the guards yanked open the back doors of the lorry and flashed their torches inside the rear compartment that held medical supplies.

Seeing only blankets, bandages, and mattresses, she imagined his relief, when the German guards motioned for the gates to be opened, to let him pass. Dismissed and told to drive on through, she believed Federico had politely tilted his hat and continued slowly across the border. But once his tires had rolled onto Italian soil, and he was free and clear, how he must have yelled out in triumph to have outsmarted the Germans and be back home again with his precious cargo still in tow.

When Luca ended his story, Nora blinked a few times when they came to Piazza San Jacopo, noticing the crowd of people milling about and the elegant displays in the shop windows. "I have to say, hiding the paintings in a medical van was very creative. Your grandfather was indeed a clever spy! But he couldn't have been working alone. Where did he get the paintings in the first place?"

"They were given to him by Paul Rosenberg."

"The French art collector who represented Pablo Picasso?"

"Yes, it was Picasso who introduced Federico to him. Rosenberg bought a couple of my grandfather's paintings. From what I understand, they still hang in his New York gallery."

"Rosenberg had a keen eye for modern art and was always making new discoveries."

"It's true he was one of the most influential men at the time—he was also very astute. Being Jewish, he saw the signs and red flags and had an idea what was coming. Even back in the early thirties, when Hitler first rose to power, he quietly moved his collection out of Paris to his London and New York galleries. And, when Paris fell, he helped hide the paintings in the Louvre to keep them out of the dictator's hands."

"I do recall reading about the effort on the part of Jacques Jaujard, the director of the museum," said Nora. "The one who organized a massive operation to move paintings out of Paris and into the countryside."

"That's right. They hid paintings in the most unusual places. Some even in Rosenberg's wine cellar. But when he was finally forced to flee to New York, he gave the remaining paintings to Federico to smuggle across the border into Italy."

"And his destination was Arezzo?"

"Right. Rosenberg was acquainted with Bernardo, and the work he was doing for the resistance. With his connections, he knew Bernardo could smuggle the paintings out of the country through the port of Livorno with his antique deliveries and get them to London."

As they reached the Santo Spirito gate, where long tables had been set up in the street, as the crowds brushed into her, Nora pressed closer to Luca's side so he could hear her better. "And was he successful?"

"For the most part. Federico arrived here with several famous paintings—a Picasso, a Matisse and one by a sixteenth-century Italian painter. He handed the Picasso and the Matisse, over to Bernardo..."

"And the third? What happened to it?" Nora asked then looked at him, suddenly suspicious. "It was by an Italian painter, you said..."

"*That* painting he hid once he got here."

"Why? Wait a minute... A famous sixteenth-century Italian painting? Which one was it exactly?"

Luca hesitated, "According to my grandmother, it was the portrait of Eleonora de' Toledo, the Medici Duchess, and Isabella painted by Bronzino."

"What?" she exclaimed incredulously.

"Yes, it's true. Rosenberg sided with the Italians and thought that Bronzino's painting of the Medici women should rightfully be kept in the Uffizi Galleries. He wanted it returned to the Italian people."

Nora stared at him in confusion. "*Your* grandfather had a hand in the disappearance of the Bronzino painting? Is it in your family's possession now?"

"Don't be silly. Of course not. If I knew where it was today, it would be hanging in the National Gallery in Florence."

"But..."

"I know. The painting is still missing," said Luca.

"What did Federico do with it and where is it now?"

"That, Leonora, is a mystery. As I said, it was hidden somewhere here in Arezzo. Most likely it hasn't turned up because it was destroyed in one of the bombing raids. Much of the city and surrounding countryside was razed. Look around you. Can't you tell this area appears newer than other parts of town? It is not like the older area where my shop is located near the Piazza Grande."

Nora focused more closely on the Santo Spirito neighborhood, noticing that the architecture was indeed more contemporary. The only reminder that once this area had also featured crenelated buildings and narrow medieval towers like in the upper part of town was the lone medieval gate.

"To think your grandfather—Federico Donati—had something to do with escorting Isabella and her mother back home. It just boggles my mind. It really is the stuff legends are made of. And after Federico arrived here, did he tell Bernardo about the Bronzino painting?"

"No. He never did."

"But why?"

"He knew he had to sit out the war, keeping the whereabouts of the painting secret. At that time, if he went straight to the Italian authorities and gave them the Bronzino painting, it would have been as if he were delivering the picture back into Hitler's hands."

Nora nodded, seeing his point.

"So, instead, to keep his loved ones safe, Federico kept the painting a secret from everyone. If anyone found out and told the Gestapo, it would be he alone who would take the full blame and punishment."

"Obviously, later he must have told your grandmother."

"He told her in private, but even with her, he never divulged the painting's whereabouts."

Nora was quiet as she pondered this new information. Finally, she said, "It is very romantic and kind of poetic, don't you think?"

"How so?"

"The French art dealer gives the lost Bronzino to your grandfather— an artist—to bring Isabella home to Italy to right an old wrong."

They looked at one another and smiled. Lost in the moment, they studied one another, once more losing track of time. It seemed the Medici Princess and her whimsical machinations was working to bring them a little closer. Nora's unspoken thoughts, however, were abruptly interrupted when a loudspeaker, set up a short distance away, gave off a piercing screech, making her cover her ears.

From across the *piazza* she could hear Claudio the deejay's voice blaring through a microphone, but he was quickly drowned out by a group of men who broke into a spontaneous chant. Soon, they were joined by the rest of the frenzied *blu* and *giallo* fans who burst into song, to encourage and cheer their team on to victory.

Overhead, more blue and gold flags waved in the evening breeze, and in the middle of the commotion, the jousters held court on a central dais. For tonight, their costumes had been replaced by crisp button-down shirts paired with jackets and blue jeans. This evening they were modern men, dressed like anyone else, but this time tomorrow, they would don medieval doublets and transport the city back in time.

Luca placed a hand on her back and guided her into the crowd. "Come on. I want to introduce you to some friends."

As they took their seats at one of the long tables, struck by a new thought, Nora said, *"Aspetta!* Something doesn't quite add up. If your grandfather was the only one who knew where the painting was hidden after the war ended, why didn't he come forward and tell anyone? At least you'd know for sure it had been destroyed by the bombs."

"I really wish he could have," he said. *"È stata una vera tragedia.* Federico was arrested and held by the Germans just weeks before the allies rolled in and liberated Arezzo. The Gestapo got a tip from an unknown source that he was working with partisan forces. The Nazis killed him in his jail cell. He took the secret of the painting with him to his grave."

Incredible, Nora thought. In the span of ten minutes, the mystery of Isabella's painting had been solved. But, like Isabella's ghost after making an appearance, it had quickly disappeared, only to be lost all over again.

Luca's words had painted a vivid picture, and here in the middle of the Santo Spirito crowd, amidst the noise and confusion, Nora's senses were heightened. She could feel once again voices from the past calling out to her, mingled with those of the present.

When the music started up, and the drum core struck up again their heart-palpitating medieval beat, she heard instead, the roar of fighter planes and the sound of bombs exploding over her head.

Nora closed her eyes and relived the legend.

Margherita

Chapter 14

The Shop around the Corner

October 26, 1941

*T*he door banged open, and the little shop bell jangled, causing Margherita to start. She glanced up from the cash register but smiled when she saw a familiar face looking at her apologetically.

"*Mi dispiace! Faccio troppo rumore.* Sorry to make such a ruckus," said Corrado. "It is windy out tonight, and the door got away from me. How are you, *mia cara*? Is your father somewhere about? We are planning on finishing your hope chest tonight." Smiling at her, he added, "He's probably in the backroom—am I right?"

Lowering the volume of the radio, she tilted her head backward. "*Sì,* he's just starting to unpack some crates that just arrived."

"As I thought, puttering around, stirring up some kind of trouble, no doubt." Taking off his coat and hat, he approached the counter. "You are looking especially lovely this evening, Nita" he said. "I came a few moments early because I need your advice. It's Signora Michelozzi's birthday tomorrow, and I want to pick up a small gift. I thought perhaps you could help me select a special little bauble from this treasure trove of yours."

"*Certo,* Signor Michelozzi," said Margherita. With a wave of her hand, she indicated a nearby table. "We have a lovely collection of Limoges teacups that I've just put out on display. Perhaps the matching teapot might please her, too."

Before he could focus his attention on the delicate china invitingly showcased on a silver tray, the sight of her hand caught Corrado's attention. Narrowing his eyes, he said, "You aren't wearing your engagement ring tonight, *la mia piccina*. I thought you liked the design I created for you.

Your fiancé spared no expense when he ordered it."

Margherita self-consciously wiggled her fingers. "*Sì, sì, sì. Mi piace molto,* Signor Michelozzi. It is a lovely gold band." She hesitated, then added, "It's grown a bit loose, and I took it off for safekeeping. I've been doing chores and didn't want it to slip off and lose it."

Signor Michelozzi nodded and patted the back of her hand affectionately. "I see. Take care of that ring, my dear, gold is in high demand these days. I'm certainly keeping mine under lock and key."

He gave her a wink, and he said, "I've come to see your father and have a drink, maybe two. *Oh mio Dio,* given today's news, maybe we will drink up an entire bottle!"

"Well then," said Margherita, "I won't wait up for him tonight. Maybe *I'll* even have a drink."

Michelozzi chuckled and turned to inspect the delicate pieces of china. Humming softly under his breath, he tested the weight of a teacup in his hand. Both his studio and the antique store were located on the same street, just around the corner from the Piazza Grande. When he needed a break or a bit of inspiration, he enjoyed stopping by unannounced to take a look around his friend's shop.

Since the age of the Etruscans, Arezzo had been renowned as a center for goldsmithing, as its hills were filled with precious ore. The city's reputation had continued to flourish, and more recently it had received even more praise and acclaim due to the lovely pieces that designers like Signor Michelozzi and his son Egidio produced.

But these days, due to the fighting abroad and the Germans who had taken up residence in their sleepy little town, the jewelers in Arezzo were lucky to remain in business. Most of the silver and platinum supplies were being confiscated by the fascist government, who said it was needed to fund the war. Many contended, among them Bernardo, that the money from the appropriated metals was used for other purposes—such as lining the pockets of corrupt government officials.

Despite the shortages, several businesses had managed to keep their doors open, and Michelozzi's atelier was one of them. His elegant pieces were especially popular amongst the local Italian bureaucrats as well as the Nazi officials, and he was kept busy producing small gifts and trinkets for their wives.

Peering beyond the jumbled assortment of lamps and tables, Corrado could see the light spilling from the open door in the rear. They both listened a moment, and Margherita could hear her father humming the tune of *"Ciao bella! Ciao!"* When he reached the refrain, he sang out softly but with conviction, *"One morning I woke up, O bella, ciao! Bella, ciao! Bella, ciao, ciao, ciao. One morning I woke up and found the invader. And if I die as a partisan, you must bury me on the mountain, under the shadow of a beautiful flower. And all who pass will say, 'What a beautiful flower' Questo è il fiore del partigiano! Ciao, bella!'"*

The two exchanged a knowing look. "Bernardo sounds quite pleased with himself. So the new shipment of paintings has finally arrived, ehi? I know he's been waiting weeks for it. With Melchiori in charge of customs these days, tying everything up in knots and red tape, it seems there are always delays. The man is a fool, that's for sure, and the Germans have him under their thumbs."

Letting his gaze drift around the shop, Corrado added, "But this place. Oh, my goodness. *É fantastico!* Such an inspiration. Every time I cross the threshold, I feel as if there is always something new to see."

Picking up a translucent Chinese vase, he held it to the light, admiring the milky hues, and said, "I think if I tried hard enough, somewhere in all this lovely confusion, I might just find a Fabergé egg or, at the very least, Napoleon Bonaparte's hat—perhaps even the little general himself."

Margherita was pleased by his comments. She, too, loved the family antique business, having grown up among the Queen Anne tables and Savonarola chairs her father acquired for their clients. Even at a very early age, she could rattle off facts about Pietra Dura Marble tables and successfully date the Capodimonte porcelain figurines on display. She surveyed the shop, trying to see it all through Michelozzi's eyes.

"Oh, it may seem like a jumbled mess to you, Signor Michelozzi, but believe me, my father knows where every piece is. He has many treasures here. It would only take him a moment to locate any item you might desire, and if it isn't here, he knows exactly where to go to find it."

"*Ah, sì.* I can see the apple doesn't fall far from the tree. You take excellent care of this place, just like you fuss over that old fossil of a father of yours."

Walking to a glass case, he pulled out a medieval Book of Hours. Without looking up, he said, "It's rather late—I'm surprised to see you are still open for business. Egidio is just locking up our place and should be coming along any minute now. I told him to meet me here."

"I had some things to finish up so I thought I'd stay open just a little longer." Just then, Margherita heard a rap on the front window and saw Egidio waving at her through the glass. Calling her by her nickname, he said, *"Ciao, Nita!* Is my dad in there?"

Margherita tilted her head in the direction of Signor Michelozzi, who was still admiring the illustrations. "Yes, of course, come in."

Crossing the shop, Egidio gave her a bright smile and kissed both of her cheeks. Taking off his coat, he neatly draped it over his arm and said, "How's it going?"

"Bene! Tuo babbo is over there trying to decide what to give to your mother. Maybe you should pick out a birthday gift for her." Stepping lightly in time to the swing music playing on the radio, she moved behind the cash register. He followed her and began snapping his fingers.

"What are you listening to?"

Turning up the volume, she said, "At this hour, sometimes I can pick up an English radio station." Swinging her hips to the beat, she sang, *"He was a famous trumpet man from out Chicago way; he had a boogie style that no one else could play. He's in the army now; he's blowin' reveille, he's the boogie woogie bugle boy of Company B."*

Egidio watched her dance, nodding his head in time to the beat. Reaching for her hand, he twirled her into his arms, and they continued dipping and swaying in time to the music. "I like it," he said. "I miss hearing decent music on the radio these days."

"Uffa!" Margherita exclaimed. "Tell me about it. It's horrible the

drivel they play on the Italian stations, only stuffy songs and stupid marches. You know what I miss the most?"

"No, Margherita, what do you miss the most?" Egidio asked as he twirled her around again.

"I miss hearing Nilla Pizzi and Pippo and all those fun jazz groups. I liked the songs they played, always upbeat and lighthearted. They made you feel good, you know, like this one, not like the songs Mussolini and the brownshirts want everyone to hear."

"I love Nilla's songs. It's such a shame she was taken off the radio."

"*È vero,*" agreed Margherita. "Things are out of control these days. Can you believe they think she is too modern and—"

Egidio cut her off. "She was banned because Mussolini thinks her voice is too exotic and sensual."

Stepping out of his arms, Nita returned to her ledger and, pulling a pen from behind her left ear, she began re-tabulating figures. *"Oh, mio Dio,* what is this world coming to if an innocent girl can't sing a song on the radio?"

Watching her, Egidio lightly beat his hands on the counter top as if it were a bongo. Resting her chin on her hands, she said, "Oh, Egidio, wouldn't it be grand to visit America? I want to go to California someday. *Che sogno!* I want to visit Hollywood where they make all the films. Do you know there is also a city called San Francisco, just like the *basilica* here in Arezzo? They have a Golden Gate Bridge that spans a bay, and the city is built on a hill. But it is so big, nothing like our hill here in Arezzo—someday I'm going to travel the world. *Ti giuro, lo farò.*"

Leaning over, Egidio whispered, "It's always great to have a dream, Nita. Me, I'm going to be stuck here for the rest of my life, hammering out gold for my father. Hey, have you seen the new film at the cinema, the new detective thriller?"

Glancing toward the back where she could see her father moving about, Margherita whispered, "Yes, I snuck out last night and took in the late show. But don't tell *papà...*"

"Don't tell *papà* what?" asked Corrado, walking toward the two.

"What secrets might you possibly be keeping from your old dad, Nita?"

Margherita put her hands on her hips and said, "That's a good question, Signor Michelozzi. I might ask the same of you."

Slyly, she asked, "Have you *really* come to help my father finish that chest of drawers the two of you are building in the attic? Recently, the two of you have been spending a lot of time together. It seems to me you might be doing something more than just sanding wood."

Corrado, the picture of innocence, said, "Don't worry about us, my dear, nothing cloak and dagger going on in the workroom upstairs. It is just a bunch of harmless old men tinkering about, not anything that would interest you in the least."

Hearing the voice of his friend, Bernardo Lancini called from the back, "Corrado, you old dog, it's about time you showed up. Come back here. I want to show you something."

"*Arrivo, amico mio.*" Turning to his son, he said, "Egidio, go on up. We will join you in a minute."

Egidio obediently saluted his father, and as he turned to climb the stairs to the rooms above the antique shop, the radio transmission faded and the American swing was replaced by crackly static. Margherita attempted to dial in the station again, but instead of lively music, the air was filled with the blare of military horns, and a radio announcer reminded everyone they were listening to the EIAR, the voice of Italian radio.

After another fanfare of music, the strains of *"Giovinezza"*, one of the fascists' anthems, started to play, and a voice thundered out, "I believe in God, Lord of Heaven and earth. I believe in justice and truth. I believe in a pure Italy. I believe in Mussolini and an Italian victory."

Next came the crackly sounds of the dictator himself: "Citizens of Italy, I come to you tonight..."

Corrado reached over and switched off the radio. "Time to turn that swill off," he said. Giving her a pat on the hand, he went to join his friend in the back room.

Alone again, Nita entered a few more numbers in her ledger and then stashed it away. In the quiet, she could hear Egidio walking about over her head and something heavy being shoved across the floor. Nita wasn't sure what they were up to, and perhaps it was wise she didn't pry into their affairs.

There were reasons her father kept secrets from her. He didn't subscribe to the fascist politics of il Duce's current government, and when he read the papers, he grumbled and sometimes became so enraged he slammed his fist upon the table. It was a travesty what was happening all around them; people were disappearing, and every day ridiculous rules were placed upon them.

And now books and even paintings were being confiscated, and if they didn't comply with the current regime's tastes, they were destroyed and burned. It was degrading to be subjected to such tyranny and live each day in fear.

But what infuriated her father most was the brainwashing and false news—propaganda—that was printed in the papers, and that spewed from the radio. If you believed the government's words, this was all done for a greater good and the triumph of the Italian people. It was unconscionable. Who gave such a small group of people so much power over a large population of souls, dictating what they could and could not like, or what they should believe?

When Paris fell, Bernardo had been horrified when he learned of the Nazi plundering. The arrogance and cruelty of a foreign nation raping another and then stealing its art was simply intolerable, and he feared greatly for Italy's national treasures.

Putting down his paper, he would say to his daughter, "Margherita, it is a dangerous world we are living in. If we are to survive, we must be cautious. But I will not sit idly by and bow my head and let things that I know are wrong happen in my own town—in my own country. I will choose to walk tall and, if need be, stand up to the forces that be."

She was proud of her father, but still, she was concerned. Her mother had passed away years before when she was just a girl, and with the start of the war and the escalating tensions, he was declining. The fight to survive was turning him into an old man before her very eyes. That was why she had decided to marry. Her father needed a business partner, and she hoped that together she and her husband could ease his burdens. But at the end of long days like these, Margherita wondered if she had made the best decision.

As she was tidying up the counter, she saw a murky shadow passing by the window. The American tune she had been humming died on her lips and her heart beat faster. With dismay, she remembered she hadn't yet locked the door.

When she saw the face of the man peering through the dark window, she exclaimed in relief, "*Oh Santo Cielo, sei tu.* Ruggero, you gave me such a fright!"

"*Ciao amore,* I've missed you." Grabbing his fiancé around her waist, the man twirled her about in a circle, just as Egidio had done, but this time, she quickly disengaged herself.

"Stop, you are making me dizzy! I didn't expect you back tonight."

"I just got off the train from Rome and couldn't wait to see you again." Kissing her on the mouth, he said, "Did you miss me?"

Margherita stepped back, smoothed her hair, and ran her fingers unconsciously over her lips. "*Sì, sì.* I missed you." Moving back to the cash register, she pulled out her engagement ring and slipped it on her finger. "I thought you'd be gone until the day after tomorrow."

"I know, but I couldn't wait to get back to your side. *Aspetta!* Hold on. I've brought you a present."

She observed the slim dark-haired man before her, dressed in an expensive overcoat. In his hands he held a large box with an elaborately tied ribbon. Extending it to her, he excitedly urged, "Go on, open it!"

Taking it from his outstretched hands, Margherita set the box on the counter, undid the ribbon, and lifted the lid. Inside was a green felt hat. It was an elaborate affair, decked out with netting and an enormous purple feather. Seeing his delighted expression, she knew the hat hadn't come cheap, and although it was not quite to her taste, not wanting to hurt his feelings, she gave him a brief kiss on his cheek.

"It's the latest rage in Rome, you know. Only the best for my Nita." Pushing the hat box aide, he said, "So tell me, how is my beautiful girl?"

Margherita felt a small pang of remorse. He was always buying her presents, and she never knew what he'd show up with next. Last week it had been a necklace, and the week before that a pair of kid gloves, and now, this ridiculous hat. He tried so hard, but it worried her where he came by the money to shower her with all these things. He certainly couldn't afford them on the wages her father paid him each week.

Like Egidio, she had known Ruggero forever. Although she lived in Santo Spirito and he lived on the opposite side of town in the neighborhood of Porta del Foro, they had been schoolmates and had later attended *liceo* together. When he was a young boy of twelve, he had brought her small bouquets of daisies or sometimes a piece of chocolate.

As he got older and grew into a handsome man, she had been quite flattered to be courted by him and receive bigger bouquets of red roses and bottles of fancy French perfume. At first, Margherita enjoyed the gifts and being squired about town to dinner or the theater, but she couldn't entirely overlook the fact that she found his conversation a bit dull, and regarded him more as a brother. She wondered if she would ever love him the way he adored her.

But when the war started, and she saw her father declining, she had decided to accept Ruggero's proposal of marriage. The young man had been very persistent, asking her countless times and, finally, she conceded. And yet, despite being engaged a year, she still hadn't set a date.

Coming from the back of the shop with Signor Michelozzi just behind him, Bernardo said, "Ah, Ruggero, my boy, I see you've returned. How did that business with Balduccio go? Did he agree to our terms?"

Hearing the sound of her father's voice, Margherita thought, *Silly girl. Of course, given time I'll learn to love Ruggero as he loves me.*

"*Sì,* Signor Lancini. By the time I left Balduccio, he was eating out of the palm of my hand. Trust me, I know how to get a deal done."

"Well, take off your coat, *giovanotto*. It's time to roll up your sleeves and get to work. There is a new order in the back that I've started to uncrate. It will save us time in the morning."

Ruggero removed his hat and coat and tossed them haphazardly onto the back of a fragile chair. Blowing a kiss to Margherita, he walked to the end of the shop, whistling an out-of-key tune. The song sounded so familiar, and she closed her eyes, trying to recall when and where she had heard it before. As it came to her, Margherita's eyes flashed open. She had heard it earlier that morning on her way to the market to buy some bread, being whistled by a German patrolman.

Catching her father's eyes, to hide her dismay, she quickly looked back down at her ledger.

Bernardo's gaze moved from his daughter to the younger man's rumpled coat and sighed tiredly. He had observed Ruggero for years and knew him to be a smart boy, and given the right guidance, Bernardo felt he had considerable potential. Lately, though, there were other things that troubled him. Sometimes the young man could be brash and overeager, cockily pretending to be an expert on matters in which he was not.

Just the other day, Bernardo had arrived late and had found Ruggero extolling the features of a lovely ceramic vase to Signora Castellani. As he listened, however, he realized Falconi had mixed up his facts, claiming it to be an antique piece from the Ming Dynasty.

When the woman had asked him the price, he stated an outrageous figure. Hearing that, Bernardo stepped up to set things straight, letting his client know it was a considerably more modern piece dating from the Qing Dynasty. Ruggero, realizing his error, had apologized profusely.

But later, observing the young man ring up the sale, Bernardo couldn't quite shake the feeling that perhaps it hadn't been an innocent mistake but rather a cunning ploy to dupe the poor old woman. That was only one of many incidents. While the young man's affections for his daughter seemed genuine, if not excessive, the young man's moral integrity distressed him.

At this moment especially, when trusting someone meant living or dying, he wasn't sure on which side of the fence his future son-in-law stood. To him, it seemed entirely possible Ruggero might be persuaded to support any political party or jump through any hoop necessary if given a few extra *lira* for his trouble.

Hearing Ruggero whistling in the back room, Bernardo gave Corrado a questioning look.

Margherita saw the telegraphed message that passed between her father and Corrado. She knew he worried, but she had made her decision and would abide by it. Closing the cash register with a brisk click, she took a key from a hook on the wall and walked to the front door to secure it for the night. Before she could, however, the bell jingled again, and a tall stranger entered the store.

He was an older man—she guessed he was in his mid to late thirties —and was dressed in a tweed overcoat with a scarf wrapped around his neck. His tall frame overpowered the room. Carefully, he shut the door, removed his hat, and nodded briefly at her. Turning to the two men, he said, *"Salve, sono* Federico Donati. I'm here to see Bernardo Lancini. I have some business I'd like to speak with him about."

Bernardo stepped forward and shook the man's hand. *"Sì, sì* we've been expecting you, Donati. Benvenuto, welcome. Let me introduce you to Corrado Michelozzi. His son Egidio is also here and anxious to meet you."

The stranger returned the older man's greeting then looked at the young woman behind the counter. Seeing his questioning look, Bernardo quickly made introductions. "And this is my daughter Margherita. She helps me here in the shop."

Leaning in, Bernardo whispered into his daughter's ear, "Run on home now, *cara.* I will be here very late. I'll see you in the morning."

Turning to Donati, he said, *"Viene qua.* Follow me."

Allowing the two older men to lead the way, the newcomer paused briefly. With one foot on the bottom step, he turned around and made eye contact with Margherita. When Bernardo spoke again, he swiveled his head back in his direction.

"So, you are the famous Federico we've heard about? You've just arrived from Paris? Tell me, amico mio, what news have you for us?"

Chapter 15

The Artist Upstairs

*O*ver the following days, Margherita watched as the man called Federico made frequent visits to the Lancini shop. Each time he entered the store, he courteously tipped his hat and moved directly to the stairs. When he went out, he passed by her without comment. He never wasted his time in idle chit-chats, like Signor Michelozzi, or commented on radio shows as Egidio liked to do. From what she could determine, he was considerably older than she, and half the time she felt entirely invisible. Margherita wondered if he even realized she was there.

After a few days, she asked her father what type of business he and the man were involved in. Bernardo off-handedly replied, "Federico is an artist. He has just come from France, Nita. You know what it is like there these days—not the best place for a painter to be. He's a good man, and I've hired him to do a bit of restoration work, and I've given him full use of the studios to work on his paintings."

Before he turned to go, he told her, "And I told him he could live with us for a while, in the attic above the shop."

This arrangement seemed a little strange to Margherita. Her father was quite capable of making repairs and refurbishing old pieces, and he had never before invited anyone to live in the rooms in the attic. Although Signor Donati had only just arrived, it seemed he had already won the trust of her father, something Ruggero was still struggling to do.

Curious to learn more, she continued to ply her father with questions. "How long will Signor Donati be staying with us?"

"As long as it takes, I imagine."

"To do what exactly?"

"Oh, this and that. I've got a few projects I need help with."

"I see." But she didn't really. "And where is he from, and where will he go next?"

"Well, his people are from Rome, so I expect he will make it back there eventually. In the meantime, I have also agreed to provide him with a few meals. Perhaps from time to time, he will come to dinner with us, or you can bring him some soup and pieces of bread. But," he cautioned her, "don't disturb him. If he doesn't answer the door, just leave a basket outside. He will get it eventually. You know how artists are—they don't like to be interrupted when their creative ideas are flowing."

"If you ask me," she said, "this all seems a little mysterious. What could Signor Donati be doing up there behind locked doors?"

Bernardo only patted her hand and said, "*Cara figlia*, I think you have seen one too many detective movies at the cinema. Stop being so nosey. Relax, he's a painter. Painters paint!"

Margherita cocked her head to one side and waited for a better answer. Realizing he hadn't pacified her, he patted her hand lightly and said, "You take after your mother, Nita. Not only do you resemble her, but you inherited her imaginative mind. Federico is simply our house guest for a short while. Most likely he will get bored with us, and he will be gone by the end of the month."

He pulled out his pocket watch, then said matter-of-factly, "Now, it's time to get to work. Can you get me that stack of invoices? Let's see which ones we should pay today."

Margherita did what he asked regarding shop business but couldn't dismiss her thoughts about the mysterious man upstairs. At the end of the month, the man was still there and had become a familiar fixture in their lives, and it didn't seem like he was in a hurry to depart.

Over the next several weeks, he came to their home for dinner a couple of times, but for the most part, he preferred to remain in his rooms. When she climbed the stairs to deliver a bit of broth and a carafe of wine, she often stopped and placed an ear to his door. But she never heard a sound. Things remained quiet on the other side, and she wondered again what kept him so completely occupied.

Finally, she couldn't contain her curiosity any longer. The following morning, she took advantage of a moment when Ruggero and her father were out of the shop and decided to confront Donati herself. If the man was up to something suspicious, something that could endanger her father, she needed to know—at least that's what she told herself.

When the man returned from his errands late one morning, he removed his hat as always and politely acknowledged her. But this time, before he slipped past her to escape up the stairs, Margherita called out, *"Signor Donati... aspetti un momento. Ha un minuto per me?"*

The tall man turned around and looked at her questioningly. Taking a few steps in her direction, he said, *"Certo, Signorina Lancini. Che posso fare per Lei?"*

Now that he stood directly before her, Margherita was suddenly at a loss for words. The man watched her for a moment, then raised an eyebrow and asked, "Yes, was there something you wanted? Or should I go now?"

Standing a bit taller, she managed to say, *"Sì, allora...* I understand you are a painter. *Papà* says you were trained in Rome and that is where you are from."

"I studied at the *Accademia delle Belle Arti*, but that was a long time ago." He regarded her curiously. "Have you ever been to Rome?"

"Of course, I've been to Rome," she exclaimed.

"Well, that is a good thing for you, then," he said, smiling at her. "I believe anyone who appreciates art or wants to paint should start their education there. You don't even have to step foot into a museum or gallery. On every corner and in every piazza—well, there is something amazing to see. I learned a great deal at the *Academia,* but I learned more by simply wandering the streets and into churches. There you can find the finest teachers—Michelangelo, Raphael, and Bernini, just to name a few."

"You talk so passionately about art. I'd like to see some of your work," she said boldly.

"Really?" Federico asked. They studied one another for a moment, and then slowly he gestured with his hat, indicating the stairs. "Well, come on, then. Let me show you."

Margherita was taken aback. She looked at him in surprise, never dreaming he would invite her into his rooms. When she didn't move, he chuckled and said, "I thought you wanted to see my work? I promise I won't bite."

She tilted her head, assessing his motives, not entirely convinced by his last statement. Signor Donati asked again, "Well, are you interested to see the work of this poor artist or not?"

Glancing at her watch, she saw that it was almost noon. Cautiously nodding in agreement, she moved to the door and locked it. When she faced about again, she saw Signor Donati was already climbing the stairs. Following in his wake across the silent room, she felt a rush of anticipation. *Finally,* she thought, *I'll have some answers.*

When they arrived at the top of the dim landing, she watched as he unlocked the workroom. Looking back at her, he smiled before pushing the door open. Gesturing politely, he invited her to enter before him.

Margherita hesitated once more. For all her previous bravado, once again it seemed she was fearful of taking the next step. Seeing her reluctance, Federico walked into the room, then, turning around, he held out his hand to her. Cautiously, she placed her hand in his and let herself be drawn over the threshold into his studio.

The light from the large front windows was a sharp contrast from the darkened hall. She blinked a couple of times to bring the room into focus and then, bracing herself for what she might see, she glanced around quickly, but everything seemed to be in order. Perhaps there were a few more canvases stacked against the far wall than the last time she had been allowed in the room, but that was not all that unusual. In the center of the room, she noted the large hope chest her father and Michelozzi were in the process of building. She wasn't sure why, but suddenly she felt a little deflated.

Giving him a questioning look, she couldn't help but ask, "So, what exactly have you been up to all these weeks, Signor Donati?"

He indicated a large easel that had been set up nearer the windows, and she saw that it held a large painting. Next to it was a small table filled with artist's tools, tubes of paint, and solvents. She wrinkled her nose and breathed in the scent of turpentine and linseed oil.

Stepping closer, she saw the picture was a perfect replica of Raffaello's Madonna and child. Studying it for a moment, Margherita asked, "You did this?"

The artist gestured about the room. "These are all my paintings, yes."

"Well, it's quite lovely—I'm impressed! You could have fooled me, I would have thought it was the original. May I take a peek at those over there, too?"

Unwrapping the wool scarf from around his neck and shrugging out of his coat, he said, "Yes, please, do. That is why you came up here, isn't it? To see my work."

Margherita moved to the stack of paintings and tilted them at various angles so she could see them better. The pictures were mostly of Madonnas holding pudgy babies, mixed in with a couple of religious martyrs. Holding one painting up, she saw it was a version of Santa Margherita. The saint's face was a little too pale and sweet for her tastes. Aside from the little dog at Margherita's feet, that was rather cute on the whole, the picture was dark and melancholy.

Peering back over her shoulder, she said as politely as she could, "As nice as these pictures are, they are a little oppressive. I guess I expected something a little more modern."

The man appeared crestfallen, and when he didn't say anything, feeling a little nervous about having criticized his work, she hastened to say, "*Papà* tells me you have recently come from Paris. I just thought your work would be a little different than this."

"I spent several years in Paris," said Federico, "and in Rome before that I was trained by academicians. Don't you like the classical style?"

"*Certo!* I admire the old masters. I'm particularly drawn to Raphael, Leonardo, and I adore the paintings done by Bronzino. I think he painted beautifully and used such brilliant colors. I've always loved the painting he did of Eleonora de' Toledo in her golden gown. And then there is the one of her and her daughter Isabella. It is in the Louvre now. I saw it once when I accompanied my father a few years ago to Paris on one of his business trips. Such a pity it is kept there and not here in Italy."

Federico said nothing, just regarded her thoughtfully.

Looking back at his paintings, she added, "Classical paintings are very nice, and you are a talented painter..."

"But..." he said.

She hesitated, then said, "I particularly admire the work of a contemporary artist that I'm sure you would absolutely hate. He isn't like the painters I just mentioned, and he doesn't do work like this. In fact, he is on the complete opposite end of the spectrum."

Turning to face him, she said boldy, "I rather like the work of Picasso. He communicates volumes in the simplest stroke and a minimal swash of color and..."

When Federico laughed, Margherita looked at him in surprise. She hadn't expected her statement to be met with such hilarity, nor by the warm regard with which he was now observing her. She looked at him suspiciously, waiting to see what he would say next.

"What if I told you that Picasso is a friend of mine?"

Margherita gaped in disbelief. Was he mocking her in retaliation for the comments she had made earlier about his work? When he continued to stare at her with an amused grin, she narrowed her eyes. "*Non ci posso credere.* I don't believe it. You! You, Federico Donati, know Picasso? I highly doubt that."

"It's quite true. I did know Picasso. We were practically neighbors and lived on the same street. I had a small place near Rue Delambre. Nothing all that spectacular, mind you, but it was cheap. I had many friends there—Picasso was just one of them."

Margherita sank down into a chair close to the window. "*Caspita!*"

"We used to meet at La Rotonde late at night. It didn't matter who you were or where you came from, what was important was the art—and the ideas."

Smiling, he added, "I can't tell you how many late nights turned into early mornings when I could still be seated at a table deep in conversation with someone. We talked about creativity and politics—we talked about everything and nothing. We challenged each other's perceptions of beauty. It seemed the sun of inspiration burned most brightly in Paris. But then the Germans marched in, and the city fell. Sadly, it is just a pale shade of its former self. So I left."

Walking to the canvas on the easel, he picked up a paintbrush and wiped it with an oily rag. He looked out the window, recalling better days. "You know who some other great friends are? Man Ray and Gino Severini. One was a surrealist photographer and the other a leader of the Futurist Movement. I enjoyed those two very much and found conversations with them extremely thought-provoking."

"Severini is from Cortona, the next town over. Did you know that? And Man Ray! I can't believe you knew him, too. That time I was in Paris with my father, I saw some of his work. What happened to him?"

Shrugging his shoulders, Federico said, "Because of his work, he was forced to leave. Like me, he left Paris. I believe he said he was returning to Los Angeles."

Margherita sucked in her breath in astonishment. "Really. That's where he is from? I've always wanted to go to California."

"Yes, he is an American." Running his fingers through his hair, he added, "There were so many times we had to cover each other's debts. One of us was sure to bail the other out."

"And Picasso, what was he like?" asked Margherita.

"I met him one night while drinking with Modigliani. From that moment on, our friendship continued to grow. He was a fascinating man. I've never met anyone quite like him. At times, Picasso could be ferocious and brutish, and at other times sympathetic and kind. Often he talked your ear off, but he could be quiet and moody. I left Paris, but he decided to stay. He is still there now."

Setting down his brush, he asked, "Have you seen the *Guernica*? Do you know what that is?"

"Yes, of course! I may live in Arezzo, but we aren't all *that* backward here."

Federico was amused by her indignation. "What if I were to tell you that I saw it with my own eyes in Picasso's apartment?" Holding up his hands, he added, "Okay, maybe not the actual painting. But I saw the studies he did as he planned out the larger painting. He kept many of them tacked to his wall in his studio."

Margherita's eyes widened in astonishment. "You saw the sketches?" She had known about the *Guernica* from the newspapers. It was the enormous mural that had shocked the world with its blatant criticism of war and fascism a few years ago. She was also familiar with the images of his painting—the raging bull, the fallen soldier, and the screaming mothers with their dead babies that condemned the useless destruction of life. But, amongst the desolation, she thought Picasso had purposefully included symbols of hope.

"In fact," said Federico, "shortly after the Germans took over the city, I was there one day when the Gestapo banged on Picasso's door. They thought he was a crazy artist, a foolish, insane man who only stirred up people with his horrible paintings."

"Well, what did they do?"

"After he let them in, they barged around his studio, upending tables and rifling through his drawings. Before turning to go, one of the Germans stopped and pointed to the images of the gored horse and the dead babies pinned on his wall and asked Picasso, 'Did you do that?'"

"Do you know what Picasso's response was?" he asked.

She looked at him expectantly. "What?"

"'No, you did!'"

Amusement lit her eyes, and she said, *"Touché!* Good for Picasso."

Federico appeared pleased by her response. "It was soon after that I knew I had to leave the city. Paris changed overnight from being a place where artists could speak and paint freely to a city of tortured souls."

After a moment's consideration, he said, "So you think my paintings are pretty tame, not all that original? Bland, I believe, is the word you used."

Margherita, amused by his tone, said, "No, the word I used was oppressive."

"Ah, yes, oppressive." He was quiet for a moment. "Tell me, can you keep a secret?"

She tilted her head and considered him for a moment. "*Certo,* of course, I can keep a secret."

Federico beckoned her to the other side of the room and lifted a cloth that was draped over the table. "This is what interests me. I may have started out as a classical painter, but the time I spent in Paris gave me so much more to think about."

She gasped in amazement. What she saw was nothing like the paintings of virgins and saints she had seen earlier. These pictures were bold, airy, and light. And, although there was no clear subject matter, the swashes of colors were vivid and raw, and the pictures vibrated with expressive emotional energy.

Margherita looked at the man standing next to her with new appreciation. There was more to him than met the eye, and when you scratched the surface, a whole new side of him was revealed. Without saying a word, they exchanged glances and Margherita felt something quickening inside of her. It was as if she was peering into a new universe, seeing for the first time galaxies that had never existed before.

Holding out her hand to shake that of the artist, she said, "I believe I owe you an apology, Signor Donati. Your work is... *Santo Cielo!* I don't even know where to begin. I find these paintings incredibly beautiful."

After that day, Margherita invented excuses to remain in the shop long after closing hours, and every time Federico came into view, her laugh was a bit brighter and she sparkled a bit more than usual. He, too, seemed more at ease in her company, and when he passed by, he took a moment to talk with her or hand her a book to read. The man she had imagined to be reserved was really quite funny and talkative.

Lost in a fascinating world of their own making, the two were unaware of the pain they were causing another. From across the shop, Ruggero watched the two with their heads bent together over a magazine or a book and noticed how Margherita's disposition changed. It was becoming more evident by the hour she found greater enjoyment in the company of the older man than in his. Ruggero wasn't quite sure what the artist's business was with Bernardo, but his presence worried him.

When no one was watching, Ruggero snuck upstairs and, using a spare key he had stolen long ago, he opened Federico's door and poked around the artist's workroom. Like Margherita, he too was curious to know what the artist was hiding behind locked doors. Gazing about the attic, he found nothing out of the ordinary. All he discovered was a stack of paintings of patron saints and a bunch of brightly-colored canvases.

Tracing a finger over the surface of the painting that Margherita had so admired, he regarded it thoughtfully. To him, it was a meaningless jumble of colors, something a child could do. The artist was quite mad. Closing the door and returning to work, he shook his head, completely mystified as to why Margherita avoided him yet was drawn to the artist who lived upstairs.

Chapter 16

Two Hearts Aligned

*F*or Margherita, the following weeks passed by in a blur of pastel colors, but for Ruggero, they dragged by slowly in a blaze of red. From the shadows, he continued his surveillance. Desperately seeking Margherita's attention, he showered her daily with flowers and boxes of chocolates and even acquired expensive tickets to the opera. When she left the shop, he'd call out, "Nita, don't forget to wear the hat I brought you from Rome. It is much prettier than the one you have on."

One afternoon, when Ruggero picked up her hand and played with the ring on her finger, she felt a stab of panic. It only increased when he looked into her eyes and said, "The days are slipping by so fast. Don't you think it's time we set a date? I know the officials at the Perfecto—they would be happy to perform a legal ceremony. Then we can have a big wedding later in the chapel in San Donato."

Hearing Federico coming down the stairs, Margherita quickly disengaged her hand and turned her attention back to the accounting ledger. Glancing up, she saw her father shake his head wearily. She knew he didn't entirely trust Ruggero. The other night, he had even intimated that he had seen her fiancé in the company of German officers and their fascist cronies. She knew the potential danger in that.

As November slipped into December, she noticed with increasing frequency that her father was finding reasons to send Ruggero out on errands far away from the shop, to Florence and various neighboring towns. With Ruggero out from under them, everyone seemed to relax and breathe a little easier.

At closing time one evening, Margherita turned on the radio, filling the shop with swing music, and by the time Signor Michelozzi arrived to collect his friend for dinner, even her father was humming along to one of the American tunes. Delighted by his good humor, Margherita watched as he placed the hat on his head and bantered good-naturedly with his friend.

Before taking his leave, he walked over to her and kissed her on her cheek. His mood grew serious as he picked up a photo of his wife displayed in a silver frame on her desk. Studying Margherita, he said, "You resemble your mother so much. She was a remarkable woman. I loved Lucrezia very much, you know."

Margherita waited for him to continue, already knowing what he was about to say. "*Senti*, Margherita, up until now, I've tried my best to protect you and keep you out of harm's way, but things are happening too quickly. Your engagement to Ruggero... Well, I have many concerns. I know you worry about me, and I fear you have accepted his proposal for the wrong reasons. But I think..."

"*Aspetta, papà,*" Margherita interrupted him, "I've been doing a lot of thinking recently, too, and have come to a decision which I believe will relieve your mind." Looking over at Corrado, who waited by the door, she said, "Go now with Signor Michelozzi, *babbo*. You two have a nice dinner. We can discuss this later at home."

Bernardo pondered her words, and as their meaning sank in, he smiled in relief. "You are a fine, strong girl, Margherita. *Una brava ragazza.* Your mother would be so proud of you."

He hugged her and turned to Corrado, saying, "*Andiamo.*" As the two men left the shop, Margherita's heart felt lighter to hear them carrying on again like old times.

Silence descended upon the shop and, finding herself alone for the evening, Margherita turned up the radio, and soon the strains of an American love song filled the air. *"Kiss me once and kiss me twice, then kiss me once again. It's been a long, long time. Haven't felt like this, my dear, since I can't remember when..."*

She hummed along to the song under her breath as she twisted the gold band around her finger. Slipping it off, she held it up to the light, admiring the design Signor Michelozzi had made. She now realized the ring, as well as the man who had given it to her, no longer fit, and it was time to give back the symbol of betrothal. She had known Ruggero a lifetime yet had never entirely fallen in love with him. It had taken only a matter of moments in Federico's studio that day for her heart to awaken and for her to discover where her true feelings lay.

Placing the ring gently into the drawer of the cash register, she picked up the shipping bills stacked neatly beside it and sat down at a small desk to sort through them.

At the sound of Federico's footsteps on the stairs, she turned around. "*Buonasera*, Signor Donati. I thought you'd already gone out."

Seeing her sitting at her desk, her face illuminated by the lamp light, Federico's heart stopped. She was lovely. "*Ciao*, Nita. No, I'm still here. I thought I heard the voice of your father."

"You just missed him, but if you hurry, you can catch him. He just stepped out the door on his way to dinner with Signor Michelozzi."

Federico walked to her side. "No, no. I much prefer your company to his." Seeing the figures she was recording, he asked, "So what keeps you here so late this evening? Don't tell me you've remained behind to work on these boring numbers?"

Leaning back in her chair, she said, "Well, yes and no. Someone has to make all these numbers agree." She boldly persisted, "But if you want to know the truth, I was thinking about having dinner with a fascinating artist who lives upstairs."

"Ah, is that so?" Reaching over, he took the pen from her hand and set it gently next to the ledger, then, clasping her left hand, he drew her up until she was standing in front of him. Entwining his fingers with hers, he noticed she wasn't wearing her engagement ring. He traced the back of her hand and studied it for a moment, then gave her a questioning look.

"Can I ask you something, Federico?"

"Of course, Margherita. You can ask me anything."

"I've been doing a lot of thinking lately... About so many things, particularly about my future. And I'm wondering, well, where do you see yourself in ten or twenty years? What is it you want out of life?"

Federico contemplated her question a moment. "Well, I believe the decisions we make move us closer to what we want in life. They can move us toward what our hearts desire or, just as easily, they can move us farther away. Each small decision, no matter how inconsequential, determines our future."

The two were quiet for a moment, caught in the soft glow of her desk lamp.

"And you, Margherita?"

Taking a step closer, she said, "I think I'm on my way to where I want to be."

Drawing her even nearer, he asked, "And where is that, dearest Margherita?"

Holding his hands firmly, she said, "This is where I want to be, Federico. Right here, looking at you."

A smile broke out over his face and, reaching behind her, he pulled the brass chain on the lamp. Instantly, the shop was bathed in shadows. In a pool of golden moonlight that poured in from the shop window, he cupped the back of her neck and slowly lowered his head to kiss her.

Raising his head and losing himself in her eyes, he said, "This is where I will always want to be—here in your arms, my darling Margherita."

Later that evening, when Margherita told her father she had fallen in love with Federico and that they had decided to marry and make a life together, he beamed with contented pleasure. In her heart, Margherita had already known Bernardo would not be the slightest bit disappointed by this turn of events.

Hugging her tightly, her father whispered in her ear, *"Mia cara,* you have made this old man so very happy with your choice. Federico is the kind of man who is deserving of you and your love."

When Ruggero returned from Florence later the next day, she drew him aside, prepared to tell him her feelings had changed. She had rehearsed her words, but as she started to say them, looking up at his ashen face, she stuttered to a stop. Slowly, she held out his engagement ring and placed it in the palm of his hand.

He said nothing, only stared at her in disbelief, trying to fathom what she was saying. And then, as reality set in, she saw the light leave his eyes and something broke inside him.

"Don't do this," Ruggero whispered. "Can't you see we are meant to be together? I don't want anyone else. It has always been you."

Knowing she was hurting him terribly, she blundered on. "I realize now I can't marry you. I could never love you the way you need or should be loved. It wouldn't be fair to either of us to continue with this..."

Suddenly, his eyes flashed wide and two bright spots burned his cheeks. Then scrutinizing her intently, he furiously challenged, "It is Donati, isn't it? You are throwing me over for a perfect stranger, who swoops in from God knows where and turns your fickle head. Why are you such a gullible, stupid girl? What can that old man provide you that I can't?"

Margherita took a step backward, frightened by his tone and the insults that poured from his mouth.

"So, it has come down to this! You choose that miserable, depraved artist over me, someone who paints like a child, hiding his hideous paintings in the loft upstairs!"

Seeing her apprehension, Ruggero said, "Oh yes, I've known for quite some time what that artist of yours does behind closed doors. He doesn't just paint holy saints and Raphael Madonnas. I might just let a few words slip to the right people. Believe me, it won't sit well with the current regime."

A terrible fear sparked inside her. Grabbing his arm, she said, "Ruggero, please! If you love me at all, don't do this. I care for you as a friend. Please don't."

Ruggero regarded her for a moment and bent his head sorrowfully. "You have broken my heart, Margherita. You know I would never do anything to hurt you intentionally... I can't turn off my feelings so easily. It's always been you..."

With heavy misgivings, Margherita watched him turn away. He quit the shop that day, breaking all ties with the Lancini family. After a few weeks, she learned that he had opened a small furniture business of his own. Arezzo was a tiny little town and news traveled fast. When they passed one another on the street, instead of flashing a smile and calling out to her, he only nodded curtly. If she was in the company of Federico, her arm linked with his, Ruggero's greeting was far less cordial, if he acknowledged them at all.

Glancing over her shoulder as he passed them by, Margherita could sense the bitterness was still there, slowly boiling under the surface.

Chapter 17

End of Days

*W*earing her mother Lucrezia's white satin ankle-length wedding dress and holding a bouquet of white tea roses, Margherita married Federico on New Year's Day in 1942. The air was crisp, but the sun sparkled through the stained glass windows as they exchanged their vows in front of a small group of close friends in the church of San Donato.

Afterward, they celebrated with prosecco and almond cake, and Corrado and Bernardo presented Margherita with the hope chest filled with secret drawers they had built together in the workroom above the shop. That evening, before slipping out of their wedding finery, Federico gave his new bride a picture he had painted of the holy family. It was very Raphaelesque and sweet.

He told her that one day the Madonna would bring them good luck. Kissing her on the neck, pulling the satin gown over her head, and drawing her to the bed, he promised her it would be a blessing for the family they hoped to start. It seemed the painting was indeed a good omen, and later that year they welcomed into the world a son they named Edoardo.

Ruggero, too, eventually married. He chose the daughter of a visiting government dignitary to be his bride, and for all intents and purposes, it was an advantageous merger for him. Due to his connections, he was rising quickly in the eyes of the local politicians, as well as the German commandants.

As 1942 moved slowly into 1943, Ruggero's business took off and was thriving while Bernardo's declined. Signor Lancini acknowledged the younger man's success tiredly, knowing full well who was helping Ruggero prosper. It was now common knowledge amongst the partisans that Ruggero was working in cooperation with the Nazis, receiving bribe money for being a paid informant, and that the Germans were using his business as a front.

The fascist regime continued to dominate all their lives, forcing them to talk in whispers and live in the shadows, making things miserable. It seemed no one could be trusted and almost daily they heard stories of people being caught and tortured for working in collaboration with the resistance forces. But, although he rarely had customers, Bernardo hadn't shut down his operations. He, too, continued to use his business as a cover for his secret activities.

Behind closed doors, Federico sided with the partisans forces and helped his father-in-law protect the art of Arezzo. By day, he painted religious subjects to keep up appearances, but at night, in secret, he created colorful expressionist paintings. It pained him to keep them hidden from sight, but it was far too dangerous to thwart the powers in charge. He played the game of deception well, and every time the Gestapo banged on their door, all the heavy-booted thugs found was a shop full of antiques and Federico's paintings of saints hanging on the wall.

One painting in particular, of Santa Margherita and her dog—the one Nita had initially found so distasteful—Federico hung in the back room of the shop. At first, Nita had protested, but when he told her it represented everything they were fighting for—Margherita, after all, was the patron saint of the downtrodden—she relented.

"Keep Margherita safe," he said. "Like the painting of the Madonna I gave you on our wedding night, Margherita is your patron saint, and one day you will be surprised by the secrets she keeps."

Things continued unfolding desperately, and every day a new sorrow filled their hearts. By the summer of 1943, it seemed the world had reached a tipping point. After years of fighting and subjugation, the tides of war were turning in their favor. That was the summer the Americans landed in Salerno and began beating their way up the peninsula.

But as the allied forces approached Arezzo, instead of fleeing, the Germans hunkered down, determined to hold their ground, patrolling the streets in more significant numbers and building machine gun nests in the ditches leading to town. Arezzo was a strategic military holdout, situated along the main rail artery connecting Rome and Florence; it became a fierce battleground between the allies and the Nazis. The bombs rained down upon the city, razing medieval towers and crenelated buildings. The very structures that had once been erected as military defense, to serve and protect the Aretini, were quickly decimated and turned to dust.

By the end of the summer, the local fascists, realizing they were losing the upper hand, commanded all partisans to lay down their arms or face death. But, instead of giving up, the rebel forces intensified their attacks.

In retaliation, the Germans stepped up their surveillance of those who remained in town, knowing full well there were those among them working to support the rebel forces. They held innocent people hostage to obtain information about anyone who might be aiding and abetting the partisans. In the process, they injured or mercilessly slaughtered old men, defenseless women, and children. One particularly brutal attack occurred in San Polo, northeast of Arezzo, where sixty-five Italians were tortured and killed.

When Bernardo, Margherita, and Federico learned of the massacres, they bowed their heads in grief, believing things couldn't get any worse. But, they did. With British troops just miles and only a few days away from liberation, the world crashed in on the Donati family.

Before daybreak one gray morning, Margherita awoke next to her husband to the sounds of bombs and shattering glass. As she did her best to sweep up the shards and put things in order, in the distance, she heard the sound of sirens growing louder, announcing the arrival of the Gestapo.

Without invitation, they stormed through the door and kicked over a table filled with china dishes. Advancing into the shop, one man upended a platter of silver teapots, making a deafening clatter.

Her father cried out for them to stop, but the officers only sneered at him and said, *"Halt die Klappe, alter Kerl!* Shut up, old man."

When Federico tried to intervene, they ignored Bernardo and

focused their attention on him. "You are the one we want," the man in charge said. The other soldier dragged Federico into the middle of the shop and, holding a gun to his head, shouted out a terse mixture of German and Italian.

When Federico didn't respond, the soldier demanded, *"Sprich, du dreckiger, abartiger Künstler. Beantworte die Frage! Wo sind die Gemälde? Wohin hast du sie versteckt?"* When Federico remained mute, the guard punched him in the gut with the end of his rifle and repeated, "Speak up, you filthy deviant. Answer the question! Where are the paintings? Where have you hidden them?"

The force of the blow caused Federico to double over in pain. Margherita advanced to help him but stopped when the guard pointed his gun at their child. She froze in horror and clutched a crying Edoardo to her breast.

"Bring das Kind zum schweigen, oder ich erschieße euch beide!" shouted the guard. Seeing she didn't understand, he repeated slowly, through clenched teeth, "Shut the kid up or I'll shoot you both."

Margherita panicked and reached out to Federico. She was about to speak, but with a slight nod of his head, he warned her not to do anything foolish. Locking eyes, they communicated a lifetime of words in an instant. He then drew himself proudly upward to his full height, and at that moment her heart burst with the love she felt for him and all he stood for. With another indiscernible signal, he silently promised he would be all right and would return to her side again soon.

Margherita did as he requested but observed in silent agony as the guards bound and gagged him and shoved him roughly into the back of a van. The soldier, seeing Bernardo bending down to pick up a shattered dish, with a flick of his head, ordered him to be put in the van too. "We'll use the old man, to get more information out of Donati."

As the truck bearing her father and her husband pulled away, with sirens wailing, Margherita leaned limply against the door frame. When the noise grew fainter and eventually died down, regaining her wits quickly, she ran down the street in search of Signor Michelozzi and

Egidio. "They've taken my father and Federico. *Aiutami!* Help me. We must do something." The two men exchanged a grim look. Seeing their faces, she demanded, "What is it? Tell me! What do you know?"

"We are waiting to find out, but if they have been taken to Villa Godiola, they must think your husband is a spy working with the rebels. We believe they are using your father as a means to force a confession out of Federico."

"Surely there is someone who could reason with the German commanders." Wildly, she swiveled her gaze from one to the other. "Ruggero knows them."

Both Corrado and Egidio contemplated her skeptically, not convinced Ruggero could be so easily relied upon. "Nita, you are not thinking clearly. Just leave things to us. We promise you we will handle it."

But Margherita pushed past her limits, refusing to be dissuaded, said, "Ruggero cared for me once. Perhaps I can reason with him again. He is my only hope. Federico is my husband and a man worth fighting for. I will do everything within my power to get him released. I'll get down on my knees and beg if I must."

Feverishly, she ran out the door. Bursting into Ruggero's shop, Margherita found him seated in a chair, bent over. In his right hand, he held a glass of amber liquid; in the other, a cigarette. When he saw her standing in front of him, his heavy-lidded eyes flashed wide, and he stood up quickly. Slurring his words slightly, he exclaimed, "Margherita! *Che ci fai qui?* What are you doing here?"

Noticing his puffy face, wild, messy hair, and the smoke-clouded room, Margherita hesitated a moment. But the concern for her husband was far greater, and in a rush of words, she said, "Ruggero, they have arrested my father and my husband! I need your help to save them from the Gestapo. Please... You have to talk to them."

He took a sip of his drink and set it on the table, but said nothing. They regarded one another in silence.

Finally not able to bear it anymore, she moved a step closer. "You have to help us. We have a child. Edoardo is so small. He needs his father." Taking his free hand, she placed it on her midriff. "I'm pregnant again."

Ruggero looked at her, the women he had loved—the woman he *still* loved. He pulled his hand away as if it had been scalded, and his face drained of color. He took a puff of his cigarette but still said nothing.

Shaking his shoulders, Margherita urged, "Listen to me. I will forgive you for being a German spy if you to talk to the officials. Don't lie to me now. I know you have connections. Tell them they are mistaken. Tell them you know they are honest men. Only you can get them released."

"It is too late," Ruggero said flatly, downing the last contents of his glass. "They have already been arrested." To further punish her for not loving him enough, he spat out, "By now, they are probably dead."

Margherita swayed slightly. "Was it you who turned them in? Ruggero, please, have you no soul? Listen, if I had money, I'd give it to you."

Emboldened by the whiskey, he said, "I don't want your money—or your pity. The only thing I ever wanted, you took away from me. You made your choice, and now you must live with it. You have brought this upon yourselves, you and your artist!"

Margherita slapped him then stepped back in shock. How could he have changed so much? Was he actually filled with such hatred? She remembered him as an innocent boy, but the man standing before her was a monster.

Angrily, she hissed, "If you don't do this for me, then do it to save your own skin. The allies are coming and the Germans are fleeing. Soon you will be left with nothing, and no one, to protect you. If you don't speak to them now, I will expose you for the traitor that you are to your own people."

Ruggero returned her unflinching gaze and blew out a stream of smoke. He believed her. Time was running out for him as well. After Mussolini was shot, it had been all over the papers how the partisans had gleefully mutilated his corpse. If the resistance forces got hold of him, he knew he would meet a similar fate.

The bravado left him, and he sagged and bowed his head. Staggering forward, he said, "I'm sorry, Nita. I never wanted to hurt you. Please..." Choking on his words, he continued, "Please forgive me for what I have done."

They stood studying one another for a long moment. Finally, he broke the silence and said, "I'll see what I can do."

She could smell the alcohol on his breath and knew he was drunk, but still, she believed him. She was convinced somewhere inside of him there was still something good. He would help her. She was sure of it.

But, in the end, there was nothing that could be done. Ruggero returned the next day and told Margherita that when he arrived at the Villa Godiola, he had found Federico already dead.

"They say he got into a fight with one of the guards. He died immediately from trauma to the head after being slammed against a stone wall."

"And my father?" Margherita whispered, the tears slipping down her cheeks.

"I talked to the commandant. He is still being held for questioning. But I vouched for Bernardo. He'll be released later today."

Staring dully at Ruggero, she said, "For that, I thank you. Now, please go away."

He started to go, but, hesitating, he turned back as if to say something more. Closing the door in his face, she locked it and sank to the floor, feeling her life ebbing away. A part of her died that afternoon, along with her husband.

As she lay on the cold floor listening to the sounds of the bombs in the distance, she also heard the cries of her two-year-old son. Picking herself up, she went to hold him. She hadn't lost everything. There still remained her darling baby boy, as well as Federico's unborn child to care for. She couldn't afford the luxury of giving in to her pain and sorrow now. There would be a lifetime to grieve for Federico.

As the sound of the bombs grew louder, raining down in greater force, she knew she had to act. "We must leave town. It's not safe for us anymore. We must get out of here."

For the people of Arezzo, the war ended on a bright July day in 1945. The Germans had held a tight death grip on the entire area, but finally, the allies broke through their line of defense, causing them to turn tail and run north to the Alps. But when the British troops finally rolled into town and stopped their tanks, they were greeted by an eerie silence and the wind whispering through the deserted piazzas. No one ran out to meet them. What greeted the troops instead was a town that resembled a desecrated cemetery. All that remained was rubble. Everyone, including Margherita and her family, took refuge in the hills outside the city.

When it was safe to do so, Nita and her father returned to Arezzo and reopened their shop, rebuilding their shattered lives. Margherita did the best she could for her little family, preparing for the arrival of her second child. But later that fall, the last part of Federico she had clung to, a tiny baby girl, died in her arms the day she was born. The only things that remained of her husband were his precious son Edoardo and his beautiful paintings.

Over time, the echoes of the bombs that had fallen on Arezzo became a distant memory. Bernardo passed away a few years later, and eventually, Margherita remarried a nice man who helped her with the family business. But he too died of a heart attack in 1965. Left to her own devices, she grew to appreciate her independent lifestyle, cultivating her love for the arts and sponsoring local artists.

Margherita would be the first to say she had found her peace by focusing her attention on her family. For this, she was rewarded with a son who grew into an intelligent businessman, a delightful daughter-in-law, and two beautiful grandchildren whom she loved well.

Ruggero's family lived on the opposite side of town near the Porta del Foro, and Margherita's lived near the Porta Santo Spirito. The two families coexisted peacefully; Ruggero even offered Margherita a loan to help restore the family business. Eventually, they were all reunited again by the marriage of their grandchildren Gianluca and Carlotta. It seemed grudges and grievances had been buried and put to rest.

The years turned Margherita into an old woman, but she still carried in her heart a picture of a man who had opened her eyes to new horizons. She never for one moment forgot him. With all her heart, until the day she died, Margherita continued to love the brilliant artist who had once known Picasso.

Nora

Chapter 18

Waking Beauty

July 26, 2010

*T*he stories Luca told Nora over the following weeks about his grandparents consumed her thoughts for days. It was becoming more and more apparent how people's lives, energy, and actions had resounding effects flowing down through the years, touching, inspiring and sparking change.

Once again, she felt the universe was sending her messages. First Isabella, and now Margherita, seemed to be reaching out to her, guiding her by example. Although worlds apart and separated by centuries, these women were connected and intertwined by similar tenacious strands of fearlessness and courage. Each in her own way had struggled to be independent during restrictive times—they had also fallen madly in love with sympathetic men, only to have their *storia d'amore* end tragically. They too had lost children, yet each had learned to be happy and had gone on to lead meaningful lives.

Nora realized she would do very well, if she could muster up half the moxie of these two women.

Looking back at her computer, she returned to the work at hand, making adjustments to the audio track. She winced only occasionally at the sound of her voice, thinking, *Oh God. Do I really sound like that?*

Hearing the coffee gurgling on the stove, she paused the video and poured herself a cup. Drawing back one of the drapes that partially covered the window, she peered down at the scene below in the piazza and observed a man on a bicycle precariously balancing a boy on his handlebars. Across the way, a woman was cleaning the window of her clothing shop, and in front of the newspaper kiosk, two men were gesturing in a heated debate.

Before she turned away, she saw Salvatore, the neighbor who lived above her, coming home for his noonday meal. She watched in amusement as he dodged a gaggle of school kids who had skipped into his path. When he glanced up and saw her in the window, he waved and shouted out, *"Buongiorno, Nora!"*

Hastening to crank open the window, she called down to him, *"Ciao, Salvo! Come stai?"* She could count the weeks she had been in Arezzo on one hand, but she already felt more at home in this neighborhood than anywhere else she had ever lived.

She returned to her computer, and fortified by the caffeine, she critically viewed the entire film from start to finish. *Not bad*, she thought.

Rewinding to the final scene, she watched as a lovely young woman dressed as the Medici princess seated on top of a horse greeted a cheering crowd. On the anniversary of Isabella's death, July 16, she, Juliette, and Marco had gone back to Cerreto Guidi to take part in the historical reenactment celebrating Isabella de' Medici's life. It seemed a perfect way to end her film by featuring the princess in all her regal glory, in command of her stallion once again.

On their way back home to Arezzo, they stopped in Florence, where Nora filmed the streets where Isabella might have walked and took pictures of buildings the princess would have known. After lunch, they crossed the bridge to the Oltrarno to visit the Pitti Palace, home to the Medici, and where Isabella had lived as a child. Inside, they explored all the rooms, and then they strolled through the sprawling gardens behind the mansion, which had once been Isabella's exotic playground.

Originally, the Boboli gardens had been the brainchild of her mother, Eleonora, and it reflected the woman's Renaissance fascination with anything unusual and misshapen. While the grounds astounded the adults with its artifice, to children it represented a fantastic fairy tale world. It was full of shady grottoes and bushes trimmed into elaborate labyrinths. Around every corner, one could find fountains shaped like seashells or turtles and statues carved to resemble sea nymphs.

The Medici brood, at an early age, had been encouraged to engage in play, to make jokes and mirror the adult lives of their parents. So when their studies concluded, they entertained themselves with games of hide-and-seek and charades in the grottoes behind their palace. The gardens were a perfect backdrop for Isabella to take center stage and star in performances, scripted by herself, that flowed from her unbridled imagination.

Aside from shrubbery and fanciful topiary, the grounds were also stocked with exotic monkeys, zebras, and ponies to delight and entertain the children. But the eccentricities didn't end there. It was also populated by unusual people—the dwarves—who were often gifts to the Medici court. Isabella's confidant Morgante was just one such little person; the lives of such small individuals were short in those days before modern medicine, and when one Morgante died, he was replaced by another and given the same name.

As Nora wandered the grounds with Marco and Juliette, she imagined what it must have been like to play here as a child, having a faithful dwarf follow her around, ready to protect her and carry out her every whim. Walking up the path ahead of her friends, Nora swore she heard the laughter of children and the lamenting of an exasperated dwarf.

"Come here, you little man, today you shall play the role of Fata Morgana, the evil witch of the north. Here, drape this about your head."

"But, m'lady! Must I dress in women's clothes again?" grumbled Morgante.

"Hush now! I am the one inventing this scene. Besides, it is only a lace shawl." Surveying the shady grotto, Isabella said, "Now, let me see. Ah, yes. You shall enter from over there."

"Where?"

"There, next to the fountain." Swinging around, she pointed a short distance away. "What's wrong with you today, Morgante? Where is your imagination? Have you no fantasy left?"

"I left it on my bedside table. Perhaps I should return to the palace and retrieve it."

"Oh, no you won't," she said firmly. "You won't escape me so easily. I know your tricks, my dear little man." Without giving him time to invent another excuse, she continued. "Come now. Can you not see it?"

"See what?" muttered Morgante, gazing around the shady grove.

"Why, we are on an enchanted island, surrounded by a lake containing magical fairy creatures, of course. You have cast a spell upon me and have placed me in your crystal dungeon." She placed her hands on her hips and said, "And I... Let's see, where shall I be?"

She brightened. "Ah ha!" Isabella skipped over to a nearby bench. "I shall lay here, still as a stone, waiting for my handsome prince to row across the water to rescue me."

Extending herself on the marble bench, she placed one hand upon her heart and the other on her forehead. Crying out in despair, she said, "Only he, the one most true to my heart, will be able to wake me."

Looking dreamily over at Morgante, she added, "That is, if he can steal from you the golden orb containing all the beauty in the world. But alas! The task will not be an easy one. The waters are filled with lily pond creatures and—"

"Lily pond creatures? And what might they be, M'lady?"

"Silly fool, they are the beautiful wood sprites who, if you gaze upon them, will steal your very soul and hold your heart hostage."

"Ah, so it will not be an easy feat, for your chivalrous knight to rescue you?"

"I should say not!" Shooting up to a seated position, she said, "By the way, where *is* my noble hero?" Pausing to listen, she scanned the emerald green bushes. "Giovanni! Are you there?"

Turning impatiently to Morgante, she asked, "Where has my little brother got to? He is to be the hero who saves me."

"I saw him last on the other side of the grotto sailing his boat."

"Well, go find him, you little goblin. Bring him to me. We cannot start without him."

"As you wish, m'lady."

Nora was brought back to reality when she heard the sound of laughter again, this time emanating from the bushes to her right. As she circled a marble fountain where a graceful goddess poured out water from a Grecian urn, she spied Marco and Juliette leaning against a tree. As the two kissed, Nora turned her camera upon them.

"*Beccati!* Gotcha. You've been caught in the act."

Marco flashed her a playful grin and spun Juliette around in a circle. "You know what they say: What happens in the garden, stays in the garden. They also say too much work makes Nora a dull girl! Now turn that thing off and take a break with us."

"But it doesn't seem like work if you really like what you do. I'm rather good at this," she said.

"Come dance with us anyway."

Happily, she put her camera away and complied. How could she pass up the chance to twirl about the Boboli gardens, enjoying the present moment?

She sang along to a song Marco played on his phone and identified with the Italian lyrics. "*Viaggi che ti cambiano la vita e non lo sai, parti senza immaginare neanche un po' chi sei...*"

To Nora, it seemed the song had been written about her. It was true. There were trips that changed your life. Like the Italian singer, she too had set out on a journey not really knowing who she was or what she wanted, but somewhere along the way to find Isabella, things had started to change. She was beginning to forget past disappoints and cease agonizing over her choices. On the contrary, it felt as though her senses were awakening and she was discovering she was quite happy to be savoring all the flavors, sights, and sounds Italy had to offer.

In this relaxed frame of mind, Nora could forgive anybody, almost anything. Joining in the refrain, she sang out, "*Salute e pace pure agli stronzi.* Health and peace even to all..." substituting her own lyric, she added, "Ex-husbands."

After so many years, finally, she was flying solo. The weight of a complicated relationship and past disappointments was now lifting off her shoulders, and she found she could soar higher than ever before.

Lightening her burdens and helping her along on this new journey of self-awareness were the friendships she was cultivating in Italy. She couldn't discount her attachments to Isabella and Margherita, as well as Marco and Juliette... And then, of course, there was Luca.

From the moment she fell into his arms, and he called her his *principessa*, she had felt an instant connection, and over the past couple of weeks, the feeling had only grown stronger. Over the course of just a few weeks, they had discovered they shared many mutual interests, aside from partisans, paintings, and the past. Over drinks or sometimes dinners, they engaged in lively discussions in which they debated their favorite books and films, even the state of the world's economy.

At first, she had been amused that instead of calling her Nora like everyone else, he insisted on calling her Leonora. When he had asked her why she had been given such an Italian name, she told him she wasn't exactly sure.

"I guess, like me, my mother had a vivid imagination," Nora said. "She used to read a lot of romance novels. But you know what's funny? I never really liked my name. It was already a nuisance having to tell people how to spell my last name. You know, Havilland with two Ls and not just one. So to make life easier and avoid the double hassle of confusing them again with my first name, I shortened it. The only time I was ever called Leonora was when I got into trouble... And believe me, that was never a good thing."

But Nora realized she had developed a new appreciation for her birth name. Not only had it been the name of Isabella's favorite cousin, she liked the way Luca pronounced it drawing out all the syllables, saying it with an Italian lilt. Instead of sounding formal, coming from his lips it seemed charming and filled her with a sense of anticipation of what he might say next. As of yet, he hadn't disappointed her—his witty remarks and astute comments were a constant source of delight.

Like earlier, when she heard him call out to her in the Piazza Grande. She whirled around, infinitely pleased to see him. She waved back and cried, *"Ciao Luca, come va?* How are you doing?"

"*Bene,* I saw you coming up the street. How is the film coming along?"

"I'm nearly finished, so it is almost time to celebrate."

"That's wonderful, *complimenti!* When you are done, I must see it. I'll bring the *prosecco.*"

"I'd love that. I'll let you know when it is a complete wrap. But right now, I've decided to take a little break from work." Giving him a mysterious smile, she said, "I'm on a quest."

"That sounds intriguing," he said. "And what are you searching for?"

"Beauty, of course."

"Well," he said, gesturing about the piazza, "just take a look around you. Life is beautiful right here."

"Yes, of course," Nora readily agreed. "You are absolutely right. But today my journey is taking me just across the way to see Piero della Francesca's frescos. Do you have time to join me?"

Checking his watch, he said, "I think I could be persuaded." Then, without further prompting, he fell into step beside her, and they walked the short distance from the piazza to the church. After admiring the paintings in the central apse, they settled on a bench at the back and quietly observed the tourists flowing in and out of the basilica.

"It's incredible to think your *bisnonno* Bernardo and your *nonno* Federico helped protect these amazing frescos during the bomb strikes on Arezzo. It would have been a terrible shame to lose them."

"Even after all these years, when I look at them, I see something new. They remind me that something astounding and beautiful still exists in the world."

Nora thought about that. "*La Bellezza.* It is such a difficult concept to express, yet a word that is often overused. I'm curious, how do you define it? What does it mean to you?"

"That's a tough one—one of the fascinating riddles of philosophy."

"Oh, come on. Don't think about it too hard. Give me the first thing that comes to mind."

"*Allora.* Here goes. Beauty by Gianluca Donati," he said in an overly scholarly tone.

Smothering a laugh, Nora rocked into his shoulder. "Come on, don't tease me. *I'm* serious. I really want to know."

"I was trying being serious," he replied with a grin. Then drawing a straight face, he continued, "Okay, "let me think. Beauty? Well, perhaps it is a means of arousing the senses. It could be something that makes you feel positive and joyful, or makes you feel simply alive."

"I like that," Nora said. "See, it wasn't so hard after all."

They sat for a moment, and then he said in an exaggerated stage whisper, "What do you think, Leonora? What is your definition of *La Bellezza?*"

"Oh, great—my turn, ehi?"

Not looking at her but smiling, he continued to regard the frescos in front of them. "You put me on the spot. Fair's fair."

"Okay," Nora began. "I believe everything has beauty, even the most simple of things. It is all around us, but not everyone sees it or takes the time to uncover it. So, for me, it exists in looking at something with the only purpose being to appreciate it and really see it, as if for the first time."

She waited for his reaction.

Turning from contemplating the frescos to studying her, he said, "Go on."

Encouraged by the warmth in his eyes, she continued, "I think it can also be found in the appreciation of many things that involve the senses, like a silky piece of marble or the way sunlight illuminates the leaves of a tree. It could also be in listening to Puccini's 'La Bohème', or even drinking cool water on a hot day. I think, though, if I were to sum it up, beauty is the ultimate expression of hope."

Falling into a contented silence, Luca and Nora sat side-by-side and continued to admire the pastel frescos painted centuries before. As light filtered through the stained glass windows, surprised by the connection they were starting to feel, they contemplated the beauty in each other.

Like a midnight lake, Nora thought Luca had depths she was just starting to fathom. He had the kind of intelligent beauty an Italian

Renaissance painter would have captured in dark smoky strokes and translucent layers of paint. Breathing in deeply, she inhaled his scent and thought it hit all the right notes. She enjoyed his sense of humor and their conversations. It was refreshing to spend time with a person who valued her opinions and shared similar interests. He was also opening her up to new ideas, and ways of doing things, and that was a quality far more appealing than any other.

Despite what she had told herself about wanting to live an independent life free of entanglements, he touched her mind and heart. She had come to Italy hoping to wake Isabella, but sitting in the church next to Luca, she wondered if another kind of beauty had just been awakened.

Chapter 19

Star of Florence

Nora relished the moment when her documentary was finally finished, wrapped up, and sent back to the university in California. On the one hand, she was thrilled to have realized her vision, having brought Isabella's story to life, but on the other, she was filled with regret. In just a few weeks, she would be returning home, back to her old job and life.

She hoped to spend the remaining time with her friends, but as the harvest approached, Juliette's afternoons were busier than ever, and Nora knew it would be pointless to call Luca. He had just received the "big shipment", as they all referred to it now, and she knew he had his hands full uncrating and cataloging the items.

One afternoon with nothing better to do, she decided to visit the fifteenth-century home of Giorgio Vasari in the Porto del Foro neighborhood and pay her respects to Arezzo's famous artist. Vasari had been a talented Italian painter, architect, and notably the first art historian, who, like Bronzino, had been employed by Isabella's father. Here in Arezzo, he had designed the lovely loggia that graced the top of the city's main piazza.

Nora was not disappointed by what she found after entering the artist's house. As she wandered through each of the rooms, she craned her neck to study the ceiling frescos Vasari himself had designed. Every soffit and arch, it seemed, was crammed full of Roman prophets and pastel goddesses, and the walls were hung with fifteenth-century portraits. After Nora circulated the house and had her fill of tumultuous allegorical scenes, she decided it was time to leave and perhaps take a stroll in the park. But, turning the corner on her way to the door, seeing a life-size portrait of a woman dressed in a velvet gown, she stopped in her tracks.

"*Ciao, bella!* Well, hello there. Fancy meeting you here."

Once again Isabella seemed to have popped up unannounced, and Nora was standing face to face with the Medici princess. Walking over to the portrait, she said, "I'm so glad I ran into you today. Your documentary is finished. You lived as the Star of Florence, now you are the star of my film. I hope you are pleased."

Nora studied the painting and noted once again the woman's proud demeanor. Unlike some of her other portraits, however, the artist had captured something in this one that didn't quite express mirth. It seemed as if something weighed heavily upon the Medici princess's mind. At the time of her portrait, Isabella could never have known how her life would end, but looking at her sad smile, Nora believed that perhaps she did.

Nora glanced to her left and saw Leonora, Isabella's cousin, next to her. An ordinary viewer would never have imagined that these two young women, dressed in velvet gowns with their hair caught up and entwined with pearls, were capable of carrying on clandestine affairs and throwing wild parties. But Nora knew full well the Medici cousins had certainly misbehaved.

With Isabella presiding over her Florentine court, her well-populated salons were rowdy and boisterous. Male and female guests often partnered in flirtatious dances or sang together, their hands caressing as they shared a single sheet of music. As the wine flowed freely, there were gambling and games of chance, as well as those that tested a partygoer's memory.

Some of the games would be known today, seemingly harmless in nature: charades and *"sosperi"* in which verbal messages were whispered from one person to another. But once the sun went down and the night progressed, as inhibitions lowered and with Isabella as the ringmaster, the games grew wilder.

Nora could well imagine the twinkle in the Medici princess's eyes as she introduced her party guests to the "game of slaves" in which male and female players would be "sold" into service to whoever wanted them most. If that became boring, she would invite them to play a game called "insanity" in which someone declared himself maddened by unrequited love, requesting to be locked up and well-tended by a willing female.

It was no wonder that Isabella and Leonora were a cause of concern to their husbands, as well as Francesco, the new Medici Duke. They were losing the upper hand, and their women were becoming an embarrassment. Something needed to be done to bring them to attention and let them know who was really in charge.

Not to be deterred and unafraid of the men and their blusterings, the unsuspecting women had continued on their merry way, never imagining they were kicking a hornet's nest and about to be stung.

Hearing the swishing of skirts and the tittering of laughter, Nora closed her eyes and drifted back to a fifteenth-century drawing room and relived an intimate conversation Isabella and Leonora might have had the morning before a party, preparing their naughty games for their enthusiastic and receptive guests.

"Isabella, because of your father's wishes, I came to Florence to marry Pietro. But, my goodness, he is an odd little man. When I first met him, he stared at me with such disdain. And now here it is three years after we have been married and he has yet to come to my bed."

Yawning widely, Isabella stood up and moved to the window. Looking down at the shrubbery in the gardens below, she said over her shoulder, "My dearest Leonora, think of that as a blessing. My brother has always been a bit slow. Even when we were children, I considered him a simpleton, and now he is no different."

With a dismissive wave of her hand, she continued, "He spends his time, like my husband, in the brothels, showering his mistresses with gifts bought with Medici money. My recommendation, dear cousin, is to do as I have done. Be content to live an independent life and take a lover of your own."

Leonora came up behind her and hugged her cousin around the waist. With a giggle, she said, "Isabella, tomorrow night at the party we must play that delightful game Signor Bellini invented last time we were all together."

Isabella turned around and kissed Leonora lightly on the cheek, then stepped back and regarded her quizzically. "And which one might that be, my sweet?"

"Ah, I believe you know the one," she said. "It's the one in which a guest is placed in a chair, and another who is blindfolded must use his hands to touch the other person to figure out who they are."

Waving her fan in front of her face to hide her blush, she boldly suggested, "Or better yet, we could play the French kissing game—*Le Baiser à la Capucine*—where instead of our hands, we must use our lips to guess who the person might be!"

Isabella tilted her head and considered her cousin's mischievous grin. "As you wish, my sweet, but perhaps you will like another I have just invented."

"And what might that be, pray tell?"

Taking a sip of wine, she said, "I am calling it the Game of Devil's Music. It is simple, really. Each of us must make the sound of an animal. Marcello makes the noise of a pig, Maria brays like a donkey. It is really quite diverting."

"And you, my love?" asked Leonora. "What animal will you be?"

"I will growl loud and long, like a lone wolf. He is a fierce beast and I will let them all know I am not afraid!" Isabella cried out.

"*That*, cousin, is why they call you the Star of Florence. You are simply brilliant and shine the brightest of them all. It frightens you not to growl at adversity and dare to live your life to the fullest, regardless of what anyone tells you. I so admire you."

"Yes, dearest. A life is wasted if not lived completely, or if one does not love well. But if truth be told, it is my creative pursuits that make me happiest. For it is when I am writing a verse or composing a song I am most content and fulfilled. So heed this advice, my sweet: Don't live in the shadow of another. Embrace your life, Leonora. Find what is most important to you and makes you the happiest and do it with great ardor."

Gradually, Nora opened her eyes and regarded Isabella thoughtfully. She studied princess' lovely features and then let her gaze drift from her beautiful face down her slim neck to the hand that delicately fingered a sensational necklace. The chain was made of intertwined strands of gold and clusters of rubies, and featured a misshapen opalescent pearl, stunning in its imperfection. She blinked, and when she glanced back at the portrait, it seemed the princess had lifted the necklace just a touch higher, holding it out for her inspection.

Nora took out a small notebook and sketched the design. As she drew, she felt the rush of creativity and shivered imperceptibly at the heady sensation. Looking at the drawing she had just completed, she was struck by a fantastic idea. The Star of Florence had once again whispered into her ear.

It had always been there, lying dormant and buried deep inside her, but hearing Isabella's words of encouragement, Nora now knew precisely what she needed to do.

Chapter 20

Portrait of Love

*F*illed with a new sense of urgency, Nora left Vasari's house, and when she was on the street, she pulled out her phone and called Juliette. Misdialing the number several times, she cursed under her breath. *"Cavolo."*

When the call finally went through, she couldn't contain the ideas and her words flooded out of her mouth.

"Hold on, slow down," Juliette said. "I can barely keep up with you."

"I know I'm not making much sense, I've got a thousand ideas in my head. Juli... *Oh, mio Dio*, you should see the jewelry those women used to wear. Wouldn't it be something to recreate those necklaces? Remember, like the ones I used to make in Florence?"

Juliette replied, "Yes, you've always had a gift with gold."

"Do you want to grab a bite to eat?" Nora asked. "I'm dying to talk to someone about my ideas."

The voice on the other end of the line sounded muffled, as if Juliette had put her hand over the receiver. Indistinctly, Nora could hear Marco's voice in the background.

When Juliette came back on the phone, she said, "That would be great, but some things have come up at the winery tonight..." She was interrupted again, and Nora could hear a smothered laugh, imagining perfectly well what those "things" might be. It was obvious to her they had nothing to do with grapes.

When Juliette spoke once again into the phone, asking for a rain check, Nora said, "Of course, I'm happy to be on my own. I can always find something to do."

Before she hung up, she said, "Be sure to give Marco a kiss from me."

Juliette laughed, realizing just how transparent she had been, and said, "Will do."

Nora tossed her phone back into her bag and looked up and down the street, thinking about what she would do next. Before she fully acknowledged where she was going, she found herself headed in the direction of Luca's shop.

When she entered his store, the bells over the door jingled. Hearing the sound, he glanced up briefly from signing papers that a delivery man had handed to him. When the *fattorino* left, Luca explained that the last of the crates had just arrived. "It's been one of those days. Problems on top of problems."

"For instance?" asked Nora.

"Well, for starters, one of the crates was delivered to the wrong place, and I was just clearing things up with the shipping company."

He continued to vent about his day, and then finally looked over at her and apologized. "I didn't mean to go on so long. Thanks for listening. It's great to see you again. To what do I owe this unexpected pleasure?"

"I was hoping to entice you to dinner tonight. We can drown your business worries in a glass of red wine and some pasta smothered in *cinghiale* sauce."

"*Ah, sì?*" he said, clearly tempted. "Well, I think I could be persuaded. But first I have a couple of things to do in the back. I just want to check the last box."

Nora followed him to the far end of the store where a pile of empty wooden boxes lay scattered about, and the floor was littered with loose straw. She observed with interest some of the pieces he had already uncrated, as well as a few paintings he had set against a far wall.

She hadn't been in the back room before and peeked around curiously at the clutter. There was a chair missing an arm and an armoire with broken moldings. On each wall, pictures were haphazardly hung. One, in particular, caught her attention. It was a painting of a female saint. Studying it in the dim evening light, she thought it particularly dismal.

Seeing her interest, Luca said, "That's been around here for years.

Ever since I can remember, it's hung in one place or another in the shop. It's something my grandfather painted. He was quite good at copying original masterpieces, but in my opinion, he did his best work in Paris."

Nora took a step closer to see it from a better angle. "Excuse me for saying so, but it is rather hideous. I can see why no one ever bought it."

Luca chuckled and said, "Oh, I won't take it personally. It *is* kind of dark and mystical. It is a picture of Santa Margherita of Cortona." Turning back to the crate, he added, "I think my grandmother kept it only for sentimental reasons—that and because Margherita was her patron saint."

"Do you see the dog at the saint's feet?" Nora asked, gesturing at the painting. "All saints have a symbol with which they can be identified. Like Santa Agata carries a plate of eyes because she was martyred by having hers poked out. And here's Saint Margherita, who has a little dog that represents fidelity."

Luca mumbled something she couldn't make out because he was bent over one of the large open crates. She watched a moment as he dug around inside, tossing the packing contents onto the floor. Seeing he was thoroughly occupied, she took the opportunity to continue snooping around the back room. When she heard him cry out: "Nora! *Guarda.* Check this out!" she turned around guiltily.

Curious, Nora stepped closer. When he threw an armful of straw in her direction, she jumped back in surprise. Spitting out pieces that had landed in her mouth, she retaliated by scooping up a handful of her own and throwing it back at him.

"*Mi arrendo!* Okay, I call a truce." Reaching into the box again, he drew out what appeared to be a small painting wrapped in thick paper and tied with string. "So far, from what I can tell, everything arrived safe and sound. I'm just starting to sort through and catalog things, but all in all, I'm quite pleased."

"What is that painting you just pulled out of the box?"

"I'm not sure," he said as he ripped away several layers of brown paper. As the painting was revealed, Nora saw it was a picture of a woman in a fifteenth-century-style dress standing in front of a musical instrument.

Next to her was a man seated in a chair, smoking a pipe.

"Ah, this is interesting," she said. "Look. This painting has a little dog too, and here again, he is a symbol of fidelity."

"And the spinet?" Luca asked.

"Well, it could be interpreted as either sacred or profane love, but the fact that the man sits with his legs widely spread, pointing his pipe directly at the woman, I'm going to say that it is a clear sign of lust."

She peered over her shoulder and saw she had Luca's full attention. Smiling, she continued, "But the key the woman holds represents true love. The painting is a message warning viewers to be faithful and not waste time romping around with a pretty woman in bed."

Luca laughed. "Well, there's nothing wrong with a roll in the hay now and then."

He ducked when she tossed another handful of straw in his direction. Brushing pieces off his shirt, he complimented her. "You're a sleuth when it comes to paintings. Very impressive."

Nora responded, "Well, research and fact finding—that is what I do for a living."

Pointing to a small piece of furniture in the painting, he asked, "And the chest of drawers, what do you make of that?"

Nora bent a little closer. "It reminds me of the treasure chests my dad used to make." She added coyly, "I would say that the lady has a secret. Perhaps she isn't as innocent as she appears."

"Really, now. What kind of secrets might they—?"

Luca was interrupted by the bell at the front of the shop. Hearing a familiar voice call out a greeting, Luca raised his own and said, *"Buonasera, Egidio! Come va?* Come join us. We are in the back room."

When an elderly gentleman crossed the threshold from the shop into the storeroom, Luca reached out a hand to shake his, then pulling him near, he gave him a warm embrace. Turning to Nora, he said, "Leonora, I'd like you to meet a family friend, Signor Michelozzi. Egidio and my grandmother went to school together. He and his sons make gold jewelry in a shop nearby. He is one of Arezzo's most talented jewelers."

"*Quanto mi lusinghi.* How you flatter me!" said Signor Michelozzi. "It's a pleasure to meet you, Leonora. I just stopped by to see if Luca would be attending the town meeting tomorrow. I hoped we could sit together."

"I think I can arrange that," said Luca. "In the afternoon, my schedule should be a bit more open. The shipment I was telling you about has arrived, and I've almost finished with unpacking it. It is proving to be quite a lucrative lot."

Pointing to the canvas they had just been talking about, he said, "Nora was explaining the iconography in this painting. Do you see the chest there next to the man with the pipe? Interestingly enough, she thought it contained secret drawers. She told me her dad used to make them too."

Signor Michelozzi smiled approvingly at Nora. "Well, my dear, it seems you have an eye for details. I too know a few things about secret compartments and hidden drawers. Here in Italy, we call them *cassetti dei segreti.* Back in the fifteenth-century, they were all the rage. They came in handy for concealing secret letters and whatnot."

With a bit of pride, he told her, "They have always been a fascination of mine. You know, there is quite an art to building one." To Luca, he said, "Do you remember the boxes and chests your Bisnonno used to hand-craft in the upper rooms of this shop?"

"Of course—to me, they are collector's pieces," said Luca.

Signor Michelozzi said a little indignantly, "When we made them, they were new and modern—and now, like me and most things, they are considered antiques."

Luca chuckled and cleaned up some of the loose straw, kicking it into a pile with his foot to be swept up later. Calling over his shoulder, he said, "Tell me, Egidio, how goes the Golden Lance?"

Clarifying for Nora, he said, "For each joust, Signor Michelozzi creates *la Lancia d'Oro*—the prize that is presented to the winning team. Egidio is currently working on the lance for the next event in September."

"Really? I'd love to see it. It sounds like you are a man of many talents:

woodworking and gold jewelry."

Fingering the necklace she was wearing, she added modestly, "I too have an interest in jewelry design. I made this piece several years ago. I worked with Signor Martelli in Florence. I did a brief apprenticeship with him."

"*Ah, si?* I know Martelli's work. He is a friend and a colleague."

Adjusting his glasses, Egidio leaned over and studied the delicate pendant nestled in the hollow of her throat. "It seems, Leonora, you too have many hidden talents. This is quite lovely, and the craftsmanship is exquisite."

Pleased by his reaction, she said, "May I show you something else?" Digging into her bag, Nora withdrew her sketchbook and flipped back the pages to reveal the necklace she had sketched earlier in Vasari's house. "I just did this drawing this afternoon. It is a pendant that Isabella de' Medici wears in one of her paintings."

The old man looked at her thoughtfully. "Perhaps we should spend some time getting to know each other better. Do you have time, say this Saturday, to stop by my studio? I'll show you the lance I'm working on and I can show you around my studio. Don't forget to bring more of your designs to show me."

"Be careful what you ask for, I'm always sketching and have hundreds of ideas."

"Excellent. *Brava!* Well, bring some of your sketchbooks and let's have a little chat on Saturday." As Michelozzi took his leave, he called over his shoulder, "Luca, I'll see you tomorrow."

When the door closed, Nora turned back to Luca, and she saw that he was observing her with clear amusement. "What? What's so funny, now?"

"If you must know, I'm a little jealous of Michelozzi. He walks in here, and after only ten minutes crooks his fingers, just mentions the words 'gold' and 'jewelry' and presto! He has a new girlfriend!"

Nora rolled her eyes.

"Well, I can't blame the old guy," Luca added. "He has quite good taste, it appears, in jewelry and women."

"Oh, please," she said. "He's just being nice. I'm sure he has a million other things to do than look at my designs..."

"Don't sell yourself short, Nora." Looking at the design she had just drawn, he said, "This is remarkable. I think it is a splendid idea for the two of you to get together. He's also been a bit lonely since the death of his wife, so he could use a cheering up."

Turning out the lights, he added, "So many funerals lately—first *nonna*, then Signora Michelozzi, Antonio, my mentor and coach—and then Carlotta..." He hesitated but didn't continue.

Nora waited for a few moments, hoping he might say something more. Instead, he shuffled a few papers, cleared the counter, then locked up the cash register. Then looking at her, he asked, "So, where do you want to eat?"

Later that evening, after dinner at a trattoria near Piazza Grande made more relaxing by several glasses of wine, Nora and Luca strolled through the upper part of town. A cool evening breeze blew, but the stones they walked upon and the buildings around them still radiated warmth from the late July sun.

Nora turned her face up to the inky blue sky and saw a full moon was on the rise. "Look at that," she said. "I've never seen the moon so heavy and full. It is splendid. I think they call that a *superluna*. They say anything can happen on a night like this."

"Really? Did you have anything specific in mind?" Luca asked.

"It doesn't work like that," she said, glancing at him provocatively. "It has to be utterly spontaneous, you see. When you least expect it—boom! *Magia*. Something magical happens."

Luca looked at her speculatively, considering her words. "*Ah, sì*? Is that how it works? *Un po' di magia?*" Smiling, he gestured to the steep steps in front of the church, inviting her to sit for a moment. Leaning back in contented silence, they continued to admire the silhouette of the cathedral, illuminated by the ghostly light. In the distance, Nora could hear the baying of a dog and the whine of a motorbike.

After a moment, he said, "Did you know right here in the Piazza del Duomo they created movie magic? This is where they filmed one of the scenes from Benigni's movie?"

"I remember it well," said Nora. "It was the scene when he throws out the endless red carpet so that his leading lady can descend the stairs without stepping in puddles. It was raining hard in the scene."

"They actually manufactured that rainstorm. The film crew brought in huge water trucks to make it seem like it was a full-on deluge."

"Really? So did you see the filming?"

"No, I was away at the time in Rome, but many of the locals around here got bit parts as extras. Everyone was quite thrilled when it won a couple of Oscars."

Slowly standing up, he looked down at her. *"Sei pronta, principessa? Are you ready to go?"*

Taking hold of his hand, she let him pull her up. They stood for a moment and regarded one another thoughtfully. Then, as gallant as Cary Grant ever was, Luca offered her his arm. She readily accepted, thinking his grandmother had taught him well. Together they walked arm and arm down the street, each contemplating their own private thoughts.

When they reached Nora's building, Luca turned on a light in the entryway that was set on a timer, giving the occupants just enough time to unlock their doors before the hallway returned to darkness. He escorted her to her apartment on the third floor, where Nora stopped and dug around for her key ring. Holding it up to the light, searching for the right one, she inserted it into the lock. It didn't work.

"You'd think I'd know which one to use by now, but I always seem to choose the wrong one."

She held up the bunch again to see better, but the automatic light blinked off. Temporarily blind, she dropped the entire ring, which clattered noisily onto the stone floor. *"Accidenti! Cavolo."*

At the same moment, they each bent down, and in the dark, they bumped into one another. Nora swayed slightly off balance, and Luca reached out a hand to steady her. Fumbling around in the dark for the missing keys, their hands met.

"*Eccole,*" he said. "Got them."

Leaning into each other for support, they slowly rose up together.

"Luca... *Dammi le chiavi*—give me the keys," Nora said with a laugh, reciting another memorable line from the movie.

He held them out and jangled them slightly, and when she reached out to take them, he continued to hold them, causing her to glance up. When she did, she was caught by the gleam in his eye, barely discernible in the moonlight. Her heart quickened as they stood for a moment in the shadows studying one another. Then, placing his hand at the nape of her neck, the keys now forgotten, he drew her closer, and they kissed.

Their interlude was cut short, however, as the hall light flashed on again and she heard her neighbor Salvatore thundering down the stairs. As he passed by, he waved good evening to them, calling out, "*Ciao, Nora!* I'm going to the bar to meet up with friends, see you later."

Disoriented, as if the world had suddenly spun off its track, Nora stepped back, feeling a flush rising from her neck to her forehead. Distractedly she pulled the keys from Luca's hand and, picking what she hoped was the right one, she jammed it into the lock. With a gentle click, this time the door swung open. Turning around to face Luca, she paused, again arrested by his magnetic expression.

He slowly traced his finger along the line of her jaw and over her lips. "*Buonanotte, principessa...* It has been a wonderful evening, but I have to tell you I'd much rather be standing in this very spot wishing you *buongiorno* tomorrow morning..."

She looked at him, realizing she too didn't want the evening to end. Feeling Isabella give her a small push from behind, she took Luca's hand and pulled him into her room, kicking the door shut with her foot. There, bathed in the light of the *superluna*, on a night when anything could happen, she wrapped her arms around his shoulders, and they gave into the magic.

Chapter 21

Urlo alla Luna

A few days later, out at Marco's winery, Nora gazed out over the fields of maturing grapes. The air still smelled of summer and a purple mist clouded the horizon just where the sky melted into the distant turquoise valley. Raising her wine glass, she said, "Just look at this place! *È bellissimo,* it's simply gorgeous. I can't believe this is where you work. I don't think I'd ever get anything done with this view distracting me all day."

"I hate to admit it, but I've grown used to it." Juliette turned to Nora and grinned. "No, I'm lying. It never gets old. It *is* beautiful here."

Earlier that afternoon, Nora had driven the winding roads to reach the winery located in the hills surrounding Arezzo about ten minutes outside of town. After her arrival, Marco and Juliette had given her the grand tour, showing her the modern facility he had built, which integrated seamlessly with the natural landscape. Inside, the entrance was decorated with wood beams and large canvases of contemporary art, and toward the back were the corporate offices and a large kitchen. The most spectacular aspect of the place was the tasting room, which boasted an entire wall of glass that showcased the valley below.

As they walked back through the ripening fields of grapes, Nora let her hand trail along the dusty leaves, revealing the heavy clusters hidden beneath. On a whim, she gave her phone to Marco and told him to take a picture. Standing arm and arm with Juliette, she held up a bunch of grapes, posing as if she were about to eat the entire succulent bunch.

Juliette pulled off a couple of grapes and gave one to her to try. Nora closed her eyes, enjoying the sensation of the warm, sweet liquid that exploded in her mouth like a burst of sunshine. Juliette tossed one high into the air for Marco to catch. She laughed when he missed, and the grape bounced off his forehead. "Here, try again," she called, throwing him another.

"In just a few weeks, the *vendemmia*—the fall harvest—will be in full swing," she told Nora. "That's when things will get very busy for us. This is the lull before the main event, so to speak."

Marco surveyed his property proudly. "Originally, my family came from a long line of *contadini*. They were farmers who tilled the land. The property has been in the family for generations." Pointing out over the horizon, he added, "They owned everything on this side of the hill and just a bit beyond."

"So the Orlando family goes all the way back to the days of the Etruscans?"

"Well, I don't know about that," he said with a grin, "but it's been in the family a long time. Someone has always been on this hill growing one thing or another—or at least up until the war, that is. This area got hit hard with bombs. The ridge over there was the German line. When we replanted the fields, we found shells all over the place."

"Ehi, Nora," called Juliette. "See this?"

Nora swung around and saw her friend gesturing to a large planter at the entrance of the parking lot. "When Marco and the workers began digging up the bombs, we decided to turn them into art."

"I like that," said Nora. "Turning something ugly into something beautiful."

Turning back to Marco, she asked, "So what happened to your family after the war?"

"Things were pretty much a mess back then. It took years to reconstruct the city."

"Did your family go back to farming?"

"No, after my folks moved into town, they found jobs doing other things. The land here was abandoned for the most part. Still, my dad didn't have the heart to sell it. He put a large *orto*, a vegetable garden, and I used to ride out with my grandfather in his truck, and I'd help him with the heavy lifting and digging. It was during those hot afternoons he would tell me family stories, and he is the one that made me appreciate this piece of land."

Marco gazed out over the valley. "You know, Luca and I used to come up here and camp when we were kids. We were a bit wilder back then, and of course, there was Carlotta, too."

At the mention of the woman's name, Nora asked, "Yes, what about Carlotta?"

"We were much younger back then and did a lot of stupid things. We used to gather kindling and light it on fire, drink wine, and tell ghost stories. When it got really late, we would let off bottle rockets, sing, and howl at the moon. It was the kind of crazy stuff kids do."

Juliette laughed. "I can only imagine you and Luca getting drunk way out here, back in the good old days."

Marco shrugged. "Well, as I said, we were all much stupider then. But that's why I decided to call this place 'Urlo alla luna'. It means 'I howl at the moon'. Did I ever tell you that before, Juli?"

"Yes, only a hundred times. But I still think it's fabulous."

Nora waited for Marco to return to the subject of Carlotta and the good old days, but once again it seemed that Marco was sidestepping the issue. Carlotta—their so-called "childhood friend"—was starting to annoy her. What was it about her that made both Luca and Marco become evasive at the mention of her name?

In an attempt to turn the conversation back to his younger days, Nora asked, "So, you, Luca, and Carlotta were pretty tight back then, right? What happened to everyone?"

"After *liceo* Luca went off to university, I stayed here and messed around..." Marco stopped. He picked up a twig and snapped it in two. Then shrugging his shoulders, he said, "I guess I finally realized I had to face reality, grow up, and get on with my life. So, I thought, why not grow grapes? I kind of felt I owed it to my grandfather, too."

He launched the mutilated twig over the cliff and wiped his hands. Turning back to Nora, he said, "As they say, once a *contadino*, always a *contadino*. And the rest is history. End of story."

Her ploy hadn't worked. Nora watched in exasperation as he grabbed Juliette's hand and said, "One of the best things I've ever done was hiring this girl. Juli has been a godsend. She has saved me more than once."

Juliette said, "Trust me, he can't plan his way out of a paper bag. He'd probably be in jail if it weren't for me."

"*Meno male ci sei tu.* Thank goodness you are here," Marco said and kissed her. "*Amore mio,* I'm going to leave you two alone for now. I've some appointments in town—but never fear, I opened a bottle in the tasting room for you to enjoy. *Mi raccomando. Divertitevi!* Relax and enjoy yourselves."

Juliette and Nora needed no further encouragement and promptly did as he suggested, pouring two glasses of one of the winery's most beautiful blends. Then, settling into wooden armchairs on the lawn, they relaxed and enjoyed the view.

Nora took a sip of wine and savored the flavor, letting it roll around in her mouth before swallowing. Hearing Marco's car rev and skid on the gravel in the parking lot, she said, "It appears you found *your* piece of paradise."

Juliette gave her a meaningful look. "Well, seems to me you might have found a bit of your own around these parts. I know someone else who is especially warming to your charms."

Nora raised an eyebrow and grinned a bit wickedly. "Well, let's just say we aren't just discussing antiques anymore." Leaning over, she clinked her glass with Juliette's.

"You know," Juliette said, "I originally came to the winery thinking I'd only stay for the summer. It hadn't been my plan to stay too long. I was here initially just to do a bit of consulting. Remember back in Florence? My goal was to manage a prestigious wine retailer in a big city."

She glanced over her shoulder at the winery building. "And now here I am instead. Stuck in this start-up winery. There is dirt perpetually on my face, and my nails are forever broken. My job is basically paying vendor bills and answering silly client questions."

Letting out a low groan, she lamented, "Can you imagine people actually ask stupid things like, 'Why don't you sell Bordeaux wines?' Seriously? We are in Italy, and people come here looking for French wines? And talk about traveling—what travel? I make an occasional trip to Florence, or once in a blue moon I go to Rome, but even then it's just for work. For the most part, I'm stuck on this hill and have to deal with Marco's *mamma*."

She took another sip of wine and said, "You haven't met her yet. She is quite a character —regularly shows up on our doorstep bringing baked pasta dishes, telling me I need to eat more."

Arching her back, Juliette pushed out her stomach. "Can you believe this? I can barely zip my jeans."

Nora laughed and said, "You silly girl, you're as thin as a rail. But I'm happy for you that you've found work you like as well as someone like Marco, even if he comes with a *mamma* who pops up announced. Despite your complaining, I think you're doing just fine."

Juliette raised herself up on an elbow and said, "Do you want to hear something crazy?" When Nora gestured with her glass to continue, she said, "When I sent you that friend request on Facebook, I have to admit I was quite impressed, and visiting your page made me jealous."

Nora shot her a dumbfounded look.

"I know it's stupid but, when I read you were newly divorced, living in California, near San Francisco, and an assistant at Stanford University... Well, I imagined you had finally figured everything out and had the perfect single life."

"Funny. I had similar thoughts when I scrolled through your feed," said Nora. "I couldn't help but compare my life with yours, and truthfully, mine just didn't stack up. Your friend request put into motion so many things, and it made me reevaluate my entire life and every decision I ever made. I have a little confession to make."

"Such as...?" Juliette asked.

"I was particularly intrigued by one of the pictures you posted."

"Really? Which one?"

"You know... The one of you standing between Marco and Luca. It was taken out here somewhere about a year ago."

Juliette thought for a moment. "I remember now. That was taken last year during the harvest. Now *that* was a great day. We were all feeling so happy and relaxed. That was the day I got to know Luca a lot better. Before that, he hadn't been out to the winery much. It seems he and Marco had a falling out a couple of years ago, and get this, it was over a woman."

"Was it Carlotta who came between them? It had to be."

When Juliette bobbed her head in confirmation, Nora mused, "From the first day I arrived, I could sense something was a little off between them. But no one wants to talk about her. When her name is mentioned, Luca goes *muto come un pesce*—mute as a fish—and Marco is always changing the subject."

"Apparently the three of them—Luca, Marco, and Carlotta—were best friends once upon a time. From what I gather, though, things changed when they got older. Seems Carlotta dated both of them at one time or another."

Swatting away a mosquito, Nora said, "I kind of imagined that was what happened. Nothing louses up a great friendship faster than a love triangle." Propping up the cushions in her chair to make herself more comfortable, she leaned over and asked, "So, what else do you know?"

"Well, let's see... Carlotta was the granddaughter of Ruggero. I'm sure you've seen the old guy around town."

"Yes, I've had the pleasure of making his acquaintance. He doesn't seem to like Luca very much."

"That's an understatement," said Juliette. "I asked Marco about it, but he didn't have a whole lot to say. When I couldn't get more out of him, I turned to his sister Mariella. When she gets bored, she can get rather chatty. One afternoon, out here scrubbing down wine barrels, I got quite an earful."

"You clever girl, I knew there was a reason I liked you. What did she tell you?"

"For starters, she said the old man holds Luca accountable for his granddaughter's death."

Warmed by the wine, Nora encouraged her, "Go on."

Needing no further prompting, Juliette began with a bit of backstory, telling Nora that at the age of seven, Carlotta lost her mother to cancer, and later the same year, her father had been killed in a hunting accident. For a couple of years, Carlotta had been parceled out to various family members, and after a series of misadventures—it seemed the girl tended to act out—had ultimately been taken in by her grandparents.

"Poor thing. What a nightmare. It must have been quite a trauma losing both parents, one right after the other. At least she had her grandparents to help her through her grief."

"Yes, but according to Mariella, they let her do whatever she pleased. Ruggero was especially guilty of buying Carlotta expensive things. She was spoiled rotten and totally *pazza*—crazy as a loon. Well, that's how Mariella described her. The three of them were free spirits. Always getting into trouble—reprimanded by their teachers for some stupid stunt or another."

Pushing her sunglasses to the top of her head, Juliette said, "They were boys, after all, and Carlotta apparently was a tomboy. From what I gather, though, she's the one that called most of the shots. As a kid, she was always egging them on. She didn't know when to stop and was always pushing the limits. It was all fun and games until they hit the teenage years."

"Let me guess," said Nora. "She went from rough and tumble classmate to alluring vixen overnight. Probably had a sensational figure, too. Am I right?"

"According to Mariella, that about sums it up. Apparently, she was really pretty—*una bella ragazza*. You know—long straight hair, perfect cheekbones, and a great figure," Juliette said.

Hearing that, Nora rolled her eyes and couldn't help but groan to learn her predecessor had been such a knockout. She had been afraid of that. "*Semplicemente fantastica*. Great. Just great. With each passing minute, I'm starting to like Carlotta less and less," she said morosely.

Juliette laughed at her exaggerated reaction. "Well, you can just imagine, can't you, how those two reacted? For that matter, how any red-blooded boy would react when faced with such a dramatic transformation! Up until then, Luca and Marco had mainly been interested in the typical stuff: horses, watching the jousters practice, and pranking their teachers. But when they turned eighteen, and both became jousters themselves, they started seeing Carlotta through a different lens."

Reaching for the bottle, she poured out more wine. "Here, drink up. You're going to need it to get through this story. Come to think of it, I need another splash, as it involves Marco, too."

"So how did it play out?" Nora asked. "In the beginning, who chased after who first?"

"Turns out it was Carlotta who first set her sights on Luca. Luca's team was on a winning streak, and all the girls were crazy for him. She was super possessive and wanted to steal him away and keep him all for herself."

Nora took a sip of her wine. "So that's when they decided to get married?"

"Oh, we are just at the beginning of the story," said Juliette, settling back in her chair. "When Luca went away to Rome to study at the university, Carlotta got bored and didn't lose any time hooking up with Marco. From what I gather, they were pretty serious, but it all changed when Luca returned home for good. It took only two seconds before Carlotta dumped Marco and started running after Luca all over again."

"That seems rather cruel," said Nora.

"I know," agreed Juliette. "From what Mariella told me, Carlotta was a tease but also a hopeless romantic. She was intrigued by Luca's stories of Rome and wanted to travel and see the world. It also didn't hurt that Luca had a good job, was making great money, and traveled for business. So that's when they decided to get married."

"Luca told me that Ruggero was once his grandmother's fiancé, but she threw him over for another man. Is that why he doesn't like him?"

"No, actually at first, he approved of the marriage. Seems he still carried a bit of a torch for Margherita Donati, but by then he had forgiven her, and it was all *acqua passata*—water under the bridge."

"So why and when did Ruggero turn against Luca?" asked Nora.

"Well, here's the thing," said Juliette. "At first, it seemed to everyone in town that Luca and Carlotta were the picture of a happily married couple. After a few years, however, that image faded. Carlotta got bored when the reality of marriage set in. She didn't want to stay in Arezzo. She wanted to move to Rome."

"That makes no sense. She knew Luca's family antique business was here," said Nora. "She really thought she could pry him away from Arezzo, a town he obviously loves very much?"

"He tried to please her, and even took her with him sometimes to Paris or London, but things didn't turn out so well. Carlotta ran hot and cold and embarrassed him in front of clients. She craved attention and knew men found her attractive, and she capitalized on that. It fueled her ego, but in the end, it had a disastrous effect on their marriage."

Juliette filled her in on a couple of particularly juicy incidents that Mariella had told her about. "It was about that time their real problems set in. Luca stopped taking her with him on his trips, but cooling her heels in a small apartment in town wasn't doing it for her. She constantly harped about buying a big house with a pool in the country, where they could keep horses. At that point, she also began running up lots of debt—buying expensive clothes and jewelry, things like that."

"What did Luca do then?" asked Nora.

"He put his foot down and cautioned her to stop. When that happened, Carlotta turned to Ruggero for money. Instead of the horses and a house in the country, he bought her a red Ferrari and an apartment in Rome, just off the Piazza di Spagna."

"Apparently," she continued, "the woman was obsessed with that red car of hers and got off on its speed."

"Bet that didn't sit well with Luca," said Nora. "She sounds high-strung. Pretty unstable."

"I asked Marco about that once," said Juliette. "All I got out of him was that Carlotta had a few emotional issues."

"A few emotional issues! Maybe it runs in the family because when I first met Ruggero, he seemed pretty nutty to me."

"Marco did say Luca tried to get her help, but Carlotta didn't want anything to do with treatments or therapy. Eventually, she just wore Luca down. When he realized he couldn't do anything more for her, he finally asked Carlotta for a divorce."

"Divorce? He's never mentioned that to me. After telling him about mine, you would think he would have opened up and told me about his," said Nora. "So how did she actually die? What happened? There was an accident of some sort..."

"She was killed in her car coming home from one of her party weekends. Mariella told me she lost control in a thunderstorm and slid into the oncoming lane where she ran smack into a truck. It was after her death Luca and Marco stopped talking and parted ways for almost a year. After I got here, they started gradually working things... Over time, things have gotten a lot better."

"And Ruggero?" Nora asked.

"Mariella says that after the accident, he just snapped. He criticized Luca for not keeping his granddaughter safe and off the road that night, blaming him for her death. It was soon after the funeral he began punishing Luca in public, saying rude things to his face and spreading false rumors."

"Obviously, the old man was devastated by grief—but, really, wasn't he the one to buy her that car, and didn't he get her that apartment in Rome?" asked Nora. "Seems he is partially to blame himself."

"Could be," said Juliette. "It certainly seems the pain of remorse is still there and he is looking for a scapegoat."

The girls were quiet for a moment, then Juliette glanced over at Nora and said, "I don't believe this... So, take it with a grain of salt" She took a sip of wine before continuing. "Mariella told me some things she overheard after the funeral. I gather she was there in a chapel after everyone else had gone home. Luca was in the front, and she overheard him say some things in front of the altar."

"Things? What things?" asked Nora.

"According to Mariella, by the tone of his voice and his actions that day, and every day after her passing—she thinks Luca has never gotten over her. She told me she believes Carlotta was the love of his life and that he is still haunted by her memory."

And there it was, the thing that Nora had started to wonder about. Was she, and would she always be, competing with a beautiful ghost?

Chapter 22

A Golden Passion

*A*s Nora pondered the story of Carlotta, she felt a little guilty for gleaning information from second—well, really—third-hand sources and not from Luca himself. It troubled her that he hadn't been the one to talk to her directly about his wife. After her conversation with Juliette, she tried to broach the topic with him several times. Her efforts, however, had been met with stoic silence. He continued to be uncommunicative about the life he had shared with a woman who had been a whirlwind force of nature.

Standing in her bedroom in front of the mirror, Nora assessed her appearance and wondered how she stacked up to Carlotta's beauty. The woman reflected back at her was average height with symmetrical features and long wavy hair, and she could only guess what Luca saw when he looked at her.

She had a pretty good idea, but they hadn't precisely expressed sentiments of undying love, although they had become a lot closer. *Well, actually, incredibly intimate,* she thought, warmly recalling the previous night. Their moments together were intoxicating and lying entwined together in the darkness afterward was as equally gratifying, caressing one another with words and heated kisses.

Yet among those words, there had been no promises or commitments. Neither one had dared move beyond the present moment or entertained thoughts of what would happen to them in a month's time. Perhaps neither wanted their hearts to be trampled upon, or maybe it was just all too soon. Yet, deep inside her was the niggling concern that Marco's sister was correct in her assumption and that Luca would never get over his dead wife's memory. Was she setting herself up for failure?

What does it matter, anyway? Nora told herself. She would be returning to California in a couple of weeks, and most likely living on two separate continents would put an end to their *storia d'amore.*

And yet... Nora thought as she picked up the note he had written that morning. She had been incredibly groggy but still felt him brush the hair off her face and kiss her before slipping off to take care of an early consignment. When she eventually rolled out of bed, she found his note on the table propped up next to her coffee cup. She smiled at the thought of him as she studied his strong, decisive handwriting: *"Buongiorno, principessa! I really wanted to wake you... but you looked so beautiful sleeping. Ci vediamo più tardi. See you later."*

Folding his letter in half, she placed it inside the drawer by her bed. In spite of her misgivings, deep inside her another voice whispered. It told her something profound and beautiful was happening between them, and she harbored the hope that this little voice spoke the truth.

But aside from the attraction she felt for Luca, since her arrival in Italy, other sentiments just as meaningful were awakening. Just the other day, when she had visited Vasari's house and stood in front of Isabella's portrait, something clicked in her head. Looking at the Medici princess's necklace had been a pivotal moment, and at that instant, she made a decision almost as definitive as when she decided to separate from her husband.

To some, resigning from a well-paying job at a prestigious university to enter into the field of jewelry design might seem crazy, but at this point in her life, it was now or never. Empowered by the stories of Isabella and Margherita, she decided it was time for her, too, to start writing hers more boldly and expressively.

To help her turn the page and begin the next chapter, what she needed now was advice and a bit of direction from an expert. Fortunately, someone who could help her had presented himself the other day—Luca's friend, Signor Michelozzi.

The following Saturday at the appointed hour, she rang the bell of his shop. But instead of Signor Michelozzi, a man about her age greeted her, introducing himself as Carlo, the jeweler's grandson. He ushered her into a showroom lined with glass cases displaying necklaces, rings, and pins.

"Just one moment, I'll let my grandfather know you are here. He's been expecting you."

Before he could turn around, Egidio walked through the door. "Leonora, I'm so glad you are here. I've been looking forward to seeing you again. Let me start by showing you some of our work."

He opened a cabinet and drew out velvet trays, placing them on top of the counter. Picking up a necklace with an ornate design, Nora questioned him about how he had crafted the delicately etched design and applied the gold beadwork, further probing him about the tools he had used.

Seeing she was quite knowledgeable and delighted by her questions, Egidio said, "*Vieni*. Come with me. Instead of describing how this was made, let me show you."

Together they walked through a door at the back of the shop that led into the studio. Scattered about the room were sizeable wooden drafting tables outfitted with ring clamps and vises. Seated at one of the stations, a man in his late fifties was working with a small torch, melting a tiny nugget of gold. When he saw her, he turned down the burner and lifted his glasses. "*Ciao!*"

Egidio said, "This is Pietro, my oldest son. *Lui è il capo.* He's taken over the family business and runs things now. Of course, I can't stay away, but my eyes aren't what they used to be. I prefer to work with wood these days. We are training Carlo together, but he has more of a head for business and not design, so I still help out from time to time."

Picking up his reading glasses, he sat down on a stool and reached for the piece he was currently working on. Nora watched in fascination as he reheated the metal and then, with a small tool, worked the surface. She noted how, by using his pincers, he delicately fused tiny beads of metal onto the surface of the medallion. "This is a technique used by the ancient Etruscans, did you know that?"

Nora nodded, watching in fascination as he worked the small metal piece. When Signor Michelozzi noticed her eagerness to take over, he motioned for her to take a seat next to him. Without hesitation, Nora accepted his invitation. Following his lead, she made little cut marks in the soft metal to which she applied the small beads. Soon she was deep in concentration and barely felt him touch her lightly on the shoulder.

"*Aspetta*. Hold on a minute. Let me show you a little trick. Hold your file in your hand like this and tilt the pendant... *cosi*." Returning the piece to her, he said, "Now try again."

After a few moments, Nora glanced up and caught him studying her. "I'm starting to get the hang of it. What do you think?"

"*Brava!* I can see you are a natural. Keep going."

Nora worked a few more minutes and, realizing she was being a bit rude to focus entirely on the gold in front of her and not the man beside her, she asked, "So, you have always lived in Arezzo?"

"*Oh, sì!* I learned all this from my father, Corrado." Gesturing to his son, he said, "It makes a man proud to have family around him who want to carry on the family traditions. For that, yes, I am fortunate. I was also lucky in love. It's been a good life, and I have no complaints."

"I'm so sorry about your wife. Luca told me she passed away recently."

Egidio smiled sadly. "*Sì, mi manca la mia Benedetta.* I miss my wife."

"How did you two meet?" she asked.

"It was 1949, several years after the war ended when my future wife arrived in Arezzo from Florence on the train. As I recall, she was here visiting a cousin, and I was at the station because my father Corrado had sent me on some errand to Florence."

He pushed his glasses to the top of his head and said, "I was just about to board a train going in the opposite direction, but as I passed by the open train compartment, I happened to notice this girl who was struggling to free her skirt, which had become caught in the door as it slid shut."

"What did you do then?" asked Nora.

"Well, what *could* I do? I rushed over and picked up her case and reached out to help her down the stairs. Holding her gloved hand and looking into her eyes for the first time, I knew she was someone I wanted to get to know better." Winking at Nora, he added, "Seeing a bit of her shapely leg when her skirt was caught in the door didn't hurt either."

On the other side of the studio, Egidio's son Pietro groaned. "*Dai, papà!* How many times have we heard that story?"

Nora smiled over at Pietro. To Egidio, she said, "Well, *I* think it is a lovely story." Motioning for him to hand her the tiny torch so she could heat the metal a little more, she commented, "I can see you take much pride in your designs. It's so lovely to see. So many things are mass-produced these days. Understanding more fully what you do here, well, I think it must be very satisfying work."

"Are you not happy working at the university in California? Making a documentary is no small thing, *vero*? You must take pride in that?"

"Yes, yes, I do. My work is fine, and research at times can be fascinating. But the world of academia, well—well, it is just so *academic*! It's just different. Writing can be quite creative, and this film, it's been a lot of work but very rewarding at the same time."

Holding up the gold piece she was working on, she examined it intently, then continued, "But when I'm thinking about a piece I want to design, and I'm actually handling precious metals, it's an entirely different feeling. I get so involved in the process, I don't even notice time passing. That's when you know you love what you do."

Egidio said encouragingly, "*Sì, mia cara,* I can see you are *un'artista* and have real passion for the work."

"You know, I brought some things to show you," said Nora. "Would you still like to see them?"

Signor Michelozzi took the sketchbook and turned the pages. "Molto bello. Very beautiful, not only are you a talented goldsmith—*una brava orafa*—but you have a gift for design, too."

He stood up and motioned for her to follow him. "Come. Perhaps you can help me with something else I'm working on. I need some fresh ideas."

Following him, Nora stepped into an adjacent room, similar to the other, but this one was filled with odd bits of wood, and the floor was carpeted with curly shavings. Taking a deep breath, Nora could smell the fragrant scent of freshly cut cypress. On the far side of the room, several lances leaned against the wall.

Glancing up, Nora noticed a bulletin board that hung over the workbench covered with pictures and old newspaper clippings. She saw many images of Signor Michelozzi shaking the hand of the mayor as they stood next to one of the lances he had carved. In several of the pictures, she could also see the smiling faces of the jousters, still dressed in their medieval costumes, holding up their lances.

"These pictures are wonderful. Look at all the lances you have designed," exclaimed Nora. "Each one is so unique and unusual."

"*Certo*, of course, each lance has a different motif or is dedicated to a special person or an event. You should have Luca take you to the Santo Spirito headquarters where they keep all the Golden Lances they have won over the years. I'm sure you know by now he won six of them. Among them was one I created to honor Giuseppe Verdi, the great Italian musician, and another to celebrate Garibaldi, the general who united Italy."

Leaning in, Nora studied the yellowed newspaper clippings more carefully. "Well, well, well. I recognize that jouster! That's him, right there? That's Luca seated on his horse in his medieval costume."

"*Sì, hai ragione,*" said Egidio. "He was very talented, and an excellent rider. They used to say he had a gift for talking to the horses."

"Look how young he was. Is this him in this picture, too?" asked Nora, pointing to a photo of Luca standing next to a man with wavy white hair. In the photo, he stood with his arm draped around the other man's shoulders, and both appeared to be sharing a joke. "And who is the older man?"

Egidio adjusted his glasses again and peered over to get a better look. "That is Antonio Giorgeschi. He was one of Arezzo's finest horsemen and coaches. He died several years ago from pneumonia. It was unfortunate, and a tragic loss for all of us in Arezzo. He was the one who first taught

Luca to ride a horse. The two of them were very close. When he was a teenager, Luca was a bit of a loose cannon. He was about to go off the deep end at one point, but Giorgeschi was a good influence on him and pulled him out of trouble. His coaching had a lot to do with grounding the boy, not only for Luca but others as well."

Signor Michelozzi pointed to another photo of a lance that featured a carved likeness of the coach. "To commemorate Antonio's memory, last year I designed a lance for him. I thought it the least I could do to honor the man, as well as an entire generation of men he had coached."

Shaking his head, he continued, "Yes, it was a terrible loss for the town, and Antonio's death hit Luca hard, following so closely on that of his grandmother, and then his wife, Carlotta."

"Did you know her well?" Self-consciously she corrected herself. "Carlotta, I mean? Well, of course, you must have known her. I'm sorry to be so direct or pry into things that aren't my business. It's just... Well, Luca doesn't talk about her much, and I've only heard a few bits and pieces, just rumors from other people."

Egidio regarded her sympathetically. "Carlotta was a beautiful girl, but looks can sometimes be deceiving. She was quite a handful, and certainly gave Luca a run for his money."

Nora regarded him thoughtfully, and when he saw he hadn't sufficiently answered her question, Egidio said, "Luca went through some difficult times for a while. Now I'll leave it at that. He will tell you his side of things in good time, but I think it will be sooner than later. During the last few weeks, a welcome change has come over him. I see a new light in his eyes."

He patted her shoulder affectionately. "At first, I wasn't sure who or what to attribute that to—now perhaps I do."

Nora was pleased by his words. Glancing around the room, she noticed several cabinets in various stages of completion. "Are those the famous chests that contain the hidden drawers?"

"They are indeed. I'm teaching Carlo the craft, so he can pass it on to his children. We've made several together already, and he is proving to be very adept at building these chests. He's just like my father, Corrado. My grandson even resembles him."

Signor Michelozzi looked at her mischievously. "I know you said your father back in California used to make similar secret chests. I invite you to try your hand at opening one."

"I warn you, I'm pretty good at this. He tried very hard, but my dad never could outsmart me."

"So you think you know the tricks of an Italian master carpenter, too? You think you can unlock this *cassetti dei segreti*?"

Nora simply smiled, accepting his challenge. After examining the piece for a moment, she pushed and slid the small hidden sections in the molding. As she did, she could hear a series of clicks. *This is child's play,* she thought, and deftly solved the puzzle. Soon, a small drawer at the bottom popped open.

She looked up at the older gentleman, and he smiled approvingly. "*Complimenti!* Well done, my dear. It seems you do indeed have a knack for solving mysteries and puzzles. This has certainly been a delightful and enlightening afternoon. It is a shame you have to return home so soon."

"Yes, it's starting to make me sad, too." Caressing the top of the wooden chest, she added, "But I am also rather excited because I've made a rather big decision. Like this chest with secret drawers, I've been keeping something precious inside—something I've wanted to do for years."

Nora glanced over at Michelozzi. "And, really, it's another one of the reasons I wanted to meet you today. I need someone knowledgeable to talk to—someone who can help me unlock it and bring it out of hiding. Can I steal a little more of your precious time and ask you for some advice?"

"This does sound rather intriguing," he said. "*Allora...* What can I help you with?"

"When I get back, I'm quitting my job. I want to go back to school or find an apprenticeship with a jewelry designer in the States. I thought with your connections, you might be able to give me some advice."

"Well, now. I think that it is a marvelous idea. You have an excellent eye for design and, observing you today, I see you learned a lot from Martelli in Florence. You just need to practice more, Nora—that, and more time working with a goldsmith who knows his craft." Reaching out for Nora's sketch of Isabella's necklace, he studied it for a moment. "You're staying until the end of September, am I correct? Well, how about getting your new career started by working on this design with me?"

"Signor Michelozzi, really?" she asked excitedly.

"It would mean, of course," he said a bit modestly, "spending more time with this old man."

"Believe me, there is nothing I'd like more. I feel like I've already learned so much just this morning. It would be a pleasure to continue," said Nora. "I'm also pretty sure you have many more stories up your sleeve to keep me entertained."

Signor Michelozzi's eyes lit up and he regarded her with keen interest. "*Sì*. I think creating this pendant will be a fitting tribute to the Medici princess and the documentary you are making. It will be our little project."

He paused a moment. "In the meantime, I will contact a couple of colleagues in the States and make some inquiries—come to think of it, I actually *do* know a few people who are located in California."

With his finger, he thoughtfully traced the lines of the pendant Nora had sketched on paper. Looking over at her, he said, "This has been a very enlightening afternoon. You know, Isabella was an excellent horsewoman and now I believe you have both just given me an idea for the next lance."

Smiling, he added, "Come back tomorrow, and we will work on both designs together."

Chapter 23

The Bitter End

*F*erragosto, the mid-summer festival celebrating Arezzo's patron Saint Donato, had passed, and the town had come to a lethargic standstill. To avoid the blistering Tuscan heat, it preferred to draw its blinds and slumber until it would be awakened again in a few weeks' time by the fanfare of trumpets and the booming of cannons heralding the beginning of the September joust.

Instead of splicing film clips and editing voiceovers, Nora spent her afternoons in the company of Signor Michelozzi in his studio, designing in gold. She was a quick study, and in just a few short weeks with Egidio as her teacher, she was learning new techniques and honing her skills. With his help, she was translating the necklace she had seen in the Medici princess's portrait into a precious piece of wearable art.

As she worked at her station in the corner of Michelozzi's studio, she tried her best not to think about returning home. The weeks, however, were dwindling down, and saying goodbye to Luca was too bittersweet to contemplate. Her mood was further dampened by the fact that there remained so many unanswered questions hanging between them. What had started out as light-hearted and joyous had suddenly turned tense, and a bit strained.

Just the other day, in fact, they had quarreled over the stupidest thing. It was shortly after she had told him that one of Egidio's contacts had paid off and that she was being considered for an apprenticeship with a goldsmith in Oakland. At first, Luca had been supportive and listened with interest. But, after a while, a black cloud fell over them, and they had exchanged heated words. Now she couldn't even remember what they had disagreed about; it had been over a trivial thing fueled by fear.

To smooth things over, she prepared what she had hoped would be a romantic late-night dinner. But as she unfolded her napkin, she could feel the stress of their inevitable goodbyes floating between them. It seemed as if they were not eating alone, but rather an uninvited dinner guest had just sat down between them.

Toying with her food, Nora waited for Luca to speak, but when he remained stonily uncommunicative, she eventually pushed her plate away, re-filled her wine glass, and glared at him. *Two can play this game,* she thought.

But, in the end, she discovered she had misplayed her cards, and he left her apartment earlier than usual that night; her compensation prize had been to sleep alone in a cold bed.

Turning restlessly onto her side, she wondered if they could make a long-distance relationship work. Luca had a life here in Arezzo, and she had a new career waiting for her in the Bay Area. Could their love survive the distance of a vast ocean and a continent?

If, on the other hand, they managed to keep things going, it depressed her to think their meetings and time together would diminish to a trickle of infrequent vacations, him visiting her occasionally in San Francisco and her returning to Italy in the summers. Would Luca write her letters? Would they be passionate and heartfelt like the ones Troilo had penned to Isabella?

Perhaps he would, Nora thought, consoled by the love notes he had left her on her pillow before he left her each morning. Cheered by the thought, she felt they could sustain their affair for many years, despite the distance that separated them, just as the fifteenth-century couple had.

Turning onto her back and staring at the ceiling, Nora was distracted for a moment thinking about Isabella's torrid long-distance affair with Troilo and their passionate exchange of love letters.

"M'lady. Wake up. Come now, you mustn't sleep all day. All of Florence has already risen."

When Morgante pulled back the heavy drapes from the window,

Isabella groaned. Shielding her eyes from the bright morning light, she griped, "Let me sleep, you little imp. I was up most of the night—can't you see I need my rest?"

"But m'lady, it is almost midday." When she focused her gaze on him, she saw he was slowly waving two envelopes in front of her face. Yawning broadly, she said, "Is this why you wake me, to bring me letters? Who are they from?"

Isabella stretched languidly in her bed before reaching to take the parchment from his hand. After studying the penmanship on both, she dismissed the first, tossing it absently onto her nightstand. The second she kissed lightly before ripping it open.

Rising out of bed she walked to the window where the light was better, and her lips curved upwards as she read Troilo's words. Glancing back at Morgante, who had returned with a pitcher of water, she said, "Come here! I need you to write my response."

Dutifully, the servant complied. Sitting down at the desk, Morgante took out a sheet of paper and dipped his pen into a bottle of ink.

"I need to warn him," said Isabella. "He mustn't sign his letters to me, as he did in this last one. He also must never speak freely about our relationship, especially to those who have the ear of my brother."

She studied Morgante for a moment. "There are spies among us ready to reveal our secret."

Nodding, he said, "You are right. Now then, m'lady, how should we begin?"

Isabella flopped onto the bed, and the down comforter billowed up around her. Rolling over onto her stomach, she regarded her friend thoughtfully. "Let's start the letter in this way..."

Dear Sir, You can be assured that I will not lose you for anything. Every hour seems like a thousand, and if it were not for the high hopes I have of seeing you again, I would be finished at this time. And do tell me that your return will be the quickest possible, so dear is it to my life.

Looking over at Morgante, she asked, "How does that sound?"

"Beautiful, my lady, very heartfelt. I'm sure Troilo will enjoy your sentiments very much," he said, his voice tinged with sarcasm.

"Shush, you don't say his name!" Suddenly alert, she glanced quickly at the door. In a whisper, she asked, "Did you hear that?"

The dwarf paused, his pen hovering over the page. After a moment of intense listening, he shrugged, and Isabella relaxed back into her satin pillow, satisfied no one was lurking on the other side.

Then, as a thought occurred to her, Isabella raised herself up on her elbows. "What rumors do you hear from the servants' quarters?"

Morgante was silent.

"Come on, out with it. I know you all talk."

"Well, m'lady, it is universally believed the Grand Duke of Tuscany is a prideful man, and he is merely toying with you at the moment. Everyone thinks it is but a game of wit and power. When all is said and done, the duke will provide for his own kin. No one believes he would ever harm you in any way. He is your protector now."

Isabella chortled, but there was no mirth in her laughter. "My protector, you say. You are all daft. My brother would just as soon see me kicked out of Florence."

Rolling off the bed, she walked to the window and gazed down at the narrow streets of Florence outside her rooms in the Medici palace. "Since my father died, my true champion is gone. My brilliant papà left me a wealthy woman, but Francesco refuses to honor our father's agreement. Instead, he keeps the purse strings drawn tight, and now every day I fear for the well-being of my children: my darling baby girl Nora, and her sweet, sweet brother Virginio."

Sweeping around to face Morgante, she haughtily reminded him, "My brother is a power-hungry man who is jealous of me. It irks him that his sister is more intelligent and could do his job better than he."

Pulling on her dressing gown and tying it firmly at her waist, she continued, "No, he must never have proof of my affair. He is sure to retaliate in the vilest of means. Look what happened to my cousin

Leonora! She was caught red-handed with a letter from her lover, Bernardino, that lovesick fool."

With her hands on her hips, she demanded, "You know what he did to her, don't you? Pietro had her beaten, for God's sake, and Francesco only encouraged him to flail her even harder."

Isabella trembled with indignation. "How dare a man beat a woman! It only shows his weakness. What kind of cowardice is that? If one should ever lay a hand on me, I swear I will haunt him to the end of time—he would never be rid of me."

Pacing the floor, she added, "And that... that... puttana, that Venetian whore that warms my brother's bed. Mark my words, she whispers evil things into his ear each night, telling him lies about me. I fear Bianca Cappella has enchanted Francesco so completely that he no longer thinks with that dull brain of his, but instead with his engorged lower regions."

Abruptly, she came to a halt in the middle of the room. "Francesco has withheld my inheritance once, and now he is ready to double-cross me again. His word is meaningless to me. I no longer trust him. But what can I do?"

Isabella started pacing again but stopped to stare up at the portrait of her mother. Here in Florence, she hung it over her bed. "*Mamma*, this situation is untenable," she said to the woman in the painting. "Francesco is but a passive beneficiary who inherited our family's fortune. What did he do to earn the title of duke? If only I were a man, I would be the one controlling the Medici fortune."

Morgante patiently listened to his mistress's tirade, and when she paused, he asked, "What do you desire that I write next?"

When Isabella didn't respond, he prompted again, "M'lady?"

"Where was I?"

The dwarf reread the opening lines of the letter. "You said you wanted to warn him..."

"Yes, that's right. Tell him I am especially worried by the rumors that Signor Spina may know about our affair—the man knows not how to keep a secret."

As she watched Morgante penning the last lines of her letter, she said wistfully, "Ah, Morgante, what has the world come to? I am bound to one man but am desperately in love with another. My husband and I live separate lives, he in Rome and I in Florence, and now there is such bitter feuding with my brother over money."

Not expecting an answer, she asked, "Have you finished?"

"Yes, m'lady, and have signed it, 'Your slave in perpetuity.'"

It pleased her to no end thinking of Troilo reading her secret code words. She had never written them to anyone else, and she most definitely hadn't used them with her husband. Paolo, for his part, would never have had the creativity or passion for penning similar romantic words to her.

"That's all for now, Morgante. You may go."

When the door closed, Isabella moved once again to the window. Leaning her brow against the cool glass, she thought about her mean-spirited brother. She wasn't sure what the next few days might bring, but she could sense an ill wind rising.

Picking up the second letter, Isabella saw it was from her husband. Unfolding the parchment, she read,

Sweetest Isabella, my darling wife, the light of my life, I urge you to join me in Cerreto Guidi. I have assembled a hunting party. It has been an age since we last saw one another, and it is my fondest desire to be reunited with you again. I am on my way from Rome. Come as soon as you can, my dearest lady.

The letter seemed straightforward enough, an invitation to join him at their hunting lodge, but it was oddly filled with romantic words that he never usually expressed. Very well, it would be good to take a journey and leave Florence for a few days. She needed to clear her head.

Perhaps when she returned, she would find her brother in a better frame of mind, and she would be able to reason with him. She promised herself she would also visit Leonora. Indeed, she thought, it was high time for a tête-a-tête. They could both do with a bit of cheering up. Looking at the picture of her mother, she squared her shoulders and stood a bit taller. She was a Medici princess, and she would figure things out.

Filled with renewed confidence, humming softly, Isabella continued to read her husband's letter. After a moment, her breath caught, and the song died on her lips.

Fear filled her heart as she read his closing words: *Dearest lady, never forget...I am your slave in perpetuity.*

Chapter 24

Drunken Confessions

*B*y the end of the month, once again blue, yellow, green, and red flags fluttered from the rooftops in Arezzo, and the sound of horse hooves clip-clopping up the streets could be heard. In the Piazza Grande, the spectator stands had been erected, and the wide-open space had been turned back into a jousting track, presided over by the Saracen dummy. People had pulled out their neighborhood colors, and competitive barbs were being tossed about freely over the counters in the local coffee bars.

After their silly argument, Nora hadn't seen Gianluca for a couple of days. She had learned through Juliette that he had gone out to the Santo Spirito *scuderia* to check on the horses, and after that, he and Marco had spent an afternoon on horseback visiting their favorite haunts.

Riding hadn't really been her thing, except during the summer days she had spent at Girl Scout camp in the hills of northern California. Knowing full well it was a passion of Luca's, being an ex-jouster and having practically grown up in the saddle, Nora decided that when she got back to the States, it wouldn't hurt to brush up on her riding skills. In anticipation of climbing back up on a horse, she had already picked up a fabulous pair of equestrian boots in a shop just off the Piazza Grande.

They were golden brown with antique brass buckles, and they encased her calves perfectly from the curve of her ankles all the way up to her knees. Seeing them in the shop window had nearly made her swoon, but it was the smell of the rich leather from which they had been made that finally convinced her to buy them. She sincerely hoped she would get to model them for Luca and that they would be put to good use in the future when she returned the following year.

Nora also figured Isabella would have approved of her choice of footwear, as she had been an excellent rider. It pleased Nora to no end that Egidio was paying tribute to her and her horsemanship, and had watched in delight as he had translated her design, whittling away at a block of wood until it revealed the profile of the Medici princess.

When the members of the Golden Lance Society visited Egidio's shop, they were delighted with the concept. After being introduced to Nora and learning about her documentary, they invited her to participate in the upcoming joust, marching in the procession as the Medici princess herself.

Egidio said, "You can sit next to me in the booths. We will have completed Isabella's necklace by then. It will be a fitting addition to your outfit."

With a new goal in mind—to complete the pendant in time for the parade—Nora spent long hours in Michelozzi's studio. Fixated on her delicate project, she sometimes worked through dinner and often finished around ten. A week before the next joust, just as she had turned off the burner and was about to quit, she heard her phone buzz. Glancing at the screen, she saw a text message from Juliette.

"*Ciao N.* Looking for M. Have u seen him? Supposed to meet 2 hours ago. Getting worried."

That's odd, thought Nora. It wasn't like Juliette to keep tabs on Marco.

Nora promptly texted back, "No. Haven't seen M all day. Maybe he is with L."

As she grabbed her bag and turned off the light, she heard her phone buzz again.

"No luck. Home now. Hitchhiked with a neighbor in his truck. M is such a jerk! CRETINO!"

Nora was amused by the thought of Juliette sitting in the bed of a small three-wheeled Italian excuse for a truck, bumping over the potholes in the back roads of Tuscany all the way up the hill to the winery. She quickly typed, "Have a glass of wine. Chill. M will turn up. LOL" She followed her text with a series of smiley faces, hearts, and wine glasses.

When her phone dinged again, she read, "Check to see if he is at the bar *Piccolo Cinghiale*. Thx."

Nora closed and locked up the shop then headed out. As she walked down the street, she heard someone cry out from a few streets over, *"Forza gialloblù!"* That, in turn, was followed by a roar of approval from the crowd. When the cheering died down, someone else countered, *"Forza Porta Sant'Andrea!"*

It was Saturday night, music was blaring, and people were out having fun. Instead of joining the throngs on the main drag, she continued down a quieter side street in search of the bar Juliette had instructed her to check. At this time of night, with its shops closed and no one around, it had taken on a desolate air. She glanced around nervously, and then laughed at her apprehension. Still, when she heard the explosion of a bottle rocket go off around the corner, she jumped.

She was heartened when, up ahead, she saw the lights were on at Il *Piccolo Cinghiale*. As she approached, a man with an apron came out and collected the tables he had set up on the street earlier. With most of his usual clients celebrating in the main piazza just a block over, it seemed he, too, was ready to call it quits for the night.

Walking in, she called out, "Ehi! Marco. There you are. Juli's been worried about you."

Marco turned around and gave her a lopsided grin. *"Ehiiii, ciaooo,* Nora. I can't believe you are here! *Vieni qua!* Come join me."

Nora stood for a moment, assessing him. From the way he slurred his words, she could tell he'd been drinking—and more than a little. "What's up, Marco? Should I call Juli to let her know I've found you?"

"No, no... I'll call her, just give me a sec. I'm not sure where I left my phone. Let's see... It was here just a minute ago. I was supposed to meet Juli earlier—she must be madder than hell. But I met some friends... and weeeelll... We had maybe a few drinks."

Marco rolled his head in the direction of the bartender. "Tommaso, this is Nora. Nora, this is Tommaso." Raising his glass, he continued. "I came into town to drop off some cases of wine to my friend here, but got a little sidetracked. Lucky for him, I made it just in time before he closed."

The bartender shook his head in amusement and asked Nora if she wanted something to drink.

"Here, let me buy that for you," said Marco. Opening his wallet, he held it up close to his face and counted out a few euros. As he placed the money on the counter, a couple of coins rolled off the bar and clattered noisily to the floor.

"*Cazzo! Scuuuusami* Nooora," he said.

Leaning down to scoop up the change, he lost his balance and tipped slightly off the chair. Marco looked at her sheepishly. "I may have had a liiiittle tooooo much to drink tonight, but I got it."

She had never seen Marco quite this far gone. Realizing he couldn't drive back to the winery on his own, given his present condition, she said, "Listen, I'll send Juli the message. She can come and get you."

Without waiting for him to reply, she typed, "Found M. *Ubriaco*. Drunk at Cinghiale."

When she put her phone down and glanced up, a smile spread across his face. "Thanks, Nora. You are a real friend. It's soooo good you came."

"Sure thing. I'm glad I found you. Juli said you might be here."

"No, no, no, that's not what I meant," said Marco. "What... What I meant... It is good that you came here. Here!" He stabbed the bar emphatically with his finger. "Here to Arezzo."

When Tommaso placed a glass of wine in front of her, he gave her a knowing look and she answered with a conspiratorial smile. They silently agreed they would both take care of their friend until Juliette arrived.

Still looking at Tommaso with the glass halfway to her lips, she felt Marco suddenly grab her arm. She turned to him in surprise when he said, "Don't go, Nora. Stay. Don't go."

Confused, she turned to look over at him. "Relax, I just got my drink. I'll stay and wait until Juli gets here."

"No—don't go home. Don't go back to California."

"Don't worry," she said. "I'm here for a few more weeks. You know that. I'm not going back home until after the joust."

"No, what I meant... mean—don't go home." Gesturing to an unseen person on the other side of the bar, he said, "He needs you."

"Who needs me?"

"I saw him the other day. Didcha know that?"

Mystified, Nora asked, "I'm not following you. Who exactly are we talking about here?"

"Luca! We went riding. Just like old times. It was Leonora this and Leonora that... Luca couldn't stop talking about you." He leaned over and grinned lopsidedly. Waving a finger at her, he said, "*Avete litigato vero?* You guys had a fight? Didn't ya?"

Nora let out a disgusted sigh. "He was being a jerk."

Marco nodded sympathetically, then his smile gradually faded. "*Anch'io sono uno stronzo.* I've been a real ass, too. I've been a terrible friend—the worst."

Concerned, Nora put her hand on his shoulder. "Marco, did something just happen? Is that why you're drinking tonight? Are you talking about Luca? It seems like you guys are getting along. I've seen you together... Did something happen when you went riding the other day?"

"Noooo," he moaned. "Things are better. But that's because of... of... you and Juli. What I'm talking about happened..."

He took a gulp of his beer and swore softly, "*Cazzo.* What I did was so bad. Do you know what today is? Do you? Try and guess."

Not really following him, Nora played along. "Um, let's see... it's Saturday...?"

"*Sbagliato!* Wrong! Try again."

When she didn't respond, he continued, "I'm celebrating the anniversary of *stupidità.* STU... PI... DI... TÀ" Weaving a bit to the left, he said, "*Sono un vero cretino!* Take a closer look at this face. I'm the real jerk here."

"What's gotten into you, Marco? What do you mean?" Nora finally asked.

"On this date, three years ago, I made the biggest mistake of my life. Yep. That's right. Me, good ol' Marco here, really screwed things up. I should have known better... But Carlotta—she couldn't be reasoned with."

Nora sat back and grabbed her glass and took a drink. This had to do with Carlotta. Of course.

"She was soooo craaazzzy about all those creepy fantasies she dreamed up. Carlotta really had an imagination! The scarier and more gruesome the better."

He gestured broadly with his arms, adding, "And that stupid ghost story... The one about Isabella. Just like you, ya know, it intrigued her. Even as a kid she was always babbling on about that *maledetto fantasma*. She was forever chasing after that damned ghost."

Breathing in quickly, he hiccupped slightly before continuing, "Remember... 'member when I told you about the times, we used to build those... those big bonfires out at my place?"

He laughed mirthlessly. "But she didn't care about the history. *Oh mio Dio, no.* The tragedy—that's what she liked. She liked the idea of dying for true love. Every time she told the story about the murder at Cerreto Guidi, it got gorier and gorier..."

Marco paused and gazed off into space. Nora imagined he was conjuring images of a brightly blazing campfire and the lithe figure of Carlotta dancing around it. Of course, to keep the boys thoroughly entertained, Carlotta would have fabricated grisly details about the Medici princess's murder.

Perhaps she embellished her fantastic tale, telling them that Isabella had been hoisted up on a rope until her face turned blue and her eyes bulged out of her head. While her husband had left her to dangle in the breeze, he danced around her body gloating. But instead of slipping away peacefully, Isabella's wrathful ghost had escaped her body to bludgeon the man, leaving him to drown in a pool of his own blood. Once the crime had been committed, however, Isabella's tortured and moaning soul had been suspended between heaven and hell.

Carlotta would have concluded her story in a voice dripping with romance and intrigue: "...and now the white lady is trapped in the walls of the villa, waiting for her lover to save her. When he returns, Isabella and Troilo will spend all of eternity together wrapped in one another's arms."

Marco let out another dejected groan and Nora came back from her fantasy. "She was perfect back then. She seemed so strong and invincible... and...." Sadly, he added, "But she wasn't. Not at all. She had us all fooled."

He played with his beer mug, spinning it around and around on the counter until Nora feared it would slide off the counter and break.

"I loved her once. Didcha know that, Nora?" He looked up quickly. "Oh, not like I love Juli. I realize what real love is now—what love *should* be now. Back then, what did I know? I was just a dumb kid. You understand what I'm sayin', don't you, Nora? "

"We all get fooled by love at one time or another," said Nora. "Believe me. I've been there."

"Did you know Carlotta and I talked about getting married?"

Nora didn't respond. She felt a confession coming on, and she wasn't sure she should be the one to hear it. "Marco, I think it is time to stop now. Juli will be here in a minute."

Ignoring her, he said, "I gotta talk. I know you'll understand... please hear me out. Just listen."

Against her better judgment, Nora nodded for him to continue.

"She... Well, something happened to Carlotta when her parents died. She was never the same. She was a crazy kid, and when she got older..."

"What happened when she got older?" Nora prodded, despite herself.

"Obsessed, that's what Carlotta was," he said. "She wanted a love like Romeo and Juliet. She wanted a man to be so head-over-heels in love with her he'd..."

"He'd what?" asked Nora, fearing the answer but needing to hear it.

"Oh, I don't know. Maybe he'd be pushed over the edge, blinded by jealousy... He'd... he'd kill for her... Or kill himself. Whatever. It would be some dramatic gesture—some kind of proof of his undying love."

Marco stared back down at his drink. "But ya know what? That girl didn't know what love was. It was staring her in the face and she never even recognized it. Not once. Not with me. Not with Luca. When they started having problems... I was kind of glad. She had dumped me for Luca, after all. She'd call me on the phone, y'know, and she'd tell me things she shouldn't. Things... things... like her marriage was a *bugia*... nothing but a *grossa menzogna*. It was a big fat stinkin' lie, and that Luca didn't love her. She complained he cared more about horses—even talked to them more than he did to her."

Marco wagged his head from side to side. "When I heard her say stuff like that, I said to myself, 'Marco, man, she's made a mistake. It was you all along...'"

Turning to look at Nora, he said, "Then, one night, after a particularly brutal fight, she called sobbing and... Wait, can you guess the date?"

"Um... let's see, three years ago today?" Nora said hesitantly.

"BINGO!" he said, so loud Tommaso glanced up from the glasses he was drying at the far end of the bar. "You got it! She called sayin' Luca had just asked for a separation and that if it didn't improve their marriage, he was ready to finish things for good. She was madder than hell and told me she needed to get out of town. She said, 'Let's go drinking, Marco. Let's go catch a ghost.' She even dared me to go. But I was used to it... She was always making us do things we'd regret later."

"So you went with her to Cerreto Guidi in the middle of the night?" asked Nora.

"Yeah, that's about it. Carlotta knew how to flatter, mope, and even coerce to get whatever she wanted. Anyway, we never did make it there. *Cazzo,* we didn't even make it that far out of Arezzo. We stopped off, and things got... Well, we drank some—more than some. We drank waaaay too much."

He closed his eyes, and his head weaved back and forth again—this time not from the beer but from guilt and remorse. "We ended up in a hotel in bed together."

He said bitterly, "I realized immediately it had been a mistake. I... I... hated myself. Not only had I cheated on my best friend with his wife, when I sobered up I realized Carlotta used me. She knew exactly what she was doing. I thought I had been the one to take advantage of her, but all along she had just been using me to get back at Luca. It had been her plan from the start to punish him."

With pain in his eyes, he said, "But this time—*this time* she knew she had gone too far. The next day, she called me over and over, asking me to forgive her, saying she hadn't meant to hurt me, but she also didn't want to break up her marriage. She wanted to make things work with Luca."

Nora squeezed his arm compassionately and said nothing.

Encouraged, Marco said, "I didn't know what to do. I certainly wasn't going to tell Luca. So I agreed to keep things quiet. Do you wanna know what she did then? She went and told Luca. She *told* him! She was like that, ya know. She swung like a pendulum. Hot. Cold. Hot. Cold. I couldn't believe her. She had just... just... threw it all in Luca's face. That day she betrayed both of us."

"Oh, Marco, I'm so sorry. How did Luca take it?"

"Not the way she hoped. I think she wanted to prod him into doing something...oh, I don't know... Something dramatic and big, like I said before. Instead, he just retreated into silence."

Sighing tiredly, Marco admitted, "That's when I knew she really needed help."

He reached out to take another drink, but Nora gently pried the glass out of his hand. "I think you've had enough for tonight."

"I should have known that Luca was doing the best he could, trying to get her to see doctors—you know, get her the help she needed. But she refused it all. Impossible woman."

The story that had been bothering her for days was starting to make sense. Although she had hoped it would be Luca to tell her first, she understood now why there was still residual tension between the two men. Still, there were pieces of the puzzle missing, and she couldn't help but ask, "What happened after that?"

Marco slumped back in his seat. "Carlotta did what she always did. She dumped the mess on us, and to avoid the fallout or deal with any of it, she ran back to Rome. Again."

"And Luca? Did he follow her?"

"He did nothing. Well, not 'nothing' nothing. He let her go, but this time... it... well... It broke their marriage completely. It was then he decided to divorce her."

"And you and he..."

"Oh, we went at it. He confronted me for being such an idiot for taking advantage of Carlotta. He punched me out, and I let him do it. We didn't speak for months after that."

Nora put her arm around his shoulders and hugged him, not knowing what more to say.

"After Carlotta's accident, after the funeral, things got a little better. We cleared the air and called a truce, and then Juli came into my life and... She is fantastic, she is amazing."

Seeing Juliette enter the bar as if on cue, Marco's face lit up, and he flashed a charismatic smile. *"Ciao, amore."*

Nora signaled to her friend that Marco was more than a little drunk. She was about to stand up and let Juliette take over, but when he grabbed her arm, she looked back at him.

"Thanks for listening," he said. "It's time to tell Juli all of this, but I wanted you to know too." He kissed Nora's cheek. "There are still moments like tonight when it feels like Carlotta's ghost returns," he added. "She's always there, floating between us."

Nora squeezed his arm and said, "I know the feeling."

Chapter 25

Exorcising a Ghost

Nora helped Juliette get Marco to the car, and when she got home later that night, she found a note under her door. It was from Luca. She felt a rush of pleasure seeing his familiar handwriting.

Unfolding the letter, she read, "*Ciao, principessa. I stopped by tonight, but you weren't home. I expect you are finishing up things at Michelozzi's. Meet me tomorrow in the Belvedere after lunch near the fortezza. Mi manchi. See you then. L*"

After not having seen him for a few days, she was relieved he had surfaced again and was missing her.

The following day, Nora climbed the hill to the cathedral. When she reached the *Prato*—the park next to the church, with its panoramic view of the Tuscan countryside—it was practically empty except for two teenagers who had their heads bent over their cell phones. The girl was sitting on the boy's lap, and every so often she leaned over to kiss him; he in return nuzzled her neck. Across the lawn, she saw a couple of boys on skateboards doing tricks. Their friends egged them on, watching from the shaded lawn, smoking cigarettes.

She glanced around but didn't see any sign of Luca. Looking toward the far end of the park where the fortress of Cosimo de' Medici rose up in the distance, she thought maybe she had misunderstood and she was supposed to meet him inside. Fishing out her phone from her bag, she dialed his number when she felt someone grab her from behind and squeeze her waist.

"Hey, you," she said. "I've been wondering where you were."

"I just got here." Leaning down, he kissed her. "*Figurati! Mi mancavi tanto.* It's only been a few days—but it seems longer than that."

"I've missed you too," she said. "What have you been up to?"

"I've been spending a lot of time out at the *scuderia* these past few days. We are getting ready for the joust and practices have picked up. The boys are looking really great, even after Michele's leg injury last month."

"I heard through Juli that you and Marco went riding the other day." She eyed him thoughtfully. "You know, I think I need to take a few lessons myself to keep up with you guys."

"Really now? That should prove to be interesting."

"I'm serious! I've already got my riding boots. You could give me a few tips on how to handle a horse. I warn you, I might be a little rusty, but I'll give you a run for your money. I'll even challenge you to a race."

"Dare accepted," he said with a grin.

Holding hands, they walked toward the Medici fortress. The park around them was shaded by trees, but from this high vantage point, Nora could see that the valley floor far below them was illuminated by bright afternoon sunlight. As they climbed to the top of the ramparts taking in the rusty red, amber brown, and dusty green colors that painted the floor below and smelling the smoky, sweet air, she could feel a change in the seasons. The countryside was preparing for harvest, and soon the grapes would be ready for collecting.

Sadly, Nora thought she wouldn't be here for the *vendemmia*. By the time Marco and Juliette were harvesting grapes at the winery in October, she would be back in California. She was going to miss her friends and Arezzo. In her heart, she knew she would never feel more at home anywhere other than in this hill town filled with history, art, and *antico ardore.*

She felt an additional wave of nostalgia realizing how much she had missed Luca during the last few days. If she felt like this after such a brief intermission, she could only imagine how hard it would be once she returned home and they faced a nine-hour time difference.

Nora shook her head, trying to lighten her mood. Nimbly, she slipped up onto the wall and settled herself on the warm stone ledge.

"Look down there," Luca said, directing her gaze to the foot of the castle's steep wall. "You can see the town's cemetery. That's where my grandparents are buried."

Nora peered down at the grave markers. Here on this wall, built by the Medici, she felt the undeniable presence not only of Isabella but that of Margherita. Closing her eyes for a moment, Nora enjoyed the sensation of the late summer sun upon her face and imagined Luca's grandmother visiting her beloved artist over the years, tending his gravestone, bringing him flowers. From the valley below, Margherita's voice floated up to her, and she could hear her telling Federico about shop business and how she continued to treasure his paintings.

"You will be pleased to know, *amore mio*," Margherita whispered, "your paintings of saints and Madonnas are still with me. But the pictures I cherish the most are the ones you did in Paris. How I love the colors that remind me of a late summer afternoon, just after a rainstorm. Now I no longer have to hide their beauty and have hung them prominently for everyone to see."

Luca touched her lightly on the arm, and Nora refocused her attention on the man in front of her, willing herself to live in the moment.

Smiling apologetically, he said, "I'm sorry we got into it the other day. *Colpa mia.* I was kind of a jerk."

"Yeah, but so was I. We all have our moments. *Acqua passata.* Water under the bridge," Nora said. Wrapping her legs around him, she drew him closer. Willingly, he let himself be pulled into her embrace, and she savored the feel of his lips on hers.

When he leaned back, she slowly opened her eyes and found him watching her thoughtfully. "I've been so busy lately with the horses—but I've also been curious about Isabella's necklace. How is it coming? Are you almost finished?"

She was glad they had let go of their silly argument, and it also made her happy he continued to show interest in her work. "It's almost done. I'm still learning, and it's been a little tricky, but all in all, I like it. Working with Egidio—it's been an unexpected gift."

Studying him a moment, she continued, "This summer has been good for me. It's been a real eye-opener."

When he gave her a questioning look, she explained, "I feel like I'm finally waking up and figuring out what I want to do when I grow up. I've met some incredible people—perhaps even a few ghosts—who have made a lasting impression on me."

He held out his arms and said, "*Ed io?* What about me?"

Nora leaned back and regarded him skeptically. "Well... I guess you make the list, too."

He kissed her again, and when they parted, she smiled. "Okay, I'm putting you on the top of the list for making the best first impression, followed closely by Isabella."

"I'll take that. It seems I'm in good company," he said.

Entwining their hands, Nora said, "You know, I'm going to miss Arezzo and everyone here. I'm already planning on coming back next spring. How could I stay away? When do you want to come visit me in San Francisco?"

She waited for him to reply, but he said nothing. Nora could tell something weighed heavily on his mind, but once again his reluctance to speak about what was bothering him was frustrating. She had been a reasonably patient woman up to this point and had been very accommodating about his personal feelings about his dead wife, giving him plenty of room. But enough was enough. She needed some answers.

Instead of backing off, Nora decided to take a different approach. Placing her hand on his cheek, she guided his gaze back to hers. "Luca, look at me."

When he faced her directly, she continued, "I've been thinking about a lot of things lately, but mostly about my future—our future—and I'm wondering what you want out of our relationship and if we are moving in the same direction. It is going to be hard enough to keep all this up long distance, but even harder if we aren't on the same page."

Taking a deep breath, she said, "I need to know. Are you okay? I mean are you happy? Not just on the surface. I mean deep down inside? I can tell something is bothering you."

She paused a beat before continuing. "I've told you about my marriage. You know I've had my share of ups and downs. I've also told you about some of the saddest moments of my life, but you've never told me anything about your marriage or life with Carlotta. I've tried to ask you before... but now I really need to know."

When Luca said nothing, she groaned, "Oh, come on! Don't pull the silent treatment on me again. Look, you should know I ran into Marco last night. He had quite a lot to drink, and told me some things about Carlotta—he told me about his affair with her three years ago."

Gauging his reaction carefully, she added, "I know you both loved her, and perhaps you still do, or maybe you haven't really gotten over her and—"

Luca interrupted, "Things aren't always the way they seem."

"Well, tell me then," she implored. "How *are* things? You must know by now I care deeply."

Picking up a small stone off the wall, he played with it for a moment. Then, tossing it up a couple of times, he threw it down into the valley. "You are so different from her. With you, I feel the world makes sense. Remember that day in the church when I told you beauty is something that makes you feel alive and joyful? Well, that's what you have come to mean to me. With Carlotta..."

"Yes?" she encouraged.

Luca gazed over her shoulder, but when Nora squeezed his hand, he turned his attention back to her. "Most of the time between us there was just anger, sadness and guilt. Don't get me wrong, there will never be anyone like her. She was bright, funny, amazing—but there was also this lonely, dark part deep inside that consumed her. There was no middle ground."

He sighed and then, as if a dam had broken, without reserve, he told her things he had never told anyone else. He described for Nora the golden days when he, Marco, and Carlotta had been the best of friends and life had been sweet and innocent. As he continued, she heard tales about their secret forts and silly dares. He even admitted that once the three of them had cheated on tests, copying from one another's papers.

He laughed softly at their juvenile stupidity and continued, "Sometimes we stole pastries from the *pasticeria* in via del Corso, other times we skipped school to gallop our horses through the hills outside of the city. On Saturday afternoons, we used to ride our skateboards at breakneck speed down the main street, just to scare the old ladies."

Glancing out over the valley, he said, "That was the girl I fell in love with, but things change and people grow up. Carlotta had things buried deep inside that she could no longer contain. She was a reckless girl who grew into a troubled woman. After we got married, she spiraled into a dark place, and as much as I tried, I couldn't pull her back."

A shadow passed over his face. "We fought often. Not like the stupid argument you and I had the other day. These were blistering, horrible battles. They wore me out emotionally. She couldn't be reasoned with."

He paused a moment and studied Nora. Tucking a piece of hair behind her ear, he said, "I tried to get her the help she needed, but in the end she ignored me. I couldn't take it anymore. Finally, I asked for a separation. I thought maybe that would be a wake-up call and she would see reason, and we could begin to work things out..."

Shaking his head as if he still couldn't believe it, he murmured, "Right after that, when I found out she had slept with Marco, it hit me hard. I forgave her, it fit her erratic pattern, but I had a more difficult time forgiving Marco. He should have known better. She fled back to Rome, and things remained the same. I'd had it by then. For me, there was no going back, so I asked for a divorce."

Already knowing the answer from Marco's recounting the other night, but wanting him to tell her in his own words, Nora asked, "What did she do then? What was her response?"

He stopped to collect his thoughts, choosing his words carefully. "Carlotta ignored me, of course. Weeks went by, and then I finally called her and told her to come home. I didn't ask. I demanded that she come back here to sign the papers."

He took a deep breath and said, "It was on her way back home that the accident occurred. It had been raining hard that night. The *Polizia*

Stradale who first reported in at the scene couldn't tell if it had been a routine casualty—just another car slipping out of control on the slick tarmac that night... or..."

"Or what?" Nora asked carefully.

"There was a car following behind hers. According to the driver's report, Carlotta's speed had been irregular that night, randomly accelerating and slowing down, but still, it seemed she had been in control of the car despite the slick weather conditions. When the police questioned the driver specifically about that, he said the car ahead of him had deftly swerved a few times to avoid debris on the road and a couple of fallen branches. Even so, he was worried and had kept a safe distance between his car and hers. He also said..."

Luca paused and Nora looked at him curiously. "Go on."

"The witness didn't think Carlotta had lost control of her car or that it had been an accident. According to him it seemed she had intentionally turned into the other lane and..."

Nora's eyes widened. "You can't think that she really tried..."

"Given her state of mind and her instability," he continued, "who knows what she was thinking that night. At any rate, the results of the investigation were inconclusive. Both vehicles were totaled, and there were no survivors."

Leaning forward, Nora rested her head on his chest. She could hear his heart and felt their bond growing stronger with each beat. Closing her eyes, she could see Carlotta driving like a maniac through the Tuscan rainstorm. In the distance, she heard the thunder and the rain pelting down on the car as the windshield wipers clacked back and forth like sparring swords. As Carlotta's tears coursed down her face, causing her mascara to drip in dark smears across her cheeks, Nora could also hear the angry insults and curses she shouted out at Luca as she drove on through the inky night.

Falling into a hypnotic trance, lulled by the steady beat of rain on the car shield, Carlotta probably hadn't even been aware she had been pushing steadily down on the accelerator, causing the car to continue racing through the night. Or had she? Nora winced as she saw the flash of lightning and the beams of an approaching truck and wondered if Carlotta's car had slid out of control or if the desperate woman had, in one final grandstanding act, turned the wheel into its path.

Nora finally understood why Luca hadn't been able to tell her any of this; the guilt he carried was far too great. "And have you been blaming yourself all this time for making her return home that night?" she whispered.

Clenching his jaw, he said, "Yes. I blame myself completely. Ruggero is right in his accusations. I was responsible for putting her on the road that night and not keeping her safe."

In a steady voice, he said, "The truth of it is, I wasn't a good husband to Carlotta. I didn't love her enough, and I didn't do enough to pull her back from the edge."

He took a deep breath. "In answer to your question, 'Do I still love Carlotta?' A part of me always will, but I miss the girl, not the woman she became. When she died, I felt a sense of release. Because of that, to this day, I feel incredibly guilty."

Digesting all the things he just told her, she finally asked, "And what about you and Marco?"

"For a long time, I didn't think I could ever trust Marco again," he said. "But things started to change. It was about the time Juli arrived. I could see how good she was for Marco and I remembered the better days. At that point, I started to forgive him."

He smiled at her. "And then you came into my life. You've made me believe in things that I stopped trusting or hoping existed. You've shown me there is still beauty in the world."

Nora slipped off the wall, and he pulled her into his arms. "So, in answer to your other question, 'Am I happy?' the answer is yes, Leonora. I am just starting to learn how again."

He kissed her lightly and then leaned back so he could see her better. "I don't want to keep you from doing what you need to do back in the States. I know you are making plans and have new things to focus on when you get back."

He paused. "But I also don't want to wake up and find you thousands of miles away. I tried to make it work with Carlotta, but in the end, I let her slip away. I won't make that mistake again. I want to hold on to you. You know what would make me truly happy? Don't go. Stay here in Arezzo... I think we are better together."

With each word Luca spoke, Nora had begun to feel lighter. Now as she looked up at the sky, at the wisps of clouds high over their heads, it seemed a ghost had finally been set free and was floating off into the distance. Standing next to him, she knew he felt the same. There was no more unspoken tension, just a beautiful sense of well being of two people who had fully opened their hearts to one another and knew where they belonged.

If she was honest with herself, the decision to remain in Arezzo had been made long before she had met Luca. Perhaps she'd known from the moment she set foot on Italian soil back in June. Or perhaps it had been even years before that, when she had come here the first time with Juliette and had fallen in love with the joust.

There was a reason Isabella had called her here to Tuscany, and to this particular hill town. She knew without a doubt there was no turning back. She wouldn't make that mistake again. Unlike Carlotta, who hadn't a clue when love was standing in front of her, Nora clearly recognized it and embraced its joyous complexities and imperfections. This time there would be no regrets and misgivings about the life she should have lived.

This was a choice she made boldly and willingly.

Smiling up at him, she said, "I most certainly could be persuaded to stay. After all, a thought has just occurred to me... Now that Isabella's film is completed, I think I should stay around here and make a new one about Arezzo's joust."

Putting her arms around him, she whispered into his ear, "I believe you have already passed the first audition... How would you like to be cast as my leading man?"

Chapter 26

Prayers to Margherita

"*Ehi, Juli! Aspetta!* Wait up." Nora doubled over, trying to catch her breath. She looked up at her friend, who was several paces ahead of her on the path. In sync, they had started out climbing the hill in Cortona to reach the church dedicated to Santa Margherita, but before long, her friend had outstripped her.

She shaded her eyes and looked up. From her vantage point, it seemed they still had a ways to go before reaching the *basilica* perched at the summit. Nora marveled at Juliette's stamina. The climb from the *piazza* below was enough to send the soundest of hearts into cardiac arrest.

Marking the ascent to the church were the Stations of the Cross, done in colorful bits of glass by Gino Severini, the local artist from Cortona whom Federico had known in Paris. Luca had told her that Margherita had known him too and that she had once helped organize an art show for him in Arezzo in the early sixties.

From several paces ahead of her, Juliette called back, "Nora! Come on! It's just a little bit farther. See? Here is another mosaic."

"You know, we could have driven up to the church," she yelled up at her friend.

Juliette called back, "Oh, stop complaining. Anyway, it's the only way to see Severini's work. Luca's grandfather would be proud of you climbing all the way up here to see his friend's art. Besides, a little exercise is good for you. You could use it—love and pasta are making you fat."

"Luca doesn't seem to mind," Nora said with a smile. "There is just a little more of me to hold on to and love."

During the first part of their journey, when she had still had the breath to tell her story, Nora had explained everything to Juli. Her friend had listened, and at the end had confided, "Marco and I talked as well. It's good we have finally cleared the air. Now we can all move forward."

Glancing over at her friend, she said, "And, for the record, I would have stolen your passport and hidden it just to keep you here."

"I think Signor Michelozzi was about to do the same thing. When I told him of my decision to stay, he couldn't have been happier. He said it was about time I came to my senses and remained. He said the contacts he gave me in California were just okay, but I would do better studying with him. He also said, if I left, who was going to help him design next year's Golden Lance."

Nora continued, "Luca may be right. Egidio might have a little crush on me, but that's okay because I have a little crush on him as well."

Trudging along in the wake of her friend, she called up, "I'm going back to the States in November to present my documentary. Want me to bring you back a t-shirt from Fisherman's Wharf? I'm taking Luca with me, too. I want to introduce him to my..."

The words died on Nora's lips when she reached the summit—not from exhaustion, but because of the spectacular view of the Valdichiana below her. Like a magnificent jewel-toned tapestry, it continued for miles, melting into the horizon. In the distance, she could see Lake Trasimeno, and to the other side, she saw the Cetona Mountains.

Looking up at the crest, she saw the silhouette of yet another Medici fortress. Climbing the hill, she walked along with Margherita and Federico, and here at the summit of a mountain in Cortona, she was greeted again by Isabella and her father, Cosimo.

Suddenly she didn't feel tired anymore. On the contrary, the exhilaration she felt yesterday after fully acknowledging where she wanted to be and knowing her true place in the world came rushing back. Flinging out her arms, she spun around in a circle. "This place makes me happy. How could I leave *this* behind?"

Catching her arm, Juliette said, "Come on, you crazy girl, let's go inside the church—and you absolutely must keep your composure when you step in front of the glass casket. Remember, a saint is no laughing matter—here in Italy, they are sacred and holy."

Nora crossed her heart and promised. Since the first day when Juli had mentioned Santa Margherita to her, Nora had been curious to visit her. Her interest in the saint had only intensified after seeing Federico's painting of the saint in the Donati antique shop.

Now as they entered the church dedicated to Santa Margherita, Nora peered toward the altar to see the saint's glass coffin. As she did, she was struck by the Gothic arches, and the high-vaulted ceiling painted lapis lazuli blue. Slowly, they wandered closer to the front, passing by statues and paintings depicting Margherita's life. Finally, reaching the high altar, they paid their respects to the lady, displayed in all her glory inside her lighted box.

Knowing she would be seeing Santa Margherita today, Nora had asked Marco to explain more about the local saint and he had been happy to oblige. As he began his story, Nora learned Margherita was the patron saint of women, the falsely accused, the homeless, the mentally insane, as well as the prostitutes, single mothers and widows.

Nora had quipped, "In any particular order?"

"No, but as you can well imagine, she was *and* continues to be a busy lady."

He then proceeded to tell Nora the legend of Cortona's patron saint and Nora had discovered that originally Margherita had been a beautiful girl who had fallen in love with a local boy. When his dog returned home one day without him, she followed it into the fields, only to find her lover murdered in a ditch. Pregnant and unwed, the girl was abandoned by the boy's family, left to beg and wander the streets of Cortona. But even in such a humiliating state, she continued to do good deeds for others, never once accepting defeat.

Standing before the Saint now, Nora whispered to Juliette, "At least, now the lady finally had a home and a place to rest her head. And keeping Margherita in a glass coffin is one way to keep a close eye on her... you know, seeing as she had a propensity for wandering around town and the surrounding area."

Juli smothered a smile, and as they left the main altar, her phone began to vibrate. She checked the screen and saw it was Marco. In a hushed voice, Juliette said, "I need to take this call, it's about the equipment we ordered. I'll meet you outside the church in a few minutes."

Nora didn't mind; after the effort she had exerted to get here, she was in no hurry to go and still wanted to explore the church a bit more on her own. Walking down the side aisle, she noted the gray-and-white patterned floor and the walls decorated with stripes so typical of the Neo-Gothic style. Stepping into a small alcove lit with candles, she pulled out her cell phone to take a picture. As she framed her shot, a familiar man stepped into the viewfinder. Slowly, Nora lowered her, phone recognizing him; it was Ruggero Falconi.

She wondered what he was doing in Margherita's church in Cortona. It wasn't that far from Arezzo, but still, in his condition, it seemed like an unnecessary journey. Respectfully, she observed the man as he gazed up at a statue of the pious saint. Was he here to say a prayer to saint Margherita and seek a bit of solace?

Or, Nora wondered, did he still harbor feelings for Luca's grandmother? Perhaps, even after all these years, he had a special affection for the girl he once hoped to marry. Had he made a special pilgrimage here to honor his lost love?

The former, perhaps, but she doubted the latter. During the past couple of months, she occasionally saw Signor Falconi around town. Sometimes when she was visiting Luca, the old man peered into the shop window. He would look at them for a moment and then, with a disgusted shake of his head, continue on by. Other times, when she and Luca were walking together, as he passed by, he'd mumble a nasty remark—but mostly he chose to ignore them entirely.

He seemed a bitter and reclusive man. Still, Nora couldn't help but feel a bit sorry for him. Ruggero had been thrown over by his fiancé and had lost his wife, his daughter, and then his granddaughter. That alone might have been enough to tip anyone over the brink of sanity or perhaps to drink.

Not wanting to interrupt his reverie, Nora was about to turn away, but when she saw a younger man walking briskly down the side aisle in his direction, she stopped and watched curiously. At first, she thought he was another tourist, so she was surprised when he ended by Signor Falconi's side and spoke with him in hushed tones.

She studied the second man, noting his close-cropped hair and the tattoos that emerged from the sleeve of his t-shirt and ran down the length of his arm. The design interested her, and without thinking, she raised her phone and took a picture. Perhaps she'd post it to Facebook coupled with a clever comment like: *Santa Margherita pulls in the most colorful crowd.*

Nora zoomed in on the picture and busied herself with cropping and framing the shot, trying to think of an even wittier comment. When she looked up again, she realized the men had stopped talking and were now shaking hands. Their meeting had been brief, and Nora viewed the man with the tattoo with a speculative eye as he moved away from her, down the far side of the church. When the wooden door banged shut, she turned back to Signor Falconi. Watching from her vantage point a few steps away, she wondered if he too would leave the church and return to Arezzo.

Instead, the old man seemed in no hurry to go. He turned his gaze back to the image of Santa Margherita and bowed his head as he made the sign of the cross. He stood for a few moments as if transfixed. As she continued to watch him, however, Nora saw him stagger slightly, and she thought he was going to fall. Reacting quickly, she moved toward him, intending to give him a hand. Seeing he had caught himself on the back of a pew, she hesitated and stepped back into the shadows.

From a distance, she watched as he gingerly lowered himself onto the wooden bench. Sitting alone in the dark church gazing up at Santa Margherita, he seemed a tired, subdued man.

Thinking about the things she had just seen, Nora left the church undetected.

Chapter 27

A Princess is Awakened

"*I*t's almost finished, Nora, what do you think?" asked Egidio.

Nora walked to his workbench and watched as he applied gold leaf to the intricately carved base of the lance, burnishing it into the wood with a flat metal tool. The gold clearly enhanced the Medici princess's distinctive profile. It also made the beads that encircled the handle more elegant and distinct, as if they were crown jewels.

"*Che bello,*" said Nora. "It's lovely. I believe Isabella would have been very pleased."

"I have something to show you, too." From her table, she picked up a heavy gold chain. "Look, the pendant is done. I was here late, but I finished it last night."

Egidio fingered the gold medallion and admired the oversized drop pearl. "*Complimenti!* It is a thing of beauty and indeed a necklace fit for Isabella. I think today we both have made our Princess very proud."

"*Senti,* if you don't mind, I'm going to take the pendant over to show Luca. I wanted you to be the first to see it, but it's important that he be one of the first to see it as well."

"Go, go!" Egidio urged.

"*Grazie, Maestro,*" she said, then kissed him on the cheek. She slid the necklace into a silk pouch and headed to Luca's shop just around the corner. But her excitement was instantly curtailed as she drew nearer and saw two police cars parked in front. *What now?* she wondered. *Had there been another burglary?*

When she entered the shop, she saw Luca standing behind the counter, and all thoughts of her necklace were forgotten. In concern, she observed the two officers wearing thick dark boots interrogating him. When he noticed her standing near the window, he smiled grimly. With a nod of his head, he indicated she stay where she was, then turned his attention back to the *carabinieri*.

"Can we have the rest of the documents, please?"

Luca reached under the counter, pulled out a thick file, and shuffled through the papers. Finding the one he was looking for, he handed it to one of the officers. The man scrutinized the contents and then nodded brusquely at Luca. "We will need to take this with us. Please come by the *questura* this afternoon. It's all just routine, you understand. We want to make sure everything complies."

When the policemen passed by her on the way out of the shop, they acknowledged her with a courteous tip of their hats. Through the window, she watched as they got into their car and drove slowly down the street until they turned the corner.

Turning back to Luca, she asked, "What's happened now? Was there another break-in?"

Luca looked disgusted. "*Che palla*! Seems the local officials got a tip that has put into question some of my business dealings. 'Someone' has suggested that I might be passing off fraudulent pieces. They are questioning the documentation of a painting I recently sold."

By the way he said "someone", Nora knew he meant Signor Falconi. "Which piece are they referring to?" she asked.

"The painting we were discussing a while back, the one of the girl at the spinet. They need to review the painting's provenance. The man who bought it from me a few days ago went to the authorities, saying I cheated him. Now they want to open a full investigation."

"But you went through and verified everything," she said.

"Yes, I know. I had everything thoroughly inspected and documented before purchasing the lot, and everything checked out."

"Well, then. Why has this blown up in your face all of a sudden?"

"That's the million-dollar question."

"What are you going to do now?"

"As you just heard, I have to go in later with all the documentation of other items I sold last week. Then I'll need to re-verify the size of the painting to see if it agrees with the original dimensions. They will want to know if the painting has been cut down from a larger canvas or if there are signs, like old nail holes on the mounting, to show whether the picture was removed from the frame or doctored in any way. Most of the time, forgeries are just clumsy copies that try to imitate a master's hand, and usually they can be easily detected."

At that moment, Egidio entered the shop. "I saw the police pass by and saw the commotion. Is everything alright?"

Luca quickly caught him up on the recent turn of events, explaining what he had just told Nora.

"And you think Ruggero Falconi is behind it?" asked Egidio. "I've known him for years, but lately, he has just become an old fool, and his judgment is clouded."

"Want to hear something funny? I saw Signor Falconi the other day in Santa Margherita's church when I went to Cortona with Juli. I thought it a little strange at the time. I see him so rarely around here, and then I run into him there and..."

Luca looked up curiously. "Falconi was in Cortona?"

"I got the impression he was there to pay his respects to Santa Margherita. But while he was there, he also met a man in one of the alcoves of the church."

"What did the other guy look like?" asked Luca.

Nora thought a moment. "It was kind of murky, and I really couldn't hear what they were saying, but the man had very short hair, almost baldish... And get this, he had this really wild tattoo on his arm. I thought it interesting he should be talking to Signor Falconi. They seemed a mismatched pair."

"A tattoo—what kind of tattoo?"

"Here, let me show you. You know me, always taking pictures of the weirdest things—seagulls, tattoos, saints in glass cases." Taking out her phone, she flipped through her photos. "Look! Here's Santa Margherita..." She held up the screen for Luca to view, but by the expression on his face—saint or no saint—it wasn't the image he was hoping to see.

"Okay, okay," she said, as he gestured impatiently for her to hurry up. "Here it is. It's not the best picture I've ever taken, but I enhanced it and lightened it a bit so it would show up better."

Luca took the phone from her, and both men studied the image. *"Beccato!* That's the guy who bought the painting. It *proves* Falconi had something to do with this. He has been a thorn in my side for the past two years, but this is the first time I've got the proof to make him back off. Falconi must be getting sloppy. Like you said, Egidio, he's an old fool."

"Yes, some of us age better than others," Signor Michelozzi said with a wan smile. "He's never been one to listen to me, but all the same I think I'll drop by his place and have a little chat with my friend Ruggero. We go way back. You know—there's a lot of history between us. Maybe this time I can talk some sense into that crusty old brain of his."

"Tell him Donati is on to him. Tell him I'm tired of his mean little games and to back off once and for good."

After Egidio left, Nora said, "You know, I felt sorry for him the other day. He seemed so alone."

"I don't have time to worry about the old man now. I'm more concerned he might have done something else detrimental."

"Like what?"

"What if Falconi has inserted a fake painting into the lot somehow, to further slander our good name? Okay. That does it. I'm going to go back through everything to make sure I didn't miss anything. I can't afford to have an actual forged painting on my hands."

Assessing the shop, Nora rolled up her sleeves and asked, "So, where do we begin? How can I help?"

He motioned her to follow him to the back room. "You can give me a hand checking over these paintings against this back wall."

She glanced at the stack of canvases then bent down to view them better. Over her shoulder, she asked, "What am I looking for?"

"Look for signs of tampering at the frame's edge," Luca replied.

Nora studied one painting, then picked up another. But seeing nothing out of the ordinary, she stood up and found herself face to face with Luca's grandfather's picture of Santa Margherita.

"Want to hear something interesting?" Nora called out to Luca again. "I just recently learned from Marco that Santa Margherita is the patron saint of the falsely accused. Perhaps you should treat this painting a little better. Maybe it is time to pay her some respect and find a better place to hang her. After all, she's your grandmother's namesake, and your grandfather painted it."

As she continued to study the painting, a ray of morning sun broke through the window, striking the canvas as if a spotlight had been directed upon it. Nora watched the light play over the surface, revealing an uneven texture. Tilting her head to one side, she regarded it thoughtfully.

"Hey, Luca, come over here a minute," she said excitedly.

"What is it? Did you find something?"

When he was standing directly behind her, he said, "I'm not interested in that painting, Nora. Check the ones over there..."

"Hold on," Nora said. "Look closely at this one first." Pointing to the right-hand corner, she asked, "What does that seem like?"

Luca narrowed his eyes at the canvas. "What are you thinking?"

"Maybe it is just my imagination, but it almost seems like you can see a bit of *pentimento*."

He leaned in closer and asked, "You see some of the underpainting bleeding through?"

"Yes," said Nora. "See? Right there. It might mean something. Then again, maybe not."

"Let's get a better look at this," Luca said as he lifted the painting off the wall. At closer proximity, Nora observed how the saint glanced heavenward and clutched a hand to her breast. Margherita, indeed, seemed the picture of piety. The mysteries of her religion were preserved and protected within her generous heart. Perhaps, however, the lady was keeping another secret.

"This was one of your grandfather's paintings, right?" asked Nora. "So what do you think he was up to?"

"Maybe he was recycling canvases and painted over one of his earlier pictures. Or maybe he was doctoring up someone else's work..."

Nora and Luca exchanged a glance. "You don't suppose..."

Without another word, Luca went to the back room and returned with a soft cotton cloth and a mild restorative solvent that he often used to clean paintings he acquired for sale. He applied a bit of liquid to the fabric and rubbed the corner of the canvas, working in small even circles. After a moment, he examined it, then held it out for Nora to see. The cloth showed traces of dark smudges, but it wasn't years of grimy dirt. Instead, some of the top pigment had been removed.

"This is obviously not your typical oil paint," said Nora. "The consistency is more like thick tempera paint, and it's coming off far too easily."

Looking back at the canvas they could just make out the hint of an indigo background starting to be revealed in the far corner. Eager to discover what lay beneath the top coat, Nora picked up a second cotton rag and swiped the surface in gentle strokes.

"This is unreal," said Luca in amazement. "For as long as I can recall, the painting of Margherita has hung here in the back of the shop over the workbench. I remember seeing it as a boy but never thought much about it."

They continued their efforts and fifteen minutes later, as the thin surface layer dissolved and the pious face of Santa Margherita faded away, it was replaced by another—that of a woman with an alabaster complexion and pearls entwined in her hair.

"I don't believe it," whispered Nora, rubbing her cloth over the surface of the canvas in deft movements. Together they worked diligently and after another ten minutes passed, they stepped back in unison, then, wide-eyed, they looked at one another.

"Incredible," Luca murmured. "Who would have guessed...?"

With a fourth of the top coat removed, they saw the painting's original subject matter, a Medici princess and her mother: It was the Bronzino painting Luca's grandfather Federico had smuggled out of Paris in a Red Cross truck between two mattresses. The canvas hadn't been destroyed in the war after all. Federico had made sure the Nazis would never find it by painting over the surface, essentially hiding it under their very noses.

In stunned silence, they gazed at the lost painting of Isabella.

"Buongiorno, principessa!" Nora finally whispered. "Fancy meeting you here, too."

Chapter 28

Tutta la Verità

*E*gidio stopped in front of a door in a neighborhood of Porta del Foro. It was midday, and except for a dog that was stretched out in the shadows trying to escape the heat, the street was deserted. As he shielded his eyes from the glare of the noonday sun that glinted off the sides of white buildings, he noticed the sky was dotted with cumulus clouds. He hoped they would bring rain and a bit of relief during the evening hours. Otherwise, it would be a hot afternoon tomorrow sitting in the bleachers watching the joust, dressed in medieval costumes.

Resolutely, he turned his attention back to the reason he had come to be standing in this particular street, in front of this particular door. It was a part of town he rarely set foot and where he knew he wasn't welcome.

As he raised his hand to knock, Ruggero wrenched the door open.

"I saw you from the window. What do you want?" the man demanded.

"It is nice to see you, too, Ruggero. May I come in? It's time we talked."

Ruggero said nothing. He observed the other man and narrowed his eyes, saying, "Come in if you must, but I've got nothing to say to you."

Turning, he shuffled down the hall, and with a wave of his hand, he indicated Egidio should follow him. "Close the door, you idiot, you are letting in the heat."

Egidio followed Ruggero down a short hall and found himself in a dark parlor, cluttered with papers and trays of food. It appeared a hermit's cave, dismal and depressing. On the walls were pictures of stallions, and draped over the back of a chair was a red and gold sash, the colors of Porta del Foro. Scattered about the table were framed photographs and in one he recognized Ruggero's wife holding the hand of Carlotta, at the age of about seven.

Walking to the window, he cracked open the shutter. Looking down, he saw the mangy dog had moved out of the shadows and was limping down the street. He imagined it was hungry and would be rooting around searching for scraps to eat. Over his shoulder, he asked, "Do you mind if I open this up and let a little more light into the room?"

Without waiting for an answer, he folded back the shutters. A shaft of light sliced through the darkness, creating a rectangular square on the floor. Dust danced crazily in the air, and the silence was broken. From across the street, he could hear plates rattling and the distant voices of the neighbors as they called back and forth across their terraces.

Raising a hand in front of his face, Ruggero shuddered as if the sudden burst of light disturbed his eyes. He blinked a few times before demanding again, "Well, you didn't come here just to open my windows, did you?"

Egidio regarded him for a moment. He removed his hat and brushed a piece of lint from his carefully pressed pants. Again, he noted that the other man did not appear at all well. They were the same age and had attended school together. Noticing the dry spots of wine on Ruggero's shirt, and his untidy hair, Egidio realized how far they had come from that time. Here he stood upright and still took pleasure in his appearance and his work, while Ruggero seemed rumpled and broken.

"Well," demanded Ruggero impatiently. "What are you waiting for? I can see you have something on your mind. Out with it... I've got things to do."

"Ruggero." He paused and indicated a chair. "You seem tired, you should sit down."

When the other man ignored him and continued standing, Egidio sighed. "Suit yourself. I think you know why I have come. I need to speak with you about Luca Donati."

"What about him?"

"Recently there has been some unpleasantness," replied Egidio. "Today, Luca received a visit from the police, and he is now under investigation. He sold someone a painting, and now the buyer is claiming it is a fake."

Ruggero grinned. "Well, he should be scrutinized. He deserves it."

"That is absurd, and you know it," replied Egidio. "Someone saw you the other day in Cortona having a meeting. The man you spoke with—he's the one who bought that painting from Luca, isn't he? Haven't you done enough damage over the years? Why are you continuing to wage this war?"

Ruggero replied angrily, "What are you talking about? What war?"

"I know you are plotting things as usual. You are up to your old tricks. Come on, Ruggero! You are too old for this. It is time to let go of the past. You need to let her go."

Stabbing the floor with his cane, Ruggero said, "I will never let go of Carlotta and the pain he put her through. He's to blame for her death."

"I'm not talking about Carlotta. I'm talking about Margherita."

He watched Ruggero as he took a step back and then sank deeply into a cushioned chair next to the hearth.

"You *know* Carlotta's death was an unfortunate accident. Luca is a good man, and it wasn't his fault. He tried his best to help her."

Egidio peered around the miserable room, then gazed directly back at the other man. "But you, old man, you have sins that need accounting for."

"What are you talking about?" Ruggero's face displayed belligerence, but by the way his darted about the room, Egidio knew he had touched a nerve.

"You know very well what I am talking about," said Egidio. "You need to take accountability for your past actions. All the blame and the resentment you have been harboring all these years... In the end, it's just been misplaced guilt. And it's been eating you alive."

Ruggero slouched back in the chair, at a loss for words, and Egidio continued. "Haven't you punished Margherita enough? You can't continue to blame her for not loving you, but loving Federico instead. I know how much you cared for her and she always had a fondness for you. I've also been aware of the one thing you could never admit to her. I'm the only one who has ever known your secret."

"Known what... What secret?" Narrowing his eyes, he said, "Tell me, Michelozzi, what exactly do you know?"

"I know you were the one who turned Federico into the Germans. I also know it was you who killed him."

The ticking of the mantel clock seemed to grow louder, and the air was thick with old grievances and ghosts.

At last, Ruggero exploded, "That's ridiculous! Preposterous! You are an old misguided buffoon. You think me insane? Well, it is you who should have his head examined."

Raising his cane in the air, he yelled, "Everyone knows I did everything I could—that is why I was there that day. I told Margherita I would talk to the German commandant. I promised her I would do everything in my power to make up for my mistake. I was true to my word, and it was *me* who got her father released."

Smugly, he boasted, "That alone is all the proof you need I was there that day to help Margherita. I'm not responsible for the death of that miserable painter. Everyone knows it was the Germans who killed him. He was dead when I got there. I did everything..."

Egidio cut him off. "I was there. I saw it happen."

Again, the ticking of the clock filled the room with a deafening sound as Ruggero regarded him in disbelief.

"I was at Villa Godiola the day Federico died," Egidio said flatly. "I know what really happened."

"How could you have seen anything?"

Steadily holding the other man's gaze, Egidio explained, "My father sent me there that day to deliver a pendant one of the German officers had ordered for his wife."

"So what does that have to do with me?" demanded Ruggero.

"Margherita came to us shortly after Bernardo and Federico had been taken by the Gestapo. She held out hope that you alone could help her get them released."

Ruggero said, "See... I told you..."

Egidio interrupted him. "But we didn't trust you. No one did back then. We knew you were collaborating with the Gestapo."

When he remained silent, Egidio said, "We needed a plan to get someone inside the German headquarters to find out what had happened to Bernardo and Federico. Delivering the package of jewels provided the necessary cover. After dropping off the package, I was dismissed, but instead of leaving the grounds, I pedaled down the road and re-entered the property from a hidden side lane. We knew prisoners were detained in the outer buildings, near the scuderia, in the horse stables."

Gazing over Ruggero's shoulder, he envisioned that day long ago. "As I approached the barns, I heard your voice. I slipped into one of the stalls and saw you at the end of the barn, talking to Federico. At first, I was relieved to hear his voice and know he hadn't been sent up north to some prison camp. I was glad he was still alive, but when I saw him, I shuddered at the way he had been treated. His artist's hand had been tightly bound with a rope, and his face had been beaten to a bloody pulp."

Clearing his throat, Egidio withdrew a handkerchief. "I wasn't sure why you were there talking to him. I hoped you were helping to set him free. But as I watched and listened, I heard your insults and your taunts. At first, Federico didn't react. I watched him take your abuse, but he seemed to hardly hear you."

Using the cloth to wipe his brow, he said, "But then I saw you jerk the rope, causing him to stumble to the ground. Finally provoked, he rose up and struck you with his two fists still tied together. It was then the two of you began fighting."

Egidio waited for Ruggero to say something, but he remained mute. Closing his eyes, Egidio saw the scene play out in his mind, as he had a hundred times before. He watched as Ruggero grabbed a block of wood from the pile stacked in the barn. When Federico had sidestepped to avoid being slammed in the chest, he lost his balance; he'd fallen backward and hit his head on the stone wall.

Opening his eyes, Egidio said, "I watched Federico collapse and saw the blood pool around his head, and I knew instinctively he would never stand up again." Slipping the handkerchief back into his pocket, Egidio added, "I truly believe you didn't intentionally set out to kill Federico that day in the stalls. I could see how horrified you were. I watched you throw the block of wood away and try and help him to his feet. But your efforts were useless."

Shaking his head sadly, he said, "It was a terrible fight that spiraled out of control."

Ruggero said not a word, but his posture betrayed him. His head hung heavily from the unnatural curve of his spine as if his body could no longer bear its weight. He was a portrait of a defeated man.

"I wanted you to be the one to tell Margherita," said Egidio. "But instead of coming clean, you covered up the whole thing. You returned to her, stared her straight in the face, and lied to her. It was *you* who made her a widow that day... not the German guard like you told everyone. You have lived with that lie ever since."

Breathing slowly, Ruggero raised his head and said, "If that were all true, why didn't you come forward years ago with this ridiculous accusation?"

Egidio said, "It was a time of war, and things were confused. I was standing in Nazi headquarters and no one would have cared. I couldn't call attention to my father's business or put my family in harm's way."

"And after the war? Why didn't you say anything then?"

"Perhaps I should have, but there were simply too many deaths fresh in our minds. After the war ended, we had to pick up the pieces and move on. At first, I was going to say something. But then I watched you reach out to Margherita and her father—all driven by the guilt you felt, I imagine—and I saw how you offered them assistance and money to rebuild their business.

"It was then I realized I couldn't find it in my heart to tell her what had happened that day. She needed your support, not to be burdened by more grief. So I kept quiet. Time went by, the years passed, and the grandchildren united, and once again it seemed better to forget and let things remain in the past."

The two men sat for a moment in silence. Through the open window, they could hear the clanging bells of San Donato. Egidio walked back to the window. "But recently something has gotten all twisted up inside of you. Perhaps if I had said something and you had been held accountable, maybe it would have helped you find some mercy."

Ruggero mumbled something under his breath, but Egidio couldn't understand him. "What did you say? Speak up."

Ruggero whispered hoarsely, "I never meant for him to die. You have to believe me. I went there to do as Margherita had asked, but I was drunk, I got angry... Things got out of hand. I just meant to rough him up..."

Egidio studied the man for a moment. "Now is your chance, Falconi. *È l'ora per tutta la verità*. It's time for the whole truth to come out. Do it for Margherita's sake. Start by dropping the false accusations you've brought against Luca. He's got nothing to do with this."

As he turned toward the door, he said, "It's time, Ruggero. It's time to forgive Margherita and let her go. Then perhaps you will be able to forgive yourself for your ultimate betrayal."

Chapter 29

The Joust

*N*ora's heart pounded in rhythm with the drummers. She was at the back of the long procession with the other lords and ladies, marching up the street to the Piazza Grande to the tournament. Ahead of them rode the jousters along with the members of each of their contrada. Even from the back, she could hear the crowd cheering wildly for its heroes.

Luca was also up there with them, dressed in a long blue cloak, walking alongside the horses and the other coaches representing Santo Spirito. Today, as in the past, he would be guiding the riders down the track and into position at the starting line.

Decked out in her own Renaissance costume, Nora felt quite at home amongst the jubilation and fanfare. Unlike the previous joust, after she had just arrived in June, instead of being merely an interested observer, she was now an avid participant representing the Medici princess.

Walking next to her were Marco and Juliette, and directly ahead of them was a troupe of men dressed in brightly colored tunics, tights, and plumed hats. Momentarily distracted by a blare of trumpets, the entire assembly came to a halt and watched as the *sbandieratori* ahead of them twirled and launched their banners high into the air. Nora marveled as the men caught them with precision and skill.

She waited for the spectacle to finish, and as she did, Nora looked around and waved to the cheering crowd lining the street. When the procession started to move again, she caught a glimpse of herself in a nearby shop window, and it almost seemed as if Isabella was greeting her from the sidelines.

Nora regarded her image with pleasure. She couldn't have been happier with the gown the costume makers of the city had chosen for her to wear. It was a tight-fitting affair made from dark blue velvet and trimmed with beadwork. It featured a full skirt that parted in the middle to reveal a gold embroidered silk underskirt. The V-line cut of the dress dipped rather provocatively, and the neckline was trimmed with frothy lace that perfectly framed the pendant she had created to honor Isabella's memory. She seemed a perfect Renaissance lady with her hair caught up and secured with a jewel-encrusted comb that Egidio had surprised her with earlier that morning.

As the entourage continued up the street and into the Piazza, they broke rank. With Marco's assistance, holding both their hands, Juliette and Nora climbed the stairs to the Grand Dais. There they took their places next to the other delegates. Shading her eyes, she directed her gaze toward the other side of the Piazza, and at the start of the racetrack, she saw Luca holding the reins of one of the horses.

Turning her attention back to the center of the piazza, she watched the pregame spectacle. Another dramatic blare of trumpets announced the arrival of the city's dignitaries. Following close behind the mayor and his wife, Nora saw Egidio. As he settled into his chair a few rows below her in the section reserved for prominent business leaders, she called out his name, greeting him warmly.

As she surveyed the scene, she noticed there were a few seats around him that were still empty. When she pointed this out to Marco, he shrugged and said, "One of those is reserved for Falconi." Looking around, he said, "I don't see him here today. Ruggero never misses the joust. I wonder why he isn't here?"

But Nora didn't have time to ponder Ruggero's absence any further and was soon diverted by the start of the joust. She, along with the frenzied crowd watched as the first jouster raced up the slope. After the horseman struck the target, men dressed in Arabic pants and headdresses raced up to grab the scorecard, careful not to be beaten with the twirling flail of the Saracen dummy.

There was a brief pause while the results of the rider's accuracy were judged by a small group of men and women dressed in flowing red robes and white caps. The crowd impatiently held their breath, many hoping their neighborhood hero had earned them more points and others hoping he'd failed, leaving their own team an opening. As they waited, they stomped their feet on the metal bleachers, making a deafening noise.

Finally, the results were posted, cheers filled the piazza, and the next jouster took his turn. As each rider struck the wooden mannequin, it spun wildly on its stand, a blur of chaotic colors.

After an hour, it came down to two teams. If Porta Santo Spirito took the next round, Luca's team would be the winner. On the edge of her seat, Nora watched as Luca walked alongside the mounted cavalier to the starting line. As the men passed by, Nora could see the pride and determination on their faces. They looked neither to the left or to the right, so focused were they on their mission.

When they reached the other side, she saw a commissioner dressed in black and white on horseback approach them and hand the rider the officially inspected lance. She then observed Luca move to the side, to stand in an advantageous spot where he could see the Maestro de Campo clearly and relay to the horseman he could take his mark.

But when the master of the field lowered his scepter and Luca signaled to the young man it was time, instead of approaching the white line, the horse danced back and forth, shying away from the loud clamor coming from the stands. The crowd chanted all over again, causing the animal to frighten even more. The man tried to steady his mount, but just as it was brought to the start line, it reared up on its hind legs and thrashed its hooves high in the air.

It seemed the horse was out of control, and a collective cry of dismay emanated from the piazza. It was then that Nora saw Luca come to the cavalier's aid. Grabbing the horse by the bridle, he whispered into the animal's ear. Then, speaking directly to the young man, he rubbed the horse's nose, and slowly the stallion settled into position.

Confident once more, the jouster clutched the reins, in control of the animal again. Then he dug in his heels and, in an impressive bolt of speed, he tore across the piazza. Horse and rider were united as one. It was a joyous sight to behold—a moment of pure beauty. As the jouster neared his goal, the crowd roared its approval, and the square was filled with exhilarated pandemonium.

Across town, a quieter scene was unfolding in a house in Porta del Foro. Standing by the window, listening to the commotion coming from the Piazza Grande, an old man gazed down at a black and white photo of a woman whom he had once adored. He rubbed his fingers over her face, recalling how happy he had been once, and his subsequent years of misery. He had been blinded by rage, consumed by a terrible hatred—and because of that, he had robbed her of something beautiful.

The years had blurred together, but still, he loved her, and now it was important for her to know.

The man glanced up when he heard the crowd roar, and just as the noble horseman's lance pierced its target, Ruggero clutched his heart in pain. Stumbling forward, he grabbed the back of his chair, and as his cane clattered to the floor, he felt the pressure in his chest increase.

As the photo slipped from his hands and fluttered to the floor, he sank slowly to the ground, and with his last dying breath, he called out to Margherita, asking for forgiveness.

Chapter 30

A Piece of Picasso

*L*uca drew Nora to her feet and swung her around in a circle, then, pulling her to him, they moved together. A week had passed since the joust, and the neighborhood had gathered together again to celebrate their *contrada's* victory.

"It's the same old festival," he said, "the same old traditions. The past seems to keep repeating itself, but because of you, I feel like I see things with new eyes."

"I can't think of any place," Nora responded, "I'd rather be at this moment than dancing with you in this piazza."

"*Sei stata mandata dal cielo.* From the moment you fell into my arms," he said, "you have proven to be my good luck charm."

"*Ah, sì?*" Nora said. "If you ask me, I think we owe our current good fortune to *La Dama Bianca*, not me. Isabella has been very good to both of us. I'm so glad she decided to show up and finally join the party. She couldn't miss her final curtain call."

Nora thought back over the events of the past week. Since the discovery of the painting, there had been a flurry of activity and Luca was now something of a local celebrity. The charges he had been faced with a week earlier had been dropped without any further complications, and his name had been cleared of any misdemeanors or unethical business transactions. Articles had appeared in the paper, causing quite a stir. Overnight, it seemed, his business picked up, and he was even busier than before.

The Shop around the Corner had been inundated by museum personnel from the Uffizi, and Nora and Luca watched in amazement as the painting that had hung for so many years at the back of the showroom, hardly given much consideration, was now the focus of everyone's concern.

A certain Lorenzo Conti, the curator of the museum's prestigious Renaissance collection, was particularly pleased with the find. After several hours, he, along with his staff of experts, authenticated it, verifying that it was indeed the Bronzino painting.

Speaking with Luca and Nora, he said, "I'd given up all hope of ever seeing this painting being recovered. It's quite a significant find, historically and economically. A real gem. Bronzino eclipsed himself—just look at the intensity of the colors."

When he had the conclusive proof he needed, he contacted the Louvre. After a lengthy conversation, one of many more to come, Nora imagined, the authorities in charge had agreed to let the painting be restored and remain in the Uffizi, under the condition the princess and her mother would be allowed a special exhibition in Paris the following year.

"Tell me the entire story from start to finish," Lorenzo had urged, and he had listened with great interest as Luca explained the details of how his grandfather had smuggled the painting out of Paris under the very noses of the German Gestapo. Hardly containing his enthusiasm, he then turned to Nora and together they discussed the importance of the iconography, and how unusual it was to have the two Medici women depicted together.

After learning of her participation in the recovery of the painting, and that she had just finished a documentary for Stanford University about the princess called *Waking Isabella*, Conti invited her to speak at the public unveiling of the picture.

Not too bad for one summer's work, Nora thought. Not only would she make her presentation in California later in the fall, she would also present her film at the Uffizi.

As Luca and Nora watched the museum curators finish their work, carefully wrapping and crating the painting to be taken back to Florence, they chatted with Signor Conti's wife, Sophia. In her arms, she held the couple's five-year-old daughter.

"I was curious to have a first glimpse of the painting," Sophia admitted. "I've always had a soft spot in my heart for Bronzino's portrait of Isabella's mother." Smiling conspiratorially, she explained, "It was Eleonora, after all, who whispered into my ear and convinced me to take a chance on Italy. And now the portrait of her with her daughter has been found and reunited with Italy again. I wanted my daughter to share in this moment as well."

Continuing to slow dance with Nora around the piazza, Luca teased, "And what did Conti's wife say, when you told her that Isabella was the one to call you to Italy?"

"We agreed it took a special kind of woman, to channel the voices of the past, and bring such role models back to life to be appreciated by a new generation."

Leaning back in his arms, she said, "You know what else I told her?"

"What?" he asked, smiling at her.

"That it is especially fitting that you, Federico's grandson, should be the one to carry out his mission to give the Bronzino painting back to the Italian people. He would have been very proud."

"Well," said Luca, "I'm sure our leading lady is happy to be back in Florence, where she will reside in the Uffizi Gallery."

"Isabella is known for popping up when you least expect her, and then disappearing all over again. I'm going to have to keep my eye on her to make sure she stays here for good."

"So, am I correct in assuming you are still planning on lingering a while longer here in Arezzo?"

"I'd say that's a pretty good assumption," agreed Nora. "After all, I've got a new video to work on that will require some in-depth research. In fact, I have a particular interest in an ex-jouster, and I'd like to interview him more thoroughly."

"I seem to recall, you are also interested in learning to ride a horse."

"That's right. There's going to be plenty to do—I couldn't possibly leave right now. I think life with you... Well, let's just say it's going to be full of surprises."

When the song ended, she whispered into his ear, "Tell me, do you have any more famous works of art hidden in some dark corner waiting to be discovered?"

Luca shook his head and said, "Sorry, fresh out of mystery paintings. But dark corners—I can find lots of those."

"That sounds intriguing. I'll let you in on a little secret—I'm no pious madonna. Rather, I'm feeling a little like Isabella tonight. I think I should warn you I've read her diaries, and that woman was no saint."

"*Ah, sì?*" he said as he caressed the gold necklace that hung around Nora's neck, the one she had created to resemble Isabella's. "*Sembri così innocente.* You could have fooled me with that beatific smile. But now that you mention it, I'm starting to see a certain gleam in your eye. Why don't you and I..."

He stopped mid-sentence, and an odd expression crossed his face, as if he had just had an amazing revelation. Taking her by the hand, he said, "Come on. It's time to go!"

"Where are we going exactly?" she asked, amused by his sudden urgency. "We've got all night, why the sudden rush?"

"You'll see in a minute."

Nora, thinking he was leading her back to her apartment in the neighborhood to spend a spontaneous and romantic moment together, was surprised to find Luca had led her to a quieter street a few blocks closer to the original gates. He stopped in front of an elegant apartment building and, digging a key out of his wallet, opened the main door.

Seeing her questioning look, he said, "My family owns this building. This is where I grew up. When my grandmother Nita was alive, she had her private apartments on the third floor."

"We're going to your *grandmother's* apartment? *Now?* That's not exactly what I had in mind."

Luca laughed. "You and Isabella have just given me an idea. I have a hunch we are about to find another hidden treasure." As he climbed the stairs, Nora did her best to keep up with his pace. When they reached the landing outside his grandmother's apartment, he turned to her and said,

"Let's see if I am right."

Without saying anything more, he opened the door and flipped on the light. Nora looked around but saw nothing out of the ordinary. The apartment was quite lovely. She noticed there were lace curtains at the window and against one wall there was a polished cherry curio filled with ceramic vases and small treasures.

She stepped over to an end table next to a love seat and picked up a photo. It showed a smiling girl and a handsome man standing in the Piazza Grande, and Nora recognized the Vasari Loggia behind them.

"That was my *nonna* Margherita, and next to her is my grandfather Federico." He indicated the far wall. "And *that* is one of his paintings."

Nora walked over to stand in front of the large canvas. The colors were bold and evocative, lovely in their asymmetrical confusion. The explosion of paint on the canvas made her think of the moment when a storm had passed and sunlight pierced through the dark clouds.

"That one was my grandmother's favorite. I'd often catch her sitting here lost in thought, admiring it. There are more paintings downstairs, and I have a couple in my apartment as well."

"This is beautiful. I'd love to see the rest," Nora said.

Taking the photo that Nora still held in her hand, he studied the image of his grandparents. "I wish I could have met him. But this place... It is just as I remember it from when I was a boy."

Luca surveyed the room. "We've left things as they were. No one has had the heart to remove anything. With my sister being gone, studying in England, and my parents traveling so much these days, the rooms haven't been needed."

Gesturing to the cabinet, he said, "*Nonna* always kept a tin of chocolate *biscotti* for me over there. She'd offer me one along with juice she made herself from lemons. As I drank my *limonata*, she'd tell me stories about her father Bernardo, my *bisnonno*, who started the Donati family business. She used to say that we had been entrusted with a gift of curating beauty and that it was our responsibility to protect it."

He was quiet for a moment, thinking about the memory. "Through her words, she brought them alive, describing them as men who stood tall and never backed down when confronted with injustice."

He looked at his grandfather's painting again and said, "She said I reminded her of them."

"She was right," Nora replied. "You are like them."

"Margherita took such pride in my grandfather's art. I can still hear her say, 'Luca, always remember that creative expression is the ultimate freedom, and it should not be taken lightly. If a person can't speak his mind, openly practice his religion, or paint what he wants, he can never truly be free.'"

He added, "She was always a tenacious lady, charming but determined as well."

"I can well imagine. From the stories you've told me about her, I feel as if I know her too. So, tell me again exactly why we are here. Something about hidden treasure?"

Luca turned to her and smiled. "Look over there," he said. Reaching over, he pulled the brass chain on a small lamp, chasing the shadows away and illuminating an alcove set into the far corner of the room.

"Do you see that hope chest? It is the one with the secret compartments that Bernardo and Egidio built for Margherita to keep her most prized possessions."

Nora walked over to the chest and, kneeling, she fiddled with the panels, searching for a spring to open the door. "So this is it? You think something is hidden inside and that I will know the secret of how to open your grandmother's chest?"

He looked at her and laughed, "No, not at all. I used to play with that as a kid. I've opened every one of those drawers. There is nothing hidden inside."

"Well, what then?" she said in an exasperated tone. Standing up, she placed her hands on her hips and turned to face him. "Where else could there be hidden treasure in this apartment?"

"Do you see the painting hanging above it? My grandfather Federico gave it to my grandmother on their wedding night. He told her to take care of it and never let it leave her sight."

Nora noticed for the first time a modestly-sized painting, which she estimated to be about three feet by three feet.

"It has always hung right there," said Luca. "I've seen it all my life and never thought much about it... That is, until tonight. What you said back there when we were dancing, about saints and madonnas? Then seeing Isabella's necklace around your neck and thinking about our recent discovery. Well, it came to me in a flash."

Nora gave him a puzzled frown. "It is just a painting of the virgin and child."

"Take a closer look. Come on, Nora. Don't you see anything particular about this painting?"

Rising to his challenge, Nora focused her attention on the picture. She noted again the serene Madonna holding a chubby baby and the little dog curled up at her feet. Fluttering above her head was a small dove. In the tranquil pasture behind the holy family, she could make out the details of a small bull.

"It seems like a typical eighteenth-century painting, sweet and bucolic. The only thing unusual is the little dog."

Turning back to him, she added, "Usually you don't see dogs paired with the Virgin Mary... But then again, it isn't unheard of."

"And..." Luca prompted, as he opened a drawer in the kitchen and pulled out a small flashlight, some tweezers, and a pair of pliers. He aimed the beam at the painting. "What else do you notice?"

"I don't know," said Nora. "It doesn't seem all that remarkable to me."

"What do you think about the face of the Madonna?" he inquired.

Nora mentally sifted through all the images of the Madonna she had seen in the past. As she carefully analyzed the virgin's alabaster cheeks, rose-colored lips, and delicate nose, she was struck by an odd sense of familiarity.

"Well, now that you mention it, I *have* seen her before..." Leaning in closer, she said, "In some ways, the Madonna here reminds me of the Santa Margherita that your grandfather painted over the Bronzino canvas... And the dog—it is the same dog!"

Nora stopped and turned around. "No! You don't suppose..."

Lifting the painting off the wall, Luca examined the back of the canvas. Carefully, he laid it on the dining room table and pried off the plywood backing. Nora watched as, with pliers, he loosened the nails that held the frame together. After a bit of gentle tugging, he pulled out the pins, and the frame broke apart. Beneath the painting of the Madonna and child, wrapped in paper, was a concealed package.

Luca smiled at Nora's wide-eyed expression. "It seems my hunch was right. You really are my lucky charm."

"Well, what is it?" she asked excitedly.

"Let's find out." As he spoke, he pulled off the protective wrapper, and Nora caught her breath. It was a painting done in black, gray, and white gouache paint. The bold, expressive strokes that defined the images of the bull and the dove were all too familiar.

"It is a study for the *Guernica*," whispered Nora, overcome with awe. "But I thought the Picasso painting that your grandfather smuggled out of Paris was sent on to Rosenberg's gallery in New York."

"Yes. Yes, it was. Bernardo and Federico managed to get it out of Italy undetected, and now both it and the Matisse painting are on display in the Metropolitan Museum."

"Then why," Nora asked, "is *this* painting here? Why didn't he send this one along with the others? Who does this one belong to?"

Luca raised his eyes to meet hers and shook his head. "I don't know."

They gazed at the painting a few moments longer, and then carefully Luca turned the sketch over. Together they read the note written in a bold hand on the back.

To Federico — Amico mio. No man is
truly free if he cannot express his thoughts freely
Your friend...

Luca looked at Nora, and a slow smile spread across their faces. Unbelievably, they held in their hands a small piece of Picasso. Blindsided by the enormity of their discovery, they merely stared in disbelief at the bold design. It seemed once again Isabella had pointed the way, helping them uncover another painting that had been hidden.

They realized this powerful drawing, a masterpiece in itself—denouncing tyranny and oppression—had been a gift to Federico from the legendary Spanish artist himself. Not wanting to endanger his family, once again Federico had taken great pains to hide this legacy, until a time when the world was a safer and saner place, and artists could once again express themselves freely.

"Art is the lie that makes us realize the truth," Picasso had once said, and he had been right. One should never underestimate its impact, for the simple swash of color on canvas, words courageously stroked with a pen, or the strains of an eloquent song have the power to change a man, a nation, even the world.

How incredible, Nora thought, *that together Luca and I should play such a pivotal role in uncovering two masterpieces that couldn't be further apart on the spectrum of beauty and creative expression.* In that quiet moment, she felt a part of something bigger than herself. It was as if she could hear the voices of countless people—Isabella's and Margherita's the loudest of them all—and could feel their joy, knowing their sacrifices hadn't been in vain.

Nora thought about something else Picasso had said: "There are only two types of women in the world—goddesses and doormats." He had been right on that account as well. Some women stood up for what they believed and lived big, bold lives and loved intensely, and then there were those who let life wash over them, fearful and afraid of realizing their full potential. After this past summer in Arezzo, she felt she had successfully graduated from the latter category to the former.

Her quest to awaken the Medici princess had introduced her to two remarkable women—Isabella and Margherita. The struggles and triumphs of a princess and those of a partisan had encouraged and inspired Nora, helping her unleash her own inner goddess. In the span of a few months, she had gone from sitting alone on a desolate beach, haunted by her choices, to the top of a mountain crest in Italy shouting out in jubilation at the top of her lungs, confident she was headed in the right direction. She liked this new version of herself.

Making eye contact with the man at her side, she could feel the love emanating from deep within him, as warm as the colors of his grandfather's painting. Nora knew life in Italy wouldn't always be smooth and without complications, and Luca might not always be easy to live with, but she was willing to accept a perfectly imperfect life if it meant growing stronger together.

This time she wouldn't give up so easily because this was a man, and a relationship, worth fighting for.

When Luca put his arm around her shoulders, Nora acknowledged to herself, yes, this was the path she chose gladly, and Italy was the ship she willingly boarded. Where it would take her in the future, she couldn't predict, but she knew in her heart if she were true to herself, life would always be beautiful.

Waking Isabella is based on facts—for the most part

Fiction

Isabella's story is based in fact and well-documented historical details, but as this is a fictional work to bring the princess to life, her conversations and scenes have been invented. And while it is true there are many portraits of Isabella de' Medici painted by Bronzino and other fifteenth-century artists, there is no actual painting of Isabella and her mother, Eleonora de' Toledo. (Or is there?)

Cimabue's crucifix in Arezzo was not hidden in a railway spur during the war. The idea was invented based on the true story of Ghiberti's bronze Baptistery doors in Florence, which were hidden from the Nazis in a tunnel near Incisa.

The Fiera Antiquaria is held the first Sunday of each month in Arezzo in the Piazza Grande. The joust is held twice a year: the third weekend in June (evening) and the first weekend in September (afternoon). Only in September do the Fiera Antiquaria and the joust coincide. Because the Piazza Grande is set up for the joust, the Fiera is located in the park next to the Duomo. For fictional purposes, the fair and the joust in June occur the same day, the third weekend in June.

Facts

Isabella de' Medici, the Medici princess, was murdered by her husband Paolo Giordano Orsini on July 16, 1576, in the hunting lodge built by her father Cosimo I in Cerreto Guidi, just outside of Florence. Isabella's lover was Troilo Orsini, Paolo's cousin. Francesco de' Medici, Isabella's brother and Grand Duke of Tuscany, was thought to be complicit in her murder. Her husband claimed she had died early one morning while washing her hair. Troilo, Isabella's lover, fled to France, but was pursued by assassins and shot dead while trying to escape on horseback.

Leonora de' Medici, Isabella's cousin, was murdered by her husband, Isabella's brother Pietro, a few days before Isabella was killed, in another hunting villa a short distance away in the Villa Medici at Cafaggiolo. Leonora was having an affair with Bernardino Antinori. Her lover was beaten and sent to the Bargello prison in Florence.

Isabella and Troilo did write secret letters. Several of Isabella's exist, and while there are references to Troilo's, only one survives. The letters in the story are fabricated except for an excerpt from a real one on p. 65 (Chapter 8, La Dama Bianca) For the full letter, reference: *Winspeare, Fabrizio, "Isabella Orsini e la corte medicea del suo tempo." Florence, 1961, p. 97, from ASF, MDP, 6373, ins. 1.*

There is an urban legend that Isabella's ghost haunts the Medici hunting villa in Cerreto Guidi. Isabella's ghost was documented most notably by a troupe of American actors in 1953 and the story was picked up by the American press.

Agnolo di Cosimo Bronzino was the court painter to the Medici from 1539-1570.

Hitler wanted to be an artist but was rejected twice from the Vienna Academy. During World War II, he attempted to amass a large collection of art to create the world's largest art museum in Berlin—the Führermuseum.

Pablo Picasso lived in Paris during WWII. There, he painted the *Guernica*, an anti-war painting. It was displayed for the first time at the 1937 World's Fair. He created numerous preliminary studies of the final piece, which eventually measured a monumental 11'6" x 25'6".

Paul Rosenberg was a French Jewish art collector who represented Pablo Picasso. In the late 1930s, alerted to the signs of an approaching war, he began quietly moving his collection from continental Europe to London, and to storage in America. He escaped to New York in 1940.

Jacques Jaujard, director of the Louvre, France's national museum, organized the transportation of 1,000 crates of ancient artifacts and 268 crates of paintings to the Loire Valley to hide them from Hitler. The *Mona Lisa* was transported in an ambulance, on a stretcher fitted with elastic suspension to keep it as safe as possible from jostling. It was moved about seven times during the course of the following years to keep it out of Hitler's hands.

Art historians called Monument Men located and worked tirelessly to identify, document, and return paintings that resurfaced after World War II.

"Bella Ciao" was sung by the anti-fascist resistance movement active in Italy between 1943 and 1945

The film *La vita è bella (Life is Beautiful)* was filmed in 1997 in Arezzo. Roberto Benigni co-wrote the story and directed and starred in the film. The film was partially inspired by the book *In the End, I Beat Hitler* by Benigni's father, who spent two years in a German labor camp during WWII. The film won numerous international awards, including three American Academy Awards, including Best Actor for Benigni.

Acknowledgements

To Patrick, Ryan, Michael, and Kyle: *Thank you for your love and support and for letting me slip into the "black hole" of writing and waiting patiently for me to emerge again. Thank you for believing in my Italian dream. Special thanks to Patrick, who made the journey with me to Cerreto Guidi to visit the Medici hunting lodge where Isabella de' Medici spent her final days.*

Paula Testi: *Director of Cultura Italiana Italian Language School in Arezzo. A dear friend and the one who first reached out to me and invited me to Arezzo. Since that day, I haven't wanted to leave.*

Roberto Bondi: *Italian teacher at Cultura Italiana and guide to Arezzo and Cortona, who first introduced me to San Donato and Santa Margherita.*

Monica Brizzi: *Program coordinator at Cultura Italiana, who first introduced me to Cimabue's cross in San Domenico and Cosimo's fortress in the Belvedere.*

Barbara Lancini: *Owner of Le Antiche Mura B&B, located just a few steps away from the Duomo—San Donato. With her, I always have a home in Arezzo.*

Signori Carlo and Matteo Badii: *Thank you for welcoming me into your gold jewelry studio in Arezzo and showing me how you create beautiful gold and silver works of art, just like the Etruscans did.*

Roberto Turchi: *Thank you for opening up the Santo Spirito Jousting Museo and Headquarters and for showing me the costumes, lances, and banners and teaching me more about the history of Arezzo's joust.*

Giampiero Bracciali: *Owner of the bookstore il Viaggiatore Immaginario. Thank you for helping me with my research and for finding photos and videos of Arezzo during the war. Your kindness and gifts were invaluable.*

Gianmaria Scortecci: *Jouster for Santo Spirito. Thank you for answering my numerous questions about the joust and the rules of the game. Forza Gialloblù!*

Arezzo, special thanks to the town itself: *The people are warm and welcoming and the town is full of history and art. It is a city easy to fall in love with and a place that inspires my creative process. Special acknowledgements to all the hard-working people in each of the four neighborhoods who help bring the joust to life twice a year, and to all the talented jousters.*

Kara Schleunes: *First reader and friend who shares a similar passion for Italy, Italian, Arezzo, and the joust. Thanks for being the best traveling partner and kindred spirit.*

Elizabeth Bosch: *Creative editor and fearless reader of the book in all its various stages from conception to finish. Thank you for accompanying me on this journey again!*

Robert Schirmer: *First Story Editor.*

Gloria Acerboni: *Italian Editor.*

Amber Richberger: *Second edition copy editor.*

Melissa Muldoon is the author of three novels set in Italy: *"Dreaming Sophia," "Waking Isabella,"* and *"Eternally Artemisia."* All three books tell the stories of American women and their journeys of self-discovery to find love, uncover hidden truths, and follow their destinies to shape a better future in Italy.

Melissa is also the author of the *Studentessa Matta* website, where she promotes the study of Italian language and culture through her dual-language blog written in Italian and English (studentessamatta.com). *Studentessa Matta* means the "crazy linguist" and has grown to include a podcast, *Tutti Matti per l'Italiano* and the *Studentessa Matta* YouTube channel, Facebook page and Instagram feed. Melissa also created *Matta* Italian Language Immersion Programs, which she co-leads with Italian schools in Italy to learn Italian in Italy. Through her website, she also offers the opportunities to live and study in Italy through Homestay programs.

Melissa has a B.A. in fine arts, art history and European history from Knox College, a liberal arts college in Galesburg, Illinois, as well as a master's degree in art history from the University of Illinois at Champaign-Urbana. She has also studied painting and art history in Florence. She is an artist, designer, and illustrated the cover art for all three of her books. Melissa is also the managing director of Matta Press.

As a student, Melissa lived in Florence with an Italian family. She studied art history and painting and took beginner Italian classes. When she returned home, she threw away her Italian dictionary, assuming she'd never need it again, but after launching a successful design career and starting a family, she realized something was missing in her life. That "thing" was the connection she had made with Italy and the friends who live there. Living in Florence was indeed a life-changing event. Wanting to reconnect with Italy, she decided to learn the language again from scratch. As if indeed possessed by an Italian muse, she bought a new Italian dictionary and began her journey to fluency—a path that has led her back to Italy many times and enriched her life in countless ways. Now, many dictionaries and grammar books later, she dedicates her time to promoting Italian language studies, further travels in Italy, and sharing her stories and insights about Italy with others.

Melissa designed and illustrated the cover art for *Waking Isabella, Dreaming Sophia,* and *Eternally Artemisia.* She also curates the *Dreaming Sophia* blog and Pinterest site: *The Art of Loving Italy.* Please visit the Pinterest page for pictures of Arezzo, the *Giostra del Saracino,* and all the places we go in Italy in her books. Visit MelissaMuldoon.com for more information about immersion trips to learn the language with Melissa in Italy, as well as the Studentessa Matta blog for practice and tips to learn the Italian language.

MelissaMuldoon.com
ArtLovingItaly.com
Pinterest.com/ArtofLovingItaly
StudentessaMatta.com

Dreaming Sophia

Because dreaming is an art.

Winner of the 2018 Reader View Best Adult Fiction Novel Award

Dreaming Sophia is a magical look into Italy and art history as seen through the eyes of a young American artist. Sophia is the daughter of a beautiful free-spirited artist who studied in Italy in the 1960s during a time when the Mud Angels saved Florence. She is brought up in the Sonoma Valley in California, in a home full of love, laughter, art, and Italian dreams. When tragedy strikes, she finds herself alone in the world with only her Italian muses for company. Through dream-like encounters she meets Renaissance artists, Medici princes, sixteenth-century duchesses, Risorgimento generals, and Cinecitta movie stars, each giving her advice and a gift to help her put her life back together. *Dreaming Sophia* is the story of a young woman's love for Italy and how she turns her fantasies into reality as she follows her muses back to Florence.

Sheri Hoyte for Blog Critics: Author Melissa Muldoon presents spellbinding artistic expression in her delightful story, Dreaming Sophia. Not your typical Italian romantic adventure, Dreaming Sophia is a wonderful multifaceted story that pushes through several genres, with layers and layers of exquisite entertainment. The development of her characters is flawless and effortless, as is her ability to draw readers into her world.

Dianne Hales, author of La Bella Lingua: In Dreaming Sophia, Melissa Muldoon weaves many strands of Italian culture into a delightful blend of fantasy, romance, art, and history. With an artist's keen eye and deft touch, she brings to life the titans of Italian culture in a touching tale of a young woman reeling from loss who discovers that Italy is the answer. The many Italophiles who share her belief will revel in the adventures of this kindred spirit.

Eternally Artemisia

Some loves, like some women are timeless.

They say some loves travel through time and are fated to meet over and over again. For Maddie, an art therapist, who wrestles with the "peculiar feeling" she has lived previous lives and is being called to Italy by voices that have left imprints on her soul, this idea is intriguing. Despite her best efforts, however, proof of this has always eluded her. That is, until one illuminating summer in Italy when Maddie's previous existences start to bleed through into her current reality. When she is introduced to the Crociani family—a noble clan with ties to the seventeenth-century Medici court that boasts of ancestors with colorful pasts—she finally meets the loves of her life. One is a romantic love, and another is a special kind of passion that only women share, strong amongst those who have suffered greatly yet have triumphed despite it. As Maddie's relationship develops with Artemisia Gentileschi—an artist who in a time when it was unheard of to denounce a man for the crime of rape, did just that—Maddie discovers a kindred spirit and a role model, and just what women are capable of when united together. In a journey that arcs back to biblical days and moves forward in time, Maddie encounters artists, dukes, designers, and movie stars as well as baser and ignoble men. With Artemisia never far from her side, she proves that when we dare to take control of our lives and find the "thing" we are most passionate about, we are limitless and can touch the stars.

Dianne Hales, author of La Bella Lingua: A true Renaissance woman, Melissa Muldoon weaves her passions for art and Italy into a stirring saga that sweeps across centuries. As her time-traveling heroine Maddie reconnects with kindred souls, we meet Artemisia Gentileschi, the 17th–century artist who overcame rape and ignominy to gain respect and acclaim. Historic figures such as Galileo and Mussolini also come to life in this intricately plotted novel, but the women who defy all constraints to take control of their destinies are the ones who prove to be eternally fascinating.